# BIG
# CHERRY
# HOLLER

ALSO BY ADRIANA TRIGIANI

*Big Stone Gap*

# Adriana Trigiani

# BIG CHERRY HOLLER

A BIG STONE GAP NOVEL

BALLANTINE BOOKS

NEW YORK

A Ballantine Book
Published by The Ballantine Publishing Group

Copyright © 2001 by The Glory of Everything Company
Reader's Guide copyright © 2002 by The Glory of Everything Company and The Ballantine
Publishing Group, a division of Random House, Inc.

This book contains an excerpt from the forthcoming hardcover novel *Milk Glass Moon* by
Adriana Trigiani. This excerpt has been set for this edition only and may not reflect the final
content of the forthcoming edition.

www.randomhouse.com/BRC/

Library of Congress Control Number: 2002090322

ISBN 0-345-44584-8

This edition published by arrangement with Random House, Inc.

Cover illustration by Danilo Ducak

Manufactured in the United States of America

First Ballantine Books Edition: April 2002

10  9  8  7  6  5  4  3  2  1

*For my mother,*
*Ida Bonicelli Trigiani*

# BIG

## CHERRY

### HOLLER

he rain is coming down on this old stone house so hard, it seems there are a hundred tap dancers on the roof. When Etta left for school this morning, it was drizzling, and now, at two o'clock, it's a storm. I can barely see Powell Mountain out my kitchen window; just yesterday it was a shimmering gold pyramid of autumn leaves at their peak. I hope the downpour won't beat the color off the trees too soon. We have all winter for Cracker's Neck Holler to wear gray. How I love these mountains in October: the leaves are turning—layers of burgundy and yellow crinolines that change color in the light—the apples are in, the air smells like sweet smoke, and I get to build big fires in Mrs. Mac's deep hearths. As I kneel and slip a log into the stove, I think of my mother-in-law, who had fires going after the first chill in the air. "I love me a farr," she'd say.

There's a note on the blackboard over the sink in Jack Mac's handwriting: *Red pepper sandwiches?* The message is at least three months old; no one should have to wait that long for their favorite sandwich, least of all my husband. Why does it take me so long to fulfill a simple request? There was a time when he came first, when I would drop everything and invent ways to make my husband happy. I wonder if he notices that life has put him in second place. If he doesn't, my magazine subscriptions sure do. *Redbook* came with a cover exploding in hot pink letters: PUT THE SIZZLE BACK IN YOUR MARRIAGE! WE SHOW YOU HOW! Step #4 is Make His Favorite Food. (Don't ask about the other nine steps.) So, with equal measures of guilt and determination to do better, I'm roasting peppers in the oven, turning them while they char as dark as the sky.

I baked the bread for the sandwiches this morning. I pull the cookie sheet off the deep windowsill, brush the squares of puffy dough with olive oil, and put them aside. Then I take the tray out of the oven and commence peeling the peppers. (This is a sit-down job.) My mother used to lift off the charred part in one piece; I've yet to master her technique. The vivid red pepper underneath is smooth as the velvet lining of an old jewelry box. I lay the thin red strips on the soft bread. The mix of olive oil and sweet hot bread smells fresh and buttery. I sprinkle coarse salt on the open sandwiches; the faceted crystals glisten on the red peppers. I'm glad I made a huge batch. There will be lots of us in the van tonight.

There's big news around here. Etta is going to be on television. She and two of her classmates are going on *Kiddie Kollege,* the WCYB quiz show for third-graders. Etta, who loves to read, has been chosen for her general knowledge. Her fellow teammates are Jane Herd and Billy Skeens. Jane, a math whiz who has the round cheeks of a monarch, has been selected for her keen ability to divide in her head. Billy, a small but mighty Melungeon boy, was chosen for his bravery. He recently helped evacuate the Big Stone Gap Elementary School cafeteria when one of the steam tables caught fire. No one could come up with a prize big enough to honor him (an assembly and a medal seemed silly), so the school decided to put him on the show. I guess the teachers feel that fame is its own reward.

Jack Mac borrowed the van from Sacred Heart Church because we're transporting the team and I've promised rides to our friends.

The television studio is about an hour and a half from the Gap, right past Kingsport over in Bristol, Tennessee. The show is live at six P.M. sharp, so we'll leave right after school. Etta planned her outfit carefully: a navy blue skirt and pink sweater (her grandfather Mario sent it to her from Italy, so Etta thinks it's the best sweater she owns, if not the luckiest). She is wearing her black patent-leather Mary Janes, though I pointed out that you rarely see anyone's shoes on TV.

I make one final pass through the downstairs, locking up as I go. With its simple, square rooms and lots of floor space, this old house is perfect for raising kids. Of course, when Mrs. Mac was alive, I never dreamed I'd live here. For a few years, this was just another delivery stop for me in the Medicine Dropper. I remember how I loved to drive up the bumpy dirt road and see this stone house sitting in a clearing against the mountain like a painting. If I had known that Mrs. Mac would one day be my mother-in-law, I might have tried to impress her. But I didn't. I'd drop off her pills, have a cup of coffee, and go. I never thought I would fall in love with her only son. And I never thought I would be looking at my face in these mottled antique mirrors, or building fires for heat, or raising her granddaughter in these rooms. If you had told me that I would make my home in this holler on this mountain, I would have laughed. I grew up down in town; no one ever moves out of Big Stone Gap and up into the hills. How strange life is.

I check myself in the mirror. Etta is forever begging me to wear more makeup. She wants me to be a young mom, like her friends have; in these parts, the women my age are grandmothers! So I stop in the hallway for a moment and dig for the lipstick in the bottom of my purse. My youthful appeal will have to come from a tube. You would think that someone who has worked in a pharmacy all her life would have one of those snazzy makeup bags. We have a whole spin rack of them at the Mutual's. Maybe Etta's right, I should pay more attention to the way I look. (Covering up my undereye circles is just not a priority.) Folks tell me that I haven't changed since I was a girl. Is that a good thing? I lean into the tea-stained glass and take a closer look. Eight years with Jack MacChesney have come and gone. It seems once I fell in love with him, time began flying.

Someone is banging on the front door. The thunder is so loud, I didn't hear a car come up the road. With one hand, Doris Bentrup from the flower shop juggles an umbrella in the wind and with the other, a stack of white boxes festooned with lavender ribbons. Two pairs of reading glasses dangle from her neck. Beads of rain cover the clear plastic cap she wears on her head.

"Come on in!"

"Can't. Got a wagon full of flowers. Got a funeral over in Pound. I'm gonna kill myself if this rain done ruined my hair."

"It looks good." I'm about a foot taller than Doris, so I look down on her tiny curls, each one a perfect rosette of blue icing under a saran-wrap tent.

"It'd better. I suffered for this look. I sat under that dryer over to Ethel's for two hours on Saturdee 'cause of the humidity. She sprayed my head so bad these curls is like tee-niney rocks. Feel."

"They're perfect," I tell Doris without touching her head.

"Etta all ready for the big show?"

"Yes ma'am."

"We hope they win this year, on account of no one from Big Stone ever wins."

"Didn't the Dogwood Garden Club win on *Club Quiz*?"

"Yes'm. But that was a good ten year' ago. And they was grown-ups, so I don't think you can count 'at. Wait till you see who these is from. I nearly done dropped my teeth, and you know that ain't easy, 'cause I glue 'em in good."

I pull the tiny white card bordered in crisp pink daisies out of the envelope. It reads: *Knock 'em dead, Etta. And remember, the cardinal is the state bird of Virginia. Love, Uncle Theodore.*

"That there Tipton is a class act. He ain't never gonna be replaced in these parts," Doris announces as she tips her head back to let the rain drain off her cap. "Sometimes we git a ferriner in here that makes us set up and take notice. How's he doin' at U.T.?"

"He says he's got the best marching band in the nation."

"Now if they'd only start winning them some ball games."

As Doris makes a break for her station wagon, I open a box. There, crisp and perfect, is a wrist corsage of white carnations. Nestled in the cold petals are three small gold-foil letters: WIN. I inhale the fresh, cold flowers. The letters tickle my nose and remind me of the homecoming mums that Theodore bought me every year during football season. For nearly ten years, Theodore was band director and Junior Class Sponsor at Powell Valley High School. He chaperoned every dance, and I was always his date. (Parents appreciated that an experienced member of the Rescue Squad chaperoned school dances.) Theodore always made a big deal of slipping the corsage onto my wrist before the game. Win or lose, the dance was a celebration because Theodore's halftime shows were always spectacular. Besides his unforgettable salute to Elizabeth Taylor prior to her choking on the chicken bone, my favorite was his salute to the Great American Musical, honoring the creations of Rodgers and Hammerstein. Each of the majorettes was dressed as a different lead character, including Maria from *The Sound of Music* and Julie Jordan from *Carousel.* Romalinda Miranda, daughter of the Filipino Doctor Who Was on the Team That Saved Liz Taylor, was the ingenue from *Flower Drum Song.* Theodore pulled her from the Flag Girls; there was a bit of a drama around that, as folks didn't think that a majorette should be drafted out of thin air for one show just because she looked like she was from the original cast. Once the controversy died down, the Miranda family basked in the glory of the celebration of their Asian heritage. (Extra points for my fellow ferriners.)

I gently place the boxes on top of my tote bag full of things we might need for the television appearance. Extra kneesocks. Chap Stick. Comb. Ribbons. My life is all about collecting things for my family and then putting them back. Lists. Hauling. And I'd better never forget anything. Even Jack relies on me for tissues when he sneezes and quarters for the paper. Sometimes I wonder if all these small details add up to anything.

Big Stone Gap Elementary is a regal collection of four beautifully appointed beige sandstone buildings, built in 1908. In mining towns, the first place the boom money goes is to the schools; Big Stone Gap was no different. There is at least an extra acre of field for the kids to play in, a glorious old auditorium (with footlights), and a newly refurbished cafeteria (since Billy the Hero). I wait at the entry fence as my own mother did for so many years.

As the bell sounds and the green double doors swing open, the kids pour out onto the wet playground like beads from a sack. Etta stands at the top of the stairs, surveying the fence line. When she sees me, she hops down the steps two at a time and runs toward me. She has a hard time holding on to her red plaid umbrella in the fierce wind. Her rain slicker flaps about. I give her a quick kiss as she jumps into the Jeep.

"Did you remember my socks?"

"Are you nervous?"

Etta peels off her mud-splattered white kneesocks and pulls on the fresh ones. "Very."

"Uncle Theodore sent you a present."

Etta rips into the box. Her light brown hair hangs limp and straight. (I'm glad Fleeta can put it up in a braid tonight.) Her little hands are just like mine, made for work. Her face is her father's, the straight nose, the lips that match top and bottom, and the hazel eyes, bright and round. Etta has freckles — we don't know where those came from. Jack told Etta a bedtime story about freckles when she was very little, which she believed for the longest time: God has a bucketful of freckles, and when he's done making babies in heaven, he lines them up right before they're born and sprinkles freckles on them for good luck. The more freckles, the better your luck. Let's hope the freckles do their job tonight. Etta holds up the corsage. "I shouldn't wear it if Jane doesn't have one."

"Not to worry. He sent one for Jane and a boutonniere for Billy."

"Just like a wedding," Etta says. "But I ain't never gonna marry Billy Skeens. No way. He's too short."

"He's probably gonna grow," I tell my daughter, sounding like someone else's annoying mother. "And we don't say 'ain't never.' Do we?"

A horn blasts next to us. "Daddy!" Etta shouts, off the hook for her bad grammar. The van from Sacred Heart Church careens into a parking spot. My husband smiles and waves to us. Etta climbs out of the Jeep and runs to the van, where Jack has thrown open the door. She shows him her corsage, which he admires. I watch the two of them through the window as they laugh. They look like an old photograph, black and white and silver where the emulsion has turned.

Jack must feel me staring through the rain and motions for me to join them. He shoves the van door open, and I jump in and climb into the seat behind him.

"How was your day?" I ask.

"Fine."

"Daddy, kiss Mama." Jack kisses me on the cheek. "Why do they misspell 'college' in *Kiddie Kollege?*"

"I don't know." Jack defers to me.

"Maybe because it matches the 'K' in 'Kiddie,' " I tell her.

"That's a dumb reason. If you're smart enough to go on a show called *Kiddie Kollege*, you're smart enough to know that college starts with a 'C.' "

Jack looks at me in the rearview mirror. The corners of his hazel eyes crinkle up as he smiles. He finds Etta's know-it-all tone funny; I think her loud opinions are just nerves before competition. Or maybe it's confidence. I'm not sure.

My family cheers when I announce I've brought along red pepper sandwiches. As I cross to the Jeep to get the cooler, Jack gets out to help me. He looks beautiful to me, fresh-scrubbed from the mine. He's gotten better-looking as he's aged. (Men are so lucky that way, and in others—don't get me started.) His hair, which receded in his late thirties and looked like it might fall out, stayed in. It's all gray now, but with his hazel eyes, it looks elegant. He lost some weight, determined not to be Fat and Forty. I smooth down my hair, which has frizzed in the rain.

"I've got it," Jack says as he lifts the cooler over my head.

"What's wrong?" I ask him.

"Nothing."

"Something is wrong. I can tell."

"Ave. Nothing's wrong."

"Are you sure?"

"I can't talk about it right now. I'll tell you later."

"Tell me now."

"No. Later." Jack looks at me and then through the window at Etta. She looks out at us. "I don't want to get Etta all riled up."

"Okay," I say impatiently. "But you can tell me." Why won't he tell me what's wrong? What is he protecting me from?

"The mines closed."

"No!"

"Yeah," he says under his breath angrily.

"I'm sorry." That's all I can say? I don't throw my arms around him? I don't comfort him? I just stand here in the rain.

"I am too." Jack turns toward the van.

"Let's not ruin Etta's night," I say to his back. Jack turns around and looks at me as though I'm a stranger; it sends a chill through me. He straightens his shoulders and says, "Let's not."

The day we have dreaded has come. My husband is out of work. But it's worse than that; Jack's identity and heritage is tied to the coal in these hills in a deeply personal way. The MacChesneys have been coal miners for as far back as anyone can remember. My husband is a proud miner: a union man who worked his way up from a pumper to chief roof bolter. Some say it's the most dangerous job in the mine. Now what will he do? What kind of work can my husband find at his age? He has no degree. How are we going to make it? I only work three days a week at the Pharmacy. We count on his benefits. Sure, we own the house, but it doesn't run on air. I wish we didn't have this show tonight, or all these people coming. Why do I always have to make an event out of everything? I had to arrange the van, fill it with friends, make sandwiches. I couldn't let it be just the three of us.

Iva Lou Wade Makin pulls up and parks across the street. Her glorious blond bouffant is protected by a white polka-dot rain cap with a peak so pointy, it makes her seem medieval. Actually, Iva Lou looks more like the state bird as she puddle-hops across Shawnee Avenue. Her lips, her shoes, and her raincoat are ruby red. She hoists herself into the van (hips first) with a Jean Harlow grin. Her gold bangle bracelets jingle as she lifts the rain cap off her head.

"Whoo. That storm is a bitch." Iva Lou turns to Etta. "Now, don't use that word 'bitch,' hon. It's a grown-up word."

"Thanks for the clarification." I give Iva Lou a look.

"Nellie Goodloe ain't coming. She's gonna watch the show with the Methodist Sewing Circle at the Carry-Out."

"Is Aunt Fleeta coming?" Etta asks.

"I saw her at the Pharmacy. I got the last rain bonnet. She'll be along presently."

Etta's teacher (and mine way back when), Grace White, a petite lady of almost seventy, holds an umbrella over Jane and Billy, dressed for television in their Sunday finest. Jack gets out and helps them into the van.

"Jane, we got corsages!" Etta squeals. "Billy, you got a carnation."

"Okay," Billy says, less than enthused.

Fleeta Mullins's old gray Cadillac with one bashed fin pulls up next to the Jeep. She barrels out of it quickly, tossing off the butt of a cigarette. Fleeta is small, and she's shrinking; smoking has ruined her bones. I try to get her to take calcium; I'm sure she has osteoporosis.

She's still a nimble thing, though. Fleeta leaps up into the van after Iva Lou pulls open the door for her, then wedges into the middle seat next to Mrs. White, bringing a waft of tobacco and Windsong cologne with her. "I had me a line at the register, and folks was surly. Pearl Grimes needs to hire more help over to the Pharmacy," she announces over her foggy reading glasses. I shrug. I am not the boss, haven't been for almost ten years. But old habits die hard with Fleeta.

"No problem. We're right on schedule," Mrs. White promises.

"Pearl made peanut-butter balls." Fleeta gives me the tin. The kids beg for them, but I tell them, "After the show. Okay? We don't need your winning answers sticking to the roofs of your mouths."

As the kids chatter, Fleeta sticks her head between Jack and me. "I done heard. Westmoreland's out."

"Don't say anything, Fleets. The kids," Jack says to her quietly.

"Right. Right. I got me half a mind to get on the bus to Pittsburgh and go meet them company men myself and tell 'em to go straight to hell. After all we done for 'em. Sixty years of profit on the backs of our men, and now they're just gonna pack up and clear out." Fleeta grunts and sits back in her seat.

As we drive out of our mountains and into the hills of East Tennessee, Billy regales us with the capitals of all fifty states in alphabetical order. Jane divides fractions aloud. Etta squeezes into my seat with me and faces her father.

"Are y'all mad?"

"No," Jack and I say together, looking straight ahead.

"Then what's wrong?"

"Nothing," Jack tells her as she shuffles through her homemade flash cards.

"Daddy, the coal of Southwest Virginia is . . ."

"Bituminous."

"That's right!" Etta smiles. "I hope they don't make me spell it."

"If they do, you just stay calm and sound it out," I tell her.

"And if you can't, we love you anyway, darlin'," her father tells her.

"I want to win." Etta's eyes narrow.

"Etta, do you know how much coal there is in our mountains?"

"How much, Daddy?"

"Enough to mine for the next seven hundred years."

"That much?"

"That much."

"If they ask me that, I'll know," Etta says proudly.

"I don't think they'll ask you that," Jack tells her.

"You never know." Etta hugs his neck and returns to her seat.

I look over at Jack, who keeps his eyes on the road. I wish I could fill up the silence between us with something, anything, a joke maybe. I used to know what to say to my husband; I used to be able to comfort him or cut to the center of a problem and dissect it. I could always make him feel better. But something is wrong. Something has shifted, and the change was so subtle and so quiet, we hardly noticed it. We pull against each other now.

"Jack?"

"Yeah?"

"Is there really seven hundred years of coal in our mountains?"

"At least," he tells me without taking his eyes off the road.

The WCYB television station is a small, square, brown-brick building nestled in the hillside outside of Bristol, just off the highway.

"Is that it?" Etta asks as she wedges between us and looks through the windshield.

"That's it?" Jane echoes.

The building does look lonesome sitting there on the side of the road. It's hard to believe that it's the center of communications for the Appalachian Mountains. The kids were expecting WCYB to be a comic-book skyscraper with mirrored windows and an oscillating satellite dish shooting menacing green waves into the sky.

"Now, see, that's not so scary," Jack Mac says to the team.

"That ain't scary at all. It looks like a garage," Billy adds, disappointed.

"It ain't how big it is. It's if they got cameras. All you need is a camera and some wires and some electricity. That's what makes TV," little Jane says definitively. (I hope Jane doesn't get any questions about modern appliances. If she does, we're in big trouble.) Mrs. White leads the kids into the studio.

Fleeta needs a smoke. Iva Lou is so tense from the trip, she bums a cigarette. The rain has stopped in Bristol, but it's still damp, and the fresh smell of the surrounding woods makes the place feel like home.

"I don't know how you people with kids do it." Iva Lou lights up, folds an arm across her waist, and perches her other arm with the cigarette in midair. I've always liked how she leans in to smoke, sort of like the cigarette might be safe to smoke if it's off in the distance a bit.

"It weren't easy, let me tell ye. That's how I started with these." Fleeta holds up her cigarette like a number one. "My nerves was so bad from the day-in-day-out with my younguns, I turned to tobacky and it's been my friend ever since. Thank you Jesus and keep the crop pure."

"Our kids are well prepared for the show. Sounded like," Iva Lou says hopefully.

"I want 'em to whoop the asses off Kingsport," Fleeta says as she stomps her cigarette butt. "I been watching every week, scopin' out the competition. I had Ten to Two Metcalf run some stats for me." Fleeta exhales. (Ten to Two is a bookie out of Jonesville. He got his name because he has a permanent tilt to his head, forcing his neck to crick over his shoulder at the ten-till mark.) "I got twenty bucks ridin' on our team. And I don't like to lose."

If the exterior of WCYB is a big fat disappointment, the interior doesn't do much to impress the kids either. The check-in desk is an old wooden table with a backless stool on wheels. A fancy plastic

NBC peacock sign spreads over the back wall. A wide electrical cord dangles down from it like a hanging noose (it must light up). I peek in the small rectangular window of a door marked STUDIO. The familiar *Kiddie Kollege* set, an old-fashioned schoolroom with six desks for the contestants, is positioned in front of the camera. The portable bleachers for the audience fall into shadow. The host's desk, complete with a large spinning wheel full of tiny folded question cards, is bathed in a bright white light.

A perky young redhead with a small, flat nose meets us at the studio door. "I'm Kim Stallard. Welcome to the WCYB studio."

"We can read, lady." Billy Skeens points to the sign.

"Aren't you smart?" Kim says sincerely. "You must be from Big Stone Gap. Would you like to see the studio?"

"You better do something with them damn kids. They're squirrelly as hell, cooped up in that van for pert' near two hours," Fleeta tells Kim, popping a mint.

"Right. Okay. Follow me." Kim motions us into the dark studio. There is a small path to the set; on either side are painted flats, which serve as backdrops for the news shows.

"Isn't this interesting, kids?" Jack asks.

"It's a mess," Etta decides.

"These are sets for the shows," I tell her in a tone to remind her that we are guests in TV Land.

"We're what you call an affiliate. We are a multipurpose studio. Is it smaller than you thought?" Kim asks.

"Much," Jane Herd tells her as she cranes her neck to look up at the rafters rigged with lights.

"Well, TV isn't all glamorous." Kim smiles.

"Look, a bike." Etta points to an off-camera bike.

"That's mine," says the familiar deep voice of Dan DeBoard, the debonair fiftyish game-show host/weatherman/anchor of the six o'clock news (he shares these responsibilities with Johnny "Snow

Day" Wood). He doesn't seem one bit nervous as he reviews his notes. He is tall and slim; his black hair is parted neatly and slicked back. The *Bristol Herald Courier* once proclaimed him "East Tennessee's Burt Reynolds." The resemblance is definitely there, and so are the *Smokey and the Bandit* sideburns.

"You look thinner in real life," Fleeta says as she sizes him up.

"So do you," Mr. DeBoard replies. (I guess he hears that plenty.)

"It's a pleasure to meet you." Iva Lou extends her hand and right hip in one smooth move.

"And you must be a former Miss Virginia?" Dan's eyes travel over Iva Lou as though he's starving and perusing the fresh pie rack at Stringer's Cafeteria.

"No, just plain old Miss Iva Lou." She tightens her grip as her eyes travel all over Dan DeBoard.

"She's murried," Fleeta growls.

"Aren't we all?" Dan winks.

Our kids swarm the stage. "It's good to let the children get comfortable on the set. It makes for a better show," Kim tells us as she checks a list on a clipboard. They catch sight of themselves on the television monitor on the floor in front of them. "Look-ee! We're on the TV!" Jane shrieks. Etta and Billy squeeze into the seat with Jane and wave to their images on the monitor.

Then the enemy arrives. Kingsport Elementary is represented by three stern boys with identical crew cuts and creases in their little navy slacks. Their matching green plaid jackets are so stiff, they look like they were pressed while the boys were wearing them.

"Lordy mercy," Jack Mac whispers.

"They look like triplets," Fleeta announces.

Mrs. White surveys the competition, then gathers our team in a huddle. The group breaks. Jane slips into her seat and folds her hands neatly on the desk. Etta smooths her hair and adjusts her nameplate so it is square on camera. Billy sits down at his desk and removes his boutonniere. The girls follow suit with their corsages. The mountain kids get it. This is for real. If they want to win, no flowers, no shenanigans.

As the theme music plays (a swing version of the alphabet song), Dan DeBoard takes a sip of coffee and spins gently on a high stool. He nibbles on the rim of the Styrofoam cup as his eyes search the bleachers for Iva Lou. When he finds her, he smiles and double-blinks (very flirty). Then he stands and casually hooks the heel of his shiny tasseled oxblood loafer on the chrome rung of the stool. He is so calm, he might as well be playing charades at home in his living room. I grip Jack's hand so tightly, I could crush a Coke can.

"Let's welcome the challengers from Big Stone Gap, Virginia." Fleeta, Iva Lou, and I applaud, and Fleeta whistles long and low, like she's calling a cow. He continues: "This is the team captain, Etta MacChesney. Etta, tell me about your family."

"My daddy's a coal miner, and my mama sells pills."

"What kind of pills?"

"It depends. What's wrong with you?"

The host stifles a laugh. "I understand you're an avid reader."

"Yes sir."

"What are you reading now?"

"*The Ancient Art of Chinese Face-Reading*. My Aunt Iva Lou gave it to me. She works at the li-barry." Etta points to Iva Lou, who straightens her spine and beams as though she's on camera.

"How interesting. What is the Art of Chinese Face-Reading, exactly?"

"Well. It's all about how your face can tell you what kind of person you are and what the future holds for you."

"A little hocus-pocus, eh?" Dan looks into the camera, raising one eyebrow.

"Not really. Like you. Your top lip is thin, and your bottom lip is thick."

"Does that mean something?" Dan rubs his chin.

"You're cheap."

"Somebody's been talking to my wife," Dan deadpans.

"I'm sorry," Etta says, realizing that she may have said something unkind.

"I'd like to crawl in a hole and die," I whisper to Iva Lou.

"I'd like to crawl into a hole with Dan DeBoard," she whispers back.

Dan tells our team that, as the challengers, they go first. He asks Etta for a number.

"Five for my cat, Shoo, who is five," Etta says.

"If you have two baskets of peaches and in one basket there are three hundred fifty-six peaches and in the other there are two hundred ninety-eight, how many peaches do you have?"

Etta squeezes her eyes shut and tries to add in her head. Jane Herd's little blue eyeballs roll back in her head and click up and down like the digits on an adding machine. Jane starts to shake; she has the answer. Etta's expression of pure panic and desperation tells me she does not.

"Five hundred fifty-four?" Etta says weakly.

"Sorry. It's six hundred fifty-four. Let's go to the Kingsport team."

Etta's cheeks puff as though she may cry. Jane is so disappointed, her head hits the top of the desk like a bowl of cold mashed potatoes. The champions look over to see what clunked. Etta pulls Jane's head off her desk by the scruff of the neck; there's no blood, thank God, so Dan throws the next question to the opposition.

The Kingsport boys take the next three questions, answering each of them correctly, including one about the state capital of Vermont. "Look at the Skeens boy. He ain't right," Fleeta whispers. "He ain't blinking." Something *is* wrong with Billy. He is frozen, staring into the distance, his eyes round and vacant like pitted black olives. Our team has totally lost focus. Jane is obsessed with the monitor. She makes circles with her head, studying her face from all angles. She is sweating so profusely in the hot lights that the barrette is slipping from her side part. Etta obsessively twists the third button on her cardigan like a radio knob; it looks to snap off any second.

By halftime, we have managed to scrape up zero points, while the Kingsport boys have fifteen. "Turr-ible. Turr-ible," Fleeta mumbles, and she goes outside to smoke. She paces in the hallway, alternately puffing and scratching her head with a pencil she found lodged in her upsweep. Mrs. White spends the break trying to thaw Billy.

As round two begins, we hope for a miracle.

"When water flows out a drain, does it drain clockwise or counterclockwise?" Dan asks Billy. Billy's forehead folds into one deep wrinkle.

"Oh, for cripe's sake," Fleeta says loud enough that everyone in the studio turns and looks at her. Dan drops his chin and rolls his head, encouraging Billy to answer. Finally, Billy opens his mouth and says, "Uhhhh," without forming words. His mouth hangs open like an unbuttoned pocket. Then his "uhhh" turns into a strange hum. "What the hell is wrong with that boy?" Fleeta whispers.

Dan looks at the cameraman, who shrugs. Jane turns to her teammate. "Dang it, Billy. Say somethin'!" He says nothing, so she turns to him and shakes him. "Guess! Take a guess, Bill-eeee!" Billy slips out of his seat like a wet noodle. Jane lunges to yank him back into the seat, but instead he latches on to her and pulls her out of her seat. Jane's desk turns over on top of Billy's. The clanging and banging sound like a four-car pileup. As Jane tries to free Billy, her foot gets caught in the metal bottom of her desk and she flips it over again. The Kingsport boys are standing now, confused by the melee. Dan runs across the set and lifts Jane off the scrap heap, and her skirt flips up like an inside-out umbrella. He yanks her skirt down, then unpins Billy and helps him back into his seat. Etta sits with a clenched smile so creepy, her upper and lower teeth form one wall of fear (I have not seen the likes of it since we watched *Mr. Sardonicus* on the Million-Dollar Movie). I look down at Mrs. White, who is dabbing her forehead with a hanky. How thrilled we are when the buzzer goes off and the game is over.

As team captain, Etta must collect the consolation prize: a case of Pepsi for their next school party and a check for ten dollars.

"Etta, what is your class going to do with the check?"

"Well, if we won the twenty-five dollars, we were going to buy a set of Nancy Drews. Since we only got the ten, we'll probably just get a *Weekly Reader* magazine or something. The Pepsi's nice, though."

"Well, good luck with all that," Dan says, and winks at the camera. The theme music plays through. "Let's do the Good-bye Wave from *Kiddie Kollege*! See ya next week!" our host says in the same professional tone he uses when he's signing off the six o'clock news or starring on a commercial for Morgan Legg's Autoworld. He places a giant yellow cardboard dunce cap on Etta's head, as she is captain of the losers, a tradition that began when the first *Kiddie Kollege* aired. The giant dunce cap is so big it covers Etta's eyes. Billy, pressure off, has revived. He jumps in front of Dan and the kids and puts his face in the camera, barking out greetings to his kin — every Skeens and Sizemore in the Cumberland Gap gets a personalized greeting. He and Jane flail their arms so hard, it looks like they're washing a car. The three automatons from Kingsport stand in front of the question wheel (which I believe should be set on fire and destroyed) and wave like movie stars. We are all relieved when the cameraman makes a slashing motion across his throat to stop this nightmare (at least he knows how we feel).

"You guys did great!" I tell them peppily.

"We lost real bad," Jane says, looking at the ground.

"I can't add in my head," Etta says sadly.

"Mrs. Mac, do you have them peanut-butter balls?" Billy asks. Finally, a child that can shake off catatonia and defeat with his sweet tooth. We know our way out of the studio, and it's a good thing. Perky Kim has disappeared. Even a television producer out of Bristol, Tennessee, knows when to remove herself from the stink of failure.

Even though we lost, the tension is gone, so the ride home is more fun than the ride over. The blue hills of Tennessee give way to our familiar black mountains as we curl through the darkness in our big green van with the Sacred Heart of Jesus painted on the side. A lot of good the religious shield did us. And what about the Saint Anthony medal that Father Schmidt gave to Etta for good luck? Did he forget to bless it? Where was Saint Anthony, the patron saint of lost things, when my daughter forgot how to add?

The kids are gathered around Fleeta in the back of the van while she tells them a ghost story. Etta has already forgotten all about *Kiddie Kollege,* and that makes me happy. Preparing for that stupid show was an ordeal, anyway. No more cramming for questions tacked on that godforsaken wheel. No more flash cards. No more watching the show every week and taking notes. Etta's moment in the sun came and went in the same night. The kids eat pepper sandwiches, chewing slowly; Fleeta cackles like a witch. Occasional passing headlights cast weird shadows on her and make her even more scary. Mrs. White has tucked her raincoat into a neat square pillow and sleeps against the window. Iva Lou hums to a Janie Fricke song playing softly on the radio. I lean across and rub my husband's neck as he drives.

"That's okay," he says.

"No. I want to," I tell him.

"Really. It's okay."

I remove my hand from my husband's neck and place it on my lap. I look out the window. I'm afraid I might cry. He puts his hand on mine. This time, I pull away.

"I'm sorry," he says softly.

"It's not my fault," I tell him without looking at him. But I don't believe it. I think everything is my fault, including the demise of the coal industry in Southwest Virginia. I am the woman in this family; I'm supposed to make everything work. What I can't seem to say aloud is that I'm failing.

"We'll be all right," Jack says, which upsets me even more. I hate when he downplays important things, the *most* important things! I'm furious with him, yet I'm also angry at myself. I saw this coming. I tried to talk to him about this many times, and he wouldn't discuss it. Why didn't I beg Jack to quit the mines when the layoffs became routine and the coal companies shrank their staffs and the train whistles carrying coal out of these hills became less and less frequent? I want to turn to him and say, "I told you this was going to happen!," but I can't. We have a van full of kids and Etta's teacher and my friends. So instead of shouting, I bury my rage. I turn to him and tell him calmly, "I can work more days at the Pharmacy."

Jack doesn't say anything. He looks at me quickly and then focuses his eyes back on the road. "Well. What do you think?" I say, realizing it sounds more like an accusation than a show of support. He does not answer me. As he drives into the dark valley, he checks the rearview a lot. But there is nothing behind us. We're the only vehicle on the road. Thank goodness the shrieks and giggles of the kids fill up the quiet.

The road to our house is so bumpy it wakes Etta, who has been sleeping since we hit the hill into town. She slept through dropping off her teammates at their houses and our guests at their cars outside the elementary school.

"We have to fix this road," I tell my husband.

"Put it on the list."

Jack lifts Etta out of the van and carries her up to the house as I clear the sandwich basket, the tote bag, and Etta's book bag. Jack takes Etta to her room, and I go to the kitchen. As I flip the light switch, I hear a thump. Shoo the Cat has jumped from his perch and is looking up at me.

"I forgot your food!" I fill the dish, pet him, and apologize over and over. There was too much to think about today. Jack comes into the kitchen and opens the refrigerator.

"There's leftover macaroni and cheese," I tell him. Jack pulls out the casserole and puts it in the oven. "We need to talk," I tell him.

"Not now. I'm tired." Jack uncaps a beer and looks out the kitchen window. I don't know what he's looking at, the field is pitch black, and tonight there's no moon.

"We need to talk about the mines." I try not to sound impatient.

"What do you want me to say?"

"Well, what's your plan?"

"My plan?"

"Yeah. What are you going to do?"

"Well, I'm going to be out of work."

"I know that. Have you thought about something else to do? Some other job?"

"No."

"Jack, maybe it's time to come up with something."

"Maybe it is." Jack shrugs. He is not listening to me.

"I know this is hard for you—"

"You have no idea."

"Yes I do."

"No you don't."

"Yes I do. I know mining is in your blood."

"Ave. Stop. Let's just forget it."

"Forget it? Why are you mad at me? What did I do?"

"You think I get up at dawn and disappear into a mountain, and ten hours later I come out and wash it off of me and come home to you. I don't tell you the half of it."

"Whose fault is that? You have to talk to me. I'm tired of pulling information out of you. I've worried every day you've left this house. Especially lately." As the bigger companies pulled out, safety became less important. I would panic every time I heard a wildcat company was coming in to reopen old mines for quick access to more coal. I knew they weren't following codes; it was common knowledge around here. I look at my husband, who is studying the label on his beer. I hear myself raising my voice; he looks at me. At least I have his attention now. "I worried myself sick. Of course, you have no idea what I'm thinking because you never ask me."

"Maybe that's because I know what you're thinking." He takes a swig.

"Look, I've had a very—" I begin to say "tough day" but stop myself. I look at my husband, and he is wounded down to his bones.

"Ave, you don't come from coal." Jack says this matter-of-factly. He's right. I'm not a descendant of these folks, even though I was born and raised here. I am a ferriner. I do have a different point of view. I don't accept the power of a big company over a community. I don't believe in waiting until the last drop of coal is pulled from these mountains before having a plan. I don't rely on anybody for anything. If I can't work for it myself, I won't have it.

"That's not fair." This is all I can come up with?

"When my grandpap took me down in the mine the very first time, he wanted me to hate it. But I got into the transport car with him, and from the first second daylight was gone and we were inside the mountain, I loved it. I loved the smell of the earth, the white dust on the walls where the coal was taken from, and the men all together in there, figuring out how to beat the mountain. How to outfox it. How to get that coal out without anybody getting hurt."

"Jack," I start to say, but he's turned away to pull the casserole out of the oven and doesn't hear me.

"When they talk to us like we're idiots, it takes a piece out of me. I saw simple men in there solve complex problems and prevail. And that's what I wanted my work life to be." Jack sits down. I sit down too and reach for him across the table.

"You can still have that. You can go back to school and become an engineer. Whatever you want."

Jack throws back his head and laughs.

"Do you have any idea who you're married to?" He tilts the kitchen chair, balancing on the back legs, and looks at me, challenging me to answer. Why do men do this? Why do they pretend to be strong when they're hurting? And why am I angry when he's hurting? I resist the urge to push him off the chair.

"I guess I don't."

"See there? We agree on something." Jack picks up his fork and eats.

I give up. I leave the kitchen and stop when I get halfway up the stairs. I didn't want to walk out of the room, I wanted to stay and work things through. Why did I leave? Why do I always leave the moment things get really hard? I sit down in the dark to think.

The storm is back, and the rain hits the house in gusts as thunder breaks over us in loud crashes. Lightning pierces the darkness, sending jagged shadows across me like sharp fingers. I pull myself up by a dowel of the old banister and take one step down to go back into the kitchen. I am determined to fix this tonight. I am going to tell him that I trust him to take care of us. But something stops me. I go up the stairs, choosing to go to my daughter instead of comforting my husband. I have the feeling it's a decision I will regret, but I do it anyway.

"Hey. You're supposed to be asleep," I tell Etta. She's looking out the window and watching the storm.

"The thunder woke me up." Etta crawls into her bed.

"It sure is loud," I tell my daughter as I tuck the blanket in; I hope it was loud enough to drown out the fight between her father and me.

"I'm glad Mr. DeBoard didn't ask me if I had any brothers and sisters. He does that sometimes, you know."

"Yeah, he does." I sit down on the bed. "Joe would've been very proud of you tonight."

"No, he wouldn't. We lost."

"Okay. Right. He probably would have teased you and called you a big loser all the way home."

Etta smiles as she turns over and looks at me. "He would have loved it when the desks flipped over." She lies back on her pillow. "Joe's been gone so long, sometimes I forget about him."

In Etta's life, three years is a long time. For me, it's a heartbeat. Joe was only four years old when he died. He and Etta were so close in age, folks often thought they were twins, even though they could not have been more different. I got pregnant with him three months after I had Etta. You should've heard the jokes in town. "Honey, must've been nice to get wet after that drought o' yorn!" one of Jack's coal mining buddies said to me at a football game. Oh yeah. They had a good old time talking about the Former Spinster turned Baby-Making Machine. I guess they thought I got myself a little taste of the honey and had to have the whole hive.

When Joe was born, Jack took one look at him and said, "The Eye-talian genes have landed!" And it was true. Joe had curly black hair and chocolate-chip eyes. He had my father's regal nose and slight overbite. His chin was square and prominent, but it curved at the bottom as though a cleft should form there. He had a deep dimple near his eye when he smiled (we don't know where that came from). He was so different from Etta. Joe was loud, funny, and exasperating. Once he even pulled down the Christmas tree. He drove me crazy. And I would give everything I own to have him back, driving me crazy.

"Don't worry. You'll never forget your brother."

"Are you sure?"

"I promise. I know."

"How do you know?"

"Because you loved your brother. And love never dies." I say this to my daughter as plainly as I might tell her to carry her umbrella when it's raining. Now if only I believed it. I turn off her bedside lamp and switch on the nightlight.

"Ma, stay till I'm asleep."

I lie down with my daughter and wrap my arms around her. She is warm and safe. I hope that, wherever my son is, someone is holding him. I have prayed to my mother to find him and take care of him. I have to trust that my prayers have been answered, but every night, even as I say them, I am not so sure.

# CHAPTER TWO

The headline on the front page of the Big Stone Gap *Post* says WESTMORELAND PULLS OUT, which causes a round of jokes in town that do not bear repeating. In the week since the announcement, *The Post* has been printing helpful articles for the miners about their benefits, insurance, and black-lung programs.

On the Almost Fame and No Fortune front: AREA KIDS TAKE SECOND PLACE ON *KIDDIE KOLLEGE* is the delicately worded headline on page two. Perhaps the editor, Bill Hendrick, placed it under PRAYERS REQUESTED FOR MAXIE BELCHER AND PEBBLE FIG so that folks could get a little perspective. We hate to lose, even at the elementary school level. The picture of our team is sweet; thank God they took it before the show, in happier times. It's taken a full week to shake defeat. Etta had almost forgotten about the loss, until she heard an old man point at her in a Buckles Supermarket, "Right 'ere's one of 'em kids that lost for us on the *Kiddie Kollege* show!" I fold the newspaper neatly into a basket filled with canned goods, fresh eggs, and milk.

It's my turn to leave staples for the Tuckett twins. Edna and Ledna are somewhere in their eighties and don't get out much. I leave the basket inside their screen door. When I get back to my Jeep, I hear the creak of their front door, letting me know that they got the basket. All these years, the sisters made pies and cakes for all the families in town: from birth to death and in between, you could count on the Tuckett twins and their cobblers. Now they find it hard to take what they consider "charity." But it isn't charity; as far as the folks in town are concerned, it's payback time.

Town is busier than usual. The first thing that happens when bad news comes out of the mines is that folks come into town to talk to the businesses where they have credit. Everyone from Zackie Wakin to Gilley's Jewelers renegotiates their terms in a time of crisis. Barney Gilley often tells his customers that without coal, there would be no diamonds; and without the coal miners, he'd be out of business, so he's happy to refinance.

My boss, Pearl Grimes, is sweeping the front walk when I pull into the parking lot of the Mutual Pharmacy. Pearl is a very mature twenty-four years old; if you just met her, you'd swear she was older. She looks polished and slim in a simple taupe A-line skirt and white blouse. Her smock is pressed and tied at the sides in small bows. Fleeta and I also wear the smocks, which Pearl designed, white with an embroidered pine tree on front (a salute to John Fox, Jr.'s *The Trail of the Lonesome Pine*). Pearl has permed her brown hair into a curly 'do, and she uses lots of spray on it. She has grown into her face, once round and girlish, now more chiseled, and she has mastered the art of well-placed rouge, which gives her cheekbones. Her soft brown eyes still have a sadness, but there is also a determination now, which is very attractive.

As Pearl has transformed, so has the Pharmacy. With Pearl's cum laude degree in business administration from the University of Virginia at Wise, she has transformed Mulligan's Mutual from a pharmacy that sold beauty aids to a full-service personal-needs department store. She began by talking to our customers and asking them how she could improve business. Then she goosed the staff (Fleeta permanent, and me part-time since Etta went to school) and set out to make the place more professional. We wear smocks (even though Fleeta rebels by keeping hers untied so it flaps like a vest on a construction worker). No more smoking behind the counter or eating lunch on packing boxes. No more Fleeta chugging back peanuts and Coke while sizing up a customer. No more putting the WE'LL BE RIGHT BACK sign on the door to hit a yard sale.

Pearl considered every aspect of the business before she made her changes, including ambience. She removed the garish fluorescent tubes installed by Fred Mulligan (the original owner and the father who raised me). "Soft light and music draw business," Pearl promised. And she was right. Some days we can't get rid of the browsers. Pearl even thought to stock Estée Lauder cosmetics, which attracted new clients who used to have to drive all the way over to Kingsport for that sort of high-end specialty item.

Pearl outdid herself with the window dressing this month. In her homage to autumn, she built a papier-mâché tree festooned with leaves spray-painted gold. A mannequin dressed like a farmer (he'll be Santa Claus come Christmas) holds a rake next to the tree. It's a simple concept, but Pearl put it over the top by burying a fan in a fake mound of dirt to blow the autumn leaves around. What a scene. It looks so real that Reverend Edmonds, in awe of the artistry, rear-ended Nellie Goodloe as he drove past one morning.

"I got an idea," Pearl says as she sweeps leaves into a dustpan.

"Fleeta and I are not doing a floor show to attract more business."

"I'm not entirely sure that would attract business."

"Thanks."

"I have a better idea. Did you know that there used to be a soda fountain back in the storage room?

"When I was little, Fred Mulligan closed it. Said it was too much work."

"The pipes are still in the wall. And they work. It wouldn't take much to put in some appliances and reopen the kitchen. We could serve breakfast and lunch. Keep the menu small at first. The only place to gather in town is Hardy's. How many sausage biscuits can you eat?" I don't want to disappoint Pearl, but the answer to that question is: a lot. Brownie Polly holds the record—fourteen sausage biscuits in one Sunday morning.

Pearl continues, "It would be fun for the town. It would be profitable for us. I think we should do it." She rattles off the list of positives with such enthusiasm, I can tell she has already made her decision.

"It sounds like you did your research."

Fleeta sticks her head out the door. And what a head it is this morning. Her hair is piled high on her head in waxy brownette curls. A tightly woven braid encircles the curls like a licorice tiara. A cigarette dangles from her mouth. In the daylight, Fleeta's rouge is so bright, it sits atop her cheeks like little orange bottle caps.

"Mornin', Cleopatra." I pat my cheeks, which makes Fleeta pat hers. She feels the two pink "X's" of tape holding down her spit curls and rips them off. The curls lie against her cheeks like commas.

"Somebody want to tell me what the hell is going on?" Fleeta pulls her smock over her head, neglecting to tie the side ribbons, as usual.

"Pearl's reopening the soda fountain."

"I ain't workin' no damn food-service job. Do you know what it is to wait on hungry people? They's beasts."

Pearl takes Fleeta's opinions seriously because Fleeta works the most hours. Ever since her husband, Portly, died from the black lung two years ago, she's been able to work more. Fleeta's kids are grown too: her son Kyle moved to North Carolina because he couldn't find a job here; her son Pavis moved to Florida because he passed bad checks in North Carolina, where he was working with Kyle. Fleeta's daughter, Dorinda, had a baby, but Fleeta told her that she wasn't raising another "damn kid." "You had the fun, now you have the baby, she's yorn, you take care of her and visit me on Mother's Day," Fleeta told her; so went the story around town. She didn't mean it, though. She takes care of little Jeanine every chance she gets. Dorinda gave her a necklace that says WORLD'S BEST GRANDMA on a little gold plate in cursive letters. Fleeta never takes it off.

"Fleeta. I think it's a great idea." I look at Pearl.

"You would," Fleeta growls. "How much more change we gonna have 'round here? Purty soon we're gonna be the Fort Henry Mall. If I wanted to work at a mall, I'd git me a job at the mall."

"With the mines closing, we need to look at ways to expand. If the fountain takes off, Pearl will be able to hire people. More jobs. Here. In town."

Otto and Worley emerge from behind the building, carrying their tools and balancing a long pipe on their shoulders (proof that Pearl's decision was made long before she asked me). Otto walks with a limp; he swears his bones got short in the one leg due to old age. He has a bright smile, thin white hair, and clear blue eyes. Their new truck has a sign on the door that says OTTO OLINGER & SON, lest anyone forget that they are father and son, not brothers, as all of the Gap believed for so many years. I notice that Worley looks good, well dressed with a certain stature. His red hair has lots of white in it. And he's had some work done on his front teeth.

"What'd Miss Ave say about reopening the soda fountain?" Otto wants to know.

"I love the idea."

"Do either of y'all two give a rat's ass about what I think?" Fleeta pats her smock, trying to locate her cigarettes.

"Not really." Otto smiles at Worley.

"You can kiss it, Otto," Fleeta barks.

"Okay, guys. That's enough," Pearl says with a smile.

"I remember old Fred Mulligan's soda fountain," Otto says wistfully. "There was a mirror on the back wall and them green leather stools that used to spin. And the cherry floats! Lord, they was good, them cherry floats."

"I 'member it too. But if I want a cherry float, I go to Bessie's in Appalachia. Let's get on it, Daddy-O," Worley tells him. (Back when

Otto confessed to Worley that he was his father, Worley stopped calling him plain Otto and invented Daddy Otto.)

I take my place behind my counter and tack up the prescription orders for the day. Pearl has left her peanut-butter ball recipe on my desk. Etta pleads for them so much, I figure they're good leverage when I want her to do something.

### COUSIN DEE'S PEANUT-BUTTER BALLS
*Blend: one box of confectioners' sugar*
*18-oz. jar of crunchy peanut butter*
*2 cups of graham-cracker crumbs*
*2 sticks of melted butter*
*Roll into bite-size balls.*
*Melt: 12-oz. package of semi-sweet chocolate chips*
*¼ box of paraffin wax*
*Dip balls into melted chocolate and wax and place on wax paper.*

"Is this it?" I wave the recipe at Pearl.

"It's easy."

Fleeta grabs the recipe and reads it. "I don't use the graham-cracker crumbs in mine, makes 'em mealy. I use crushed pea-nits. Gives 'em weight plus crunch."

"I'll keep that in mind."

"Try the crackers, then be the judge." Fleeta shrugs. " 'Course, nobody round here cares what I think."

"Pearl, can I talk to ye?" Worley asks.

"Sure."

Worley's tone is serious, so Fleeta and I look at each other. I tug on her smock and move toward the office to give them privacy.

"You can stay, Miss Ave. In fact, I'd like ye to," Worley says. Worley doesn't say anything to Fleeta, who takes this as permission to stay. She turns her back to us behind the counter, lightly dusting the outgoing prescription envelopes. Her head is cocked with her good ear toward us, so I know she's eavesdropping.

"Is something the matter?" I ask Worley.

"No ma'am. I got me a full heart is all."

"Sad-full or happy-full?" From Worley's somber expression and the deep crease between his eyes, I can't tell.

"Oh, very happy, ma'am."

"Does this have something to do with my mama?" Pearl asks.

"Yes, it do. I'd like to murry Miss Leah if it's all right with you." Worley looks at Pearl and then, struck with shyness, looks at the floor. Fleeta and I look at each other. We're stunned.

"Did you ask her yet?" Pearl asks Worley.

"We have talked."

"Did she say yes?"

"She said if you said it was all right, then she'd murry me."

"Well, it's absolutely all right with me."

Worley smiles. "I always wanted me a nice Melungeon girl like my mama was. And now I got me one." He goes back to the storage room.

"Your mama and Worley have been dating?" I ask Pearl.

"I wouldn't call it dating. You know how things are at the house— it's old, and pipes go, or something goes wrong with the wiring, and Otto and Worley know where everything is, so they come over and fix it. And then it's rude not to ask them to stay for dinner or lunch or whatever."

"Put milk out and you ain't never rid of a cat," Fleeta says under her breath.

Fleeta's got a point. Before I got married, I had so many repairs on the house, Otto and Worley practically lived there. They'd take in my mail, close the windows when it rained, and sometimes even start dinner before I got home.

"I guess Mama and Worley evolved sort of naturally." Pearl sighs.

"Why on God's green would your mama want to murry him? What does he got that's worth having?" Fleeta demands.

"Companionship," Pearl says over her shoulder as she walks back to the storage room.

"Leah will see how she likes companionship when she has him hangin' 'round all the time. She'll get tarred of that directly. A man can crowd a woman worse than a bunch of kids." Fleeta cracks a roll of quarters into the register like an egg.

"Do you think you'll ever fall in love again?" I ask.

"I had me Portly. I don't need to be goin' down that road agin. I'm old. Or haven't you noticed?"

"Love doesn't have an age."

"Yes, it do. If you heard the way my bones creak of the night, you wouldn't be tryin' to get some old man to come into my bed and creak around with me." Fleeta grabs her cigarettes and goes outside.

Falling in love with Jack Mac was almost an accident, so fleeting a moment I almost missed it. I was thirty-five and figured I'd be alone for the rest of my life. But Mrs. Mac knew better. She wanted me for her son and set about to make it happen, practically ordered me to go to the house when he would be home and she wouldn't. And I did—I went up there and waited at the old stone house with four chimneys. I often think of that night when he told me he loved me for the first time. I was so scared of it, of him, of everything. What if I had gotten back in the Jeep and driven down the mountain before he got home? If he had decided not to come home that night to find me waiting there? If he hadn't seen in me what even I didn't know was there? How did he know I could love him back when I never gave him a single sign? How fragile love is. How delicate and small in its first buds, when it's just an idea, a wish filled with hope. It is so easy to turn away from it entirely and choose to live alone in your own private fear. I had one moment of courage, and it changed my life. I didn't turn to love out of loneliness. Or out of habit. I let love change me. I see why Fleeta doesn't want a new man. She doesn't want to change.

The bells on the door ring merrily.

"Saw your Jeep outside." Spec Broadwater saunters in, leans against the counter, and starts fiddling with the viewfinder key chains hanging on a wire by the register. Spec, well into his sixties, is like a tree, seeming to grow higher and higher with age. Everything about him is oversize, his big head (mostly forehead, etched with crisscross lines from the smoking), his mighty hands, even his gold aviator eyeglass frames are so big they seem like windshields on his face. "Bad news about the mines." Spec exhales like a cartoon cloud that grows a face and blows gusts of wind. "How's Jack Mac?"

"He's okay."

"The situation stinks." Spec tears a stick of gum in two and offers me half. I decline. He chews one piece and puts the other in his shirt pocket. "You know they got this new thing now."

"What's that?"

"It's a new way to get coal out. Instead of digging it, you start at the top of a mountain and mine from the outside. Kindly like peelin' an apple. You mine down the outside of the mountain and then through."

"What happens to the mountain?"

"Eventually, it's gone. It disappears."

"That's horrible."

"Yep. It is. If a bunch of ferriners come in here and mow our mountains flat, what will we be? Indiana?" Spec leans across the counter and shakes the March of Dimes coin canister. "A job's a job, though. Maybe this here new technology is the answer."

"I don't know." I smile at him, but he knows and I know that new technology isn't going to help us. The companies have decided that they can go elsewhere in the world and mine coal more cheaply. There isn't anything we can do.

"I don't neither. Maybe some of these politicians 'round here will get off their arses and get the tourism thing going."

"Maybe they will."

"We got a lot around here to offer folks. The mountains. The beauty. Huff Rock. The Valley. Keokee Lake. Big Cherry Lake. You been up 'ere lately? Oh, it's a beauty. The Dickensons put in a boat launch—no motors up there. Only manual. It's something." Spec neatens the rack of cough drops.

"Spec. Do you need something?"

He looks at me and laughs. His laugh turns into a hack. He clears his throat. "I need you to come back on the Rescue Squad."

Spec has got to be kidding. Volunteering on the Rescue Squad when I was single was a natural thing; I was the town pharmacist trained in CPR and first aid, so soon I was assisting Spec. But it's been almost ten years since I was on board. I don't have the time anymore. "You know I can't. I've got the kids—I mean, Etta."

Spec looks away at the reference to Joe. I'm not offended by that, it happens a lot. Whenever I talk about Joe (and that's rare), folks quickly change the subject. It's not that they're being rude or insensitive, they just don't know what to say. Maybe it's too painful for people to look into the eyes of a mother whose child has died, so they'd rather pretend it didn't happen. Or maybe they think if they mention Joe, it will hurt me all over again. Joe's life was so brief, just a small piece of the landscape of our long lives in these parts. Except maybe for Spec. I believe Spec remembers Joe the way I do.

Spec was Joe's godfather, even though he isn't Catholic. In fact, I found out later that Spec had never set foot in a "Cath-lick" church on account of the way he was raised. Catholics were strange and mysterious and not to be trusted. But he bucked up the day Joe was baptized, and made it to the church, even though he was shaking so bad from nerves he almost dropped the baby.

"I hate to turn you down."

"Then don't. I can't keep nobody. I had that Trudy Qualls running shotgun with me for a while, and she just didn't work out. Tried to boss me. You know how I am. I don't mind living with one bossy woman, but I ain't gonna work with one too."

I'd like to help Spec. I would. He's been there for me on some of the worst days of my life.

"Come on, Ave. For old times' sake."

There were lots of good times with Spec on squad detail: cat rescues, setting off confiscated fireworks for all the kids in town when there was no other means to destroy them, decorating the Rescue Squad wagon to ride in the parade at the state capital when Big Stone Gap's own Linwood Holton was elected governor. And when it came to Etta and Joe, there wasn't anything he wouldn't do. He used to let Joe ride around in the Rescue wagon with the siren going and the lights flashing.

When I took my son to the hospital for the first time, it was one of those bleak January days. We came off the elevator and ran smack into Spec. It was a Snow Day, and Etta was home from school, so she came along. Spec made a big fuss over them, threw them both up in the air, then sent them off to look at the newborn babies behind glass.

"What the hell you doin' here?" Spec asked with a smile.

"Joe has a bad bruise."

"Did he get in a fight?"

"No."

"Well, you know boys, they fall a lot. Who's his doctor?"

"Dr. Bakagese."

"The Indian? He's right good. I ran Myra Poff over here the other day, and he caught the first start of pneumonia in her chest."

"That's good to know."

Spec put his arm around me, which, in all the years I had known him, he had never done. I assisted him for eleven years on the Rescue Squad; in the face of sickness and accidents, I never flinched. I followed his instructions and never panicked. I think he appreciated that I could deal with things without emotion.

"Why are you gittin' yourself all upset?"

"What if it's serious?"

"Good God a-mighty, Avuh. You can't be the mother of a son and hit the panic button every time he takes a tumble. Boys are a mess. I got me two; one was a head-banger in the crib and the other one set fires. It's just how they are."

Somehow the thought of Spec's sons, one a self-flagellator and the other a pyromaniac, soothed me. I had been fighting feelings of doom for months; maybe the long winter had me in a state. Hadn't I read that folks get depressed this time of year? That the short days and over-cast skies can chemically alter the brain into sadness? Hadn't I no-ticed that the mountains surrounded us like brown metal walls and the sky, a dismal patch of faded blue flannel, had made everything seem worse on the drive up to the hospital that day? I thought then, as Spec looked at me like I was crazy, that there was a chance I was making the whole thing up. How I wanted to believe Joe was fine. For those few seconds, I did. I gave Spec, the Mighty Oak, a big hug. He pulled away quickly, embarrassed, and said, "See ye," then off he went. That was the last time I felt hope throughout Joe's entire ordeal.

I owe Spec. He knows it and so do I. How can I say no to Spec Broadwater now?

"Okay, Spec."

"You'll come back on?"

"Yes sir. But only one week a month. I'm a mother. I can't be high-tailing it all over Wise County with you."

"I'll take you. Even one week a month. Better than nothin'. See ye." Spec goes out the door, whistling.

"You're a fool." Fleeta clucks and reloads the candy bar display.

"I know."

"You got enough on your plate."

As I load Mary Lipps's insulin into a plastic case, I am sure that Fleeta is right.

"Oughtn't you check with Jack Mac? Don't he have no say?"

"I never once heard you say you checked with Portly about any-thing, so lay off," I tell her pleasantly.

"I may never have said it, but I done did it," Fleeta says as she stuffs overflow Goo Goo Clusters into a basket. "I done did it."

It's dark in Cracker's Neck Holler as I drive home from work. I stopped at Buckles for milk and talked too long with Faith Cox, who is taking names for the bus trip to the revival of *Carousel* starring John Raitt next month. (Etta would love it, so I took a flyer.)

I take the curves of the roads gingerly. I'm crawling along so slowly, you'd think that I don't want to go home. Truth is, I'm tired and don't want to take a dip over the side. I don't drive as fast as I used to. (I don't do a lot of things since I became a mother.) I love my time alone going to and from work. It's my time to think and sort things out. Right now I'm reconstructing all the little day-to-day decisions I've made that led us to our present situation. It's what I always do when I have a big problem to contend with and feel stumped. I've been doing this a lot since Jack told me about the mines closing. I wonder if things would be different if I hadn't given Pearl the Pharmacy and the Mulligan house on Poplar Hill.

When I sold Pearl the business for a dollar (the technicality made it legal) years ago, it wasn't just to keep it from falling into the hands of my Aunt Alice Lambert. I did it because it was time for me to move on and start my new life. I shed the reputation of town spinster; I didn't know what I would replace it with, but it was going to be something! I had big plans. I was going to travel the world and find the place where I fit. I had lived my life taking care of my parents; at thirty-five, I felt half of my life was over, and I hadn't lived one day of it for myself. Folks were shocked when I sold Mama's car, then gave Pearl the store and the Mulligan homestead on Poplar Hill. I knew if Pearl and Leah moved into town, it would give them a new world-view, the very thing I was seeking. It seemed crazy to others, but I saw potential in Pearl and knew that, with a little encouragement, she could make something of a business that I merely maintained. I never felt like Mulligan's Mutual was mine, even though it said so in Mama's will. I never felt like anything but an employee. Once I knew that Fred Mulligan wasn't my father, I didn't have to hold on to the things he had built. And I didn't want to.

I never intended to become a pharmacist. After I went to Saint Mary's and got my degree, I came home because Fred Mulligan had gotten sick and couldn't run the place, and if he lost the business, what would happen to Mama? Then he died, and she got sick. I don't regret staying home to take care of my mother. She had peace of mind when she died, knowing I was secure financially. I wonder what she thought up in heaven when I sold the Pharmacy to Pearl.

It sure would be nice to have a little cushion now. I don't like myself for feeling this way. A little cushion is just a veil for what you really need. Don't we all need extra money? Is there ever a time we don't? The nest egg that I came into my marriage with has dwindled over the years. We needed extra cash to maintain the property. Things happened: the big pine tree that hit the back of the house two winters ago; a new truck for Jack when his old one broke down; Joe's medical expenses.

I began working at the Pharmacy again once Joe was in preschool. When I came back to work, I realized how much I had missed my work life. Maybe I initially became a pharmacist out of duty, but when I returned, it was by choice. I found out that I love what I do, the precision of it, learning about new medications, and helping folks look after their health. When I quit, I missed the delivery run and talking to folks in their own homes. I missed the way their houses smelled so distinctly from one another: the Tuckett sisters' of cinnamon, the Bledsoes' of lilies, and the Sturgills' of fresh vanilla. The job was something that was all mine, and I liked that. I missed being needed for my skills and my knowledge of medications. My job fills me up in ways I never knew until I left it behind.

The fifteen-minute commute seems more like ten seconds. As I come into the clearing, I figure I've taken a wrong turn or I'm at the wrong house. My home is lit up like a casino. Cars and pickup trucks are parked all around it. I don't remember planning a party.

As I climb the front steps, I look in the window like a visitor. I see my husband in the front room, surrounded by men. They drink beer and laugh and talk. I must stand there a long time, because the milk in the paper sack starts to feel wet on the bottom.

The laughter dies down a bit when the men see me in the entryway.

"I thought poker night was Tuesday," I say with a big smile.

"We ain't gamblin', Ave," Rick Harmon says with a wink. He has his feet on my mama's old coffee table. I push them off; the men laugh. Jack Mac takes the milk from me and leads me into the kitchen. Shoo the Cat makes a break for the kitchen and follows.

"Where's Etta?"

"Watchin' TV." Jack puts the milk in the fridge and turns to me and smiles. His face is full of news to share, his eyes full of hope again. I haven't seen him smile in days. Instead of being happy about this, I am curt.

"Did she eat?"

"I heated up the spaghetti."

"Did you make broccoli?"

"No."

"So she didn't have anything green?"

"She had that green banana for dessert."

"Not funny. I'm tired. I've been working all day, and I'm really really tired."

"I get it. You're tired."

"Where are you going?"

"I'm in the middle of a meeting."

"You're in the middle of a party." Why am I doing this? I want him to have a good time with his friends, don't I? Jack stares at me with disbelief.

"We got sidetracked."

"Sorry I interrupted the fun."

Jack looks back at me as he goes. I don't look up at him. I sit down at the kitchen table and cry. I just have a nice little self-indulgent cry. I want to feel good and sorry for myself. I came home to a mess, a child fed supper with no greens, and noise and beer and company I didn't want to see.

I check on Etta, who does not look up from a cartoon show. I kiss her and walk back through the old kitchen onto the back porch, through the creaky screen door, and out into the black field behind our house. It's cold, but I don't turn back for my coat.

The moon hangs between the mountains like a searchlight, making a path through flimsy clouds. I breathe deeply. The cool night smoke fills me with calm. The mountains, knit together seamlessly, form a black velvet fortress around me. The dark sky lightens to a shimmer of silver on the mountaintop, like a window shade that cannot reach the sash to keep out the light. The details are clean—bare branches with fluttery edges like curls, and strong black veins in the trunks and branches of the mighty pine trees. I am so small here.

There's a stump from an old weeping cherry tree in the back field that overlooks the side of Powell Mountain. When I sit on it, I'm nearly on the edge of our cliff, which gives way to a ravine and then the valley below. It's a wild, dark tangle of shrubs and branches and overgrown footpaths. When I first lived here, it scared me to come out back alone. But as time passed, I became less afraid and began to explore the MacChesney woods. I'm not afraid of falling off mountains anymore (at least when I'm on foot). And something about these old hills reassures me.

I don't know how long I've been sitting; it must be a while, because my hands are freezing. I hear the hum of motors starting in the field out in front. Jack's meeting must be over. I don't know why, but the sound fills me with dread. I feel a big argument coming on with my husband, and I don't have the energy to fight. I go inside and up to Etta's room. She finishes the second chapter of *Heidi*, reaches up to turn out her light, and dutifully lays her head on her pillow. There is a catch to her breathing—her nose is stuffed up, probably from the first cold spell of the season. I have to remember to give her something for that tomorrow. I give her a kiss and tuck her in.

Instead of going to the living room to collect beer bottles (great), I go to the sun porch and fold a load of laundry. When I'm done, I straighten up the rest of the kitchen and look in the refrigerator, making a mental note that we're low on lettuce. Enough procrastinating. The men left over half an hour ago, and the house is quiet. Time to go to bed. The light on the nightstand sends a warm glow up the walls of our room across from the kitchen. On the surface, everything seems safe, normal. I walk around the bed and see that the bathroom door is open, but I don't see Jack.

Shoo the Cat is asleep on the bench in the hallway in an empty box Etta uses for Barbie school. I look out the window. Jack's truck is there. Good. He didn't go out with the boys. I go to lock the front door, and through the small pane, I see him sitting on the porch steps, leaning back on his elbows. His legs drape down the stairs and are crossed at the ankle.

"I'm locking up."

"I'll take care of it."

"It's chilly out there."

"I like it."

I almost turn to go to bed, but something tells me to go to Jack. So I go out onto the porch and sit down next to him. He doesn't make any room for me on the stairs.

"I'm sorry about before. I'm just tired," I tell him.

"That's no excuse."

"Yes, it is. When people are tired, they get a little testy."

"You're more than testy."

"Not really."

"I'm not going to fight with you," Jack says plainly.

"I don't want to fight either." And I mean it. I hate fighting. "Jack.

Please. What's wrong?" My husband does not answer, but this is typical. I have to pull everything out of him, especially his feelings. "Just say it. Come on."

"Why haven't you talked to me about the mines closing?" Jack says quietly.

"We talked about it. Honey. We knew this was coming."

"Yeah. We did, didn't we."

"What does that mean?"

"You act like it's my fault. Like I wanted, after twenty-two years, to be out of a job, out of the only trade I've ever known."

"It's not your fault."

"Damn right it isn't."

"What good is that going to do? To be angry? It won't make Westmoreland reconsider. We have to face this."

"We? You're the one who hasn't faced this."

"What do you mean?"

"You think that the solution to this problem is to take care of it yourself."

"What's wrong with that?"

"Everything. You don't believe in me. I need your support."

Oh my God, he thinks that I don't support him? That I didn't admire him every day for taking such risks in a dangerous job? That I don't respect his physical strength and leadership skills? Of course I support him.

"Don't you trust me?" Jack looks at me. He's thrown a lot of questions around, but I can see that he'd like an answer to this one.

"Of course I trust you." I blurt this out instead of saying it like I mean it. Do I mean it? Do I trust him?

"Do you think I'm going to get another job?"

"Yes. Of course."

"I'm worried about my life too. But I'm not going to sit around waiting for something to happen. I'm out there making it happen."

"I never said you wouldn't."

"You said *you'd* work extra hours. As if this were about money. Do you know how that made me feel?"

"It should make you feel like you've got a wife you can count on."

"I know that. That's not what I'm talking about. Ave, I have my pride. Okay? I thought we were partners. I thought that you understood me, that you knew that whatever comes, I would find a way for us to get through it. Instead, you make me feel like I'm expendable. You don't need me around here if you're gonna do everything yourself. Why are we married if you're gonna handle everything alone?"

"I don't want to handle everything alone!" I feel my marriage sliding off this mountain like a loose rock, with me flailing after, trying to catch it and make it secure.

"You aren't the man in the family." Jack Mac gets up to go back into the house. I grab his ankle, then pull myself up and put my arms around him.

"I'm sorry. These worries overtake me sometimes. I still think I have to do everything myself." This revelation comes from the deepest part of me, and my husband knows it. He knows how hard it is for me to let go. *I* know how hard it is for me, but then why do I keep making the same mistakes? Why do I push him away when I need him? I feel my husband's heartbeat slow from an angry pounding to a sweet, steady rhythm. His arms encircle me tenderly. His great shoulders protect me from the cold; I melt into him in a way that I haven't in a very long time.

"I believe in you," I tell my husband, meaning it with every cell in my body.

"I hope so, Ave."

"No. No. I do. Here. Come on. Sit. Tell me your plans." I pull Jack down onto the step and put my arms around him. My husband's face is bathed in the golden haze of the lamplight from the living room window. I see the same expression I saw in the kitchen earlier. He is excited, hopeful, full of new ideas, solutions, even.

"Rick and Mousey want to start a construction company. The three of us. We think there's going to be a lot of development in the area. There's talk of that prison being built, and that means a new highway coming through, and that'll create a need for additional housing. We thought we'd be the first to get in on it."

"Great idea. You're terrific with woodworking."

"Yeah, and Mousey knows electrics and plumbing."

"Is Rick going to quit his job at the car dealership?"

"He thinks he can do both. Until we get busy enough that he can quit."

"Okay. This is great! When do you start?"

My husband pulls me close and kisses me a hundred times, quickly and sweetly and gratefully. This is what I love the most about being married: sometimes, even after eight years, we feel new, like there's a surprise in the familiar that I wasn't counting on; the passion comes back, sneaks up on you. You gear yourself up for what might be a doozy of a fight and reach an understanding instead; instead of jabbing at each other, you kiss. And you learn to take advantage of a moment like this, because it comes and goes and may not return for a very long time.

The moonlight blankets the porch. We lean into the pale blue, and in it I see my husband's face clearly. Every detail. The strong, straight nose, the perfectly matched lips, and the hazel eyes that can show hurt and love in the same moment. We fold into each other naturally, but it isn't like any time we've made love before. We laugh as we go for each other's buttons, zippers, lips. He shushes me, tells me not to wake Etta, then kisses my laughter away. What wonderful thing is happening? How can it be so different this time? It's romantic, yes, and a little daring (we're outside, for Godsakes), but this feels like it used to, when we were first in love. Why did that go away, and why didn't I know how to get it back? We talk too much or too little and show our love so rarely. We need to show each other more. Why do I forget this simple truth when I'm tired from work or caught up with Etta? This is the center of everything, this love right here. Without it, we're nothing but an old boardinghouse in Cracker's Neck Holler with Etta, the ghosts of those who are gone, and a box of problems. We're more than our problems, aren't we? As my husband kisses me, I am reminded of why he chose me, and how we must always come back to that, even when we've disappointed each other. Especially then. He holds me tenderly, and a night breeze settles over us. I shiver.

"Let's go inside, honey," he whispers.

"I love you, you know," I tell him.

"I know." He kisses me again.

In the warmth of our bed, Jack holds me closely as he hasn't done in a long time. We're united again under these old quilts, and I like the feeling.

"Honey?"

"Yeah?"

"Spec asked me if I could come back on the Rescue Squad a few days a month. What do you think?"

"I told him I thought it was fine."

I sit up in bed. "He asked *you*?"

"Spec's old-school. He does the right thing and checks with the husband before he goes to the wife."

Before I can object, Jack begins to laugh. I take my pillow and beat him with it. Jack grabs the pillow, and then me.

"You got a problem? Take it up with Spec." My husband smiles and kisses me.

A square of homemade fudge topped with snowy mini-marshmallows and crunchy pecans is wrapped neatly in wax paper and waiting for me on my counter. I need the sugar this morning. (I forgot how much energy the love department requires; it's like starting Jazzercise after a long hiatus.)

"Hey, thanks for the surprise," I tell Fleeta as she squirts a big blob of hand cream onto her forearm from the Estée Lauder display. (Never mind that the tube is not a sample.)

"I'm just a big ole sweetheart, ain't I?" Fleeta looks at me over her glasses and rubs her wrists together. "Nobody'll miss it." She puts the tube of hand cream back on the shelf. "What are you smilin' about?" she asks suspiciously.

"Nothin'," I tell her and shrug.

Pearl walks in carrying two big bags from the hardware store.

"What's that?" Fleeta asks Pearl.

"Contact Paper for the shelves in the fountain." Pearl goes to the back of the store.

"I ain't helping ye with nothin' back 'ere," Fleeta calls after her.

"Not a problem, Fleets," Pearl hollers back.

I grab a pair of scissors and join Pearl in the Soda Fountain.

"Pearl, I need a favor."

"Sure."

"I hate to ask, and I wouldn't if I didn't have to."

"Ave, come on. What do you need?"

"I need to work more hours."

Pearl looks at me oddly at first; it is still hard for her to be my employer. "No problem."

"Are you sure? You've got the expense of this new venture back here, and I don't want to strap you."

"Are you kidding? I need you."

"Great." I turn to go back to my post.

"Ave Maria?"

"Yeah?"

"There's something I want to tell you. And it's still real new, so I can't say too much. I'm . . . I'm seeing someone."

"A man?"

Pearl nods.

"Romantically?"

Pearl nods again, and this time she smiles.

"Good for you! Who is he?"

"I don't want to say yet. In case it doesn't work out."

"Okay."

"I like him a lot."

"That's great!"

"You know I'm sort of a late bloomer. So I'm a little nervous. You know." Pearl looks at me. I spent fifteen years in this town without a boyfriend. I know all about late blooming. I was alone so long, there are still times when I forget I'm part of a couple.

"Take your time. And don't agonize."

Pearl laughs. "I'm having too much fun to agonize."

"Good girl."

"Ave Maria! Pat Bean needs her 'scription! She ain't got all damn day!" Fleeta shouts from the register. (So much for the soothing shopping atmosphere at the Mutual Pharmacy.)

"I'm on my way," I yell back to Fleeta.

"Hey, Ave. Thanks," Pearl says, and her face flushes to a soft pink.

Pearl Grimes in love? Things around here are changing fast. I wonder if I can keep up.

The Halloween Carnival at Big Stone Gap Elementary is sold out. Nellie Goodloe thought it would be fun to host an all-county carnival to raise money for the John Fox, Jr., Foundation, which funds the Outdoor Drama. "Nellie has a flair," I keep hearing over and over as I walk through the spectacular decorations. White ghosts with black button eyes line the rail of the balcony overhead; the basketball backboards are big black cauldrons; a family of black paper bats flies over the bleachers. Nellie banked the entire ceiling in a spiderweb made of thick rope. In the center, she attached a giant papier-mâché spider that dangles down like a creepy chandelier. How does she do it?

The admissions table is loaded with straw and jack-o'-lanterns of all sizes; the ladies of the June Tolliver Guild are dressed as witches. The Foxes, who hand out programs at the Outdoor Drama, are also dressed as witches, but instead of billowing black robes, they wear short skirts (to show off their fishnet stockings, I'm sure).

Nellie hauled the oil painting of Big Stone Gap's most famous resident, John Fox, Jr., the author of *The Trail of the Lonesome Pine*, over here from the museum. Fleeta thinks Nellie has a crush on him, even though he's been dead since 1940-something. "Whenever she throws a shindig, she drags his mug out," Fleeta complains. Mr. Fox's oil portrait is eerily perfect for Halloween: he sits in profile in a dark wood study; on his long, pointed nose sits a pair of granny glasses. Come to think of it, he looks like a male *Whistler's Mother*. Nellie has draped fake white cobwebs on him. He fits right in.

Local merchants and the PTA provide the booths. Nellie is raffling off six free car washes (with wax) at Gilliam's Car Wash and a month of free dry cleaning at the Magic Mart. The money raised will go toward new streetlights in town (Nellie wants the old-fashioned-lantern look). There's a cakewalk and a costume pageant. Etta is not particular about her costume. Every year she goes as a skeleton, wearing a black jumpsuit with silver bones and a skull mask. She loves games of chance; she has spent the better part of the evening shooting at ducks on a spinning wheel.

Etta runs up to me with a glossy caramel apple covered in orange sprinkles. "Mama, will you put this in your purse for later? We need to cut it."

"This is the biggest apple I've ever seen," I tell my daughter. She hands me two pretty china saucers she won in the penny toss. When I ask her where the matching teacups are, she says, "I missed."

Etta's pals—Tammy Pleasant, a tiny, wiry blonde in constant motion, and Tara Kilgore, a tall, serious brunette with heavy-lidded brown eyes—grab her.

"You got to come *now*, Etta." Tammy tugs on her.

"They got a man that bleeds actual red blood in the Spookhouse," Tara says flatly. "I wasn't skeered."

"I was!" Tammy says, her eyes widening. The girls run to get in line at the Spookhouse. I know all about the Spookhouse because I spent the better part of this morning peeling grapes for the bowl of eyeballs the kids feel on their way in. Nellie convinced Otto and Worley to play monsters: Otto lies in a casket with blue goo on his face while Worley chases the kids through the locker area with a plastic ax strapped to his head.

"Yoo-hoo, Ave!" Iva Lou hollers. She is selling used library books in a booth decorated like a study in a historical home, and is dressed in a sexy turquoise hoop skirt and a frilly peasant blouse that exposes her creamy bare shoulders. Her cleavage forms a clean line like an exclamation point. "Is this a good idea or what?"

"The blouse or the booth?"

"The booth, silly. I'm unloading all our old stuff, making way for the new. What do you think?" Iva Lou spins like a plate on a stick.

"What a deal!" I hold up four Lee Smith paperbacks tied with string, priced at two dollars even.

"Hold off. In another hour, I'm doing a flood sale: everything must go."

Iva Lou leaves the booth to James Varner, who looks much taller in real life than he does behind the wheel of the Bookmobile. Iva Lou still turns every head in the room. (There are some women who never lose their allure.) Lyle Makin stands off with a group of his buddies. He nods and smiles at us.

"How's your husband?" I ask Iva Lou as I wave to him.

"Well, he ain't been soused this month. Of course, no full moon yet."

"What does that have to do with it?"

"He gets drunk almost exactly with the tides of the moon. It's the strangest thing. He can go dry for weeks, and then boom, he goes on a four-day bender. There's no getting around it, either. I can hide the stuff; I can try to divert his attention; I can fuss, but nothing works. When he wants to drink, he'll find a way to drink, and that's that. So I learned to live with it. He's good for weeks on a stretch; and you

know, that's more than most women git." Iva Lou unwraps a chocolate marshmallow witch and takes a bite. "How are you doing?"

"We're okay. Better than okay. Jack is fine."

"It's a big damn deal when a man is out of work."

"I know."

"They *are* their jobs. You have to be careful. He's vulnerable right
now."

"To what?"

"To getting sick. Taking to the beer. Running around. You know."

"*My* husband?" Iva Lou has got to be kidding.

"He's a man, ain't he? He's forty and change. Jack Mac's hittin' that
mortality wall."

"Aren't we all?"

"Women are different. Men ain't got markers to show them that
they're getting older. Not like us. Mother Nature takes us women by
the hand and leads us into it slowly. You got your monthly to tell you
that you went from girl to young woman; childbirth to let you know
you're in the middle; and then the Change to tell you that soon it'll all
be over. What have men got, really? Losing their hair? Losing a job?
A pot gut? What?"

"I don't know."

"You got to git a man to talk. It ain't easy to git a man to talk about
his feelings. They'd rather not have them at all. It's our job to draw
'em out."

"Ivy Loo-ee?" Lyle hollers from the Coin Toss.

"Lyle's hungry."

"You can tell what he wants from the sound of his voice?"

"I'd know that call of the wild anywheres. I don't even need him to
use words. I can tell by a grunt." Iva Lou gives me a quick hug and
goes to the Coin Toss.

Jack is shooting ducks outside the Spookhouse. As I make my way
across the crowded gym, I think about how a good woman can suss
out her husband's needs. Or how a good man can do that for his wife.

Sometimes Jack reads my mind. But do I read his? Does he know how I feel about him? Is he still attracted to me the way I'm attracted to him? My husband has a great body. Really. He has broad shoulders and strong arms. His legs are thick and muscular from years of lifting, chopping wood, mining. And though I hate guns, there is something sexy about him as he stands with a rifle cocked. He sort of reminds me of John Wayne in *Stagecoach*. (Jim Roy Honeycutt just ran the print at the Trail. Black-and-white movies are always better on the big screen.)

The crowd shifts a little, obscuring my husband. Before I can get to him, Leah Grimes stops me. I hardly recognize her. She's lost weight (must be prewedding jitters), her hair is dyed a magnificent red, and the cut is pure Dottie West, a neat chin-length bob with feathering.

"Leah, you look so pretty."

"Love done it to me."

"Congratulations on your engagement. Worley is a fine man."

"I know." Leah blushes. I look over her shoulder and see my husband putting the toy rifle down on the shelf of the duck booth. A woman I have never seen before touches him on the shoulder; he turns around and grins at her.

"Are you having a church wedding?" I ask Leah while repositioning myself to get a better look at the woman talking to my husband.

"Nope. We're gonna elope. Perty soon, too. Soon as Worley gets the pipes done at the Mutual's."

"How are things at the house?" I ask Leah. Jack is laughing with the woman.

"Good. Good. I want you to know if you ever need me to do anything fer ye, I'd like that. Baby-sit for Etta. Sew fer ye. Whatever you need."

"Thank you, Leah. But you're gonna have your hands full with a new husband directly."

Leah smiles and nods. Her friends join her, and they go off to the crafts booth. Instead of following them to check out the apple butter, or going to Jack and introducing myself to the strange woman, I go up the stairs to the balcony. I circle around the upper level so I can watch them without either of them seeing me. I feel guilty doing this (slightly). I sit down behind a family dressed as sunflowers, munching on popcorn balls. They ignore me and watch the people below. As I slide down in the seat, I can see Jack Mac and the woman perfectly.

From overhead, she looks like the Athletic Type. She is small and fit. Even though it is late October, she still has the bronzey glow of a summer tan. I thank God for the Art of Chinese Face-Reading and the bright fluorescent gym lighting, which helps me to get a good look at her. She is definitely attractive. She has deep-set brown eyes (a secretive nature, great) which flash in a way that shows a sense of humor and a certain intelligence. She has a long, angular face and a large head (means she's not hurting for money). Her short blond hair is sprayed into a casual bob, with spiky bangs. (She looks about forty, but maybe that's just the sun damage.) She is neatly dressed; even her trim, faded jeans are pressed. The collar on her pale pink blouse is turned up, as are the sleeves. The top three buttons are open, revealing a freckled chest and a high, small bust. (I quickly unfasten the second button on my denim shirt and sit up straight.)

She says something; my husband throws his head back and laughs. She holds a set of used books to her chest (good, I'll ask Iva Lou about her) and gazes all around, giving him an opportunity to take a good look at her. Isn't she a little old to be playing the coquette? It doesn't matter. My husband is enjoying this! She sways back and forth, restlessly shifting her weight from foot to foot as she chatters. She is doing most of the talking (of course she is, I'm not married to a conversationalist), then she leans in and whispers in my husband's ear. As her lips near his earlobe, I feel a stab of jealousy in my gut. Part of me wants to jump up on the balcony wall, latch on to one of the bedsheet ghosts, swing down onto the floor, and knock her over like a bowling pin. But I am his wife, so I would prefer to knock him over first and take care of her later. However, I do nothing. I sit here frozen.

Why is he still talking to her? What does he see in her? I have my answer. She laughs a final time and pats the small of his back. (That's a little low on a married man's body to pat, in my opinion.) She turns and walks away. My husband watches her as she goes. She rolls off the balls of her feet and up onto her toes to give her hips just the right swivel. Jack Mac doesn't miss one movement. I am officially sick to my stomach. Then, as if his conscience has bitten him on the ass for eyeing hers, he turns his attention innocently to the shooters at the spinning duck booth.

The popcorn-ball eaters have left. I lean forward and drape myself over the back of the seat in front of me as though I have been shot and left for dead. (I don't consider this too dramatic in light of all Iva Lou just told me!) Suddenly, as if marital radar alarms have gone off, Jack Mac feels my presence overhead and looks up at me. He smiles sheepishly. Well, maybe it's not sheepish; I don't know what it is, but whatever it is, I haven't seen that smile on his face in a long, long time. It's the kind of smile he gave me on Apple Butter Night, the night he first proposed to me. I lean back in my seat and exhale a long, deep breath toward the ceiling. (I must have been holding my breath the entire time!) The big black spider swings overhead, its crooked legs caught in the ropy web.

I'd rather die than let my husband think I saw him flirting with the Blond Mystery Woman, so I wave to him from my perch and survey the gym floor as though I'm looking for someone. He looks up at me, confused. I want to stand up and scream, in front of the entire Halloween Carnival, "Yes! Yes! Yes! I'm spying on you!" Instead I smile and give a thumbs-up to the decorations. Spec joins him. Jack points up to me. Spec motions for me as he taps the red emergency cross on his orange vest. As I run downstairs to join them on the floor, I'm hoping the kids didn't have an accident in the Spookhouse; the tile floor in there can get slick.

"We got a call up in Wampler Holler. Let's go."

"What happened?"

"Not sure. Police radiocd me," Spec tells me, handing me my gear.

"Honey, look after Etta," I tell Jack, and go with Spec. I look back as we leave. God, he looks good to me all of a sudden in his white cotton shirt and his oldest jeans. (Are all men better-looking when other women want them?)

Spec takes a road up to the holler that I've never been on before.

"So what's going on?"

"We're cuttin' through Don Wax's farm, goin' to the old Mullins homestead."

Most of the Mullins family (no relation to Fleeta) has moved out of our area; some to Kingsport, others north to "O-high" (I don't know what the industry is in Ohio, but lots of our folks have gone north to whatever awaits them there). All that's left of the Mullins family is its matriarch, Naomi, who still lives in Wampler Holler. I love this holler; it cuts into the mountain in the highest point in the cliffs, and it has a great view of East Stone Gap and the dairy farms that make up this side of Powell Valley. As Spec speeds along the ridge, I figure it's a real emergency—Naomi must be close to ninety years old. She still comes to town to trade on the first of every month; her face has not a wrinkle, and her hair is still coal black—must be that Cherokee blood.

"Is Naomi all right?"

"I ain't got no details, Ave, so don't ask me. The Fraley boy from the next house over was gittin' some firewood out of her barn and saw something and called it in."

"Fine, Mr. Testy."

Spec smiles and keeps his eyes on the road. It's just like old times, with Spec's complaining and my prying. As we approach the Mullins log cabin (which has since sprouted extra rooms and been covered in aluminum siding), we are stopped by burly Tozz Ball, a deputy in the Big Stone police department. He directs us to pull into the clearing next to the neighbors, take our gear, and approach on foot. Spec and I make our way on a small footpath that leads to Naomi's front porch.

I see a group of men, most from neighboring Norton's rescue squad, looking in the windows on the side of the log-cabin portion of the house. Spec and I join them. One of the men turns to us and motions us to be quiet.

"Lordy mercy," Spec says as he looks into the window. (He's tall enough to see over all the heads.)

"What is it?"

"You ain't gonna believe it." Spec pushes me to the front of the group so I can see in the window. There in the living room is Naomi, in a long pale green flannel nightgown, standing completely still and staring into the eyes of a six-point buck. The buck seems twice as big as any horse I've ever seen, and he doesn't seem agitated, he just looks deeply into Naomi's eyes. Naomi does not move; she stares the buck down.

"It's been pert' near an hour we been waitin'. But the buck ain't flinched, and neither has Naomi," a man holding a stun gun tells me.

"What are you gonna do?" I whisper back.

"I got ten bucks on Naomi," he whispers back.

"Boys, we'd better make a move," Spec warns the group. But no one can make a move; we're in that strange place where awe and fear intersect, and it has paralyzed us.

Naomi takes a step back without breaking her stare. As she shifts, the deer cocks his head. We hold our breath outside the window. Naomi holds up her finger.

"I'm a-gonna go, Ben," she says to the buck. "Now, you go when I go. Go on. Git." Naomi disappears down a hallway and we hear a door close.

"Who the hell is Ben?" Tozz whispers.

Then the six-point buck rears up. For a second, it looks as though he, like Naomi, may back out the open front door. Instead, in a panic, he charges the bay window at the far side of the living room and jumps through the window, tearing away the wood frame with his antlers. We hear a small yelp from deep within him as he breaks through the glass, which shatters onto the wood floor like crushed ice. In what seems like a long time but is only a few seconds, Tozz leads the charge around the side of the house to the front, to see where the buck went. As we get to the front porch steps, we see his silvery-brown rump as he leaps majestically back into the dark woods.

Spec and I run into the house to Naomi. The bay window is destroyed. The simple voile sheers are torn where the buck's antlers caught; there is fresh blood on the sash, where the glass pierced his underside. This makes my stomach turn. Spec opens the door to the bedroom for me.

"Naomi, honey, are you all right?" I ask her.

She sits on the edge of her bed in a state of calm with her hands folded neatly on her lap.

"Naomi?"

"Check her breathin'," Spec barks.

"What happened?"

"Oh, Ava Marie," Naomi says and sighs. Naomi's pale skin has a pink sheen to it; there is a little dew on her forehead (from the standoff, no doubt). Her long hair, which I have never seen outside a braided bun, is loose and hanging around her shoulders in shiny ropes. Her bedroom is small, with a bed with a red and white Irish chain quilt, a small lamp, and a table. She looks like a doll in a simple cradle as she sits. "He come to me. I dreamt it, and he done come."

"Who?"

"Ben."

"Ben?"

"My husband, Ben. Ye know."

"Naomi, we always called your husband Mule. Mule Mullins."

"His Christian name was Ben."

"I didn't know that."

"Benjamin Ezra Mullins. That was his name in full. I had a dream a while back where he was a buck and I was a doe and we was talkin' to each other like we was human." I make Naomi cough three times as I listen to her heart. "I been restless, thinkin' about him here lately. And I prayed that I could talk to him dye-rectly as I was feelin' his presence here. I been thinkin' 'bout selling this farm, and I couldn't decide on nothin' on my own, so I called on Jesus and then, o' course, my Ben."

"How did the buck, I mean Ben, get into the house?"

"He just walked right in. I had left the door open for air."

"How do you know it was him?"

"The eyes." Naomi smiles.

"What did he tell you?"

"To stay."

"Well, if that was his message, he tore up the window in the living room pretty good."

Naomi chuckles. "He never did want me to put that window in. He said we got enough light with the front windows. But I wanted me some big windows, so that I could put me some purty curtains up, like I saw in the movies. I always wanted me some big windows where the breeze comes through and moves them curtains around like fancy skirts."

"Honey, it doesn't seem like there's anything wrong with you. Your heart is beating normal, your blood pressure is good . . ."

"I wasn't skeered of that old buck."

"I know. But the excitement might've caused you some trouble."

"Aww, I feel fine," Naomi tells me, and gets up.

Spec has cleaned up the glass in the living room. Two of the men are taping cardboard along the frame where the glass had been.

"I'm gonna put on some coffee, boys. Any takers?" Naomi offers.

The men grumble appreciatively. Spec leaves his number with Naomi.

"Now you call me, youngun, if you need me."

"I will."

The ride down through the veiny roads of East Stone Gap is dark except for our high beams and the occasional jack-o'-lantern on a porch. As we speed through the black night, I have a sense that time has stopped. I am somewhere in the past, when I was younger and wore the same orange vest and sat beside Spec in this very wagon that forever smells of tobacco and spearmint.

"Ave?"

"Yeah, Spec?"

"That there was a good run."

"For everybody but the deer."

"Yup." He smiles.

"It was a mystical experience."

"Don't start that stuff, Ave."

"Spec, that was a visit from the beyond."

"It was a visit from the woods. That deer saw a light through an open door and went in Naomi's house uninvited. And that there is the end of it."

"Nope. Naomi thinks it was a visit from her husband on the other side."

"You're givin' me the creeps."

"I thought you were a believer."

"I am. If it's Bible-approved, or if it makes any goddamn sense. People don't come back as animals. That's nuts."

"I wish I knew where we go when we die."

"What good would that do?"

"I don't know. Maybe I'd live differently. Maybe I wouldn't be so afraid to lose people. I get scared that I'll never see my mother again. My son."

"I shore would like to see my mama agin. And my pap, too. 'Cause if I could see 'em agin, I would ask 'em a lot of things. Things that weigh on my mind."

"Like what?"

"Like why both of 'em died on me before I could git to 'em. Both of 'em. Ma went in her sleep, and Pap died at the hospital. But I never did say good-bye to neither of 'em. I wish that were different."

"I wish I would have made my mama go to Italy. She never went home, you know. That bothers me."

"I knew your mama. You couldn't make her do nothin' that she didn't want to do. So you got to let go of that one."

"I guess so."

As Spec drives us up the holler road, I wish for a minute that the run weren't over. There are things I'd like to talk about.

"Thank ye, Ave. You done good."

"Don't flatter me, Spec. It ain't your style."

Spec smiles. I grab my gear and go into our old stone house.

Etta must be asleep, I can see the glimmer of her nightlight from the bottom of the stairs. I place my gear on the bench and head back to our bedroom. Jack is propped up in bed, reading.

"How's Naomi?"

"How'd you know?"

"They made an announcement at the carnival. A guy from the Norton fire department called down the mountain with details."

"It was something to see."

"I'll bet." Jack goes back to his reading. When I see my husband, so comfortable in our house, in our bed, I feel as though we could last forever. I want to tell him about Naomi's dream, and I wonder if he believes in that sort of thing. We never talk about things like that, so I don't know.

"Do you ever dream about Joe?" I ask him.

Jack puts down his newspaper and looks at me, surprised that I brought Joe up. "No, I don't," he says softly. "Or maybe if I do, I don't remember it." We never talk about him; it's just easier that way. I turn to go into the bathroom to wash up for bed.

"Why do you ask?"

"I wonder where he is."

"In heaven."

"God, Jack."

"Don't you believe that?"

"I tell Etta that; I guess I'm hoping it's true."

"I thought you believed."

"Oh, I believe. I just don't know in what," I say. Jack looks at me funny. "What?"

"Ave, sometimes . . . I don't know. I don't get it." He shrugs and goes back to his reading.

"Honey?"

Jack puts down his paper. "What?"

"Sometimes you don't get *me*."

I go into the bathroom and take a good, long time brushing my teeth. Jack appears in the doorway. "Is everything all right?"

I want to say, "No. I'm scared. Who was that woman at the carnival? Are you tired of me?" Instead, I look at my husband and say, "Everything is fine." He buys it and goes back to bed. And that, I am sure, is the root of our problem.

# CHAPTER THREE

For the first time in his life, Jack MacChesney is officially his own boss. MR. J's Construction Company opened its door on November 20. MR. J stands for Mousey, Rick, and Jack. Very clever. Rick finagled a small office for them at the car dealership. Morgan Legg, the owner, was happy to oblige them, as Rick was his top salesman on the floor last year. I have never seen my husband so happy. And they're off to a good strong start. They bid on a job to renovate the Fellowship Hall at the Methodist Church, and they won. Jack is having a ball designing the new space. No money coming in yet, but it doesn't matter, my husband's smiling face is payment enough. Jack's new job frees up extra time for Etta too. When he was a miner, he left before dawn and often came home after dark. Now he controls his time, so we see more of each other. I feel our troubles lifting a bit. A real reason to celebrate come Christmas.

I'm back to working full-time, and I like it. Jack didn't like the idea at first, but I was so supportive of his new company that he let go of any misgivings he may have had about my schedule.

The grand opening of the Soda Fountain is December 1. (Otto and

Worley are practically living in the Mutual's, trying to finish the job.) We're having specials and giveaways all month. (Maybe we can unload some of that partially used Estée Lauder cream that Fleeta pinches.) Pearl has sifted through lots of employment applications, looking for two waitresses and a cook. She has decided to hire Tayloe Lassiter as head waitress, who, despite having two babies now (Misty was joined by baby Travis last year) is still a looker and can draw a crowd. Sarah Dunleavy, the high school teacher who replaced Theodore when he left for the University of Tennessee, directs the Outdoor Drama and has taken Tayloe under her wing. She gives her acting lessons, and everyone in town agrees that Tayloe has gone from amateur to semiprofessional actress beautifully. Sarah has also encouraged Tayloe to model. Occasionally, we see Tayloe in the *Kingsport Times* on the hood of a new truck or in an ad for kitchen appliances.

Pearl comes in with a large packing box. "Fleets, the tinsel is in."

Fleeta takes the box and rips into it.

Pearl comes behind the counter. "I'd like you to come over to Lew Eisenberg's with me."

"Right now?"

"Yeah. If you don't mind."

"What's the matter?"

"Nothing. Just need your help on something."

"Okay." I grab my coat and follow Pearl out.

Lew Eisenberg has gone from the best local lawyer for the coal companies to representing the townsfolk in all matters from wills to divorces. He's always busy, and he's very good. He's even happy now that his wife, Inez, has gotten back her race-car body. She is a Weight Watchers leader, having kept off fifty-eight pounds for over seven years. It's been a long time since I've heard Lew mention moving back to Long Island, New York.

Lew's hair is completely gray; other than that, you'd never guess he was flirting with sixty. "Hey kids," he says from behind his desk. "Ave, your husband was in with his buddies incorporating last week. What do you think of that?"

"If you can't keep Westmoreland Coal Company in town, we'll take it," I tell Lew.

"We're real busy over at the Pharmacy," Pearl tells Lew, cutting the chitchat in half.

"Okay, so let's get to it. This is easy. Ave Maria, Pearl wants to make you her partner at the Pharmacy."

"A partner? Why?" I turn so that I'm facing Pearl. She glances at Lew, then looks at me.

"Because I need a partner now. We've grown so much that I can't oversee everything alone."

"I can't do it."

"Sure you can."

"No I can't. I have more than I can handle." I can't tell Pearl and Lew that for the first time in three years I feel my home life is return- ing to normal, that the hole left by Joe's death is slowly being filled by time, routine, and change. How could they understand that?

"I'm going to hire more help for you." Pearl offers.

"No, I'm sorry, Pearl. No."

"But you need it," Pearl blurts. It's no secret that with the mines closed, anyone with a miner in the family is struggling.

"We're doing fine."

"Let's say that you *are* doing fine, I still need help. I'm looking to expand, and I want to keep the flagship going strong. I'd have to hire a manager; who better than you?" Flagship? Little Main Street Mul- ligan's Mutual Pharmacy a flagship? What is Pearl talking about?

I turn to Pearl. "You're expanding?"

"I'd like to open a pharmacy in Norton. I've been looking at a building."

"You're serious?"

Lew pulls out a file and shows me a picture of the old insurance building, which has been abandoned for several years, in downtown Norton.

"We're talking to the realtor right now," he tells me.

"I think my concept of a down-home variety drugstore is one that can work anywhere. And Norton needs a pharmacy. They have two hospitals but no pharmacy."

"Pearl's on to something here. You should consider this," Lew says, peering at me over his glasses.

I know I should. I'd have fewer Night Worries about the bills, college, and pensions. And the other part of all of this is just selfish. I've missed my pharmacy. I loved making the day-to-day decisions; I used to be a person who *ran* something. Being in charge gave me a sense of accomplishment that I don't get working part-time or at home scrubbing the oven. I still have to scrub the oven, and that's okay, but I love my job.

"Ave, please do this. I wouldn't have anything, I wouldn't be anything, if you hadn't helped Mama and me. It forever changed us. I owe you." Pearl looks off for a second, and then that familiar concentration crease between her eyes deepens. "And I don't like owing people. So let me at least begin to pay you back by sharing in the success of Mutual's."

"The chain," Lew pipes in.

"Let me see what you've got there."

Lew hands me papers; Pearl lets out a whoop and claps her hands. It's a simple deal. On the flagship store, I will be salaried as a manager and pharmacist and take 50 percent of the profits; the other share goes to Pearl. As I sign my name, I am thinking of my daughter and her future. She needs security. My husband will never leave Cracker's Neck Holler, and now that he's found work he enjoys, I have to contribute all I can, however I can.

As Pearl and I walk back to the Pharmacy, she chatters on about her business plans, and I think about my family. This break will help us;

I'm tired of worrying, and maybe this will help me stop. Ever since Joe died, when something wonderful happens, I have a moment of elation, then I remember my son and feel a pang of doom. What good is anything without my son to share it with? Now that I've ruined the moment for myself, I plunge further into despair. I feel a strange sense of defeat: here I go again, I'm tied down to a business I didn't choose in the first place. When I gave the Pharmacy to Pearl, it was a no-strings deal. I knew the power that guilt can have over a person because it had defined my life. How I wanted to do the choosing and be free to invent myself. I had made a plan. I was going to leave Big Stone Gap and find myself out there in the world, seek my happiness, own my destiny, have a life of adventure before it was too late. Instead of going away, though, I fell in love and stayed here. I married Jack Mac and believed that the only cage I had been in was one of my own creation. Why do I now have that old boxed-in feeling when I should feel relief?

Jack's truck is parked in front of the Mutual's when we return. "I hope Etta's all right," I tell Pearl.

When we get inside, we find Jack, Rick, and Mousey working with Otto in the Soda Fountain. Etta is wearing Fleeta's smock and painting one of the wood panels on the base of the counter.

"Hey, what's going on?" I say to the men, who look up but keep working.

"Well, we was worried that we wasn't gonna make our deadline. So I called old Jack Mac and I done tole him my troubles and he come over and here we are," Otto explains.

"I'm painting, Mama!" Etta says proudly.

"I can see that," I tell my daughter, who haphazardly streaks paint down the wood.

"Don't worry, Ave. It's just the base coat," Otto says under his breath.

"Try not to get any paint on Fleeta's smock."

"She can ruin it for all I care," Fleeta says as she stacks boxes of Christmas tree lights onto the shelf.

I watch my husband as he stands on a ladder, maneuvering a ceiling tile into place. I consider what I told Pearl about spending fifteen years in this town without a boyfriend. Suddenly, I am not in the present—I am the woman I was ten years ago, when I worked in this Pharmacy and it was my life. My husband swivels on the ladder. I don't think any man could look better in a pair of old overalls and a bandanna. We're so different; he's talented with his hands, and the last book he read was *Moby-Dick* in the eleventh grade. I can't hammer a nail, and I wait for the Bookmobile every Saturday. I must be attracted to what I don't have, but I wonder what I fill up in him. He catches me looking at him and smiles. "What are you looking at?"

"You," I tell him.

"Jack, you gots a call."

My husband and I are really looking at each other in a way we haven't in a very long time, and I don't want this moment to end.

"She says it's important," Fleeta says impatiently.

"Who is it?" I ask. My tone of voice causes every man in the room to look at me.

"Karen. Karen somebody," Fleeta barks.

"I'll be right there," Jack says, and steps off the ladder. He touches my arm as he passes; I'm going to take that as a sign of reassurance for now. I look over at Rick, who studies the trim of the counter a little too intently.

"Who's Karen?" I ask him. Without looking up, he shrugs.

Mousey interjects. "She manages the lumber store up in Coeburn. We git our lumber there."

I'm so glad I asked.

"Hel-looo?" Iva Lou calls out from the front of the Pharmacy.

"We're back here," I holler.

"Well, lookee here. This is gonna be some soda fountain." Iva Lou inspects the job. "All we need is Lana Turner on the stool and we're in business."

"Who's Lana Turner?" Etta asks.

"She was a sweater girl in the movies when I was a boy," Otto tells her.

"A sweater girl?"

"Yeah, she made me sweat." Otto laughs.

"Mr. Honeycutt shows her movies sometimes. I just haven't taken you to any of them yet," I tell my daughter.

"I got tickets over to the Barter The-A-ter in Abingdon for tomorrow's matinee," Iva Lou tells me.

"What are you seeing?"

"*Fiddler on the Roof.* Remember that Womack girl who used to understudy June in the Drama? Well, she's playin' one of the sisters. I put a group together. I was hoping I could take Etta."

"I want to go to the show!" Etta says. She puts down her paintbrush and shoves her bangs out of her eyes.

"Okay, honey."

"I'm gonna be all alone this weekend without my women," Jack Mac says from behind me.

"Really? You throwing me out?" I tease.

"Kind of." Jack kisses me on the forehead and pulls a ticket from his pocket. UNIVERSITY OF TENNESSEE VS. ALABAMA, it says in orange letters.

"What's this?"

"You're going to Knoxville to see Theodore."

"You're kidding." I'm thrilled. Utterly surprised and a little confused, but thrilled at the prospect of a weekend without chores and errands and worries. I have the most thoughtful husband in the world.

"Go on home and pack. Your bus leaves in an hour."

"Etta, you'll be all right?"

"Mama. Go," she says, and rolls her eyes.

"Okay. Great. I'm leaving." I kiss Etta and then my husband.

"I'll follow you home and give you a lift back down to town," Iva Lou says as I head for the door.

Once I'm home, I throw together a duffel bag of clothes, feed the cat, and turn up the heat so it'll be warm when Jack and Etta come home later.

"You need to git away," Iva Lou tells me as we descend the mountain into the Gap.

"I do?"

"Honey, you're worn to a nub. We've all noticed it."

"I thought I was fine."

"Not to those of us who know ye."

We travel in silence for a moment. I dismiss the fact that folks are discussing my moods behind my back.

"There was something I meant to ask you a while ago."

"Shoot."

"Do you remember a woman with blond hair buying books at the Halloween Carnival? She was small?" I was going to use the word "petite" but that sounds too pretty.

"There were so many people there."

"This one kind of had a tan?"

"Hon, I don't remember." Iva Lou looks at me. "Why do you ask?"

"I just never saw her before. I thought maybe you knew her."

"No. I could ask James. Maybe he knows her."

"No, no, that's okay. It's not important."

"Are you sure? James is a bigger gossip than any woman I know. He's carried more stories across this county than there are miles on the Bookmobile."

"Nope. It's okay."

I have always loved bus rides. When you grow up in a small town, they really are your ticket to the outside world. I've been to Washington, D.C., Cincinnati, Nashville, Memphis, and Charlottesville by bus.

Last year, I took Etta and two of her friends to Knoxville for "Holiday on Ice." Theodore showed us the town, even let the kids run on the football field at the U.T. stadium. Jack stayed home. (You couldn't pay him to go to an ice show—another one of those facts that surface after you marry someone.) I love ice shows: the cold stadium, the crowd, the smell of carmel popcorn, the pale blue ice rink, the criss-crossing beams of red and tangerine spotlights, and of course, the Stars of the Show, the skaters, lean and graceful, who shoot past in their glittering tulle skirts.

The bus is nearly empty tonight. I'm sitting behind the driver (my favorite seat), with my feet resting on the aluminum bar separating his area from the rest of the bus. As we speed along in the dark, the soft lights of the distant farms fade into the black, creating a hypnotic effect that begins to lull me to sleep. I am exhausted, so I take my duffel bag and place it on the seat next to me. As I begin to stretch out and lie down, a sudden thought causes me to bolt upright. Why did Jack rush me out of town so quickly? Does he have a date with that mysterious blond? The driver must have heard me shift quickly because he looks at me in the rearview. Honestly. Stop this, I tell myself. You're making things up. I lean over onto the duffel bag. If I sleep, we'll get to Knoxville all the faster.

"Hey. Sleepyhead. Wake up," the familiar deep voice teases me.

"Theodore!" I sit up, refreshed from my nap. "God, you look great!" And he does. He is trim; I can see the cut of his biceps through his T-shirt. "What's with the arms?"

"The beauty of working at a university is the free gym and trainers."

"Get me a job here. Immediately."

Theodore takes my bag, and I catch him up on everything as we charge through the bus station. We stop under a crosswalk light so I can show him Etta's new school picture.

"Hungry?" he asks me as he loads the bag into his car.

"Starving."

We go to a twenty-four-hour IHOP and settle into a booth, just like the old days. When Theodore lived in Big Stone Gap, we'd drive over to Kingsport after the football games and sit at Shoney's all night dissecting the halftime show and everything else going on in our lives. How simple it was! How perfect.

In the bright, warm light I can see Theodore more clearly. We talk on the phone a lot, but I haven't seen him in months. He still looks like the passionate pirate poet who moved to Big Stone Gap from Scranton, Pennsylvania, so many years ago. There is nothing boyish about him anymore, though. He is Lord of the Manor now, his strong jaw more chiseled, character and experience having given him a sort of nobility. His red hair is as full as ever, and there's some white in it at the temples; the blue eyes are a little more crinkled, but not much; overall, his face is smooth and clear. Theodore looks like a man who loves his life, and that makes me very happy.

"Tell me everything," he says.

"I've told you everything." I laugh. "Etta is great. Jack started a new business."

"Everything about *you*."

I don't know why, but that sounds like the strangest thing I have ever heard. I don't think of myself separate and apart from what I have to *do*. I think about things that need to be done. Taking care of my responsibilities. Being there for my family. When Theodore asks me about myself, I realize that I don't have anything to say.

"Come on. Talk," he says as he punches open a tiny white plastic barrel of half-and-half and dumps it in his coffee.

"Pearl asked me to partner with her at the Pharmacy. She's opening a new shop in Norton. I didn't want to say yes."

"Why?"

I shrug. "It's hers."

"Well, good for Pearl for asking you to partner. You gave her a future when you gave her your store. Let her help you now. Are you going to do it?"

"Yes. I signed the papers today. I'll be the manager and split the Big Stone profits fifty-fifty with her."

"What does Jack think?"

"He doesn't know yet."

"Oh," Theodore says casually.

"It just happened today. I haven't had a chance to talk to him." Boy that sounds lame—and it sounds lame because it *is* lame. I hold everything in, and not for any good reason I can think of!

I want to tell Theodore everything. I want to tell him that when the mines closed, I was afraid Jack wouldn't find a job; how he laughed when I suggested he take some engineering classes; how he looked at that woman at the Halloween Carnival. And how I get scared, every day, that I am going to lose him. How can I explain it to Theodore? Months after Joe died, Father Rausch came to see me. He told me that most marriages break up when a child dies. I couldn't imagine losing my son and then losing my husband. What good would that do? And Etta needed us. I still worry about her and the way losing Joe affected her. I want to tell Theodore every detail. But I can't. I want everything to be just fine. It has to be. What have I worked so long and hard for? Besides, isn't this life? Aren't things hard? Doesn't the romance come and go? Don't children take precedence over everything else? Don't all husbands stop looking at their wives instead of drinking in their beauty? Don't they learn to see past the exterior and right into our brains, where necessary facts and schedules are stored? Don't all marriages become routine? Spats? Silences? Weird openended arguments? Sex on the porch? Sour milk and burnt toast? Dirty laundry? Isn't money always a problem?

"What is going on with you? Your face looks like a Picasso, for Godsakes."

Looking distorted doesn't worry me. "Do I look old?" I ask him.

Theodore laughs.

"Do I?"

"No."

"Thank you."

"Why did you ask me that?"

"Because I live in Big Stone Gap, where people have seen me every day for forty-two years and don't really look at me."

"What about your husband?"

I can't answer. Instead, I start to cry.

"Jesus, what is wrong?" Theodore says as he yanks napkins out of the holder on the table and shoves them toward me.

"I'm scared."

"Of what?"

"That it's over."

"What's over?"

"Everything."

"What are you talking about? Are you sick?"

"No. I'm fine."

"What's over? Your marriage?"

"Yes."

"What's going on?"

"Jack is looking at other women."

"So?"

"Strange women with tans."

"Tans in November?" Theodore tries not to laugh.

"I know. It makes me sick." The word "sick" makes me weep harder.

"Who is she?"

"I don't know her name. She wears tight pants."

"You don't know her name but you've checked out her ass?"

"I can't help it. I had to watch them. They didn't see me. It's not like I stalked them or something. I just watched them fall all over each other at the Halloween Carnival."

"Your husband is madly in love with you. He'd be crazy to even think of another woman."

"You say that, but you didn't see her. She was working it! She was patting his back. Low. She's one of those predators. One of those women, and you can just tell, who only wants a married man. They're in it for the thrill. For the pain it causes people like me. She looks like one of those women who has all day to fix a strand of hair! And look at me. I barely have time to put on lipstick. I'm starting to look like Ma Kettle, for Godsakes."

"Have you asked Jack Mac who she is?"

"God no."

"Why not?"

"Because in every Bette Davis movie I have ever seen, when the woman asks the man that question, the man always says, 'I'm sorry, yes, you're right, you're so intuitive, yes, I love her. And I don't love you anymore. So set me free so at least one of us can be happy.' "

"Don't base your real life on bad melodrama," Theodore says, rearranging the sugar packets in their plastic holder.

"Do you have a better idea?" I ask him as I blow my nose.

The waitress comes over to take our order. She doesn't even look concerned. She just picks up my wad of tear-soaked napkins and dumps them in the trash on the way back to the kitchen. I guess a lot of people face their demons in the middle of the night at the International House of Pancakes.

"Why would your husband call me and brag about you and how hard you work and what a great wife and mother you are and how you need a weekend away because there isn't enough he could do to ever thank you, if he was leaving you?"

"I don't know."

"You have got to get a grip."

Theodore's exasperation soothes me. Maybe I am crazy. "I know I sound totally irrational—"

"Listen to me. This thing, this blackness and doom you feel, is just a tiny storm cloud of feelings passing overhead. You are at a crisis point. I don't think it's about Jack Mac and Etta. It's about Joe."

"I'm dealing with Joe."

"Joe isn't here to deal with. That's your problem," Theodore says tenderly.

"I hate myself. I was a terrible mother to him."

"You were not!"

"Do you know that I yelled at him every day? Do you know that he got spanked? And I swore to Jack I'd never spank the kids. But he turned on the water in the tub and left it and it overflowed and ruined the ceiling and I went crazy. I took him to sit in Etta's time-out chair. He laughed at it! In fact, he never sat in it. The thing had cobwebs on it!"

"So you spanked him. What else?"

"I was so busy trying to make him behave that I missed everything. I was chasing him all the time. Correcting him. Begging him to sit still. Whatever it was."

"He was a demanding kid."

"But I didn't appreciate him. I wanted him to be more like Etta. And he wasn't. He was a tornado. Even the way he got sick in the end. Etta gets a cold, and it takes her half the winter to get over it. I see bruises on Joe one morning, and six days later he's dead. Don't you see? He was this unbelievably vibrant color, this amazing shot of purple that flew in and flew out, and I was too busy trying to make him into something else. I blew it. I totally blew it. And now, three years later, I just want to apologize to him. To tell him I'm sorry for not seeing what he was." I'm stunned that I am not crying. Theodore looks at me.

"Feel better?"

"I sort of . . . do." The waitress refills my coffee and dumps some more half-and-half onto the table. "Really, yeah, I'm fine," I tell Theodore and then the waitress, who ignores me and checks her reflection in the window of our booth.

"No, you're not. You wouldn't be here. You wouldn't be asking me if you look old. Somehow Jack knew you needed a deeper conversation. One that cannot be had over the phone."

"Did he say something to you?" I rise up in the booth by my chin like a rattlesnake peeking out of a basket.

"No. He did not," Theodore says calmly. His tone of voice makes me sink right back down into the booth.

"How do you know so much about men?"

"I've been one for a long time."

"Right." I stir my coffee. I don't care if it's my second cup and it's the middle of the night. "You should thank God you're not married."

"I could never be married."

"Good thinking."

"It's not for me."

"You're smart."

"No. I'm gay."

The IHOP becomes very quiet. It's almost as though I can hear the pancake batter pouring onto the griddle through the swing doors.

"You are?"

"Yeah."

"Well, when?"

"Since I can remember."

The thoughts kick up in my head in a thousand different directions. Questions pop up: How? Why didn't you tell me sooner? Is there a special man in your life? That's why we couldn't take our friendship any further so long ago! I wasn't crazy! You just weren't available! "Couldn't you have told me thirteen years ago?"

"Why? I wasn't going to date men in Big Stone Gap."

"Good point."

"And we had each other."

"Yes, we did." Boy, did we have each other. For so many years, that was all I needed. Why does my single past seem so perfect now, so uncomplicated? Was it? "When did you know?"

"I guess I knew all my life. But I wasn't out all my life. I guess I thought I was a loner, and that I would never become attached to anyone because I didn't need it. I have a creative life, and it makes me whole. I wasn't unhappy. I was and am very fulfilled. I never saw that people in couples were very happy, so I assumed it wasn't for me. And when I met you, we had such a mind meld."

"Yes, we did."

"You never made me feel bad about being a loner. You were one too."

"I know. It explains a lot, though."

"Sure. Everything. It was that missing piece of information that made all the facts fall into place. I was fighting my instinct to be who I was—that's always a bad idea."

"Do you have someone special in your life now?"

"I did. A biochemist who was at UT on a grant, studying some kind of cells to cure some kind of something. He was terrific, but he lives in Boston, and I'm not moving, so it didn't work out."

"I would have loved to have met him." And I mean that. We sit quietly for a few minutes, but I'm never troubled by long silences when I'm with Theodore. That's just our rhythm.

"By the way, you didn't turn me gay."

"I like to blame myself for everything from laundry mistakes to the failure of world peace, but I won't take on that I turned you gay." I pat his hand.

"Good."

"It's a good thing you figured it out while you're still young."

"Yep. I figured it out in the nick of time."

"Maybe that's what I'm scared of. I feel like my life is ice in my hands. It's going by so fast, and I'm not any smarter. I don't have that peace that I read about in magazines. I'm old enough to be wise, and I'm not. I don't want to get old, though. I feel like I've never been young. Maybe I thought love was going to make me young."

"Before we go down this road," Theodore says, "let me say that aging is worst for two groups: women and gay men. Straight men are told they're potent all their lives, they can be ninety and have kids, and so on. I know what you mean about feeling old and stupid. I'm not a professional psychologist, so don't hold me to any of this, but I think what's going on here, apart from your communication problems with your husband and your grief for your son, is even more personal. It's about you. You woke up one day and realized that you were halfway through. You're middle-aged."

"I am not! Fifty is middle-aged."

"Okay, now we're squabbling about numbers. Here's the fact of the matter: there's a lot behind you. You've got some miles on you now. You're not a sweet young thing anymore."

"I was never a sweet young thing! And don't think I don't resent *that*!"

"Stop whining. Let me finish. Getting older is tough. It's depressing. But it happens to all of us. Look at me. I'm lifting barbells sumo wrestlers won't touch because I want pecs of steel, believing that muscles will hold up my youth like those pillars hold up the Acropolis. Well, they don't. The only thing you can do is accept it. Do the best you can. But accept it."

"Am I that shallow?"

"We're all shallow. But you're luckier than most. You don't really look forty-whatever-you-are. You can be one of those timeless beauties with the good skin. You can wear cardigan sweaters and a little lipstick, and no one will know if you're thirty or sixty. Okay?"

"I feel so stupid." I swing my legs sideways in the booth and sink down.

"Vanity will do that to you."

"I am vain, aren't I?"

"And a little paranoid. You had to take a three-and-a-half-hour bus ride to have me tell you that your husband is not having an affair. Look at yourself. You're letting one woman in tight jeans derail your entire life. You have *earned* a glorious marriage, because you and Jack have gone through the worst and come out the other side. And you still have your daughter. You are still a family, even though Joe is gone. And you love each other! Stop. Think. What are you doing? This woman who has no name has taken your self-confidence and run off with it. How can you let a stranger do that to you?"

Theodore's guest room is simple and comfortable. There is an old, rich chocolate-colored four-poster bed, a matching dresser, and a small Tiffany-style lamp. There's a luggage rack for my duffel bag and a full-length mirror behind the door. The walls, the linens, the rug—everything is white. I pull back the coverlet and climb under the cool sheets. This is the first time I have been alone in a bed since I married Jack MacChesney. I've never gone anywhere without him in all this time, nor he without me. I wonder if he is thinking the same thing at home in our bed. I stretch my arms from edge to edge in the double bed and my feet as far apart as they can go. I stay in this snow-angel position until sleep comes.

Big Orange does not begin to describe the University of Tennessee Football Experience. It should be called All Orange, All the Time. Thousands of fans descend upon Knoxville wearing the theme color, and many of them have painted all exposed skin to match; their devotion seems to begin on a cellular level. I have never seen such football mania (and I went to Saint Mary's College in South Bend, Indiana!). Painted people aside, Knoxville is a genteel Southern city famous for its Dogwood Festival and debutantes. You get a sense of times gone by when you walk the streets here.

Once I'm at the stadium, I weave my way through the tailgate parties (a man is actually roasting chicken on a spit in the back of his station wagon). Theodore let me sleep late and left without me. He meets me at the staff entrance and takes me up one of the aerial booths where the football staff films the games. This is also Theodore's perch, where he can watch the 125 brilliant musicians who make up the UT Marching Band. "Theodore, remember the county band competitions?"

"Yeah. We always beat Appalachia's Tricky Sixty," Theodore remembers.

"Enrollment took a dive since you left. Now they're called the Dirty Thirty."

Theodore laughs. I can't believe he's gone from the Wise County band competition to national television in less than ten years.

We barely watch the first half of the game as Theodore checks via headsets with the camera crews who are set to record the halftime show. He is a celebrity and honored auteur here—people stop him and ask for his autograph—because he delivers. Theodore, however, takes it all in stride; he knows his popularity rises and falls along with the success of the football team: no sense having a winning band with a losing team.

When the band takes the field at halftime, the crowd goes wild. If you could tap the energy in this stadium right now, you could win a war or move a pyramid. Theodore plays right into the razzle-dazzle. The majorettes are glorious, magazine-cover gorgeous: the whole weekend is an homage to youth, powerhouse athletics, and white-toothed sex appeal.

Theodore's shows are more technical, more complex, than they were back in Big Stone Gap. Of course, this is another level entirely. But it is a wonder to see how Theodore has grown with the challenge of college football, most of it nationally televised. He has assumed the mantle with little fuss. He has Elizabeth Taylor to thank for this opportunity, and he knows it. If it weren't for her fateful visit to Big Stone Gap, Theodore never would have been discovered.

As the band takes the field, Theodore is calm and focused. A row of small television monitors on the desk in front of us all record several angles of the performance at once. Theodore takes some notes, occasionally curses, sometimes smiles. I don't know how he keeps what he's watching straight. All I know is, when I look out of this glassy cube in the sky down onto the bright green field filled from end to end with crisp orange and white figures moving as smoothly as the intricate inner workings of a Swiss watch, I would be hard-pressed to find a mistake. I see only an astounding sculpture in motion, and the crowd agrees, thousands of them on their feet, feasting at the sight and sound of this display.

"Pretty good," Theodore says as the band marches off the field. "Let's go."

We leave the booth and head down what seems to be secret stairs into the belly of the stadium. We come out into daylight on the ground level of the field; the plastic passes hanging around our necks on chains give us immediate access everywhere. Security guards nod respectfully at Theodore; VIPs lean over the side of their boxes and yell, "Good show! You're the man!" Theodore takes my hand and leads me up a tiny set of stairs to the base of the band box. I look up, and as far as my eyes can see, this orange and white checkerboard reaches to the top of the sky. The band major and Theodore huddle, and the band members watch with interest. Then the captain blows his whistle, and they launch into "The Tennessee Waltz." The crowd goes wild. Theodore looks all around the stadium slowly, and for a moment, backlit by the orange and white musicians, with a breeze blowing through his hair, he is just a little bit Greek god, but surely all artist. He takes me in his arms and we spin to the music.

We have a lazy Sunday, and too soon it is time for me to get on the bus and head for home. I have an extra duffel bag full of UT paraphernalia and stuff Theodore bought for Etta—puzzles and games and an origami kit. Etta knows about international crafts because of Theodore. He is far from an absentee honorary uncle.

"I want you to remain calm," Theodore tells me as he hugs me good-bye.

"Promise you'll come for Christmas," I tell him, not letting go until he promises.

"I will be there. I'll bring the eggnog."

"I love you."

"I love you too."

I climb onto the bus and sit in my usual seat, right behind the driver. Theodore circles around and taps on the window. I use both hands to slide my window back.

"You're not old. You're beautiful."

"Thank you," I tell him, meaning it, restored after a great weekend. I'm not crazy, I'm okay. I'm just human. I get scared, and I can be comforted. That's the miracle of Theodore Tipton. He makes it all better.

As the bus pulls away, I'm not sad. Christmas is just a few weeks away. I want to go home. I miss Etta terribly. And being away from Jack, even with all of our problems, made me long for him. I haven't kissed him like I meant it in a long time. I will, though, as soon as I see him. I can't wait.

As the bus makes its descent into Big Stone Gap through the Wildcat, I am filled with anticipation. The apricot sun fades behind the blue mountains in twilight. The trunks of the trees, knotty and twisting toward the sky, wet with rain, look like they're embroidered in shiny black pearls. They make a fence down either side of the road; I feel protected, but I can see the mountains beyond spilling away in layers down the sides like cake batter. There is an awesome beauty to the Appalachian Trail, where the Blue Ridge meets Tennessee. Soon I will be inside the mountain again, inside the Gap, home.

Jack is waiting for me at the bus station. I am sitting on the edge of my seat like a kid, full of stories to tell. I want to tell Jack everything. I want to tell him how I went away so afraid and how I've come home full of hope again. I wave to him from the window, and he waves back. Etta isn't with him; how romantic! I stand with my bag before the bus can make a full stop. The driver's flinty brown eyes narrow in annoyance, and I lurch forward when he brakes. I thank him as I charge down the steps toward my husband. I throw myself into his arms and cover his sweet face in kisses. He accepts the kisses but doesn't kiss me back.

"What's wrong?" I ask him.

"Did you have a nice weekend?" he asks me without emotion.

"It was great. Is something wrong with Etta?" Now I'm worried. Why is he acting so strange?

"Etta is fine. She had a good time at the play," he tells me, taking my bag.

"Musical."

"Musical. Play. What's the goddamned difference?"

"Why are you yelling at me?" I'm yelling at him.

"It's all over town that Pearl made you her partner."

"What?" For a moment, I forget time and place. I was so happy to come home, I forgot all about last Friday, all about the deal and the papers.

"Why didn't you tell me?"

"Wait a second. I was going to tell you Friday night, but you had my trip planned. There wasn't time."

"You could've told me before you left. There is no excuse for this. None."

"Jack. This is ridiculous."

"You know, the things you think are ridiculous, I think are important. That, right there, is the problem with us." Jack throws my duffel bag in the back of the truck. If I weren't so angry, I'd be laughing. The word "problem"—that's my word, he never used that before. Men don't use that word about their relationships, they use it for cars that won't start or appliances that break down.

"Don't throw my things!" I holler, sounding about five years old.

"Get in the truck."

"Don't tell me what to do!"

"I'd like to find the person who tells you what to do and you do it. I'd like to meet him and shake his hand."

"What's the matter with you? I can't do anything right. I only agreed to partner with Pearl so you could be free to go off and be a construction worker, own your own business. I thought if I could take some of the burden off of you financially, you would be free to pursue your dream."

"You kill me."

"What?"

"Since when do you care about my dreams?"

I don't say a word. I get in the truck. He jumps into his seat and faces me. "You don't think I can take care of us. You don't believe I can make a go of the business, so you go behind my back and cut a deal so you'd feel secure."

"That is not true! I am not thinking about me. I'm thinking of Etta. Okay? If that makes me a bad person, then I'm a bad person!"

"You don't trust me. If you trusted me, you would have come home and discussed it with me. And we would have made a decision together. One that was best for our family. Instead, I hear about it all over town. Folks think it's pretty funny that I need a woman to take care of me, so I can have a hobby as a fix-it man." Jack leans back in the seat, defeated. I can't bear to see him own this like it's true.

"I never said you were a fix-it man. Who cares what people think anyway?"

Jack doesn't answer me; he just starts the truck and drives fast, back up into the holler. He pulls up next to the house. I jump out of the truck and pull my duffel bag out of the bed. I don't look back. I climb the steps, and Etta meets me at the door. She is happy and shows me the program from *Fiddler on the Roof.* I hear the gravel spit out under the tires as the truck bounces back down the mountain.

"Where's Daddy going?"

"I don't know."

"Is he mad?"

"I think so."

"Did I do something?" Etta's brow wrinkles with worry.

"No, you didn't. Daddy is under a lot of pressure. That's all."

I divert her attention with all the goodies from Uncle Theodore. Etta pulls apart the origami kit. We sit on the floor and make shapes with the delicate rice paper. I have to use both of my hands to hold the directions, I am shaking so. The rice paper is so thin, so delicate, I'm afraid I'll tear it. "Here, Mommy, let me." Etta takes the paper and lays them out on the floor in front of us.

I give Etta a snack and tuck her into bed. I check the clock; it's almost nine, and Jack is still not home. I made up an excuse for Etta, but the kid is smart. She knows. I switch on the nightlight in the hallway and turn to go downstairs, but instead, I go into Joe's old bedroom. We converted it into a playroom for Etta a couple of years ago. I turned his twin bed into a daybed, with a red corduroy cover; now it looks more like a couch. Etta has set up a blackboard and chairs. I go over to the daybed and lie down.

For the first few months after Joe died, I would go to bed with my husband, wait until he was asleep, and then get up. I'd wander through the house, then eventually I'd come up here to Joe's room and lie on his bed. It was the only place in the house where I could find rest. I tried the sun porch and the living room couch, but I never slept. Once I knew that I could fall asleep in Joe's room, I came here every night.

I never told Jack why I came up here. Any discussions of Joe's death were just too painful. And I couldn't tell him about The Dream, the real reason I came up here each night. I could hardly wait for night to come so I could have The Dream, the same dream, night after comforting night. Joe and I would run through the house. And we would laugh and laugh. The laughter was so real. It sounded like him, and it sounded like me. And then, as we were getting pains in our stomachs from laughing so hard, the roof tore cleanly away from the house, leaving no jagged edges, as though it were the lid of a pot being lifted off. Then the sky above our house filled with fantastic colors, usually shades of rose and deep blue that striated and glistened and moved like iridescent folds of oil in water. And then Joe opened his arms . . . it was always the same . . . he'd look at me and smile and say, "I love to fly!" And he would lift off the petit-point rug in the living room and ascend up and out of the house and into the swirl of fantastic color overhead. And he would fly around in it. I would try really hard to fly so I could join him, but I couldn't get off the ground. It was like my limbs had turned to stone. I would call to Joe but he had flown away. Sometimes in the distance, I heard his voice. And then the sky became a blueprint, the colors fading away like pencil lines, and it turned a flat blue like construction paper, with no movement and no depth, just a flat color, and I'd keep trying to fly, but no matter what I did, I couldn't get off the ground. I even climbed the walls of the house, but I kept sliding back down onto the floor. And I kept climbing and then I'd slide. And I'd wake up exhausted, but I didn't care. I was happy, because all night I had been with Joe, and it felt real. And it was, for the most part, a happy dream; he never cried or took a needle or slept. He was all mine, and we were together, mother and son, even though the background was skewed and strange; we were together.

"Ave?" The sound of Jack's voice startles me.

"Hi."

"Hi." He sits down on the toy chest. He folds his hands and looks at them.

I know my husband. He'll just sit there and look at me until I say something. Why is it always the woman's job to pull the information from the man? Why can't he tell me what he's feeling? That's just the way it is, and I'm certainly not going to try to change this worldwide dynamic tonight. So I take a deep breath and look at him. "Where'd you go?"

"I went up to Big Cherry Holler and walked around the lake."

Before we got married, we spent a lot of time up on Big Cherry Lake. We'd lie on the bank, or Jack would row me around in a canoe. That's the place where we really talked, shared everything we'd been through with each other. It was a magical place for us, totally private, just clean blue water as far as the eye could see, surrounded by a clean wall of regal pine trees.

"We haven't been up there together in a long time, Jack."

"Years."

"Maybe we should go sometime."

"Maybe."

Jack's one-word answers are typical. But typical isn't going to work tonight. We're in bad shape, and we have to talk about it.

"You know, I don't mean to hurt you. Somehow I always end up doing the wrong thing. I just want you to know that I don't set out to do that."

"I know," he says quietly, leaning against the window.

"I just don't know how to talk to you. Maybe I never did." Why am I using words like "never"?

"No. We got along good in the beginning."

A wave of panic goes through me. This sounds like the windup on one of those "I'm leaving you" speeches. "In the beginning" usually leads to "We're at the end of our road."

"Why do you stay?" I might as well ask him, since we're finally speaking seriously to each other.

"I love you, Ave Maria."

"You do?"

"Of course I love you."

My eyes meet his and I know that I still love him too. But loving him isn't really helping us make a marriage. Loving Joe didn't keep him alive; loving my mother didn't prevent her from getting cancer and dying; and loving Jack MacChesney isn't going to help us stay together. What will?

"Jack?" He looks at me, and I must say, I love that look. He gives of himself completely when he listens. (I don't think I do that.) "I guess I thought when we got married, since I had gone for so long without love in my life, that everything would be perfect. That because I had waited, time had made this perfect bubble, and you and I would climb in and float till we were old and died in each other's arms."

"Come on." Jack smiles and shakes his head.

"No, really. I did. I thought since I had been sad for so long, let's say for the first half of my life, that once I opened my heart, it would be beautiful and wonderful and . . . easy. So maybe what we have here is my unmet expectations biting us on the ass."

"What made you think it was going to be easy?"

"I believed the hard part was finding love."

"You didn't find me; you decided you deserved it."

"Do you think?" I sit up.

"Yeah."

"What about you?"

"I knew what we were in for."

"Am I that bad?"

"No, you're not bad. Not at all. You just don't think of me first."

I want to disagree with him, but I know he's right.

"You're not happy, Ave."

"I am. Sometimes."

"When was the last time you were truly happy? Be honest."

"January fifteenth, 1983. You made chili. It was snowing. Remember? You and me and Etta and Joe baked a chocolate cake. We drew a snowman in the icing. And we played Go Fish. And we laughed all night."

Jack sits quietly for a while; I can see he remembers Chili Night, and for a moment I cannot imagine that we won't work out our problems and be happy again. I am about to tell him this when he interrupts my thoughts. "He's gone, honey. But you and me and Etta. We're still here."

"I know."

"We matter."

Jack says this simply, and I know it's true. But it just makes me feel like a bigger failure. My mother was surely the center of my life and our family life, and here in my little family, I have let everybody down. I have a husband who feels rejected and a daughter who can't really be happy because she can't be herself and her brother too. She cannot fill that void. But she tries. Maybe that's what we've become, the three of us. We're trying to fill the space left by Joe and none of us are successful, and the harder we try, the bigger the void becomes.

"Ave?"

"Yeah?"

"You're not going to sleep in this room again, are you?"

For a second, I want to tell Jack about The Dream, but I can't. Instead, I tell him, "No. I want to be with you." I take his hand and lead him down the stairs. Sometimes, even when I'm failing, I do the right thing.

# CHAPTER FOUR

*I*va Lou and I sit on the old stone bench outside the Slemp Library, eating lunch. We're bundled up; it's an overcast late November day, but we need the fresh air. Besides, we have the entire winter to cram into Iva Lou's tiny office for our weekly get-togethers. The bench is a low, wide half-moon of blue slate resting on ornate concrete pedestals. It faces an old fountain, a series of jagged fieldstone steps stacked delicately up a low hill. At the top, brass cardinals hold a pitcher from which water cascades down rocks covered in green velvet moss. When it reaches the bottom, the water flows into a small triangular pool filled with pennies. It's a romantic place, hidden by poplar trees. At night it's a make-out spot for teenagers. Young lovers have thrown their pennies in the pool (lots of them), hoping their luck will last.

Delphine Moses made us meatball heroes. Iva Lou peels the tin foil down the sides of the long bun like a banana.

"Aren't you gonna eat?" Iva Lou asks me as she takes a bite.

"I'm not hungry."

"What's the matter?"

"Jack and me."

"What happened?"

"He's mad at me because I took on managing the Pharmacy without asking him."

"Why didn't you ask him?" Iva Lou takes a swig of Coke.

Iva Lou asks me this so matter-of-factly, you'd think I'd have an equally easy, off-the-cuff answer. But I don't.

"You know, men got to feel in charge. Even if they're not. You got to let them think they are."

"Iva Lou, I'm too old for those games."

"Well, I hate to tell you, but the games go on until you're in the grave. I never met a man who didn't think he was the center of the universe."

"Do you think Jack Mac is tired of me?"

"Nope. It sounds like he's mad at you."

"Good."

"No. That's actually worse. When men get mad, they don't sit with it, they do something. They act out. You know. They go out looking for . . . I don't know. Diversions."

"Other women?"

Iva Lou nods. "And I know that for sure because once upon a time, I was the best diversion in Wise County. Now I'm just another old married woman who's kept her shape." She sits up and breathes deeply, pinching in her small waist.

"Do I need to be worried about other women?" I lean back on the bench casually, yet my spine is so rigid, it's as though there is a steel pipe in place of the bone.

"If you're a woman, you always need to be worried about that. You got a good-looking husband. And there are women out there who look for, well, they're looking for company."

"I'm not going to follow him around."

"You shouldn't! No, you have to act like nothing's wrong and gently move things back in a positive direction. You have to *act* like you have a good marriage, and then, as time goes on, if you act like it's good, it becomes good."

"How do you do that?" I want to know.

Iva Lou continues, "In little ways. Make him comfortable. Kiss him when you pass him while he's watching TV. Even if he don't kiss you back, mind you."

"Okay. I can do that."

"How's the sex?"

"God, Iva Lou."

"Are you having sex?"

"Sometimes."

"Regular?"

"Not as regular as it used to be."

"Well, girl, get on it. Make it *your* idea. That'll keep you two connected until he comes around."

"You're serious?"

"Hell, yes. A man would rather saw off his arm as live without sex. We women, well, we're camels. We can go months and months without, though I don't recommend it. We like to think about sex, and sometimes thinkin' about it's enough. Why do you think women get married to men in prison and not vice versa? We're fine just having a man sayin' he loves us, even if he's locked up with a life sentence. We don't need him home in the flesh tellin' us. A man is different; he needs a woman to be there, present, takin' care of him." Iva Lou looks at me, her left eyebrow rising up to make her point. "And I mean takin' *care* of him."

"Does everything come down to sex?"

"Yes." Iva Lou sets her hero down on the bench. "A man looks at sex like a health issue. If *it's* workin', then *he's* workin'. You got it?" I nod. "Drop by the church. They're still fixin' the Fellowship Hall kitchen, right? Surprise ole Jack Mac. Bring him a slice of pie or a thermos of coffee. And look good doin' it. Be sweet. Understand?" I nod again, but part of me resents hearing this. Why do I have to do all the work?

A squirrel, his brown coat the color of the bare ground below, shimmies down the thick trunk of the poplar tree behind Iva Lou. He stops and chatters, snapping his neck, looking all around. Then the branches rustle from above, and down the trunk, like a gumball swirling down a chute, comes another squirrel. The first squirrel waits for the second to join him. When she gets within an inch of his tail, he runs away. This reminds me of something Otto told me so many years ago. He said, "Ave, you gots to decide three things in life: what you're running from and what you're running to, and why." What Otto didn't tell me and should have: no fair running in place.

Fleeta leans against the new fountain at Mutual's. "Here I stand at the gates of hell."

"How many times do I have to tell you, you don't have to work in here."

"We'll see. This is just like when I was told I wouldn't have to handle stock reorders. Now I'm the only one who handles stock reorders."

"It came out nice, didn't it?" I ask Fleeta as I spin on one of the fountain stools. Pearl found antique etched mirrors, which she framed in white and hung behind the fountain. She copied the marbleized green linoleum countertops from the original pictures. Gaslight wall sconces with brass accents throw a soft golden light on the pale green booths with white Formica tabletops.

"Yeah, it come out good. But I don't know how it did, with Pearl's attention everywhere else in Wise County but here."

"Do you have a problem with expansion?"

"I ain't talkin' about that. Pearl's in loo-ve." Fleeta rolls her eyes when she says "love." "You know 'im too. The Indian doctor up at Saint Agnes. Bakagese. Good-lookin' sucker. He's as dark as mahogany, honey. Black."

"He was Joe's doctor."

Fleeta thinks for a moment. "Right. Right. I bet they met up your place. He's dark. But tain't nothin' wrong with it. Pearl's Melungeon herself, so she's mixed. So in a way, they match. Though lots of Melungeons don't like me saying they're mixed."

"I thought you were Melungeon."

"Part."

"There's nothing wrong with you," I point out.

"No, there ain't."

"His color doesn't matter."

"You say 'at, 'course you're Eye-talian. And Eye-talians are the great mixers of the world. Ain't no country that ain't been in yorn. And everybody knows It-lee is nothin' more than a rowboat away from Africa."

"You know your geography. Maybe they ought to put you on *Club Quiz* next time we send a team out." I hand Fleeta a note regarding a prescription. "I can't read your writing."

"It was a call-in prescription. For a delivery. To . . . Alice Lambert."

"Oh."

"I know." Fleeta clucks. "She oughtn't buy her pills from here, after all the trouble she caused you." Fleeta's right. Alice Lambert is Fred Mulligan's sister. When I found out that he wasn't really my father, she claimed I was a bastard and therefore not entitled to his estate; she even tried to take me to court. That was nearly ten years ago, and I haven't seen her since.

"When you're sick, you probably don't care where the pills come from."

"What kind of pills does she need?"

"They're for nerves."

"Uh-huh. I'd say she has nerve tryin' to trade in here."

Otto comes in with his tool chest. "Hey, Otto. Can you make a delivery over to Alice Lambert's?"

"I don't see why not. But I need to hook up the stove back 'ere. Do you think Jack Mac could help me?"

"I'll ask him." Good. Just what I needed: an excuse to pop in on my husband. Iva Lou would definitely approve.

The parking spots outside the Methodist Church are filled, so I double-park behind Jack's truck, filled with plywood sheets. I check my lipstick, which I've eaten off, and reapply it. I run a comb through my hair and fluff it. I look pretty good today, I think as I climb out of the Jeep.

The tension has eased between Jack and me, and I see this truce time as an opportunity to bring us together again. There have been small signs that he's trying too. He took my hand helping me up the attic stairs to get the Christmas ornaments. He hugged and kissed me when I made ravioli from scratch. And he rubbed my neck when I was working on the bills after Etta went to sleep last night.

The door to the church basement is propped open with a barrel trash can full of shards of old Sheetrock. I should've brought Jack something to eat, I'm thinking as I go down the familiar steps; Iva Lou would give me a demerit for not planning ahead. I hear laughter and note that the new yellow paint they chose for the stairwell really brightens up the place.

"Hello?"

"In here," my husband's familiar voice says.

I walk carefully into the hall; the floor has been removed, and new Sheetrock is being applied to the walls. Jack is measuring a large flat of wood on two horses as Mousey hammers a corner of Sheetrock to the wall.

"Hi!" I say brightly, with a big smile.

"Hi, honey," Jack answers warmly.

"I love the yellow. It's pretty. This room is really coming along," I tell them, surveying the changes. And then, as if in a dream, I see a woman emerge from the hallway that leads up the back stairs to the sacristy. It's that woman. That tanned woman from the Halloween Carnival!

"Honey, this is Karen Bell from Coeburn. This is my wife, Ave Maria," Jack says to her matter-of-factly.

"What a pretty name."

"Thank you."

"She's Italian," my husband tells her. I guess he's explaining my name.

"Yeah, I'm just plain old Karen. There's a million of them out there," she says, and shrugs.

My mind races: the name Karen. I've heard that before. The Pharmacy? A Karen called Jack at the Pharmacy, before I went to Knoxville! Why do I feel as though I've caught my husband doing something wrong?

Karen Bell wears a blue-and-tan-plaid pleated skirt and a sweater set in soft blue, a shell with a cardigan over it. She is carrying a clipboard and has a pencil tucked behind her ear (all business). She is much smaller than she appeared to be at the carnival. She's one of those women a man could carry around like a doll. And the way she moves, she comes at you one piece at a time, reminding me of the goatherd girl marionette my father sent Etta from Italy. Every movement is deliberate.

"Karen's our supplier."

"Supplier?" I guess I say this in a funny way because she laughs.

"I supply the aggravation," she says.

"That must be expensive."

"Depends." She looks at me for the first time. Or maybe she just sees me for the first time. She slides one hip onto one of the horses and perches there. Then she rubs a pencil between her palms; it clacks against her rings. (But not one of them is a wedding band.)

"Karen is a salesperson for Luck's Lumber," Jack tells me.

"Yeah, that's how we met," she says.

How we met? What an odd phrase for a salesperson to use. "Did Jack ever tell you how *we* met?" I say, wrapping my arms around him.

"No, he didn't."

"In kindergarten."

"That's so cute. Childhood sweethearts," Karen says, not meaning it.

"Not really," I tell her.

"Let's say we got together later in life," Jack adds.

"Not too late, though." I pick up a hammer and hit my open palm with it. I do this a few times before Jack takes it away from me.

"Jack, do you want to take one last look at these blueprints?" Karen is asking him the question, but she's looking at me politely, like "Could you get out of the way? We've got business here."

"Sorry. I interrupted. You guys go ahead. Do your business thing," I say nicely, and go off to the far wall to examine my husband's Sheetrock technique. I lean against the radiator to get a closer look, placing my hand on it—it's actually very hot, and I think I now have third-degree burns on my palm. But I don't scream, I just shove my hot hand into my pocket.

Karen unrolls the blueprints, which, out of the corner of my eye, look like complicated geometry to me. How hard is it to take down walls and put them back up again to reconfigure a kitchen? From the size of the blue paper and the series of complicated intersecting chalk lines: very. I watch as Karen, capable and professional, shows Jack and Mousey how things are to be done. What they need. How they can save on insulation. What size wood they need to lengthen the counter space in the kitchen. My husband listens carefully to what she is saying. She makes sense when he challenges her with a good question. Respect washes across his face when she comes up with a solution to a problem he couldn't solve until she stepped in. She taps her foot and continues to roll a pencil between her hands. She has given this project a lot of thought. This is a woman with follow-through. She always has a plan.

"Well, I guess I'd better get back to the office." Karen rolls up the blueprints. She looks over at me as if to say, "Okay, he's all yours. You can talk about what he wants for dinner, what time the PTA meeting starts, and does he need new underwear." The boring stuff that wives do, not the fascinating stuff of blueprints, raw materials, architecture, and construction—the stuff of Karen Bell.

She tucks the prints under her arm like a baton and walks across the room to her coat, dangling on a nail. Mousey watches her as she goes. She's got one of those walks where her rear end makes a complete circle as she moves. Smart and Sexy, just like *Redbook* magazine says, I think as she walks. Just what I should be, I tell myself. Jack keeps his eyes on the wall.

"Y'all let me know if you need anything else. You know where to find me," she says as she goes upstairs.

"Nice to meet you!" I call after her.

"You too" is the muffled reply.

"I've got a problem, guys." Jack and Mousey look at me. I guess my tone of voice sounds oddly curt. "Otto and Worley need help installing the oven." Boy, does that sound like the lamest excuse ever invented by a wife who suddenly had to come up with a cover story when she caught her husband with a mysterious blonde.

"We could take a look at it. Later, though, okay?"

"That would be great. There's some problem wiring, and the BTUs of the oven. That sort of thing. We may have to open a wall." What am I saying? I don't know anything about opening up walls. I'm just repeating a fragment of a conversation I heard Otto having with Worley. Who am I trying to impress? My husband? "Anyway, I don't know details, guys. All I know is we have a deadline."

"We'll stop over later," Jack promises, and kisses me on the forehead like I'm Shoo the Cat.

As I climb the stairs out to the street, Karen Bell's perfume lingers in the air. It's that Charlie cologne that makes Fleeta sneeze. It's too sweet, even in afterthought. It feels good to get out in the fresh air again.

Christmas in the Gap is a month-long affair. Of course, the kick-off was the opening of the new Mutual Pharmacy Soda Fountain. (Thank you, MR. J's Construction, for your electrical assistance in the wee hours of November 30.) Pearl wisely featured prices from the original Soda Fountain days for the first week: Cokes for a nickel, sundaes for a dime, and so forth. It has become a real hangout. Even folks just passing through the Gap stop in for a cup of coffee and pie. One man on his way to Bristol from Middlesboro, Kentucky, stopped in for Tayloe's autograph. He saw her on local TV selling storm windows and was thrilled to meet the Real Thing and leave her a big tip.

Inez Eisenberg heads the committee for Decoration Downtown; she's asked every business on Main Street to hang a wreath with tiny white lights on our entrances. Everyone complied except Zackie Wakin, who hung his wreath with blue lights (he sells them, so he used them). The Methodist Sewing Circle sponsors a door-decoration contest on private homes. Louise Camblos even decorated her doghouse door, that's how competitive folks get.

The local garden clubs boost Christmas spirit with their holiday flower shows. The Dogwood Garden Club decorates the Southwest Virginia Museum; the Intermont Club takes over the John Fox, Jr., house; and the Green Thumb ladies dress up June Tolliver's House down by the Outdoor Drama Theatre. They ship judges in from eastern Virginia to judge horticulture (you should see Betty Cline's Christmas cactus), arrangements (Arline Sharpe's centerpiece of stacked Rome apples on the dining room table at the museum is a wonder), and special creations like a ceramic Madonna and Child placed amid gold gourds.

Iva Lou, Fleeta, and I are spending most of Sunday touring the exhibitions. We're about to enter the Rooms of Historical Distinction when Joella Reasor stops us in the narrow hallway.

"Hey y'all," she says in a tone that tells us there's gossip. She wipes the corners of her mouth, where the orange lipstick bled, with her thumb and forefinger.

"Spill, Joella. We ain't got all damn day," Fleeta says impatiently.

"Pearl Grimes is in the Victorian Room with her doctor friend."

"From here on in, we'll have to call it the Indian Room." Fleeta chuckles as she searches the room for Pearl and her man.

A ten-foot blue spruce is decorated with tiny handmade lace fans. The boughs of the tree are filled with hundreds of midnight-blue satin ribbons tied into neat bows. Ropes of miniature pale lavender pearls drizzle down the branches. Moravian stars punched out of old tin nestle near the trunk, throwing oddly shaped beams of light around the room. "That's a stunner," Iva Lou says. "I wonder if they'll sell it to me."

"There they is!" Fleeta clucks. Pearl and her doctor kiss under the mistletoe hung on the pocket doors between the Victorian and antebellum eras.

"Doctor B. It's so good to see you again." I give him a big hug. We ferriners should stick together. Besides, if this romance works out with Pearl, he'll be family.

"Joe's doctor." Iva Lou whispers this as though she doesn't realize she's said it aloud.

I cover for her. "Iva Lou, you remember Dr. Bakagese."

"Of course. How are you?"

"Fine. Thank you."

Fleeta looks at me sadly; she can be sensitive once every hundred years or so, and this is one of those times.

Dr. Bakagese smiles at me. I feel instantly guilty. So many times over the past few years, I meant to call him and thank him for all he did for our family and for Joe. But I have not called him to come to dinner, as I meant to do, nor did I go to see him. I kept meaning to, but I couldn't. When I look into his eyes, he seems to understand. I flash back to the day I met him; of course, that was the day that would change our family forever.

"Mama! Joe fell!" Etta hollered from upstairs.

That kid is driving me nuts, I thought. I went up the stairs.

"I'm fine," Joe said, rubbing his hip.

"Where did you land?"

"On my butt."

"Good."

"Why? It wouldn't hurt him if he landed on his head."

"That's not funny!" Joe pushed Etta. Before they could fuss full-out, I pulled them apart.

"Stop it. Both of you. I can't take it anymore!" The tone of my voice scared them (a little), so Etta went off to her room in a huff.

"Come on. Let's get you dressed."

Joe took off his pajamas and waited for me to hand him his clothes. As he climbed into the red pants, I noticed a bruise near his knee.

"What's that from?" I asked him.

"What?"

"That bruise."

"I dunno."

"You've got to be more careful."

"It doesn't hurt."

The room was dark because of the gray day outside, so I pulled open the shades to let more light in. The sun peeked out of a curtain of charcoal clouds, enough to help me see. I turned to help Joe into his shirt. There was another bruise on his back, right under his shoulder blade.

"Jesus, Joe. You're all banged up."

His skin looked a little transparent, and there seemed to be deep pools of shadow right under the skin, almost like bruises that turn from blue to yellow as they heal.

"I don't like the way this looks," I told him, and then my son wriggled away from me. I loaded the kids into the Jeep and took them up to Saint Agnes Hospital. Looking back, that seems extreme; after all, it was just a couple of bruises. Somehow, I just knew something was terribly wrong.

Joe sat in the front seat, holding on with his hands as we bounced down the holler road. I remember looking down at him and thinking how much I loved his little face. His profile was perfect; his chin stuck out like an emperor's. Etta rested her head on my shoulder as she stood between the seats. I didn't yell at her to get into her seat belt. She had her hand on her brother's neck, the way she did when we took him into his first crowd at a high school football game. For the first time in a long while, my kids were quiet. Neither of them said a word. There was only the sound of the windshield wipers, of the wheels hitting the wet road and our breathing.

Sister Ann Christine met us at the reception desk. She's five feet tall (at most) and was dressed in a white shirtwaist habit, white shoes, and a white wimple. She was around sixty then, but you couldn't tell by her skin. It was smooth and pink, not a wrinkle in it. Her small nose dipped down in a straight line; her blue eyes stood out like patches of sky against clean white clouds. As she leaned over to embrace my children, I imagined my mother holding them and almost cried.

Dr. Bakagese entered the examination room with a big smile. "What's happening, little buddy?" He spoke American slang with an Indian accent. He was tall and slim. He had beautiful hands with long, tapered fingers. His hair was jet black and cut short. His skin was a beautiful shade of café au lait. He had a small nose, full lips, and wide brown eyes. I've always had a hard time surrendering my children to doctors, but this time, I wasn't afraid. I trusted this man.

"Ave. Yoo-hoo." Iva Lou pokes me back into the present.

"I'm sorry." I look at Pearl, whose face wears an expression that I've never seen before. It's motherly. She knows what I'm thinking. Pearl always knows. "You know, I would love to have you both to Christmas dinner." I turn to Iva Lou and Fleeta. "And you too. Lyle. Dorinda. Baby Jeanine. Everybody." I turn back to Pearl. "Your mom. Otto and Worley."

"Hell. Let me check my calendar." Fleeta searches her pockets for her cigarettes. "Yup. We can make it."

"Are you sure?" Pearl asks. She knows that I haven't celebrated Christmas in a big way since Joe died. I put up a tree for Etta, but we haven't had a party or a big dinner.

"Yeah. I think it's time. Lots of things to celebrate this year. Jack's new job. The Soda Fountain. Lots of good stuff." I look at my friends, reassuring them that this is something I really want to do. They all agree to come; we'll talk about what they can bring later. Even if you throw a dinner in the Gap, it's potluck. We live to get out our pans and fill them with our best dishes. Pearl and Dr. B. move on to the Roaring Twenties room.

Iva Lou watches them go. "They're so sweet. Like a romantic postcard."

"From somewheres in the Middle East."

"Jesus, Fleeta." Iva Lou turns to her.

"What?"

"India is not in the Middle East. Git yer facts straight."

"It don't matter. The man knows he's black."

"Indian," Iva Lou corrects her.

"Black. Indian. Brown. They's all ferriners. What's the damn difference?" Fleeta, having had enough of the Victorian era, heads into the antebellum room. Etta runs in from the hallway.

"Mommy, I barely touched Mrs. Arnold's gingerbread house and the roof caved in!"

"I told you if you touched anything, we were going home."

"I just ate a little piece of the top."

"You ate the roof? Etta, you have to go apologize immediately."

"Let it go," Iva Lou says, as Etta is heading off to make amends. "It's not a big deal. Patsy Arnold needs to get a grip. You'd think her gingerbread house was the Sistine Chapel."

I work through the crowds and down to the main floor, where the gingerbread houses are on display. I see Patsy in the corner, repairing the hole in the roof of Santa's workshop with an icing bag.

"Patsy, I'm so sorry."

"It's okay. Corey Stidham tore off the door and ate it before Etta had at the roof."

"Are you sure?"

"Hon, it's a compliment. The thing is supposed to look good enough to eat."

I head through the house looking for Etta. I go to climb up the back stairs and see her sitting outside on the porch, which serves as a loading dock for the Tolliver House.

"I told Mrs. Arnold I was sorry."

"I'm sorry I yelled. But there are judges coming around, and people work hard on their crafts."

"I want to go home."

"But we haven't seen all the rooms yet."

"I don't care."

"Why?"

"I hate Christmas."

"Come on, Etta." I take my daughter's hand. "I want to show you something."

In the study, there is a display of handmade quilts by local artists. The quilts are donated by families to the John Fox, Jr. Museum. Two of Etta's Grandmother MacChesney's creations are on display. There is a colorful drunkard's-path pattern; a king-size quilt with bright cotton paisleys; red, blue, and pink ginghams; and florals in soft pastels. A red, white, and green checkerboard with a white background covers the largest wall in the room. There is a card next to her quilts:

NAN GILLIAM MACCHESNEY, 1907–1978. I point out the card to my daughter.

"Okay," Etta says, bored. To her, this room is a bunch of colorful old blankets that smell like cedar hanging on sticks.

"See the stitch work? How tiny? And how there are layers and layers of it? It took her close to a year to make one of these. And she was fast."

"How come you don't quilt?"

"I don't know. I can sew a little."

"Your mama sewed too."

"Yes, she did."

Etta walks off to look at the diorama of the Outdoor Drama. I think about what I've tried to teach my daughter about life and love and family. The one thing I wanted to give Etta that my mother couldn't give me was the example of a happy marriage. I remember Jack told me many years ago that the most important thing a father could do for his son was to love his mother. Maybe the most important thing a mother can do for her daughter is to love her father.

The trick to the Kiwanis Club Annual Christmas Tree Sale is to find out when the truck is delivering the trees to town; if your husband is a Kiwanis member, you have an in. Then you must position yourself for the unloading, and there is a pecking order. Hospitals and churches first, then regular people. The Kiwanis Club owns the market; no one else in town sells trees. You would think that because we live in these lush mountains, Christmas trees wouldn't have to be imported. Any reasonable person would assume that we'd just take an ax, go out into the woods, pick a tree, and cut it down. I don't know why, but that is just not how it's done. We don't chop down trees in Big Stone Gap. We wait for the Kiwanians to bring them from Canada.

Otto and Worley dig holes in the ground where the trees stand until they are purchased. The empty corner lot across from the First Baptist Church became the outdoor showroom by process of elimination. The Club used to sell them up the street in front of Buckles Supermarket, but when the market needed additional parking space, they blacktopped the lot, and so went the Kiwanians. Otto swears that the trees stay fresher when they're in the ground; the men water and groom them like fine racehorses. I always laugh when the trees are gone the day after Christmas. The lot is pitted with holes where the trees were, and it looks as though a team of killer groundhogs had a battle. It stays that way until Christmas comes around again.

My husband is a new member of the Kiwanis Club, because after years of working in the mines, he can finally attend their monthly lunches at Stringer's. (Evidently, this is the backbone of membership in the Kiwanis Club—you have to be available for lunch.) Jack substitutes in the pit band at the Outdoor Drama, and when the crowds are big, he spends intermission selling popcorn and chili dogs in the Kiwanis Club concession stand (the proceeds go to the show fund), so many of the Kiwanians thought Jack was already a member. They were a little surprised to find his name on their new members list. He was elected treasurer immediately.

As we drive down Poplar Hill, cars are already parked all around the Christmas-tree lot. I pull in at the Baptist Church.

"Let's pick our tree."

"You go. I'm cold."

"Come on. It'll be fun." I put on my lipstick in the rearview mirror. "Etta, don't make me beg. I don't need a sourball in my house ruining our Christmas spirit." Etta laughs. "I'm not kidding. Come on. They have hot chocolate."

Reluctantly, she gets out of the Jeep, then sees Jack. "Daddy!" Etta says, and runs to him.

"I sold three blue spruce and one Douglas fir," Jack says, kissing me on the cheek.

"I'm impressed."

"Who knew it took selling Christmas trees?" He smiles at me.

Since Iva Lou alerted me to the fact that I must put the romance back in my marriage, I listen carefully to everything my husband says. And now I notice Little Diggers. Like that one. He said it as a joke, but there's a deeper meaning. He doesn't think I admire him, so it's my job, in this period of trying to win his heart again, to resist a funny retort and instead gently correct his misconception.

"I'm always impressed with you and everything you do." I give him a hug. He looks at me like I'm crazy. (I guess my new technique needs some refining.) "Did you pick out a tree for us yet?"

"I waited for you."

"What do you think?" I follow him into a row of fragrant Douglas firs. I stop and inhale deeply. The cold air and the clean sap make a fragrant mix of evergreen and sweet pine that sends me spinning.

"You look pretty," my husband says to me. Instead of blurting, "What? Get your eyes checked," as old, insecure Ave Maria might joke, new improved Ave Maria says, "Thank you." What I really want to do is grab him and throw him up against a tree and say, "Are you cheating on me?," but I don't. Of course not. I have a plan. And the plan is: keep my emotions in check and win him back. I am going to be so adorable that there is no way he'll want any other woman. Iva Lou swears that's the only way to keep a man in love with you, and since I have no strategies of my own, I'm going with hers.

"Ma, look. Little trees!" Etta waves from the end of the row.

"Etta honey, we've got a whole attic full of ornaments. That tree is too small."

"I want a big one too. For our house."

"Two trees?"

"This one is for Joe." Etta twirls the little tree around. "I want to take it to Glencoe."

Jack and I glance at each other. We're both surprised that Etta would want to take a tree up to the cemetery.

"I can decorate it myself. But maybe you can help me." Etta looks up at me. "I know you're busy, Daddy." Thatta girl, Etta. You tell him.

He hasn't been home for dinner in weeks, he's probably grabbing sandwiches with Karen Bell—and he should be home with us.

Jack kneels down next to Etta. "I'm sorry I'm working so much. I just started the business, and it takes up a lot of my time."

"Okay, Daddy." Etta pulls a locket of mistletoe out of her pocket and holds it over Jack's head. "Mommy?" She grins.

"Excuse me," I say to Etta. Then I throw Jack on the ground, straddle him, and kiss him. I really kiss him. Not a peck. Not a swipe on the lips. No, it's one of those French Soul Kisses you heard about in high school study hall the Monday morning after the popular kids had a wild party at Huff Rock.

"Good God a-mighty! Call Spec. Jack needs oxygen, pronto!" Zackie says loudly. "Careful, Av-uh! The Baptists will throw us off the lot!" Jack's fellow Kiwanians whistle and applaud.

"Hey." I stand up and brush the leaves off my coat. "Sometimes you just have to kiss your husband."

"Just as long as that's all you're doing," Nellie Goodloe says from the hot chocolate stand. I look down at my husband, who stares at me as though he doesn't have a clue as to who I am. Good. He wants a new woman? He's got one.

*I*n the winter, the Powell River curls along Beamontown Road like a rusty pipe; red clay and gray rock and black ice make a path where the water will go come spring. I always thought this hillside by the river was a perfect place for a cemetery, but that was long before I knew anyone inside its gates.

An ornate wrought-iron arch stretches across two regal brick pillars in the entrance way. The cursive letters spelling GLENCOE CEMETERY are surrounded by black iron filigree flowers. A beautiful fountain sits just beyond the gate; in warm weather, water gushes over the marble shells and into a deep pool.

I used to bring the kids here on holidays. We came on Memorial Day, my mother's birthday, and every Christmas. When we visited the cemetery, I would tell the kids stories about their grandmothers. Jack always thought it was a little creepy, that I liked the cemetery and found comfort here. I tried to explain that this was part of my Catholic faith and my Italian heritage; our gravesites are as important to us as our living rooms. In Jack's Scotch-Irish tradition, a cemetery is a place you visit on the day of burial, and, hopefully, not often after that. So when I came here, I came with the kids or alone, sometimes just to sit and talk to my mother.

Four years ago this Christmas, I brought the kids here, and we placed green holly wreaths with red velvet ribbons and small glitter charms on Nan MacChesney's grave and on my mother's. Joe ran in and out among the stones, laughing and playing, hollering for Etta, then hiding and hooting like an owl or howling like a ghost. She pretended to be scared, and I, of course, teasingly reprimanded him for his lack of respect for the dead.

Now Jack's truck bounces over the gravel road on the way to the MacChesney plot. The little tree Etta chose for Joe's gravesite is safe under a tarp in the flatbed. She has a bag of bells she made out of birdseed to use as ornaments, and red ribbons to tie on the branches. She wrapped two bricks in tinfoil like gifts to anchor the trunk at the base.

Etta and I chat all the way in. Jack becomes somber the moment we drive through the gates. He pulls the truck up under the old tree that showers the ground with shiny black buckeyes (which we collect for good luck) every autumn. Our son's headstone, simple black marble with white swirls, rests near the gnarly roots of that tree.

I help Etta out of the truck. Jack lifts the tree from the back of the truck and positions it over Joe's headstone. Etta helps anchor it with the bricks. Then she carefully lays her ornaments out on the ground and begins to decorate the tree while Jack holds the tree.

I walk across the plot and over to my mother's grave, marked with the same simple marble. I pull some weeds from around the stone. I look over at Fred Mulligan's and pull some weeds from his too. My parents are buried just a few feet from the MacChesney plot (one of life's ironic little twists). I've been standing at Mrs. Mac's grave for a while when I feel my husband's arms around me.

"How's Etta doing with those ribbons?" I ask him.

"Just fine."

Together, we watch our daughter as she decorates the tree. The picture of her, reaching up inside the tiny branches to place pine cones coated in birdseed, reminds me of a Hümmel statuette my mother kept on her nightstand.

"You know what I think about sometimes?" my husband says as he pulls me closer.

"What?"

"How it all seems like a bad dream."

"I know."

"Remember the day we had all of Joe's school friends over?" Jack asks me. We had taken Joe out of the hospital so he could be home with us, with Shoo the Cat, in his own bed. Joe felt pretty good one morning and decided that he wanted to see all his buddies from school. So I called all of their mothers and threw a party.

"The boys were running and playing inside, and next thing you know, they took off in a pack and went outside into the snow. Joe took off after them. And he got as far as the middle of the field in front of the house, but he couldn't keep up. So he knelt down alone in that field. And he didn't call for us. He just knelt there. And waited. God, that broke my heart. When he couldn't run anymore."

"I hope we never forget him." I turn and face my husband.

"How could we?"

"I don't know. People do." I hold my husband so tight, it's as though he's in pieces and the only thing that can hold him together is me. I close my eyes and remember how close we have been. What is worth saving in this life? What is worth holding on to? Does anyone know until they lose it?

I look over at our daughter. Etta holds a red ribbon in her hand as she watches the two of us. She is smiling.

This Christmas is our best yet. Maybe it's because Etta feels it's a real celebration again; or because Theodore made good on his promise to spend the holidays with us; or that Jack and I seem to have come to a good place in our marriage (maybe it's temporary, or maybe it's the holiday spirit, I don't care, it's nice!). We're sitting on a Lily Pad of Calm amid a year full of setbacks and arguments. When I tell Jack we're on a pretty lily pad, he takes his fist to his head and mockingly pounds it. But the more I think of this image, the more apt I think it is. Lilies bloom on the surface of dark and murky water. There is a lot under the surface of this marriage, and I don't forget that for a second.

"Can I help?" Theodore stands behind me as I maneuver the turkey into the oven.

"Get the potatoes. Please."

"Sweetie, where's the wine?" Jack wants to know as he passes through to gather Etta and our guests.

"On the porch in the cooler. I needed the space in the fridge for Fleeta's Jell-O mold."

"Which no one eats," Theodore whispers.

"It makes a nice centerpiece."

"Until it melts lime-green goo all over the table."

"It's Christmas. Green is good," I tell him. "Thank you for coming. And being here. Especially this year. Thank you."

"You owe me. I stayed up until four-thirty putting that Barbie thing together for Etta."

"I know."

"I know you know," Theodore tells me, and kisses me on the forehead.

The phone rings, at least four times; just as I'm about to yell for someone, anyone, to pick it up, I hear Etta in the hallway.

"Ciao, Nonno!" she says, giggling. Jack takes over carving the turkey and motions for me to take the phone.

"Merry Christmas, Papa."

"How's my daughter?"

"I'm great. Just wish you were here."

"How is Christmas?"

"Hectic. Nuts. How about you?"

"Mama took a little fall, so we —"

"How? Is she all right?"

"Nothing broke. Thank God. She's bossing everyone from her chair."

"May I speak with her?" My father gives my grandmother the phone; she sounds hearty and robust and not broken at all. She tells me all the news of Schilpario in a run-on sentence, ending with the news that my father is seeing a woman seriously. Her name is Giacomina, and she's only forty-four years old! "Put Papa on the phone," I tell her. I know she must be important to him; my father has always had lots of girlfriends, so to bring home someone special must be a big deal, and for my grandmother to mention it, it's got to be serious.

"Yes, yes, it's true. I love this woman," Papa says to me, and laughs.

"Are you getting married?" I ask him.

"Thinking about it. Yes. I would prefer to only think of it and never do it."

"Don't you do a thing until I can be there!" I yell into the phone.

"When are you coming?"

"I don't know. But don't do anything until we can be there. Promise?"

"I promise."

Jack takes the phone and talks to my father. I go into the dining room and catch Theodore up on all the goings-on in Italy as he places serving pieces on the table.

The dining room table, a rustic farm table with thick legs, is dressed with my mother's china, a pattern I have always loved, which is called "English Ivy." I have placed crystal plates filled with celery, carrots, and black olives at either end of the table. Sterling silver open-weave baskets are filled with fresh rolls, and pats of butter in the shape of Christmas bells and fluffy buttermilk rolls (thank you, Hope Meade) are placed on each guest's bread plate. I dim the lights (my mother's simple crystal chandelier from our Poplar Hill house) and light the twisty red taper candles in their Santa holders (a special from the Mutual's).

Etta runs in and offers to ring the dinner bell. She grabs it and runs through the house, clanging it in every room as if she's a goatherd. Jack says good-bye to my father and goes into the kitchen for the turkey. The company drifts in, though they aren't company at all, really, but family. Iva Lou and Lyle take their places opposite Jack; Etta sits next to Iva Lou; Pearl and Dr. B. sit to one side of me, Theodore to the other; Fleeta, Dorinda, and baby Jeanine sit in the center; Otto and Worley and Leah fill in the rest. In the beauty of the moment, surrounded by my favorite people, I want to cry.

"Don't, Ma," Etta whispers.

"No, no. I'm happy. I was just thinking how lucky we are. To have each other. That's all."

My friends murmur in reply, no one 'fessing up to their holiday emotions, and maybe not wanting to deal with them, either. I miss my mother terribly; my father is a big ocean away; Mrs. Mac is gone. My son, who loved Christmas, is not here. I wonder if they're looking down on us, sorry they can't be with us. I stare into the candle for a second, hoping that the bright white of the flame will center me and help me from having a sobfest right here in the sweet-potato casserole with delicate marshmallow crust. Dr. Bakagese winks at me. Maybe he knows where my thoughts have taken me.

"Honey, why don't you lead the prayer?"

"Catholic or Baptist?" Etta offers us a choice.

"If we're goin' by the numbers, go with Baptist. We got you Cathlicks beat by about six." Fleeta moves her head around the table, counting Protestants. " 'Course, Doc, I don't know what religion you is but I'm perty sure it's one of them that meditates."

"Fleeta, with all due respect, my daughter is Catholic," Jack offers, avoiding the Cracker's Neck version of the Great Schism.

"Well, I don't much care. Jesus is Jesus." Fleeta takes a stand.

"Well, I'm half Baptist," Etta says, looking at her daddy. " 'Cause you're a full Baptist. So I will say a prayer in half and half. Bow your heads. God, the Baptists thank you for the turkey. The Catholics thank you for the cake . . ."

"And I'd like to thank the ABC store for the whiskey. Amen," Lyle says, finishing Etta's prayer. Etta makes the sign of the cross with me and shrugs. The phone rings. Etta excuses herself to go and answer it.

"Tell whoever it is we're eating dinner, Etta," I yell as I pass the gravy to Pearl.

"Probably one of 'em phone-solicitation deals," Fleeta grumbles.

"On Christmas?" Dorinda wonders.

"That's the best time. They know yer home." Fleeta takes the last drag off her cigarette, then dips the butt into her ice water. It is so quiet, I hear the sizzle. Then she places the soggy butt on her bread plate.

Etta runs back into the room. "It's for you, Mama."

"Who is it?"

"It's Captain Spec."

"I bet that Edens boy shoved another button up his nose. That boy is forever cloggin' up the holes of his head with somethin' or another."

I excuse myself and go to the phone in the hallway. I barely hang up the phone before running in to tell our guests, "I have to go. I'm sorry. There's a fire at the Trail Theatre." Chairs push away from the table, and our group moves into action, putting out candles, grabbing their coats and purses, gloves and hats. "Hell, we'll all come," Fleeta says. "It could spread to the Pharmacy." Instead of arguing with Fleeta, I turn to Iva Lou. "Watch Etta for me, honey, will you?"

"I'm going too, Ma!"

"Don't worry. She'll stay with me," Iva Lou promises.

"I'll drive you," Jack says, helping me gather my gear.

By the time we reach town, four fire trucks have parked in front of the theater. Black smoke billows out of the second story; flames pour out of the lobby below. Jim Roy Honeycutt, his white hair askew, is pacing behind the fire trucks, distraught.

"What happened?"

"My prints! All my movies is in there! From the beginning!"

I leave Jim Roy with his wife and duck under the hoses, which are being pulled off their giant spools and up to the building. A fireman from Appalachia taps the hydrant in front of Gilley's Jewelers. Barney and his son work furiously, emptying the window display into a sack. The sight of them tipping the velvet necks modeling pearls and chains reminds me of Cary Grant in *To Catch a Thief.* The chug and grind of the ladders as they extend to the roof drowns out Spec, calling to me. Jack, who is helping a volunteer fireman with an unwieldy hose, motions to me to go to Spec.

A crazy series of loud pops, followed by billows of black smoke, comes from the building. Cinders from the ornate wooden molding cascade from the building in small sprays of orange.

"Must've hit the storage room. The oil and popcorn has gone up," Spec tells me. How strange to smell the popcorn burning outside. Jim Roy's popcorn was so good, folks would stop in and buy a sack even if they weren't staying to see the movie.

"There's a man inside," a fireman shouts to us. Spec and I move in with our oxygen and gurney.

The streets are filled with onlookers, including all the merchants. Zackie gathers them together, and the postmaster from across the street manages the crowd, pushing them back and onto the Post Office steps.

Then, in a cloud of gray smoke, the captain of our Fire Department emerges from the side door to the ticket booth, carrying a man over his shoulder. Spec and I help him place the man on the gurney. He is not breathing; we administer oxygen. Doc Daugherty joins us and takes over.

"Who is he?" I ask Spec. I've never seen this man before. Spec shrugs.

Across the street in front of the Pharmacy, our Christmas dinner guests stand in a huddle watching. Pearl grabs Fleeta's hand as she watches Dr. Bakagese help a fireman who has taken in too much smoke. The crowd points and sighs as red sparks blow off the roof and out into smoke, disappearing into the cold blue air.

Spec searches the man's pockets for identification, finds his wallet, and opens it. "His name is Albert Grimes. He's from Dunbar." Dunbar is a coal camp over by Appalachia. What was he doing in the closed theater on Christmas Day?

"I wonder if he's kin to Pearl," Spec says, waving her over.

"I don't know."

"Let me see," Pearl says, running up behind me. She leans over the stretcher. "He's my father." Spec looks at her—"What?"—and then looks at me; I had no idea Pearl's father was alive or lived around here. I glance at Pearl, who gazes down at the man on the gurney. She isn't afraid for him; there is detached concern in her eyes, but certainly not worry. Spec and I lift him into the Rescue Squad wagon. I look at Pearl again and hold back a thousand questions—this is not the time.

"The building's empty!" the Fire Chief yells to his crew. "Let her have it, boys!" In earnest, they begin hosing the building through the windows; the gold flames disappear, replaced with thick black smoke.

Doc Daugherty rides with Albert Grimes in the back of the wagon. Spec and I speed up to Lonesome Pine Hospital's emergency room, which is not more than a five-minute drive through town and out through the southern section. The fireman whom Dr. B. treated did not require oxygen, but he is behind us in Appalachia's rescue squad wagon for a thorough check at the hospital.

Albert wakes up and moans; his blue eyes are fuzzy, and he cannot focus. As we wheel him into the emergency room, Tozz Ball wants to ask him a few questions, but Spec tells Tozz to beat it. Pearl and Leah sweep through the automatic doors and search the room for Albert. Pearl sees him through the window in ICU and goes to him. Leah joins Spec and me.

"Is he all right?" Leah asks.

"We think so. He took in a lot of smoke."

"He didn't mean no harm."

"I'm sure he didn't." I put my arm around Leah.

"He's basically good. He just had a bad run of it."

"Of what?"

"Of everything. Things didn't work out between us. He lost his job with the railroad on account of the disability and it all went downhill after 'at. He just lost his way, you know." Leah goes through the doors and into the ICU. She puts her arm around Pearl, who rests her head on her mother's shoulder.

I can't believe that Leah is making excuses for the man who left her and a baby. She doesn't love him anymore; she's going to marry Worley. Maybe she just feels sorry for him. Pity is a dangerous thing in a woman: it gives the man the power to treat you any way he wants; he can stay and be cruel, or he can abandon you. As I watch Pearl lean on her mother, I think of my own mother, who I could always count on when I was hurting. My mother pitied my stepfather, Fred Mulligan, felt compassion for a man who could not feel, and it left me in the middle, feeling sorry for a man who could not love me.

"I think we ought to run down and check on Jim Roy. This thing could give him a nervous breakdown," Spec tells me, and I follow him back to the squad wagon.

We pull up in front of the Pharmacy. Fleeta has opened it, turned on all the lights, and it looks as though the whole town is stuffed inside, where it's warm. The mechanical choir in the window nods and waves as though nothing has happened. There is one truck left on standby across the street outside the theater. Jack Mac and Etta stand on the sidewalk outside the Pharmacy, watching the firemen as they secure the building.

"Mama, look!" Etta points to the marquee, which has burned off the facade of the theater.

Before the fire, the bright white marquee used to have a green plastic pine tree anchoring it in the center, and THE TRAIL in plastic cursive on either side. Underneath THE TRAIL was always the title of the movie, or at least as close as Jim Roy could spell it. As the years went on, letters got lost or broken, and Jim Roy didn't replace them. So you'd see titles like GO WIND for *Gone With the Wind* or SUM 42 for *The Summer of '42*. Now the modern plastic is gone, and under it, in bold letters carved into the wood, is AMAZU.

"What's Am-a-zoo?" I ask my husband.

"Amaze You."

"What's 'Amaze You'?"

"That was the first movie house in Big Stone Gap. Way before Jim Roy bought the place and modernized it. My mama used to tell me about it. They saw silent movies there. Lillian Gish. Buster Keaton. Charlie Chaplin. And there was an organ and a stage. And before every show, old Possum Hodgins, who owned the theater, would get up and tell the audience, 'Today we're-a-gonna Amaze You!' "

I look up at the old marquee, and it sends a chill through me. How strange to see the past exposed under layers of the present.

"Honey, it's cold. Go inside," I tell my daughter.

"Fleeta opened up the Soda Fountain. She's pushin' pie and cake and coffee," Jack Mac tells me. I'm not surprised. As much as Fleeta complains, if she's not in the center of everything, she ain't living.

Spec is over at the Trail with the firemen. Jim Roy is standing out front, talking to them. I take Jack's hand, and we cross the street to join them.

"It's gone. It's all gone," Jim Roy says sadly. "All my movies. My prints done burned. All my years of collecting. Gone."

"We were able to save some, sir." A fireman joins us, just a kid of maybe twenty, and he shows Jim Roy a stack of black tin canisters which he salvaged and placed in the doorway of Gilley's Jewelers. Jim Roy sees the canisters, and his eyes light up with joy.

"Here, I got a flashlight," Spec tells Jim Roy, who rushes over to the canisters and runs his hands over the wheels of tin as though he were patting a baby.

"Let's see what we got, buddy," Spec says to Jim Roy. Then he reads the tape on the sides as I hold the flashlight: "*The Thin Man, Dancing Lady, My Man Godfrey, Stagecoach, The Heiress, Midnight* with Don Ameche and Claudette Colbert. That would've been a tragedy right there if they burned up." Spec shuffles through the reels: "There's *Bachelor Mother*, yeah, Ginger Rogers was sexy in that one; *The Barretts of Wimpole Street, Topaz, Pride and Prejudice, Jezebel, It Happened One Night . . .*"

"Clark Gable!" I shriek. Spec gives me a look.

"Let's see, there's *The Ghost and Mrs. Muir, Song of Bernadette, Test Pilot, Wuthering Heights, Dinner at Eight; Goodbye, Mr. Chips, The Women, Sullivan's Travels*; there's Claudette agin with *The Palm Beach Story*, the Duke in *The Quiet Man, How Green Was My Valley*, thank you Jesus, it looks like we saved most of Maureen O'Hara. And lookee. Henry Fonda in *The Trail of the Lonesome Pine*. It's here, Jim Roy!"

"How 'bout Kay Francis? I had all of Kay Francis," Jim Roy says nervously.

"They're here." Spec shows Jim Roy a neat stack of her movies, safe on the ground. He places a double reel on top of the stack. "*National Velvet* . . . that's Etta's favorite, isn't it?" I nod.

Jim Roy breathes deeply. Most of his treasure has been saved, and saved by a kid who probably wouldn't know Spencer Tracy from Joel McCrea. Seats and screens and popcorn machines can be replaced, but the prints that Jim Roy has collected all these years cannot.

"Come on, Jim Roy, let's take you and Mrs. Ball over to the Mutual's. Fleeta's made coffee." Jack puts his arm around Jim Roy. But Jim Roy doesn't move. He stands there looking at his theater.

"I can't believe it. And on Christmas." He sighs sadly.

As we enter the Mutual's, folks gather around Jim Roy and his wife. Soon we break into small groups in the booths or sit around the Fountain, reminiscing about our favorite movies or the first movie we ever saw at the Trail. Theodore, put to work as a waiter for Fleeta, serves pie off of a tray. Fleeta peels the cellophane and red Christmas ribbon off a Whitman's sampler box and passes the chocolates around.

Quietly, through the kitchen, Leah and Pearl come in; Worley rushes to Leah's side, and she explains all about Albert. Folks buzz around Pearl, who says that Albert will be all right. Folks around here don't even know the man but are concerned.

"He didn't set no farr," Otto tells me.

"How do you know?"

"Chief tole me. Said it was wiring in the sound system. I ought to tell Pearl that, oughtn't I?" Otto goes off to give Pearl the news.

Nellie Goodloe, dressed in her red velvet Christmas suit studded with a jeweled Christmas-tree brooch and glittering smaller trees on her ears, gets up and calls the gathering to order.

"I want to tell you something, Jim Roy. I want you to know that I had my first kiss in the Trail Theatre in 1942." Wolf whistles fill the soda fountain. "Yes sir, I did. Robert Taylor leaned over and kissed Vivien Leigh on the silver screen, and up in the balcony, Spec Broadwater leaned over and kissed me. I never forgot it."

The crowd cheers, and Spec turns so red, he matches his flannel shirt. Spec's wife, Leola, in a running suit with snowmen painted on it, shoots Spec a dirty look. Then she thinks better of her petty jealousy and chuckles. Fleeta stands up on a step stool behind the counter. "Nellie, I want to know one thang. Did old Spec know what he was doin'?"

The crowd turns to Nellie. "Honey, I hope to tell ye, he surely did."

Fleeta spins her dishrag in the air like a truce flag. Etta is laughing along with the crowd, and she looks so grown-up to me all of a sudden.

"I think Etta just got her first sex-ed lesson," I whisper to Jack.

"Could be worse," he whispers back.

Fire or no fire, once I'm home, I have to clean up the dishes. I'm one of those people who must have every dish washed and put away before they can sleep. Luckily, Theodore is one of those people too. My husband, however, is not. He went to bed after putting Etta down.

"How about I take Etta to Cudjo's Caverns tomorrow," Theodore says, stuffing the refrigerator with more leftovers.

"She'd love it."

"What are you going to do on your day off with your husband?"

"I don't know." And I really don't. I never have a day off with Jack.

"Maybe you can think of something fun to do together. And I don't mean clean the oven. I'll keep Etta away until suppertime. You can have a lot of wild sex while we're gone."

"Thanks."

"You don't even blush. What has happened to you?"

I look at him, and he laughs. He goes into the dining room to collect the last of the dessert plates while I scrub the sink and think about wild sex. I don't think of actual wild sex, I'm wondering where mine went. Ours. I expected, before I got married, that I would be the last person to trade passion for comfort and then for routine and now for, I don't know, privacy. I thought the need to communicate, to physically communicate, in marriage would grow. No one told me, and perhaps no one can, what the truth of it all is. Sex becomes another way of speaking to each other, and when you stop touching, it's just as bad as if you're not speaking. When you stop everything except those perfunctory hello and good-bye pecks on the cheek and the hugs, more a way to brace yourself than to express feelings, you're in Big Trouble. But there is no one day or one thing that sets the Big Trouble alarms off. At first you stop kissing because you're annoyed at him, and it's a way to communicate that. And when the message gets through that you're not kissing for a reason, his behavior seems to adjust to the new rule: you upset me, you hurt me, you disappointed me, no kissing. And when those tender kisses become further and further apart, so goes the sex. It's impossible to make love when you can't kiss your lover. Someone once said that sex is the thermometer in a marriage; only when something is wrong is sex an issue. And that is true. But what no one tells you is that once you stop connecting, it is very hard to bring it back. There are times when I see my husband doing mundane things like unloading the truck or stacking the firewood, or today, when he was carving the turkey, and my instinct is to run to him and tell him how much he means to me and how I want to make love to him, and let's drop everything. But I don't. Maybe I'm afraid he'll reject me or maybe it's just life—there is always something in the way. Time. Work. Etta. Company. Or something else that has to be done. And then you forget. And sex is always the first thing to go, because it's the one thing that can wait. Who knew the most natural thing in the world could become the most elusive?

Jack is snoring when I crawl into bed; I give him a gentle nudge, and he turns over. I am looking forward to sleeping long and late since Theodore is taking Etta spelunking. I sink down into the soft flannel sheets like a spoon in gravy. Jack turns over and opens his eyes.

"I thought you were asleep."

"I have an idea," Jack says, and lies back on the pillow.

"Yeah?"

"I think we should take Etta to Italy next summer to see your dad."

"Really?"

"Don't you think she's old enough?"

"I do!"

"They accepted our bid for the rec-center job in Appalachia. I think we'll be in pretty good shape financially. If we buy tickets now, we could get a good deal."

"Okay. I'll get on it."

"Does that make you happy?" he asks me.

"Oh my God, yes!" I kiss him good night.

Jack rolls over onto his side and yawns. Soon he'll be snoring again. I've never seen anyone fall asleep more quickly than my husband. Italy. Next summer. It seems so far away. And I'm happy that he got the job in Appalachia. But it's odd, he hasn't mentioned my partnership with Pearl since our argument about it. I thought it was best to leave it alone. No matter how well I think I know Jack MacChesney, he can still surprise me. His reactions to things. The things that hurt his feelings. Things I haven't counted on. There seems to be this gap between us sometimes; he doesn't know what I'm thinking, and I don't always know what he's feeling. I never would have thought that the family finances would be a problem for us. Both of us were so eager to share everything equally in the beginning. And when I had the babies, it seemed natural to work part-time; after all, we own this house, and his paycheck was enough. Maybe he felt empowered in an old-fashioned way when he was the chief breadwinner. Maybe he liked being the only one taking care of us in that way. Is Iva Lou right? Is this all about the male ego? Or are our fights about money really about something else—something both of us are afraid of, so we use the finances as an excuse? Sometimes there's a stranger in this bed, and I think it's me.

My post-Christmas present to myself is a call to Gala Nuccio, our travel agent. Gala became a big part of our lives after Jack found her in the New York paper years ago and she planned the trip that brought my dad and nonna to me for the first time.

Gala's tours are now the gold standard of Italian-American bus tours; she recently shot her first TV commercial (which airs in New York, Connecticut, New Jersey, and Pennsylvania). She sent us a videotape: there she was, an Italian goddess with golden skin, a beautiful teased bubble of black curls with red highlights, full, shiny maroon lips, arched black eyebrows, and a killer pale blue Chanel suit with gold chains on the pockets. Her perfectly manicured nails with French tips pointed out vistas of Mighty Italia in the background: Rome, Florence, Capri, and Milan whizzed by, a supersonic slide show of adventure. Then, at the end, Gala sat on a suitcase and pointed down to her 800 number, which pulsed in red, white, and green.

"Gala Tours," the receptionist says when she answers the phone.

"Is Gala in?"

"Who shall I say is calling for Mizz Nuccio?"

"Tell her it's Mario da Schilpario's daughter."

"Hold, please." I am on hold for barely ten seconds, then Gala bursts through the wires.

"Holy Mother, is that you, sister?" Gala barks into the phone.

"It's me. You dropped Nuccio? Now you're a one-name star like Cher or Liberace?"

"Or God." Gala cracks herself up.

"How are you?"

"I am fan-tab-you-luss." Then Gala lowers her voice and growls, "Yesss ma'am."

"Who is he?"

"His name is Toot Ruggerio. He lives in Manhattan. Little Italy. He's busy. And he's thrifty. He lives in the same apartment he grew up in. Rent control, you know. He's very close to the senator up there. Senator Pothole, they call him."

"Oh, Toot's in government."

"Nope. Construction. Honey, they call it politics, but honest to God, it's all construction."

I tell Gala all about Jack's new business.

"I cannot bee-leave that your Jack and my Toot are in the same line of work. We are linked by some giant bubble of karma, you and me. I tell you, we knew each other in another life. My psychic tells me I was a gemologist in Calabria. I have to remember to ask her what you were next time. She reads pictures too. She gets vibes off of them. I'll bring pictures of Etta from Christmas." Gala tells me all about her business, how it's growing by leaps and bounds; when she goes to the

Short Hills Mall, she gets mobbed because people know her from television. "Don't worry, hon. I keep it all in perspective. Success hasn't changed La Nooch. That's what Toot calls me: La Nooch. Okay, maybe now I have money and influence and I'm on TV. But believe me, at my center, at my core, fame has not gone to my head."

"Gala. I have a job for you."

"Let me get a pencil. Give me the dates."

As I give Gala the dates, I picture Jack and me in Santa Margherita, on the cliffs of the Mediterranean Sea, in the port by the sea with bright blue water where white sailboats bob like prizes and the nets are filled with shiny pink fish and the moon makes the cobblestones look like they're brushed in silver glitter. My husband will fall in love with me again in that light. I just know it.

I drive up Valley Road on my way to Norton. Pearl wants me to see the new building; the deal went through the week after Christmas. It's easy to find where Mutual Pharmacy II will be, as there are building permits posted in the window. Pearl is waiting for me inside.

"I wanted to hire MR. J's, but they're booked up."

"That's okay. How's your dad?"

"He's going to be just fine."

"There's all sorts of stories in town."

"I know." Pearl frowns.

"What was he doing in the theater?" I ask her gently.

"He was sleeping there."

"But they say he lives in Dunbar."

"Not really. After he left Mama and me, he went and lived with a woman in Dunbar, and then she threw him out after a couple of years."

"When was the last time you saw him?"

"About a month ago. He comes to me twice a year. For money." Pearl looks down when she says this. "And I give him a little, and he always promises to pay it back, and then he disappears."

"How did he find you?"

"He saw my picture in the paper when I graduated from UVA Wise."

"Did your mom know?"

"Yeah, and she didn't discourage me from seeing him. I feel bad. Mr. Honeycutt didn't know he was staying there. He snuck in through an old air shaft behind the screen."

"Don't worry. Old Jim Roy is just happy his collection got saved."

Pearl shows me the plans for the pharmacy—no soda fountain here, it will be strictly med counter and health and beauty aisles. She also tells me that the Soda Fountain is such a success, she should be able to pay off the bank loan within a year.

"I'd better get back to town. We have the sale running." I turn to go. "Pearl, where's your dad now?"

"I got him an apartment in Appalachia. I don't know if he'll stay, though."

"It's so complicated, isn't it?"

"I'll never figure it all out, will I?" Pearl asks me by way of answer.

"Did you ever ask him why he left you?"

"I did."

"And what did he say?"

"He told me it hurt too much to stay." Pearl shrugs. "I don't understand it. But that's the way it is."

The after-Christmas sale at Mutual Pharmacy is a circus. All holiday decorations, wrapping paper, ribbons, and gift sets are marked half off. Jean Hendrick has loaded her trunk with stuff twice. Mrs. Spivey and Liz Ann Noel nearly got in a hair-pulling fight over our last mechanical angel, marked down 75 percent (even though the angel was missing a wing). Peggy Slemp bought the remaining three boxes of Whitman's chocolates (we polished off the rest on the Fire Night) for half off (she freezes them!). "She gives 'em year-round. She is so cheap. Tighter than a truss," Fleeta sniffed, but she rang them up anyway.

The crowds have made the Soda Fountain lunches standing room only. Tayloe Lassiter was promoted to hostess during the post-holiday rush. We have two high school kids from Mr. Curry's Future Business Leaders Club waitressing in her place. Otto and Worley volunteered to be cooks on their days off. They're not bad, either.

By closing time, we are exhausted. Fleeta locks the door behind Reida Rankin, who bought the last few boxes of Christmas lights. "She'd stay all the night if I let her," Fleeta says, lighting up a cigarette.

"What a day!" Pearl says as she emerges from the office.

"Who's hungry?" Fleeta wants to know.

"I'm gonna head out," I tell Fleeta.

"No, not yet," she tells me firmly.

There is a knock at the front door. "Tell 'em to drop dead," Fleeta hollers, walking back to the Soda Fountain. But it's Iva Lou, so I let her in.

"Did you save me the cards with the Delacroix snow village on them?"

"I put the last three boxes behind the register."

"Good girl."

"Are you hungry?"

"Twist my arm."

If the sales staff (Fleeta and me) is half dead, the Soda Fountain staff is worse. Otto pours himself a Coke. Worley, who ended up waiting on customers because the Future Business Leader girls got flustered, sits in a booth with his feet up.

"I'm telling ye, people was so hungry, they'd have eaten a dead rat," Otto tells us.

"The sale made them hungry," Pearl says.

"What are ye talkin' about?" Fleeta asks, biting into a stale doughnut.

"When there's a sale, folks literally salivate, their mouths water at the possibility of a bargain. They have a physical reaction. It's exciting to get a deal, and the human body knows it."

"That's just fer women," Worley says.

"No, it's all people. Watch the men when Legg's Auto gets the new trucks in. You'll see," Pearl promises.

"I thought we was gonna have a full-out fistfight 'tween the Baptists and the Methodists over them religious cards you had out two for the price of one," Otto comments.

"The Baptists took 'em. Everybody knows the Baptists got more bite." Fleeta puts out plates. "Well, come on, y'all. It's buffet-style." Fleeta has displayed all the food that is left in the Soda Fountain. There are four wedges of pie, coconut or cherry ("Yer choice," Fleeta grunts), a plate of oatmeal cookies, two croissants with cheese, and several individual servings of Jell-O with a small star of whipped cream dead center on the squares. "The coffee's fresh," Fleeta says, apologizing for the hit-and-miss eats.

"You kept me hanging around for this?"

"Not exactly. This meetin' is hereby called to order. Now, who's gonna tell Ave what we heard up in Coeburn?" Fleeta announces. Iva Lou looks at her like she wants to throttle her.

"What did you hear?"

"Now, Ave, don't git pissed at the messenger is all I'm a-gonna say."

"I won't, Fleeta."

"All right. Here's what we know and when we knowed it. Pearl sent me up to Norton to check on a couple of things fer her at the new store." Fleeta looks at Pearl, who nods. "And when I was up 'ere, I done heard something. But as my mama used to say, you can put what I heard and what you heard together and hear nothin'." I nod at Fleeta. What she says makes absolutely no sense, but it seems like she rehearsed it, so I don't interrupt. "I got me a cousin up 'ere. I think you've met her. Veda Barker. Small woman. Vurry Christian woman. Well, she was over to the Coeburn town meeting, where they was talkin' about renovations and such of the town hall up 'ere, and they announced that MR. J's won the bid."

"I know they won the bid on a job in Coeburn."

"Yeah, but what you don't know is that Kurr-en Bell got up and spoke on behalf of MR. J's."

"She vouched for Jack's company. So what? She manages Luck's Lumber; they supply MR. J's with their materials."

"Kurr-en Bell is after your husband. And you need to wake up."

"Fleeta. Your tone," Pearl says to her gently.

"What do I need to wake up about?" I ask innocently. Suddenly, I realize how wives have done this for centuries. We buy time, pretending not to know what folks are talking about when they're talking about our husbands and how they spend their time and with whom. This pretend act will get me out of here so I can breathe and think.

"Karen Bell is going around telling folks she's in love with your husband. Maybe it's nothing. Maybe it's just gossip." Pearl puts her arm around me.

"Like hell. This is one story circulatin' through Wise County that has some meat on its bones. Now, get serious. You can't just turn yer husband loose up in Coeburn and expect him to find his way back home. That's too far from Cracker's Neck. He's lost. You got to make him come home. Or I'll tell you what, he'll be gone." Fleeta sits down. I've never seen her upset in this way.

I sit down. I have to. "Okay. I'm listening."

"I've followed the woman," Otto announces. "I ain't proud of it. But I done did it. I know where she lives. And I know what company she keeps up 'ere."

"You saw . . ." I look at Otto, and he looks away sadly. "Well."

I study my hands as though they're brand new and I'm seeing them on the ends of my arms for the very first time. I don't know what to say to my friends. Do I tell them that I've seen signs too, that I've been suspicious? That I had a feeling the first time I saw Karen Bell? I want to open up and tell them everything, but I can't. My loyalty to my husband, who has probably been disloyal to me, stops me.

"I need some air," I tell my friends. I stand up. So do they, and the sound of stools scraping linoleum is deafening.

Iva Lou follows me out to the Jeep and jumps into the passenger side. Mentally, I know I need to turn the key to start the engine, but I can't.

"Look. It ain't a done deal."

"Do you think it's true?"

"I been trying to tell ye. I heard bits and pieces of things. You know how stories travel."

"What do I do?"

"Nothing."

"Nothing? How can I do nothing?"

"We do not know the extent of it. Now, I know your husband. I don't think he loves her. I don't think he could. I don't think he loves any woman but you. Really. So that's good fer you. But you got a bigger problem."

"What?" What is Iva Lou talking about? What could be worse?

"Karen Bell is your problem. She wants him. And she wants him baaaaad. That's a fact. I heard that straight out of the mouth of her best friend, Benita Hensley up to the county library. She works up 'ere, and she told me herself."

Who are all these people, these strangers, who know my name and my business? What do they want? Why do they care about me and my situation? The noise in my head gets louder as Iva Lou goes on.

" 'Cause Karen Bell, you can't control. She's a wing nut and a wild card, 'cept she's a genius, 'cause she acts like a sure and steady professional woman. She's had a series of men too. Not that there's anything to judge about that." Of course there isn't. This is Iva Lou, the Siren Goddess of Big Stone Gap talking.

"I don't want to hear another thing."

"Listen to me. I have some experience as the Other Woman. I don't think there's a single scenario out there that I ain't in some way, at some point, been in. So you have what might be called a secret weapon in me, as your friend. I know what Karen Bell is up to. She can't pull anything I ain't seen before or done myself." Iva Lou fishes in her purse for a cigarette. "You need to listen to me, because I know what I'm talking about. There's Other Women who just want to play, have dinner, a movie, and some exciting sex; and then there's the Other Women who are husband hunting. And they are relentless. They don't rest till they got of yorn's what they think they want for themselves, and then it's too late for all concerned. Karen Bell is thirty-four years old—"

"She's forty if she's a day."

"Honey. She's thirty-four. Spec checked with the DMV."

"Spec!" I hit the steering wheel. Does everybody in Wise County know my business?

"He has a connection at the DMV. We had to tell him. Honey-o, here's the deal. She wants to git murried, and she wants kids, and she thinks Jack Mac would pass on a fine set of genes. She told Benita Hensley that Jack MacChesney is one of the smartest men she's ever known, that he's a man with a lot of Unrealized Potential. How do you like that? Karen Bell can spot potential. I almost threw up."

"I feel sick myself."

"I know. I know. I am so glad I'm murried and not foolin' around no more, 'cause I feel dirty just thinkin' about the pain I inflicted as the Other Woman. I hate myself for that, well not entirely, but certainly for your sake."

"What am I going to do?" I turn to Iva Lou. I almost want to grab that cigarette out of her mouth and smoke it myself.

"You can't let on to Jack that you know anything."

"Why? If I stop it . . ." And then I stop talking. Stop what? Their first kiss? Their first time together? Their falling in love? His packing up and leaving me? Their outdoor wedding at the lake in Big Cherry Holler with my Etta as the flower girl?

"Here's what you need to do. Are you listening to me?"

"Okay. Okay. I'm listening."

"She is counting on the fact that you are gonna blow this. She already knows, 'cause she's hooked your husband, that he ain't happy. So all she has to do is be sweet as pie. Uncomplicated. And that'll keep him coming back for more. If you go crazy and start following him and making him miserable and accusing him of things, it'll give her an advantage. You'll look like the hag wife, and she can be the sweet young thang." Iva Lou looks at me. "Bless your heart."

"How did this happen?"

"This happened 'cause there's a man involved. And they's vulnerable on account of the fact that they surrender their will to their ego. Don't forget that: their Will to their Ego. 'Cause their ego is what keeps them male. You got it?"

"I don't want this trash in my life! This sordid stuff. I don't want it!"

"Ave, there's that point in an affair where nothing's happened yet—nothing physical, that is. The man and the woman have established contact. They're friends. They work together. They probably talk about things. Personal things. She probably confides in him; maybe even, once in a while, pulls a little something where she has a problem at home and doesn't have a husband or any man around and something needs fixin' like a pipe or a wire and he says he'll stop by her house to fix it, and next thing you know, he's in the web."

"What web?"

"Her web. The little scene she puts together with her and him in it. Picture this. He fixes whatever she needs fixed. She has to thank him, so she makes a strong cup of coffee and a good sandwich for him. He sits down. And they get to chattin' about this and that, and next thing he knows, he doesn't know where the time went. So he gets up and says, I gotta get home to my wife, my kid, whatever. And she looks sad, but she understands. That's the important part. She understands."

"Understands what?"

"What his life is like. What he deals with. What he needs. What his problems are. She is His Friend. Get it?"

"Men don't talk to other men about their relationships, so they need a woman to talk to?" I ask. Iva Lou nods. Now I'm getting it. Jack Mac talks to Karen Bell about me. Etta. Work. Just like I talk to Iva Lou. (If this weren't my life, I'd be thrilled at the notion of this breakthrough in male-female relationships.)

"Now you see what I'm sayin'." Iva Lou leans back.

"Oh, I see it." Iva Lou doesn't know how clearly I see it.

"Jack Mac don't want to be in the web, but he's trapped, and he got there by being nice. Men don't understand how something innocent becomes routine, and then routine can become a relationship. You got no idea how many men I've known who told me that they're surprised when they find themselves having an affair. They didn't see it coming or plan it. But somehow, just by being nice, they got themselves yupped into bed. The Other Woman makes these innocent requests of their time, and they say, 'Yup, I'll help you out,' and pretty soon she says, 'Kiss me,' and he says, 'Yup,' and the kiss leads to the next yup."

"I don't want him to yup himself away from me."

"He won't. If you use your head. Ave Maria, that's where you've got to be smarter than her. He doesn't want this. He knows it's wrong. But you can't accuse him of something you're not sure he's done yet, or for sure that will drive him right to her because he's gonna need someone to talk to about that too." Iva Lou takes a deep breath. "I would rather be you in this situation than her."

"Why?"

"Because he's a good man. And he's gonna try to do the right thing. Now, I ain't sayin' he's a saint. But he's gonna wrassle right good with it before he gives in."

"You think so?"

"I know it."

I know I should thank Iva Lou for helping me see what I should already know. But I'm not feeling much gratitude at this moment. I feel the gloom and despair of all women who have found themselves in my position, the terrible place of not knowing yet knowing all. The tricky thing is staying in the middle. I wonder if I can pull this off. I'm not going to hand over my husband like a covered dish at a church supper. If she's going to take Jack, it will be only because I let her. I guess I will find out what sort of a fighter I am. I twist my wedding band around on my finger; it feels loose. "The world's tiniest handcuff," Lyle Makin called it once. I think he was right.

# CHAPTER SIX

One thing is for sure in a small town: if you're the toast of the town today, tomorrow you're bread crumbs. And if there are rumors that your husband is having an affair, if you wait long enough, somebody will top it with a bigger story. I'd like to thank Tozz Ball for having a second wife and family down in Middlesboro, Kentucky, and coming clean to his first family here in the Gap during a Sunday Revival at the Methodist Church. Tozz is now the headliner; I am happy to be bird feed.

Jack Mac and I talked about the rumors, in our way. I never directly named anyone (Karen), and he never admitted to anything (Karen). He told me that kind of talk comes with the territory; he works with women now, and people will talk. I told him that I understood, but I didn't want him to give anyone reason to talk, either.

I don't know if I'm getting better at following Iva Lou's instructions or if it's plain old fear that's helped me stick with my plan to be the perfect wife. I have been a joy to live with all spring: Upbeat, Warm and Tender, Uncomplicated, and Loving. I am no trouble at all. You could press me in dough and make sugar cookies out of me, I've been so sweet. I'm sure Etta wonders where my temper and occasional blue moods went this spring, but if she thinks about it much, she doesn't mention it.

It's the last week of April, which means that my wedding anniversary is coming up. April 29 will mark eight years of married life. On our first anniversary, Jack asked me what I wanted; of course, I wanted our baby to be healthy, and she was. But he wanted to buy me something. So I asked him for a book; not a book with a particular story, but one of those empty books with blank pages. He went over the mall and got me a pretty blue velvet journal and wrapped it up. When I opened it, I thanked him and then I gave it back to him. He looked confused and I told him that there was a second part to the gift. I wanted him to write me a letter every year on our anniversary, and I would write one to him, so that someday we could look back and see what we were. Now, Jack is not a writer, and neither am I, but I felt even a man of few words could come up with a page of something once a year. And he has. There are times during the year when I forget about the book, and right around our anniversary, Jack and I do this funny teasing dance with each other about writing in it; we pretend squabble and he acts like I'm asking him to yank a tooth, but we've written to each other every year, without fail.

The book has come in handy lately because I've needed reassurance. I wanted proof somehow that I didn't dream all of this, my great fortune at falling in love with a good person and having two beautiful children with him. I am trying to hang on, so I need to know why I should. I'm a woman of instinct, and my instinct keeps telling me that there's trouble ahead. I play out the scenarios in my mind: all the horrible ones, like the day he packs his clothes to go, the morning I get the divorce papers, and the day he remarries and I'm alone again. I know it's crazy, but these are crazy times around here.

The last few years have been so hard, we've written very short letters to each other. The year Joe died, Jack wrote: "I love you honey. I'm sorry." And I wrote the story of Joe's passing. But that year was the worst for us, and instead of dwelling on that, I pull the book out of my dresser and read Jack's first letter.

April 29, 1980

Dear Ave,

    I know that the world is filled with lucky men. And I know that because I have met a few. And all the lucky men have one thing in common. They have a good woman who loves them. I know you worried all your life if you were pretty enough, and I hope to tell you that pretty doesn't begin to describe you. I see more in you when you're sleeping than you could ever imagine. They say your soul comes out when you sleep and, for you, this is true. When your eyes are closed, your eyelashes lie against your cheeks and you purse your lips in a way that makes you look like you're smiling. You're a peaceful girl, my Ave. And that's what I found in you. Peace. I am the luckiest man in the world. I love you. J.

I take the book and put it on Jack's nightstand with a pen. Maybe if he looks at what he's written to me, it will remind him that there is a lot here worth fighting for.

June, the month of Our Big Trip home to Italy could not come fast enough. Now that it's here, I am filled with hope again. I want to be with my husband in a romantic place where we can be together, talk, and laugh, where no one knows us. All winter the mountains felt as if they were closing in on us. Jack has spent most of the spring working overtime. There's been very little rain, so he and Mousey and Rick have been working long hours. Construction is all about the weather.

    I remember the clothes Jack took to Italy on our honeymoon, and I try to copy the contents this go-round. I've asked him a few questions here and there about what he wants me to bring for him, and he just says, "You decide." So I pack for him.

    The night before we're set to fly out of Tri-Cities, en route to

Kennedy Airport in New York and then to Milan, I check on Etta. She had been too excited to sleep, so I allowed her to keep the night-stand light on and read. It worked. As I pull Beverly Cleary's *Fifteen* out of her grasp and shove the bookmark into place, she turns over and hugs her pillow without opening her eyes. I give her a quick kiss on the forehead. Her bags are packed neatly and waiting in a row by the door. I can't wait to see her face when she sees Schilpario for the first time.

I hear Jack park the truck in the side yard. I am looking forward to the long airplane ride. Etta can sleep, and Jack and I will finally get a chance to talk, to catch up. Our happiest memories together are of our honeymoon, and now we'll get to relive all of that.

I meet Jack in the hallway as he shuffles through the mail. I wrap my arms around him from behind.

"How was your day?" I ask him.

"Rough."

"I bought you new socks."

"Why?"

"Your old ones were too shabby for Italy."

Jack starts to move, so I let go of him. He puts his arm around me and moves toward the kitchen.

"And by the way, these aren't the socks that come in a pack. They're the good kind that hang on the rack on the little plastic hangers at Dave's Department Store. Nothing but the best for my husband."

"I want to talk to you." He sits down at the kitchen table. I sit across from him.

"What's up?" I say cheerily. I can be cheery. Tomorrow we'll be in Italy.

"I'm not going."

"Why?" I ask. He doesn't answer me. "Is it work? Are you behind on a job?"

"No. We're okay."

"Then what is it?"

"I think we need time apart." Jack leans back in his chair and looks at me intently. His gaze makes me uncomfortable, and I look away.

"Why?"

"I think you know why."

The rumors around town? The long silences in our own bedroom? The way we bury ourselves in work, emerging only to take care of Etta?

"I don't know what you mean." Let him explain this. I am tired of filling in blanks.

"I don't think you want to be married to me anymore."

"That's not true! Not at all."

Jack gets up and turns on the tap. He pours himself a glass of water and drinks it. "Ave, you don't want to face this."

"Face what?"

"You do your chores: taking care of Etta, the house, me. And you're even sweet about it. You've been great all spring. But you're not really here in this marriage, it's an act."

"I resent that. I am doing things, living this way, out of love. I'm not pretending."

"Maybe 'pretending' is the wrong word. You're going through the motions. It's rote. You do what you think you're supposed to do. You do it well. And it's all very pleasant. Aboveboard. Nice."

"I've been doing this for you. It's not an act!"

"That's not what I want," Jack says simply. He moves and stands near the windows, yet he keeps his eyes on me the whole time.

"I'm sorry I'm such a disappointment to you."

"No. I'm sorry I'm such a disappointment to you," he says, then comes over to sit next to me.

"I'm really afraid right now. These things that you're saying sound so final to me." I take his hands into mine. I love his hands, and I don't want to let go. "Don't you love me anymore?"

"That's never been the problem. I love you so much that I'm willing to live an unhappy life for you."

"I don't understand."

"I didn't think you would," he says quietly.

"Jack, you have to explain to me what you're feeling. Because I don't get it. Please help me understand."

"When I married you, I wanted to make you happy."

"You did."

"I took it on because I wanted to."

"Took what on?"

"You. Your ways."

"Nobody is simple, Jack. We're all complicated. That's how people are. And anyone out there who you think is easy, believe me, they're not." I want to come out and say, "If you think Karen Bell is a cakewalk, you're crazy." But I can't. I will not say her name in this house.

"I knew it was going to be hard. I know a good marriage is more work than not. But I thought at the time that you would dig in and work with me. I thought that no matter what happened, we would share it."

"Haven't we shared everything?"

"No."

"I thought we had." I'm lying. We haven't shared everything, and I know it. "You're talking about Joe."

"My heart broke too when he died."

"I know." Jack takes my hand.

"And it's still broken. I've felt ready to talk about it, but you seem distant so I give up. The only time you dealt with it, with me, was at the cemetery last Christmas. And I had so much hope that it was the beginning of a new time for us. I felt like maybe you were going to share with me. Grieve with me. But that one day came and went, and that was it." Jack lets go of my hand.

"You shouldn't attack me for the way I handled our son's death. That's not fair."

"I'm not attacking you," he says quietly.

"There isn't a manual out there that tells you how to handle your child's death. Even other parents who went through this, the ones I talked to, couldn't help me. Us. I didn't handle it well. But how do you handle something like that well? Is it even possible?"

Jack Mac looks at me. He closes his eyes to think for a moment, then he opens them and looks at me. "I know he came through your body, and that's something I could never understand, but you pushed me away."

"I didn't mean to."

"Let's be clear. You did mean to. You think that there's only one person in the world who can do things right, and that's you. You've never really trusted me." I start to object, and he interrupts me. "You don't think I'm capable of taking care of our family, of you. In some way, you think that I'm not up to the task. Now, maybe you'd be that way with any man, but I only know how you are with me. And you can flit around here and smile and pretend that everything is fine, but you and I know the truth. Underneath this perfectly nice surface is a lie. I really believed in us, and you never did. It's unrequited love. I love a woman, you, who doesn't love me in the same way. A thinking man would end it all right here. A thinking man would just say, 'It's over.' But I have always let my heart rule my head. I think you need to take the summer to think about what you want to do. And I need the time to think about what I want to do. And I say we talk after you come back from Italy and we decide how we're going to proceed."

"You want a . . ." I can't, won't, say the word "divorce."

"I didn't say that. I want you to think about what you want. You may decide that you don't want to be married to me anymore."

"And you're willing to take that chance?"

He shrugs. "I can't live like this."

I look at Jack MacChesney, and he is in pain. He doesn't want to say these things. He doesn't want to believe them, yet he knows that they are true. I am not really here. When we got married, I thought happiness would come naturally. I thought he could fill me up in the way that love fills people in storybooks. I thought passion would rule us, that love would overcome any problem we had, that love itself was communication. But it's not. I haven't worked on this. I'm afraid to tell him that I don't know how. And where would I learn it at this late date? He is unhappy. I am not the woman he thought I was. I have turned out to be a disappointment to him. Remote. Private. Unwilling to share. I know myself well. I've always been able to take care of people and call it work. But the real work is being honest. The real work is admitting that what I came from had a deeper effect on me than I knew. That when our son died, it was worse for me. Maybe it wasn't, but that was what I felt. Maybe I believe that mothers are more important than fathers, and Jack sensed that. Sensed it? He downright laid it out plain for me. He has given this a lot of thought. He thinks about this all the time. How much time in a given day do I think about him in this way, if ever? I usually think about him in terms of myself. I do things for him, sure. But I do them because I'm supposed to, out of duty. The same way my mother did things. If the home was orderly and the meals were prepared, she'd provided stability. But my husband doesn't want stability. He wants a real partner. Someone who is going to dig down deep and work things through with him. I have failed him. I need to own up to it.

"Jack MacChesney." I whistle low and long.

He looks at me and smiles.

"Lordy mercy. I hear what you're saying." I collapse on the chair.

"Don't kid around."

"I'm not kidding around. And it doesn't matter if I agree with everything you've said, which, by the way, I don't. It's how you feel. And I honor that."

"Thank you."

"I'm not going to cut you loose."

"Ave?"

"What?" I sound annoyed when I say this, but come on, how much more am I supposed to take?

"Don't stay in this marriage for me. Do what is right for you."

"Okay. But I want to tell you something. And it's not to dump guilt on you in any way. But I was looking forward to being together in Italy, like we were on our honeymoon. I was hoping that this trip would be a new start for us. I just want you to know that I know you're not happy. And I wanted to change that."

Jack comes to me and puts his arms around me. "We can't go back to a magic place and hope it fixes us. It don't work that way, baby," he says simply, then he kisses my neck.

"As long as there's one spark here, just one, maybe we can make it work," he says to me. I smile at him, then I bury my head in his shoulder. One spark. My marriage rests on the notion of one spark. What a delicate, tiny, insignificant little thing. A spark. One glint of light. Is that enough to see with?

Etta walks between Jack and me, holding our hands as we walk through Tri-Cities Airport. When we get to the gate, Jack hugs Etta for a long time.

"Etta, wait for me by the door," I tell her.

"Okay, Dad, that's enough," Etta says as she gives her father a final hug. She adjusts her backpack and goes to wait for me.

"Jack. Look at me." My husband looks at me. His eyes are full of pain. I can see that he is torn, that he would like to go with us. But he too has a plan, and he is sticking with it.

"Not here," he says softly.

"No, I have to say something to you. You told me last night that you want me to decide if I want to be married to you. And I promised you that I would think about it while I was in Italy, so I will. But I want you to understand something. I may always be, I don't know . . . awkward. Maybe I didn't leave that spinster behind when we got married. I don't know. Maybe I don't express the love I feel the way I should. And maybe I don't know how to love you like you need to be loved. But I believe that even with all my shortcomings, and there are many, I am still the right woman for you. Please wait for me. I think I deserve another chance." And with that, I kiss my husband on the cheek. I hoist my duffel bag on my back and join Etta by the gate. I hand the tickets to the nice man by the door, and we follow the other passengers to the puddle-jumper plane, then climb the steps. When we get to the top step, Etta turns around and waves to her daddy.

"Mommy, wave."

"You wave for me, honey." I can't look back. I won't.

My daughter's sadness at Jack's absence gives way to the excitement of international travel in a matter of minutes. Our flight from Tri-Cities connects into Charlotte, North Carolina, we make a quick change, and head on to John F. Kennedy Airport in New York. Etta is shocked at how many people race through JFK from one terminal to another. "Mama, they look like ants!" she says, pointing to the crowd of travelers, which surges at a central point where the international terminal merges into one big space. "Stay with me," I tell my daughter cheerfully. She latches her finger on to my belt loop lightly as we walk through the throng. I'm excited by the hub of activity too. I love the way the airport smells: of soap and leather and perfume from the duty-free shop. This is just what we needed, I think as I look down at Etta.

Everything about the transatlantic plane ride enthralls her: the pretty flight attendants with their long, shiny taupe nails and perfect haircuts; the Coke in small glass bottles on her seat-back tray; the kit of amenities, including navy blue cotton booties with Italian flags embossed on them. Etta sheds her small-town, Blue Ridge Mountain reserve and sits high in her seat. She is not missing one detail of this flight. How thrilled she is when they bring her dinner in courses.

"Mama, why is it so black out there?"

"That's the ocean underneath us."

"But shouldn't there be ships with lights on them?"

"I don't think ships come out this far."

"If we crash, would anyone know?"

"Let's not think about crashes."

"We better not crash. What would Daddy do?"

"We won't crash."

"Daddy told me to be careful."

"He did?"

"He told me that you and me were his life. And that I was to watch out for you and make sure that you had a good time."

"You and Daddy talk about me?"

"There's only the three of us," Etta says, looking off down the aisle as though I am the biggest idiot in the world. Maybe I am.

Milan is a city of crisp vertical stripes, navy blue, gray, and black. Everything here is angular, from the architecture to the bone structure on the serious faces that brush past us. Even the Milanese bodies are simple and spare and thin; no Sophia Lorens here. No curves. Just straight, lean, no-nonsense shapes. Etta and I, in our cotton and denim, stick out like American tourists. (Forget that we actually *are* American tourists, we just don't want to look like it.) So before we board the train for Bergamo (there is one every hour), I take Etta into a small women's clothing shop. Lightweight wool trousers, navy blue with a flat placket and straight legs, a white cotton blouse with a gold hook and catch at the collar, and a beige cardigan are exactly what I'm looking for. I am not getting on that train with this Italian face in these American clothes. I need a uniform. And here it is. Etta thinks I'm nuts. My daughter likes her American jeans just fine and has no need to be anything but a MacChesney from Virginia, U.S.A.

As the train clicks north through the Italian countryside, low mossy hills of a deep green so rich it's almost midnight blue give way to a deep and endless pink skyline, and I am amazed at how quickly we leave modern Milan behind. Soon the world chugging past turns ancient, untouched. The sun hangs low and golden, resting on peach clouds just like it does in Tiepolo's painting on our guidebook.

I look down at Etta, who gazes out the window with an expression of wonder. I've seen that expression before, on her father's face. God, she looks just like him. Even if I wanted to leave Jack Mac behind in the mountains of Virginia, I can't. As long as she is with me, her father is here too. She is so much like Jack, even though my friends say she is just like me. She is so steady and true. Even if you hurt her feelings, she forgives you and doesn't seem to store up grudges. That's not to say she doesn't suffer; she does. She feels things deeply. But like her father, she doesn't like to linger too long on things that hurt her. There is no victim in my daughter. She is wide open and yet very private. I fold my arms across my chest and lean back, placing my legs on the seat across from us. I look down at my long legs; I could work a farm here.

A man passes by our glass-enclosed car and peeks in. He drinks me in from the tip of my toes to the top of my head and then looks into my eyes. His brown hair and mustache make him seem young, but he is around fifty. He winks at me. I smile politely, quickly look away, and sit up. I grip my knees with my hands, wedding-ring-side up. He couldn't care less about the ring; I shoot him a look that he should move on. He does.

As our train chugs into Bergamo, Etta stands in awe. I have told her the story of my honeymoon many times, and how I felt when I first saw this place, my mother's hometown in all its detail: the carved wooden bench at the train station, the fountain of angels, and my first ride on cobblestone streets. How the air smells like clean straw and lemongrass.

Etta presses her face against the window, knowing that in seconds she will be with Nonno; at last she will meet her great-grandmother (to whom she has written letters since she could write); all her cousins; and of course my mother's people, the divine Vilminores of Bergamo. I have shown her pictures of them many times, and she starts rattling off things she remembers. Some of the first words she learned were their names from the "flash cards" we made of our honeymoon pictures. Etta wants to visit the magical Alta Città and see the priests in their wide-brimmed black hats and cassocks, and the post where my grandfather used to hook his donkey named Cipi and his old wooden wagon before he made deliveries up into the Alps. I want to stand and jump up and down like she is, but suddenly, I see Joe's face as he lay dying, and I cannot be happy. Quickly, I erase the picture. I'm a terrible mother. I don't focus. Focus on Etta. She's alive and well and thrilled to see Italy. Don't think about all the things you didn't do for Joe. Don't think about how he would love this train. Don't think about how you made him frozen waffles in the toaster instead of fresh pancakes on the stove. He's gone. Etta is here. Focus on Etta.

Carefully, I pull our luggage off of the wooden rack above our seats as Etta smoothes her hair. Even the luggage racks in the Italian train cars are works of art. The lush cherry wood is curved and polished smooth. Etta runs for the steps to the platform and stops short of hopping off, turning around to wait for me. My father greets us at the foot of the stairs. He pulls Etta off the steps like he's gathered a bunch of flowers and swings her around the platform. How youthful and strong he is, though his hair has more white in it now. His eyes, a clear, dark brown, dazzle against his golden skin. I feel instantly safe around him. He wears black pants (the cuffs hit his gray suede loafers in a perfect crease) and a gray cashmere pullover sweater. Papa puts Etta down and embraces me.

"How was your trip?"

"Glorious."

"You're tired."

"A little."

"I want you to meet Giacomina." My father turns to find the woman in his life. She is a few steps behind him, smiling, with her hands clasped in anticipation. Trim and small with clear gray eyes, she has a simple beauty and thick, straight brown hair that she wears in a ponytail. Her lips are full and even, her teeth white and perfectly shaped. She has a small, delicate nose with a narrow bridge. She is dressed like the Milan version of me, except she's in beige from head to foot. In English, her name is Jacqueline—it suits her.

"Ave Maria, we are so happy you're here."

"I've heard wonderful things about you."

"Thank you. I feel as though I know you. Your father talks about you all the time." Giacomina loads my bags onto her shoulders and arms without wrinkling her silk blouse.

"Where is Jack?" Papa wants to know.

"He had too much work."

"He needs a rest, though."

"Yes, he does. But you can't tell my husband anything." I say this all so gaily that my father looks at me curiously.

"The Vilminores are expecting us at Via Davide."

Etta shrieks at the mention of Via Davide, Mama's family homestead on the side street. She has heard all about the poofy beds and the hard biscuits and coffee with sweet, hot milk for breakfast. She wants to see the tiny handmade chocolates on a silver plate that Zia Antonietta left on our pillows each night.

"Giacomina and I will stay in her apartment nearby. You and Etta will stay with Meoli. Sound good?"

"Sounds great."

"When I told her you were coming, Meoli didn't want to wait until after you stayed in Schilpario. She wanted you first. Very bossy." Papa clucks. "But I don't argue."

"Schilpario will be there tomorrow," Giacomina says, and smiles.

Via Davide has not changed. The houses are close together and painted soft corals and blues. Long shutters flap against the houses in the breeze. Small, shiny cars are parked on the street.

"It's just like the postcards," Etta exclaims.

When we get to Zia Meoli's house, I jump out of the car and race for the front door. Zia Meoli, in a simple navy blue pocodotte shirtwaist dress, greets us. Her beautiful black hair is streaked with white, and she wears shiny gold hoop earrings. Her daughter, Federica, joins her at the door, wearing jeans and a T-shirt, her red hair a mop of curls and her brown eyes crinkled at the corners. Zio Pietro walks around from the side yard, having heard our noisy reunion. He brushes his thick white hair from his forehead, takes a final drag off his cigarette and tosses it into a rosebush. When I introduce Etta to them, they fuss over her like a new toy. They feel as though they know her from my letters; I am so glad that I write to my family here regularly. It's as though they live an hour, not an ocean, away. We have a bond that connects us at the soul; we don't have to be neighbors. Zia Meoli touches Etta's hair and her face and holds her hands, examining them, all the while shooting questions in all manner of Italian— fast, slow, dialect—and broken English.

"She looks like her papa," Zio Pietro decides.

"I think so too," Zia Meoli agrees.

"Where is Zia Antonietta hiding?" I ask my aunt.

"Oh, Ave Maria. I'm sorry." Zia Meoli looks down. Her face assumes the expression of grief that I know so well. "She passed away last month."

"No!" I take Zia Meoli's hand.

"She knew you were coming, and she tried so hard to stay. But she was very sick for a long, long time."

"I'm sorry." I had a deep connection with Zia Antonietta, Meoli's twin. She never married, so the chores of housekeeping and managing the family home fell to her. That is the way it goes in Italy. The one without the husband takes care of the group. Meoli's children were Antonietta's life, and she spent it taking care of them. She wasn't sad or bitter about it, though. It was as if she was only happy to have a role, an important role, in her family and in serving them. Zia

Antonietta had been in love once, and her true love died. So she accepted fate and, instead of having her own family, invested herself in her sister's. Zia Antonietta was the most unselfish person I know.

"Come. Let's eat," Zia Meoli says. I explain that Jack could not come because of work. Zio Pietro, in particular, is sad about that. He has a woodworking shop and wanted to show Jack a sideboard he made himself. (I have to remember to tell Jack this.)

The parlor is just as it was when I came here on my honeymoon. The walls are eggshell white; the rug on the floor is a simple tapestry of gold and sage green, and it looks like there's a needlepoint tree woven in the center of it. The furniture is sleek and low and dark wood, Italian from the 1930s. A rocker, painted black with gold swirls, sits in the alcove between the windows. The fireplace is full of wood, waiting for winter. The kindling next to the mantel is tied in a bundle with a white velvet bow. The windows have no shades, only long panels of ecru lace. (The shutters close out light and noise when need be.) The mantel is crowded with framed photographs, some as old as the turn of the century, others new. The faces of my mother's family give me a sense of belonging, a point of origin. Right here. In this room. In the old black-and-white photographs, the expressions are stern; as the years pass and the pictures turn to color, the mood lifts.

If only my mother could have been a part of these new days, not the old times, when a daughter would shame her family by choosing a man they didn't approve of. I would have had my parents together. My mother never would have fled and come to America, pregnant with me. And she wouldn't have had to marry Fred Mulligan. How different our lives would have been! There are several framed pictures of Etta and Joe. This moves me. I feel that we are a part of their daily lives, even though we rarely visit.

On the screened-in porch off the kitchen, where there is a cool breeze, Zia Meoli has set the table with white linen and white dishes. In the center of the table, a cluster of delicate gardenias float in a crystal bowl. Zia directs my father to the head of the table, her husband to the other. We fill in around the men.

"Madame Vilminore?" a voice says from the doorway.

"Ciao, Stefano. Come. Sit. Eat with us," she says to him. Stefano comes out onto the porch. He's around fourteen, with brown eyes, small half-moons that disappear when he smiles. His hair is thick and unruly but beautiful: gold curls that spiral into tight corkscrew ringlets. He has a broad nose, the tip of which lifts up ever so slightly. It's a big nose, but it suits his face. He walks with his hands in his pockets, more self-effacing than shy.

"I'm Ave Maria. And this is my daughter, Etta," I tell him. He smiles at us. I hear Etta gasp. Her eyes widen ever so slightly. (Oh, no. Here we go—puberty.)

Stefano takes a seat next to Etta, who is thrilled to have A Boy sitting next to her at her very first sit-down meal in the country of Italy. And I can't blame her. He is really cute.

"I speak English," Stefano says proudly.

"Where did you learn it?" I ask him.

"School. I must learn English so I can come to America and make a lot of money," he announces.

My father laughs. "Did they tell you the streets were paved with gold?"

"Yes. Paved with gold, and you ride on them in gold Cadillacs. But I like a Ford truck better."

"Then you would like my husband. He has a Ford pickup truck," I say.

"What color?"

"Bright red," Etta pipes up, happy to have something to add.

"I like red." Stefano breaks off the end of the hard-crusted bread Zia has placed by his plate.

"Stefano is a good worker. He helps me in the shop," Zio tells us.

Zia Meoli explains that Stefano is an orphan who lives up the street in a boys' school. Evidently, orphanages aren't sad in Italy. Stefano paints a picture of a happy place, with good friends and nice rooms. I have to remember to ask Meoli later if this is true. Stefano sips the Chianti my uncle has poured.

"You drink wine?" Etta asks him, unnerved at the idea.

"Every day. What do you drink in America?"

"Milk. Pop."

"What's pop?"

"Soda pop."

"Coca-Cola?" Stefano guesses.

"Yes!" Etta says, thrilled to break through the language barrier.

"Maybe someday I try to come to America and drink your soda pop."

"Anytime, Stefano," I tell him. Etta nods in agreement.

Zia Meoli leans in. "He was Antonietta's favorite. Since she died, he's come here every day."

"You were good friends with my aunt?" I ask Stefano.

"Sí. Yes. Yes."

"What did you like about her?"

"She yelled at me all the time."

"Good preparation for marriage." Zio winks.

"Zia Antonietta didn't yell," I tell Stefano.

"Only at me. She wanted me to cut my hair." Stefano shrugs.

"That's a woman for you. Always trying to change the man," Zio says.

Zia Meoli shoots him a look. But I think about Jack, and how I'm constantly trying to change him. Did I insult him when I suggested he go to college and study engineering? I said it only because I think Jack is smart and could be a great engineer. I remember something Nellie Goodloe said to me when she found out I was to marry Jack Mac. She told me that Jack and I were very different: I ran a business and my husband was a miner—how could that work? But I laughed it off at the time. I thought I knew what I was getting into; I thought I could handle our differences. Aren't all marriages a battle of wills and a compromise of different backgrounds?

"*E vero?*" Zio looks at me.

"Yes, you're right. It's true. It's true," I tell my uncle.

We feast on delicate ravioli filled with leeks and tossed in creamy butter and shallots. The bread and butter and wine is a meal in itself, but the ravioli are so tender, they're irresistible. The breeze, filled with sweet gardenia, makes everything taste delicious.

Federica shows us to our room after lunch. It's my mother's room, the very room that Jack and I stayed in on our honeymoon. Federica has pulled out the trundle for Etta. Etta pokes at the bed piled high with fresh linens and blankets and pillows full of soft goose down.

"Mama, the coverlet is full of marshmallows!"

"Wait till you sleep on it."

"Sleep now," Federica tells us. We're ready for a nap, ready to follow any orders given us on Via Davide. She closes the door softly behind her as she goes.

I help Etta into the trundle. "Can we get me one of these back home?" she asks.

"We'll see." I climb up onto the bed.

Etta sighs. "I love Italy."

I lean over the side of the bed so I can see Etta. "You do?"

"It's not like anywhere I've ever been."

"Honey, you've only been to Tennessee and Florida."

"I know. But I didn't think it would be like this."

"That's how I felt when I first came here."

"Mama?"

"Yeah?"

"Someday I'm going to marry Stefano."

I'm glad I'm in the big bed up high, where my daughter can't see me, because my jaw is on my chest. Instead of laughing, I take a deep breath.

"You are?"

"Yes."

"How do you know that?"

"I just do."

I wait for Etta to tell me more, but she doesn't. She falls asleep, no doubt to dream of the cute Italian boy with the crazy hair. Part of me wants to wake her up and tell her to stay a little girl forever. I have to remember to tell her that love is not enough. Don't be like your mother and your grandmother whose name you share. Do better.

After a day of touring Bergamo, meeting neighbors, and going out to dinner, Etta sees *la passeggiata* for the first time. Folks leave their homes to walk around the fountain in the middle of town until the sun sets. Not much happens. Just conversation. A few laughs. Card games. Chess. Checkers. Or they simply stroll and catch up. Etta is invited to play pick-up sticks with some kids from across Via Davide. Papa and Giacomina know lots of people in town, so they walk about and greet their friends.

Zia Meoli finds a place for us on a bench under the fountain, so I can keep an eye on Etta.

"What do you think of her?" Zia Meoli points across the piazza to Giacomina and Papa, who are talking in a small group.

"Giacomina is very nice," I tell her.

"Too young for him," she says.

"At least he's settling down."

"We shall see." She shrugs.

I am happy for my father. He seems content with Giacomina. She fits into his life perfectly. She owns a shop in Schilpario that sells ski equipment. My father likes the fact that she can turn a key in the front door and close the place in a flash. He likes to pick up and do things.

"We're sorry Jack could not come," Zia Meoli says.

"I am too. I wish he could see Etta's face. She loves it here already."

"She's a beautiful girl," she says sincerely.

"Thank you."

"I am sorry we never met Joe."

"I know. I always intended to bring him here."

"What was his funeral like?" my aunt asks me.

In most countries, this would be a strange question, but in Italy, a funeral is an art form. It is the last public gathering to honor a life, and therefore, it must tell the story of that life. So there are prayers and music and speeches. They even take pictures of the deceased in the casket and make copies for all to have after the funeral. It sounds macabre, and maybe it is, but it is also tradition. When Zia Meoli asks me about Joe's funeral, she isn't trying to upset me, she just wants to know.

"It was very simple. No wake. Just a Mass and burial. His friends from school came. You know that Papa came too."

Zia Meoli sits quietly as I play the morning of Joe's funeral over in my mind. And then I remember something I haven't thought about, not during the funeral and not since.

"Remember the story of Aunt Alice Lambert?"

Zia Meoli nods and makes a gesture that indicates Alice was not a nice person. I had written to her about how Alice Mulligan Lambert tried to take the Pharmacy and house away from me.

"I just remembered something. Alice Lambert came to Joe's funeral. She was sitting in the back row on the aisle, and at the end, when we were processing out of the church, I looked down at her, and I guess I looked surprised. She was the last person I expected to see at my son's funeral. But she looked me square in the eye and said she was sorry. And that was it."

"How strange that she came at all," Zia Meoli muses.

"I know. And how funny that I didn't remember it until now."

This happened to me the last time I was in Italy. I remembered details, moments, that for some reason never crossed my mind in Big Stone Gap. When I came here the first time, I was able to see my life from a different perspective. It's as though I left myself at home in the mountains of Virginia and invented this new person to have Italian adventures abroad. I can't do that now. This time I'm on assignment, and the job is to write the plan for the second half of my life. I'm not going to be able to invent it as I go along, because Jack won't let me. He wants to know where I stand. I'm not here on vacation, and every now and then, a pain shoots through my gut to remind me of that fact. I have to make a decision. Sometimes, when I think of my husband, I get butterflies; a surge of emotion goes through me, and I long for him. Other times, I'm glad he's home, where I don't have to deal with the sadness and the stress of us. This makes me feel selfish, and I hate to admit that I haven't lived my life generously. I've sold myself on the idea that I am a magnanimous person, but it was false advertising. I always do what's good for me — what makes me comfortable — and then I dictate to my family how things will go down. Usually, they play right along. I keep telling my relatives that I wish my husband were here too. But Papa could see that I was lying when I said Jack was too busy to get away. So maybe there's another element to my summer in Italy. This is the summer I tell the truth. I will begin with Zia Meoli.

"Jack wanted me to come alone with Etta."

"Why?"

"We're having problems." There. I said it. That's not so hard.

"I am sorry."

"You don't have marital problems here in Italy, do you? The love center of the universe." I wave my hand in front of me — every age of love is in the piazza: teenage lovers speed by on their motorbikes; a young wife splashes her husband as he passes the fountain; an older gentleman buys his wife gelato. Tonight, it seems, everyone is in love in Bergamo.

Zia Meoli throws back her head and laughs. "Yes, we have problems. Lots of problems."

"Well, you're spoiling my romantic notions, but I guess that actually makes me feel better."

"Problems can be good. You solve them, and they bring you back together again."

"That would be nice."

"You've had a lot to cope with. Sometimes you take things out on each other. No?"

"I guess."

"I have a friend who got a divorce. Here in Italy, that is rare. But she was unhappy, so she divorced him. She married a new man, a very nice man. And she told me that she thought she left the problems from the first marriage in the past. But it turned out that she packed them up and took them with her into the second marriage. Sometimes it's not them. Sometimes it's you."

"Oh," I say, "I know it's me."

"Don't worry."

"All I do is worry."

"You are just like your mother."

"I am?"

"She thought love was enough."

She's right. I did think love was enough. Until my husband told me it wasn't. I am like my mother in so many ways. She invested herself in me, all of her time, all of her care. I'm sure Fred Mulligan knew that. Mama kept a beautiful home and made good meals, but she didn't love her husband. Her marriage was a safe place to raise me. I wanted so much more for Etta. But how do I change? It seems I always slide back on my bad habits, my repression, my cold core, so I don't get hurt. But I am hurting everyone around me. Just like my mother did. Fred Mulligan didn't feel her love, she saved it all for me. But it hurt me to see her hurting Fred, even though I didn't like him and he surely didn't like me. But whose fault was that? I didn't have a chance with Fred because I was the obstacle to his happiness. And Mama put me there. A marriage based upon financial security and social acceptability is not what I want for my family, yet isn't that what I have? Am I my mother?

Meoli pats me on the hand, and we get up to stroll in the piazza. The night air is chilly, and I shiver. The sound of the water spilling over the marble seashells in the fountain makes soft music as we walk. The lights above us in Alta Città are dim lavender sparks behind the black trees. I am glad the sun is sinking low behind the hills of Bergamo—I don't want Zia Meoli to see me cry.

# CHAPTER SEVEN

With Papa at the wheel, we take the curve up the mountain road, out of Bergamo, north to Schilpario. Once again I am in the mountains; whether it's the Italian Alps or the Appalachians, it seems I can't escape them. As we speed up into the peaks, I am not afraid, as I was on my first visit. I look at Etta, who doesn't flinch as we climb higher and higher or even when trucks whip past us and force us over to the gravel edge of the road, our wheels inches away from the perilous edge above gaps several miles deep. I guess my kid is an old pro, having flown around the curves of Cracker's Neck Holler all of her life.

"Aren't these mountains different from ours back home?" I ask Etta, and point to the Alps.

"They're taller. And they have snow on them in the summer," she says, sounding impressed.

"Yep, they're so high up there, it stays cold and never melts."

Giacomina, strapped in by her seat belt, turns as best she can from the front seat. "We're going to take you to lots of places."

"Do you have goats?" Etta asks Giacomina.

"Many goats."

"I went to Mary Ann Davis's farm in East Stone Gap, and she had miniature goats. Do you have those?"

"We do. And they all wear bells. So when they get lost, the goatherd can find them."

"Just like Peter in *Heidi*! I love *Heidi*!"

"Etta, I will make you wear a bell!" Papa says, winking at her in the rearview mirror.

As we drive into Schilpario, for the first time in a hundred miles, Papa slows down. He has been the mayor of this village for nearly forty years. The houses with their dark beams set off by white stucco, others painted shades of pale blue and taupe and soft green, look like candy tiles glued into the rocky mountainside. Window boxes spill over with small purple blossoms and spikes of green plants I have never seen before. "Herbs," Giacomina tells me.

Etta is thrilled by the waterwheel chugging slowly around in a circle, scooping the crystal water from the stream and sending it flowing over the slats of the old wood, polished smooth from wear. I point to the stream that rushes down the mountain over clean gray stones, then widens and makes a pond next to the cabin by the waterwheel. I show her how everything is connected; I think she understands.

Nonna is waiting on a swing in the patch of grass between the street and the front door of her house when we pull up. (Nonna and Papa's home is dead center on Main Street, the perfect spot for the mayor.) She pulls herself up with a cane and opens one arm to Etta, who runs to meet her great-grandmother. Nonna's body, thick through the middle with short muscular legs, is as hearty as it was when I first met her. She is instantly in love with Etta, whom she spins around like a top, checking her out from every angle. My grandmother is as sharp as she was the day she entered my house on Poplar Hill in the Gap. I have to remember to ask Papa how old she is, because she hasn't changed a bit. What's her secret?

Mafalda, my father's first cousin, is around fifty, petite with a sweet, round face, clear, pink skin, small lips, and the trademark Barbari nose. She is bustling around the kitchen, setting the table for supper. She takes orders from my grandmother without complaint. That's just the way things are in Italy; I never hear anyone arguing with their elders. (I hope Etta makes a note of this!) Nonna runs this homestead like a general, and for her size, she packs more punch than the Italian army. Etta can't believe how loud she is, how she barks orders and seems to get angry, which then passes over like a storm cloud dissipating into mist before it can explode. My grandmother grabs Etta, hugs her, and rubs her cheeks at every opportunity. She promises to teach Etta everything about life in Schilpario—the cooking, the manners, and the family history. I have a feeling Etta will be a good student. Nonna wouldn't have it any other way.

Giacomina wasn't kidding when she told us that she has lots of plans. She brings out a calendar, and the days are full of trips and activities. She tells me when Etta leaves the room that these trips are especially for Etta, not for me. Papa wants me to rest. Only my father can see what I truly need (isn't that true of all parents?).

Nonna treats my father like a king. He is the boss, his every whim indulged. Mafalda tells me Papa has lots of company, "town business," men from Bergamo who come north with ideas for local trade. Something is always going on with Papa. He may disappear at a moment's notice, without explanation. When he returns hours later, he'll simply tell you he got caught up in a conversation. Mafalda tells me she has learned never to set the table until she sees his hat on the hook.

Papa takes us upstairs and shows Etta her own bedroom, a small, charming room with a balcony on the front and a sloped ceiling. A hand-painted yellow daybed piled high with goose-feather pillows (those poofs!) fits neatly under the eave. There is a long pillow shaped like a sausage and tied at the ends with ribbon like a hard candy. Etta holds it up and shows it to me. She's never seen one like it before. There is a trunk, an old rocker with another blanket on it, and a vase full of edelweiss that climbs out of a small silver flute. Etta loves the walls, painted beige, with the dark brown beams on the ceiling.

"Mama, don't the beams on the ceiling look like Little Debbie Snack Cakes?" She points overhead.

"They do." I laugh.

"Everything in this house looks like something to eat. Like Hansel and Gretel's house."

"You know something? You're right."

"Why?"

"Well, we're so far north in Italy, it's almost Switzerland. So you have that Tyrolean look to everything."

"What's that?"

"It's like a cuckoo clock. Gingerbread roof. Windows with shutters. Low ceilings to keep it warm and cozy in the cold. And round-topped doorways. Do you like it here?"

"I love it. I just wish Daddy was here."

I unpack Etta's things as she dresses for bed. She says her prayers and climbs under the covers. A cold breeze flaps the shutter open. I go to the window and look down on the narrow main street of Schilpario, lit only by the light that pours out of the houses in soft pools. An old man carrying a box shuffles up the street and disappears into a doorway. I can smell the tobacco from his pipe as he goes past.

On the horizon I see a rim of clouds, but I realize that they are actually the mountains' snow-covered tips, lit by the moon. The sugary caps are so close, I could lean out this little window and touch them. My face is cool from the breeze; it feels good, but I don't want Etta to catch cold, so I unfold the shutter and hook it against the frame.

I go downstairs; Mafalda is preparing the table for breakfast, Nonna has gone to bed, and Papa is watching television. I go into my father's office and pick up the phone. It's the wee hours of the morning in Big Stone Gap. As I dial our home phone number, I cannot wait for Jack to pick up. I want to tell him about our trip. The phone rings a few times, but Jack Mac is a deep sleeper. I let it ring again. And again. I count the rings. It rings thirteen times. I hang up the phone. Maybe . . . *he's not there?* Of course he's there. Where else would he be? I am not going to make too much out of this. I'm an ocean away, and there's nothing I can do. I'll try again tomorrow.

Etta is off to Sestri Levante, an old fishing village on the coast of the glorious Mediterranean. Papa's first cousins live there and want to meet Etta. The Bonicellis have a candy shop and a house on the beach. Nonna's sister has a ten-year-old granddaughter, Chiara. The girls introduced themselves to each other on the phone. Papa and Giacomina are taking her; they'll stay the weekend and get some sun. *"Bronzata,"* Papa calls it.

Mafalda lets me sleep late every morning. The only job I have is to write long letters to Theodore and Iva Lou, describing everything. I collect local postcards to send to Iva Lou. I know she'll tape them to the dashboard of the Bookmobile. I'm sending Theodore a bell for his front door—it's a small hand-painted brass bell on an embroidered rope. (Maybe next summer Theodore can come with me and see Italy for himself.) I can't believe we've been here almost a week. I'm finally feeling rested. The food makes me feel sturdy. The fragrant risottos made with saffron and sweet butter; the fresh berries drizzled in honey and served cold in sterling silver cups; and the bread, spongy and light inside, with chewy, hard crust (it's so delicious, I don't even put butter on it).

I've decided that my body could use some attention; I've neglected myself for too long. So during siesta, instead of sleeping, I climb the steep hills behind Schilpario alone. The mountain paths, worn from time, creep up through the green in all directions. I vow that by the end of the month, I will have followed most of them. Whenever I climb, I think of my mother, who loved these mountains with their emerald green fields, dangerous cliffs, and cold streams.

Today the mountain breeze is especially cool, so I borrow one of my father's soft leather car coats and wrap a red bandanna around my neck. Maybe it's just looking up at the snowcaps that makes me shiver. The sun is warm, but the ground is always cold to the touch. (I don't think the Italian Alps have ever had a good thaw.) I opt not to wear Papa's hat, one of those Robin Hood numbers: dark green felt with a feather in it. Besides, I don't want to mess up my new hair.

Yesterday Mafalda took me to the next village, Piccolo Lago, where I got a haircut. The sign in the window said MODERNA. I think "Modern" is a nutty name for anything in these parts. Everything should be called "Antica." I hadn't had a real haircut in years; I still wore it in a braid up and off of my face. Jack always liked my hair long, so I never changed it, and pulling it back is so easy. But I've needed a change for a long time. Don't I always notice women who get stuck in beauty ruts? So when Violetta, a tall blond Italian with a heavy dose of German no-nonsense in her accent, sat me down and told me to throw my head forward, I obeyed. I watched as glops of my old brown curls hit the black-and-white-checked linoleum like lengths of ribbon. When Violetta was done, she told me to sit up straight (you do whatever she tells you and fast), and the girls in the shop gathered around my chair. "Gina Lollobrigida," Violetta said and smiled, taking full credit for transforming the mouse into a va-va-voom. The other girls agreed as Violetta spun me around like a Cadillac at a car show.

The new hairdo accentuates my face. The long, boring braid is gone; this is full and thick and much shorter, with loose waves that soften my cheeks and nose, and long, delicate spiraling down my neck. One of the shop girls, a birdlike brunette with perfect lips, took a tube of lipstick out of her apron pocket. At first I was clumsy with it, so she had to unscrew the Italian top for me (different from our lipsticks, there's a latch on it). I put on the lipstick, filling out my full lips top and bottom, and my first thought was that it was too much. Too dramatic. Too purple! I felt like I was sporting a duck bill. But Violetta handed me a tissue, and after I blotted, the magenta with the little gold sparkles in it actually looked alluring. *"Bellisima!"* a customer under the dryer said, banging her head as she strained to get a look at me. I smiled and gave all the girls big tips. If I had a million dollars, I would have given it to Violetta. I needed this.

Nonna flipped for the haircut; she said, "Ornella Muti!" when I came into the house. Ornella, a Roman actress, is featured on the cover of this month's *Hello!* magazine, which has claimed a permanent spot on Nonna's coffee table. She grabbed it and pointed to the exotic green-eyed beauty, who, yes, has my haircut. Or more to the point, I have her haircut. I made Nonna take a Polaroid of me and my new hair to send to Theodore.

So it is with more than a little renewed self-confidence, a bright lipstick (God bless the kid; she gave me the tube), a new purpose, and a dazzling haircut, that I climb the Alpine trail like the Eye-talian native I would have been if my mother had not run off to America pregnant with me and without my father, Mario da Schilpario, and married Fred Mulligan instead. I look down at my thighs as I use them to power my short, quick steps up the trail. I shouldn't have such muscles in them; I've been climbing around here only a week. But they're there. I never got muscles like these hiking up Powell Mountain. The leather in Papa's coat smells like him, clean and woodsy. I feel great. Maybe it's the altitude.

I decide to take a new path today, the one that's a little more finished-looking than the rest. There are actual stones that anchor either side of the path like a garden walk. At the very top of that trail, there is a plateau that piques my curiosity.

Once I reach the top of the ridge, I have to hoist myself up and over a small shelf of ground to reach the plateau. There, high above Schilpario, in a place where only goats go, is a field of bluebells so thick, they look like a carpet stretching across the expanse. So blue, it could be a lake, or the Mediterranean Sea. Bees buzz above the sweet blossoms, so many of them that they knock into one another in midair before they dive below to drink from the flowers. Beyond the blue carpet is a green field that leads to a ledge of rock dripping with vines. I won't venture out to the edge. I know there is a drop there—probably one of those frightening gaps, so deep you cannot see the bottom. I sit down in the flowers; the only sound is the music the bees make. I think of Mrs. Mac. I must remember to bring Etta up here and tell her about the origin of the middle name that she inherited from her grandmother Nan Bluebell Gilliam MacChesney about the bluebells that bloomed in the field behind our house in Cracker's Neck the day that her grandmother "got born."

When I return from my hike, Giacomina announces that she and Papa are going to take us to a disco tonight. The whole family. (Except for Nonna, who tells me she would rather someone throw her off the mountain than make her go to a disco-tekka. Mafalda thinks Nonna is seventy-nine years old, but isn't exactly sure because Nonna won't fess up.)

Etta is back from Sestri Levante. Papa bought her a turquoise choker, which she vows she'll never take off. It lies flat and clean against her brown skin; her time on the beach brought out her freckles. Giacomina and Papa thought it would be a good idea to bring Chiara back to keep Etta company.

"Hello, Cousin Ave Maria," Chiara says to me, sounding like one of those learn-a-foreign-language-fast tapes.

"Ciao, Chiara." I give her a hug. She's a beauty, with her shiny black hair and wide brown eyes. Chiara is taller than Etta, but just as lean. She wears plastic rings on all of her fingers, a style that Etta has eagerly copied. They look like a couple of five-and-dime Cleopatras.

Then she tells my father in Italian that I am pretty and not too old. I tell my little cousin that she should have seen me before the va-va-voom haircut. Chiara looks at me like I'm crazy.

Chiara is full of mischief. In pictures, she comes off as serene and serious, but in life, her dark eyes constantly dart about, looking for excitement. She is very quick, instantly picking up English phrases from Etta. Etta is doing fine with her Italian too. Chiara is teaching her

Italian curse words, which make my daughter laugh. She is the perfect foil for Etta, who tries to do the right thing even at the expense of fun. But I instantly love my cousin; I want her to help Etta test her limits. Etta needs to loosen up. She needs to run and get dirty and play. I just want them to be careful, but I don't have to worry. Giacomina takes them under her wing like her own little summer charges, and they obey her without question.

As we drive through the mountains, Papa tells Giacomina about town business, something about tourist season come winter. Then, in a split second, he swerves off the main road and through a mass of vines and brush. We bump onto a gravel road that pitches us around like loose fruit. The girls laugh and hang on. Soon we see a clearing with tall lanterns on spikes stuck in the ground around a dance floor of portable linoleum.

I was expecting an indoor disco. When we say "disco" in America, we mean a dance club, a place where you would find John Travolta in an ice-cream suit. But here a disco can be any place there's music. The music, which sounds like Italian covers of American hits, plays out through the black night. Folks are gathered around the bar (a table set up in the field), and the kids are drinking a dark red fizzy drink, which they throw back like shots. "Bitters," Giacomina tells me. There's a crowd. A big crowd. It seems that most of the mountain villages emptied out and came here tonight. Cars are parked haphazardly along the sides of the field.

Chiara acts sophisticated and points out all the particulars to Etta. I can hardly hold on to them as they bolt from the car and head for the dance floor. Papa and Giacomina see friends from town and stop to chat. I whisper in Giacomina's ear that I am going to go exploring.

I love the way Italians look. Maybe it's because I'm relieved that there's a place in this world where I look like somebody. But I find their faces so interesting. I don't know what makes the women so beautiful—you would never see any of them on a magazine cover in

America—but they are striking. Here a strong nose is a source of pride. Most of these noses wouldn't last in America, with their length and their regal breaks in the bridge—they wouldn't be appreciated. Maybe these women are so attractive because they like themselves. They accept what they are born with; even their flaws are a source of pride, the very thing that makes them distinctive and alluring.

The men are beyond handsome. Even when they're short (I guess height is an American thing), they have a strength that makes you believe they could take one of these Alpine boulders and roll it down the hill like a basketball. They live in their skin like kings; their mothers encourage that. A son is a prized possession, more treasured than land or gold. A son means continuity. A son can become a father, and a father is the center of wisdom and policy in the home. I see it in action, in the small pockets surrounding the dance floor. Of course, the men seem to be in charge only because the women let them. Entire families are here together, enjoying the night air and the delicate paper lights and the music. (It reminds me of the Singing Convention held at Bullit Park back in Big Stone Gap. Families come with a picnic basket and stay all day listening to the music.)

"Ave Maria! *Andiamo!*" Chiara says, grabbing one of my hands while my daughter takes the other. They yank me onto the dance floor. Some Italian singer has covered an old American disco standard, and the girls want me to dance with them. At first I don't want to dance. I'm old, I want to tell them. I'm a wife and a mother and a pharmacist. There's no place for me on the dance floor; I have no business moving to the rhythm that makes the floor buckle under the impact of all these feet. But I look at my daughter's face, and she wants me to dance. She seems to be saying, "If you dance, then I can. I want a mother who is happy and free and moves without worrying about what other people think."

And for some reason, on this mountaintop, hidden inside all of these bodies as they sway and bounce, it's okay for me to let go. I feel safe in this place where I am not known. My daughter is with me, and her cousin, but really, I am alone. I'm not married in this moment, and I am not a mother. I took my wedding rings off to collect stones in the stream above Papa's house, and I forgot to put them back on. No, tonight I am Ave Maria Mulligan, the girl I left behind before I decided to give everything away to be simply a part of the Mac-Chesney family. I let the music take me to that place where I was before I knew life could be so complicated.

Chiara and Etta and I have locked arms and are spinning in a circle, laughing. People on the dance floor make room for us. I throw my head back and look at the open sky above. I am connected and at the same time completely free. I am here, in my body, in this moment, but I'm also flying overhead in the inky sky streaked white with stars.

When the song ends (and I'm so sorry it did!), Chiara and Etta giggle and run off to find my father. I breathe deeply; my heart is beating fast. I lean over and rest my palms on my knees. I am hot and winded and sweaty and I like it.

"Ciao," a man's voice says to me. I look up and into an amazing pair of blue eyes.

"Ciao," I say. He extends his hand to me. To be polite, I take it.

He looks as though he is searching for words. And he is. Italian words.

"Uh, *dove e* . . ." I do my best to follow along. In a few broken sentences, he has asked me to dance and to point him to the garage (we're in a field, there is no garage), and inquired as to what village I'm from. I'm getting a kick out of him. He has beautiful hands, which make grand gestures to help me decipher what he's trying to say in Italian.

He is also really handsome. He's tall. And what a face. He reminds me of Rock Hudson in *Pillow Talk*. Maybe it's the dark hair. Or maybe it's the look in his eyes. That's where the movie-star dazzle ends, though; he's pretty trim, but I can see he has to fight a gut. (Who doesn't? Maybe he's a little older than me, but not much.) The chest is broad; I'll bet he's a runner. He isn't wearing glasses, but I can tell he wears contact lenses, because he blinks a lot. He has beautiful white teeth, with the front teeth a little longer than the rest, which is sexy. He has thin but well-shaped lips (no cruelty there, just practicality in buckets, according to face-reading). The nose is amazing: straight, a little bulbous on the end (this is the nose of humor and wisdom—the tip is the giveaway).

"*Non capisce,*" I say to him.

"Okay, okay," he says, more to himself than to me. Frustrated, he looks off, giving up the Italian. "You're looking at me like I'm nuts. Okay, maybe I am nuts." I get it: he thinks I'm a native. I feel as though I won the Nobel Prize, I am so proud of myself! I have passed for a Bergamosque! The pants, the cardigan, and the haircut have worked. I appear to be a real Italian through and through! I could kiss this guy.

"*Sì. Sì.*" I motion that he should continue in English and, with gestures, relay that I am trying to understand him. This is so much fun!

"I saw you dancing with those kids. And well, anyway, I think you're cute. And I'd like to dance with you. I'm American. I guess you could tell that from the English I'm speaking. You've got a great face. In fact, everything is pretty fine on you, to tell you the truth."

"Yes?" I say.

Galvanized that I am making the attempt to communicate, he continues. "So you'll dance with me?"

"*Sì,*" I say slowly, sounding like Gina Lollobrigida in *La Bellezza di Ippolita.*

The American takes me in his arms and pulls me close, placing his hand on my waist, a little too low for a stranger. I reach back and put his hand above my waist. (I'm having fun, I just don't want to have too much fun.)

As the song ends, he seems to screw up his courage to say, "You have beautiful eyes."

I try to smile in a way that is enigmatic yet noncommittal.

"Could I take you to dinner sometime? I'm here for another few weeks . . ."

Okay, Ave, game over. Let the nice man off the hook. "I'm married," I tell him in a pure country accent straight out of the Appalachian Mountains.

"Say that again."

"I'm murried. Married. And I'm American. I can't do this to you for another second. I'm sorry."

"You're Southern!"

"Uh-huh. Virginia."

"You're just loaded with accents. Can you do Garbo from *Camille?*" I can't tell if he thinks my little game was funny or offensive. "Where in Virginia are you from?"

"Southwest. In the Blue Ridge Mountains. Where they meet the Appalachians. Near the Cumberland Gap." When you're from Big Stone Gap, you always have to overexplain the location. No one ever knows where we are.

"You aren't on the Appalachian Trail, are you?"

"We're right on it. In fact, it runs through our home-ec room at the high school. At least that's what I was told in ninth grade by my home-ec teacher, Mrs. Porier."

"I'm hiking that trail this fall!"

"You are? Well, you'll have to stop in."

I extend my hand to the tall American with the pretty eyes. "My name is Ave Maria Mulligan. I mean, MacChesney."

"You don't know your own last name?"

"I do. I just forgot it for a second. My married name, I mean." I'm so embarrassed. Why am I embarrassed? Why is he laughing in that conspiratorial way? Am I flirting with this man?

"I'm Pete Rutledge."

"Well, it was nice dancing with you." Nice, Ave. Could you sound more awkward?

"Thank you for the dance," he says. We stand and look at each other. I don't want him to go, but I don't want him to stay, either.

"Thank you for saying I was cute," I blurt.

"I meant it."

"I could tell. So thank you." I smile at him as one does when a stranger compliments your car.

He tilts his head and looks at me directly. "How married are you?" he says with a half smile. (And I thought the only wolves in Italy were Italian.)

I don't answer his question, I throw my head back and laugh. I turn to walk away and he grabs my hand.

"How long are you here?" Pete asks, then follows me off the dance floor.

"I'm leaving soon."

"You're lying."

"Yes, I am. But you make me nervous, and I lie compulsively when I'm nervous."

"That's good to know." He smiles.

"I'm here all month. Not here in this village. I'm with my father, over in Schilpario."

"What's his name?"

"Mario Barbari."

Pete leans down and pushes an unruly curl off my cheek. "Will I see you again?"

"No."

Pete laughs. "You're a Play-by-the-Rules girl?"

"You have no idea."

I hustle the girls to bed so I can be alone and think about what happened tonight. Why am I so jazzed, so giddy? I'm a grown woman. I'm acting more like Chiara and Company than the sensible woman I am! I feel guilty for replaying the excitement of Pete Rutledge in my mind, so I go into my father's study and call Jack. The phone rings three times.

"Hello?" he says, groggy with sleep.

"Hi, it's me."

"Ave?" Then he seems to wake up and listen. "Is everything okay? How's Etta?"

"She's great. We went to a disco. And she's made friends with my second cousin Chiara, who's ten. She's here with Etta now." Why am I talking so loud and so fast?

"That all sounds great."

"I missed you tonight. There was dancing."

"There usually is at a disco."

"Right. Right."

"I miss you both too," he says.

"Thanks." I don't mean to be selfish, but can't he just miss me? "Well, I guess that's all the news."

"Yep."

There is a long silence; I guess I'm waiting for him to tell me about his life, but he doesn't volunteer anything, so I don't press. "Sleep well." I hang up the phone. My body is shaking, but it's not chills. I'm happy! A fine-looking stranger thought I was pretty! And I danced with him. And he felt good, and he smelled like mint and clean woods. And he wasn't a local on the make, either, he was an American who thought I was an Italian goddess. I dial Theodore's number.

"Hello?" Theodore answers his phone sleepily. I've woken him up too.

"It's me—Ave."

"Where are you?"

"Schilpario."

"Jesus. What time is it?"

"Early. For you. Late. For me."

"This better be good."

"I danced at a disco tonight."

"Wow," he says with no enthusiasm.

"Don't be rude."

"I can be whatever I want when you wake me up at this hour."

"Sorry. Theodore, there was a man there. Pete Rutledge. He thought I was cute."

"You are cute. You're also married."

"I know. Can you print that on a postcard and send it over to me?"

"I think I'd better." I hear Theodore sit up straight in his bed. Now he's paying attention.

"He thought I was Italian."

"You are Italian."

"No, really Italian. Like from here. Born and raised. I got a haircut."

"I really have to hang up this phone."

"Bear with me, please," I beg him.

"I'm trying."

"When Violetta of the Moderna Salon cut my hair, I don't know, my face changed. And then I felt like I was walking differently. Then all of a sudden, when I was climbing in the Alps, I looked down and there were muscles in my legs, like the ones that were there when I was young and didn't have to work at it. And I got this lipstick that, I swear to you, is like magic—I put it on and I don't know, I'm sexy or something. Me. Sexy."

"Where was Jack when you were flirting with this Pete person?"

"He didn't come. He's back home."

"How convenient."

"It was his idea. It's not my fault I'm alone over here for a month—"

"You'd better be careful. A woman in her prime loose in the Italian Alps sounds like a setup for a spaghetti western with a bad ending."

"Theodore! I won't do anything! I never do anything. I'm a sensible, practical pharmacist, remember?" Doesn't Theodore know that it's the idea of an affair that excites me? I hang up the phone; my palms are sweating so much, they leave a print on the black receiver. I rub it off with the hem of my sweater.

Everyone in the house is asleep. I tiptoe up to my room on the second floor, a big, square room with a fireplace and four windows, and a high double bed with four carved wood posters that nearly reach the ceiling. It's a princess bed. And tonight, I *am* a princess who floated on a dance floor in Italy under a box of silver stars with a handsome prince.

I close the door and slip out of my loafers. I undress in the dark. When I am completely naked, I stand in front of the long mirror with the gold-leaf frame. The soft beam from the nightlight puts me in silhouette. I turn to the side and look at myself in profile. The gentle curves of my body, from having the babies, are suddenly beautiful to me. My skin is soft and warm, and I smell like the rosewater Mafalda left for me on the vanity. I shake my head, and my hair shakes loose away from my head in full, waxy curls, as curls were meant to be. Something happened to me tonight. I'm a girl again. And I like it.

# CHAPTER EIGHT

The rain began in the early hours of Sunday morning before I could drift off to sleep. Papa has built a fire; the smell of wood smoke, fresh rain, and Mafalda's macaroons baking in the oven woke me up. Etta and Chiara are in the basement making a mural in chalk, and I am reading all about Ornella Muti's life (she's good friends with Mussolini's granddaughter). Papa is at Giacomina's store, helping her do inventory and place orders for the ski season. Nonna went up the street to visit a friend. Papa argued with her to let her ankle heal a little longer before she went out. (Guess who won that argument?)

Jack called this morning; fully awake, he was much more animated and attentive on the phone. He had a long talk with Etta, and when she handed the phone over to me, I realized that even though she misses her daddy, she was happier than I had seen her in a long time. She is happy because she sees how happy I am. Don't I remember when I was a girl and my mother was happy? I would do anything to see my mother smile. I remember when I brought Mama to our cast party at the Drama and she sang an Italian folk song for the crowd. I couldn't believe that she had the courage to sing in front of all those people, and as I watched her, she became her best self, her most free and happy self. I'll never forget her face that night. I wished her joy could last forever. She had so much sadness, I just wanted her to forget it all and laugh. And when she did that night, I knew that it was possible for her to have a life of joy. Etta knows I'm happy here, and it brings out the best in both of us. I must not forget that I have an insight into my daughter, because I was a daughter once too.

Jack tells me about the progress he and the guys are making on the rec center in Appalachia. He catches me up on the local gossip. Leah and Worley got married by the justice of the peace; everyone thinks Tayloe Lassiter is having an affair with the jeweler from down in Pennington Gap; and Zackie Wakin, concerned that he was getting robbed, ordered a detective kit from a magazine to trap the thief. He put a special invisible powder on everything in his store and hung a sign on the door that said he was out of town ("To throw 'em off but good," he told Jack). Turns out someone was in the store at night—and when the police came and washed the powder with a special solvent and took the footprints, they belonged to Zackie. Evidently, Zackie is a sleepwalker. We have a good laugh over that one.

There is something different in my husband's voice. His tone is warm but just a touch hollow. Sort of like: you're there, I'm here, let's not talk about anything too deep. But since I danced with Pete Rutledge, all I want to do is talk about deep things. One dance made me want to dig deep and live. How dramatic, but how true.

"Ave, were you drunk last night?"

"What?"

"When you called. Had you been drinking?"

"I had bitters at the disco. But that's all."

"How much?" Jack chuckles.

"I wasn't drunk."

"You're on vacation. Live it up."

Part of me wants to tell Jack everything, as I used to do, in the beginning. We'd lie in bed for hours, and I'd share things with him I had never told anyone. It's different now. I'm not compelled to tell him everything, and I'm not sure why. When Jack hangs up, I am relieved. We ran out of things to say.

The rain is coming down so hard now, it's making a river in the street in front of the house, and it's dumping into the creek that feeds the waterwheel. The waterwheel whips around in a high-speed frenzy, throwing sheets of water everywhere. I get back to the glamorous life of Ornella Muti. Oh, the details.

Mafalda pokes her head into the study. "Ave Maria. You have a guest."

Through the door from the living room, which connects to the kitchen, I see Pete Rutledge in a yellow rain slicker, standing in the doorway. He is so tall, he has to duck his head down; his shoulders barely fit in the frame. His blue eyes stand out against the bright yellow collar of the slicker. His hair is wet, and he hasn't shaved. He reminds me of Clark Gable in *The Call of the Wild*, just a little. I wish I didn't think this man looked like all my favorite movie idols, but in certain ways, and in certain lights, he does. He's a little like my girlhood board game Mystery Date—which Etta still plays with her girlfriends—where the players spin a dial and a plastic door opens to reveal seven different specimens of young all-American manhood, one cuter than the next. I bite my lip; good, I'm wearing lipstick. (Loretta Young would never be caught without it, even in frozen tundra). Why am I worried about how I look? My heart skips, sending a flurry of butterflies through my chest, and lower. Shame on me! I take a deep breath. I am not excited he came to see me; I'm *surprised*, but I am definitely not excited. Maybe if I say this to myself enough, I'll believe it.

"Hello," I say to him as I lean in the doorway with my arms across my chest.

"Everybody in this town knows Mario Barbari." Pete smiles.

"He's been the mayor for—"

"Thirty-seven years," Mafalda finishes my sentence.

"May I borrow your Ave Maria for the afternoon?" Pete asks Mafalda.

"I cannot answer for her," she says warmly. Even Mafalda is suckered by this American male.

"There's an inn up the street. Want to get a cup of coffee?" he offers.

Mafalda instantly grabs the pot, and I stop her. "No waiting on us."

"I am happy to!" Mafalda says.

"No. If Mr. Rutledge has checked out the local coffee, then the least I can do is try it." I smile at Pete, who smiles back at me.

I grab one of my father's coats off the rack by the door. This time I wear his silly Robin Hood hat. Pete holds the door for me, and we step out into the rain. I walk ahead a few steps, and he catches up with me and opens his raincoat, pulling me inside. I resist at first, but the rain is coming down so hard that I opt to stay dry. I have to skip to keep up with him; his legs cover twice the distance mine do in the same amount of time. He looks down at me and laughs. I hope he thinks this hat is ridiculous. I do not need this man attracted to me.

Pete holds the door for me as we enter the old inn. My father has told me that in the winter, at the height of ski season, this place is packed. Today there is just me, Pete, and the proprietor, an old man with a pipe, sitting in the kitchen and reading the newspaper. The pipe smell is familiar: he's the same man who walks home late at night. I smile at him and wave, and he looks up and nods. Pete takes off his raincoat and drapes it over a chair. He helps me with my coat and hat. The proprietor comes out; Pete orders coffee in lousy Italian, and I let him. There are three stuffed deer heads over the fireplace. The room has Tyrolean touches, just like the homestead. The tables are waxed and the chairs mismatched, some with embroidered seats and some straight-backed and plain. I sit down in one of the two dilapidated easy chairs in front of the fire and stretch my legs out on the stone hearth. The chairs are so old and low to the ground, you might as well sit on the floor. Pete sinks into the other chair, scooting it to face me.

"How are you?"

"I'm fine. How are you?"

"A little wet," he says as he runs his fingers through his hair. "Why don't you wear a wedding ring?"

I look down at my hands. Why do I keep forgetting to put on my rings?

"I was helping Mafalda make macaroons."

"You weren't making macaroons last night."

"No. Last night I wasn't wearing them because I had been fishing stones out of the stream yesterday afternoon and I had taken them off."

"You wouldn't want to lose them," he says, and smiles in a way that is so sexy, I'm glad I'm sitting down: if I were standing, my knees would give out.

"No, I wouldn't," I tell him, regaining my composure, then say directly, "What are you implying?"

"Nothing."

"Good." I lean back in the chair, then shift as a spring pops up and jabs me in the center of my back.

We sit in silence for a moment. The old man brings the coffee. He looks at Pete, and then he looks at me. I can see that he appreciates the happy American couple who wandered in from the rain. You can't find a soul in this country who doesn't believe in romance. No need to further anyone's misapprehensions. I move my chair away from Pete's. I have to get this conversation on a more general, friendly plane.

"What do you do?" I ask him a bit too chirpily.

"I'm a marble guy."

"Game marbles?"

"No." He laughs. He has a good laugh—it's right up there with his smile. "Marble for houses. Mantels. Walkways. Tabletops."

"Interesting. Is there a lot of call for marble in New Jersey?"

"Are you kidding? It's the goomba capital of the world."

"Hey. I'm a goomba," I tell him.

"Me too. Half."

Half Italian. Okay. That explains the dark hair and the good nose and the hitting on married women.

"My mother was Italian," he explains. "Her people were from Calabria. They're very passionate."

"I've heard."

"You don't like small talk, do you?" he says.

We sit quietly for a moment, and I consider this stranger as he gazes into the fire and sips his coffee. Who is this guy anyway? What kind of man uses words like "passionate" and persists with a woman whether she's wearing her wedding ring or not? He eases his long legs out and rests his feet against the wall. I feel dwarfed sitting here next to him, but I shouldn't—I'm far from tiny. But there is something about this man that fills up a room. The size of him makes me want to take him on and set him straight: no, I don't like small talk. In fact, I don't like anything frivolous. I would prefer it if folks just got to the point. I learned the value of time the hard way. It's a sin to squander it.

"Maybe I don't like small talk because you're not very good at it," I tell him.

I catch him off guard and he laughs. Is there anything sexier than a man who laughs at your jokes? I don't think so. I take a sip of the coffee. I've never had a cup of coffee so good.

"Have you read *Browning's Italy*?" he asks.

"By Helen Clarke? I love that book!"

"I don't know how anyone can come to Italy without reading it."

"That's my favorite love story."

"Robert Browning and Elizabeth Barrett?" he says.

"Who did you think I meant?"

"Maybe you and me." He smiles. "I'm kidding around."

"Good." Boy, this guy is bold. "It's awfully hot in here." Let me get back to the Brownings before he says something else that makes me sweat. I push my chair away from the fire.

"Why is it your favorite love story?" he asks.

"Because it was an impossible situation. Elizabeth Barrett was living a terrible life; she was sick and housebound, writing poetry. Oppressed by a cruel father. And then Robert Browning sent her his poetry, and they began to correspond and fell in love through their words."

Pete picks up the story. "And then Browning proposed, and Elizabeth was afraid to tell her father, so they eloped and moved to Rome." The man is finishing my sentences. "You know, you can rent their apartment in Florence."

"Really?"

"I've been in it."

"You have?"

"A friend of mine rented it last summer, and I went over and checked it out."

"Did you know they had a son?"

"Penn."

"Right. And she defied the doctors; they told her that the trip to Italy from England would kill her. And that she would never have a child."

"So she followed her heart, and everything worked out. That's very reassuring, isn't it?" Pete looks at me.

"Yes, it is."

"Have you read *Casa Guidi Windows*?"

"My mother had the poem in Italian."

"It's a beaut. I think it's Elizabeth Barrett Browning's best poem," he says, then looks back into the fire. I can't believe I'm talking poetry with a man. When was the last time I did that? When did I ever do that?

"So . . . what's your story, Pete?" I ask him, feeling a jolt from the caffeine.

"You want the whole thing?"

"Sure."

"I grew up in New Jersey. I went to Rutgers. Studied theater. Set design. Graduated. Worked in not-for-profit theater in New York. Got sick of that. Hooked up with an old buddy of mine; we started this marble thing. Now I live in Hoboken. And once a year, I come over here for a couple of weeks to buy marble."

"Are you married?"

"No."

I don't know why his answer makes me smile, but it does.

"What's funny?"

"I don't know."

"You're glad I'm not married?"

"No."

"It would be nice if *you* weren't," he says, tapping my leg with the toe of his shoe. I move my leg.

"Why?" I'm only asking because I'm dying to hear what he'll come up with.

"Well, for starters, if you weren't married, we wouldn't be sitting down here having coffee." Pete's eyes travel from me to the sign that says ROOMS, with an arrow pointing up the stairs.

I don't move a muscle. I can't. Between the bad springs in this chair and my nerves shutting down one synapse at a time, I can't trust my body. "Boy, this is some haircut."

"What?"

"I never got this kind of attention with my old hair."

"It's not the hair."

"Come on. You don't even know me."

"I like what I see so far."

"Pete, let me tell you about the part you don't see."

"Please do. That's the good stuff."

"I don't know how good this stuff is. I was the Big Stone Gap Town Spinster for fifteen years."

"You called yourself that?"

"Yeah."

"So what are you saying?"

"I waited a long time to fall in love. And then I married him."

"So how's it going?"

"What?"

"Your marriage?"

I take a deep breath. "Not so great."

"Why not?"

"We're very different."

"That can be a good thing."

"Sometimes."

"What did you think it was going to be like?"

"Being married?"

"No. Loving someone. When you were a spinster—your word—did you imagine what love would be like?"

I sit back. No one has ever asked me this before. Not even Theodore. That's the sort of thing we might have talked about, but we were so busy making each other feel safe in our roles that we didn't talk about the murky, deep stuff that a potential lover might unearth. And Jack Mac doesn't talk about these things at all.

"I thought that love made everything better. I thought that it was a state of happiness and security. Yeah, that's it. And serenity. I thought love made a person whole."

"How would it do that?" Pete asks.

I think about this for moment. "It can't." Saying that almost makes me cry. I rub my eyes. I hope that Pete thinks I'm tired.

"I've upset you."

"No, no. I should think about these things more." I mean that. "You must think I'm crazy."

"I think you're fascinating."

"Me? Come on." I shift in the chair. Another spring stabs me, this time near my ribs.

"So what's the problem with your husband?"

I won't answer that because I have no answer. Instead I state the facts. "My husband was supposed to come on this vacation, and at the last minute he told me he wasn't coming because he thinks I need time to think, and he told me that I need to decide if I want to stay married."

"Do you?"

I should say yes, but I don't. "He may not want *me* at the end of this vacation."

"Wouldn't it be better if you decided what you wanted?"

"That's what he says."

"He's right."

I watch Pete drink his coffee by the light of the fire. I imagine him leaning across the chair and kissing me. I shake my head. The picture goes.

"Well, this is going to be an interesting month for you, isn't it?" He smiles at me. I wish he didn't have such great teeth.

"And busy," I tweet. Where did *that* sound come from? I breathe. "There's a big calendar at the house filled with stuff to do. Giacomina, my dad's girlfriend, came up with a month of activities. And I like a plan."

"The first thing you need to do is . . ." Pete leans toward me and puts his hand on the arm of my chair. "Throw out that calendar."

Pete walks me home in the rain. Giacomina and Papa are back from the ski shop, and it's suppertime. Where did the time go? That cup of coffee lasted for hours! Mafalda invites Pete to stay, and he graciously accepts. He instantly charms my family; he is so easygoing and fun, it's as though he's been around for years. As I watch him keep the conversation going, I think about my husband, who, in the same situation, would rather listen than talk. I like to sit back and listen, but when you're married to a quiet man, you have to do the talking most of the time. I relax back into the chair and let Pete do the entertaining.

Chiara and Etta tell Pete all about the jellyfish in the ocean at Sestri Levante. He tells them about the jellyfish on the Jersey shore. As we eat a hearty lamb stew (what does Mafalda do to the meat to make it so tender?) and bread, both of the girls develop wild crushes on him. He pays close attention to every word they say, the girls, vying to impress him, transform from kids to coquettes before our eyes. Papa asks Pete about stonework for a wall behind the house; Pete gives him helpful tips. Papa has an easy rapport with Pete, much like he has with Jack Mac. This Marble Man is just a big old American charmer. He's got everyone in this house under his spell. Everyone except me. I am not falling for him. No way. There is no way a guy this smooth can be genuine. I'm going to enjoy him and, for security purposes, I will wear my wedding band at all times. This tingling I feel in Pete's presence just reminds me that I'm alive; it doesn't mean I could fall for him; he's not a threat.

By the time I put the girls to bed, Mafalda has done the dishes, straightened the kitchen, and set the table for breakfast. (That's a good time-saver. I'll remember it once I'm home.)

Papa and Giacomina sit on the couch in the living room, cuddling and reading the paper. I sit down at the kitchen table, in Pete Rutledge's chair; okay, now I'm naming chairs after him, what is that all about? He left nearly an hour ago, though the girls begged him not to.

"How about a cup of coffee?" Giacomina says, touching my shoulder in a way that reminds me of my mother.

"Mafalda prepared the pot for breakfast already."

"I will put it back the way I found it. Don't worry." Giacomina smiles and turns on the stove. The clean mountain water makes a hissing sound in the blue-and-white-enameled pot.

"So, you met Pete at the disco last night?"

"Yeah. He asked me to dance. I wish I wouldn't have."

"Why not?"

"I'm married." Saying this aloud absolutely kills the temptation. (I must remember that.)

"Dancing with a man isn't a bad thing."

I look at Giacomina. Is she kidding? The thought of falling into the arms of another man on an Alpine cliff while music plays through the trees is a terrible thing. Giacomina doesn't know me very well. I am an all-or-nothing woman. I married Jack MacChesney the first night I made love to him. Not on paper, but in my mind, the commitment began right there. Later, when we went to the priest and said our vows, it was just a validation of what I already knew. I can't have a tall American man with a killer smile and great legs pull me away from the promises I made. What am I saying? What am I thinking? In twenty-four hours, I'm imagining a romance with someone besides my husband? Italy is a dangerous place.

"It's very complicated, no?" she says.

"What?"

"Men and women."

"No, not really. It's easy. You make promises and you keep them. That's all."

"Easy to say."

"No, it's easy to do," I insist. "I can appreciate a nice-looking man who—" why am I struggling to describe Pete? "—reads poetry and tells funny stories. But that doesn't mean anything. It's just admiration of some sort or another, I guess." I never admired any man, really and truly, until Jack MacChesney. So why I am using that word now to describe Pete Rutledge from New Jersey? "Well, I don't mean admiration. I don't know him well enough, nor will I, to use such a strong word. Let's just say I get a kick out of him."

"Who?"

"Pete."

"Oh, I thought you might be talking about your husband."

"No, I meant Pete."

As Giacomina pours our coffee, the way she holds the pot with the yellow-and-white-striped pot holder, and how her simple gold wrist-watch twists down to the inside of her wrist and dangles there, face out, and how she moves the cup toward me — scooting it on the table, not lifting it, just like Mama used to do — all make me want to confide in her. I could never lie to my mother. She would ask me questions, like Giacomina just did, and lead me gently toward the truth, so I would never *have* to lie. I could admit the worst things about myself to my mother, and she would never judge me.

"Okay. All right. Okay. I'm a little attracted to him," I confess out loud.

Giacomina smiles. "We all were. You can't be a woman and not be attracted to him. Did you see the girls?" I nod. "There are men like that out there. They sparkle. Your father is one."

I look into the living room. Papa has fallen asleep, his head lying against the back of the couch like a throw pillow. For the first time, he looks older to me. But there is an ease to his aging; a natural grace. It doesn't look like the loss of something. It's like he traded in excitement for comfort. The hair, almost completely silver now, the softer jawline, and the padding around the middle have turned him into a grandfather. And he's letting it happen. Happily.

"I have this under control, Giacomina." I reassure myself, saying it aloud.

As I lie in bed, unable to sleep because I'm wired from the caffeine (I should never have a cup of strong coffee late at night, what was I thinking?), I review my actions of the past day. This is a habit I've had since I was a child. I want to nod off with a clean slate, in case I die in my sleep. I apologize to God for my shortcomings, and while I'm at it, beg him for insight into my problems. A lot happened today. I imagined kissing a man whose attraction to me has been made abundantly clear. Bad. I opened up to him about the problems in my marriage. Bad. I allowed him to stay for dinner. Bad. I agreed to see him again. Worse. Now Pete Rutledge has a fan club at 108 Via Scalina. Now they're invested in him. Now he's a part of things! Am I falling for him? God, this is sick! What was Giacomina getting at tonight? Does she want me to leave Jack Mac and move to Schilpario and marry Pete Rutledge and start a new life? Of course not. But why do I think that's what she means?

I sit up in bed.

I realize something that makes me queasy at first, then rings through my head like a proclamation. I am still repressed! That's my problem! I hold my face in my hands. I can feel the heat rising off of my face. I thought I no longer buried my feelings and made decisions about my body and my life out of fear, but in fact, I do. Pete Rutledge unglues me, and I can't handle it! I'm afraid he's going to stir me up and then I'll really have a problem. I was so smug, so shielded from temptation, in Big Stone Gap. I was proud that I didn't want any man but my husband. That I had never wanted any man but my husband. Now I can't say that. I can't even think it, because it's not true any-more. I want Pete Rutledge. Never mind I must not have him, I want him. Why can't I tell Pete to go away? Is this retaliation for Karen Bell? No, I'm not one of those tit-for-tat people. Maybe this is what Jack Mac was talking about. Maybe he thinks I didn't live enough be-fore we married. I got married, but I didn't leave the spinster behind: I moved her from Poplar Hill to Cracker's Neck, and now I've dragged her across the Atlantic Ocean to northern Italy! But I'm still the same woman, and Jack MacChesney is right—I am not being honest about my feelings.

Pete promised the girls a trip up into the Dolomites, a mountain range that touches the Italian Alps. (I know, I know, don't get me started on how I got myself into this one; Pete came back to the house with some slate to make the girls a chalkboard, and before we knew it, we were planning a day trip.) It's a fifty-mile ride, one way, so we plan on a very early departure. He wants to show them the marble quarry. At first I think to bring Papa and Giacomina with us, but I decide

against it. Etta has been spending time with everyone but me. And
Pete is fun. I am doing nothing wrong (I keep reminding myself), and
there's no need to avoid our new friend. He makes us all laugh. Besides, I want to see the marble quarry.

As Pete drives, the girls jockey for position next to him. We finally
decide that Chiara can sit next to him on the way over and Etta on the
way home. I wasn't planning on dealing with adolescent hormones
for another five years, but here they are, in all their raging glory. I sit
by the passenger window as they chat and giggle. Pete and I speak occasionally, to ask and answer questions about the directions and how
far we have to go, but mostly I sit with my own thoughts as we speed
and swerve through the mountains.

The marble quarry is an enormous pit dug in the side of Assunta
Mountain, named for a woman two brothers loved and fought over.
She died, and neither of them ever loved another woman again. As
Pete explains this to the girls, they nod, their eyes wide with understanding. As we walk toward the marble pit, Chiara gives Etta a tiny
pot of peach lip gloss; Etta dips her pinky into it and applies it carefully to her lips. Where did she learn how to do *that*?

The marble pit is so deep and wide and black, it looks like the pit
of hell in the catechism book Mama bought me for my confirmation
so many years ago. I take a step back.

"Are you all right?" Pete asks.

"It's just so deep."

"Don't look, then," he says, and pulls me away from the edge.

We walk away from the pit and into a clearing, where trailers are set
up. These are the mining offices, and just like our coal mines in Big
Stone Gap, there is a sense that this business is temporary. No need to
build an actual office; a trailer will do.

Pete takes us into the largest trailer. He shows the girls little boxes
of samples, small, cool squares of finished marble, shell pink with
gold veins, black with white streaks, and my favorite, the rarest of the
marble, lapis-lazuli blue with accents that look like black glitter.

"You like the most expensive marble," Pete tells me. He stuffs a square into the pocket of my jeans.

"It figures." My hip tingles where he touched it. I bury my hand in my pocket to stop the sensation of that, whatever that was.

Pete lets the girls take whatever small squares they want. As we load back into the truck, Pete tells us that he has a surprise. The girls giggle and chat as we descend the mountain. Pete veers off the main road; all of a sudden, we're bouncing on an unpaved gravel road, kicking up dust.

"Mama, this is like our road," Etta says.

"Yes, it is," I tell her.

"What road?" Pete wants to know.

"Cracker's Neck Holler Road. Where we live."

"Cracker's Neck?" Pete laughs.

"Hey. Don't laugh at Cracker's Neck," I tell him.

"Yeah! Don't laugh," Etta says with mountain pride.

"If you think that's funny, you ain't been to Frog Level and It-lee Bottom," I tell him.

"I've got to see this Big Stone Gap someday," Pete says. "Yeah, right," I want to tell him, "come to the Gap and meet my husband."

At the end of the gravel road is what looks like a crude parking lot, a square of muddy field that has been driven over so many times, there is no grass, just dirt.

"Here we are!" Pete announces.

"What is this?" Etta asks, unimpressed.

"Well, not here. We have to go in there."

Pete points to the woods. We follow him in, and for a second I think, really, how well do I know this guy? He could kill us and leave us here, and we'd never be found. But when he turns around and motions for the girls and me to walk in front of him, I look at his face and trust him. It's just the trees, so high they block the sky and create a dank forest, that give me the creeps.

"Take a right," he tells the girls. They turn and we pass two big rocks; one has a red arrow painted on it.

"Look. Directions!" Etta says. I nod. Chiara nods too; her English is only rudimentary, so I don't know how she knows what Etta is talking about half the time. But they have that secret language of girls, and now I have proof that it is international. We hear a loud hissing sound, and at first it's a little scary. But it isn't the hiss of a machine, and it's too loud to be a snake.

"These are the mineral baths of Assunta Mountain," Pete announces. And there, before us, is a waterfall of deep purple rocks so dark they're almost black, covered with glistening pale green moss, leading to a natural pool of clear water. Steam rises off the top and swirls delicately upward through the trees, like cigarette smoke from a glamorous Bette Davis moment.

I turn to Pete. "Hot springs?"

"Amazing, isn't it?"

The girls circle around the edge of the pool and dip their hands in.

"It's warm, Mama," Etta says, amazed. "It's like a bath."

I sit at the edge and take off my shoes and put my feet in. The warmth settles into my entire body. This is bliss. The girls' laughter seems far away. They climb the side of the hill up to the top of the waterfall.

"Be careful!" I shout. They disappear into the ravine.

"What do you think?" Pete asks.

"I've never seen anything like it," I tell him. I wish I were alone here. I would take off all my clothes and lie in the pool and let the minerals and salts soak through my skin and replenish my soul. I can smell the salt as it bubbles in the water. Quickly, I shake off the picture of myself in this pool (just in case Pete Rutledge is a mind reader).

Pete takes his shoes and socks off and rolls up his pants legs. He wades out into the pool.

"Come here," he says.

At first I don't move. I look at him out in the mist. I like the idea of him in the mist, like a mirage, something unreal that I can't touch.

"Come here," he says again.

I roll my pants legs up, then I stand up in the water and slowly wade out to him. The bottom of the pool is filled with sand, and every once in a while something sharp, like a shell, jabs at me. Pete holds his arms out to me. Just as I'm about to reach him, my foot slides into a hole where the bottom of the pool has given way. Pete reaches out and catches me, scooping me out of the water and into his arms.

"What was that?" I look down at the water.

Pete doesn't answer me. He holds me. He looks at me. With my arms around his neck, I put my head on his shoulder, just for a second. I feel his heart beating fast; and now I know how it feels to be in his arms. I would stay here forever if I could, with the mist rising off the warm water and surrounding us. Beads of water run down my calf and onto his sleeve. He looks down at my legs; I take my hand and roll my pants legs down. When I look down, he nuzzles his nose into my neck.

I hear my daughter's distant laughter, and it brings me back to the present.

"Um, maybe, put me down," I tell him. Pete doesn't listen; he carries me back to the edge of the pool and sets me down on the ledge.

"Let's go home," he says softly.

Pete Rutledge folds into our lives in Schilpario as though he was a part of the vacation plan all along. He eats meals with us; he tours Alta Città and rides the train with us to see the Villa d'Este, the great hotel on Lake Como where the movie stars go. Since the day at the Assunta Mountain, Pete has not said or done anything flirty, and I'm relieved. Maybe fifteen years of spinsterhood taught me how to shut down suitors. I hope so.

Gala sent a telegram inviting us down to Florence. She's conducting a tour of the Big Three—Rome, Florence, and Venice—and wants us to meet her for the weekend. I wire back that we'll meet her, but I don't send details. At the last minute, Pete decides to join us because he has business in Florence. The girls are thrilled (of course). The train ride is so much fun. Mafalda packed a lunch. The girls whisper and giggle the entire trip, when they're not begging Pete to play cards or explain what they see outside the window as we speed past.

"Have you ever been to Florence?" Pete asks me.

"On my honeymoon."

Pete smiles. "Ah," he says.

When we pull into Florence, I understand why artists must come here. Everywhere you turn you see art—a painting in the way the sun hits a wall of terra-cotta tile, or a sculpture in the pattern of the cobblestone, or a poem in the way an old man with white hair feeds a flock of doves.

"Mama, can we go on the bridge?" Etta points to the Ponte Vecchio, over the Arno River. The simple bridge, a sturdy U-shaped construction of ancient brick the color of ripe peaches, waits for us in the distance.

"Absolutely. But first we have to meet Gala."

We leave the train station and find our spot in the Piazza della Signoria, where we are surrounded by rows of ornate town houses, connected but painted different shades of gray, pale blue, and beige. Only the shutters in shiny black and the touches of gold in the trim offer any glitz, but it is not necessary; the architecture is artistry enough. We stand on the corner of San Marco Street and wait for Gala.

Etta points across the cobblestone square. "Look! There she is!" Etta has never met Gala but knows her from the videotape. Boy, does she know how to make an entrance. Gala Nuccio emerges from the crowd of tourists like an exotic bird from a lake. The people in the square seem to peel back to make way for the woman who lives up to her dramatic name. Gala walks toward us in a white piqué sundress with turquoise water lilies embroidered on the hem and bodice. A wide cinch belt gives way to a balloon skirt that grazes her knees. The square neckline lies flat against her brown chest, with just a hint of cleavage peeking above the trim. She wears dark sunglasses and carries an enormous straw hat, which catches in the breeze like a flag. She manages to walk in black stiletto heels on cobblestones without tripping. How does she do it?

How happy Gala is to meet Etta and see me again. How delightful when she speaks rapid, machine-gun Italian with Chiara. How intrigued she is to meet Pete and share a couple of New Jersey anecdotes.

Pete takes the girls to the Cathedral of Saint Paul; Gala takes me for a cappuccino. "Who is *he*?" She squeals the moment Pete is out of earshot.

"Pete?"

"Who else?"

"He's a new friend."

"Where is your husband?"

"He decided not to come."

"Big mistake."

"There's nothing going on with Pete and me."

"Oh really."

"Gala, I swear there isn't."

"Maybe not for you. But there is for him."

"He knows I'm married."

"Long, tall, single lattes like that don't care about wedding rings, honey."

I feel my wedding band on my finger. Thank God I remembered to wear it today. "He's been a gentleman."

"Yeah, but you're packing two kids. Lose the kids and see how fast he jumps your bones."

"You're terrible."

"You know, your scent doesn't shut down just because you're married. Trust me. Pheromones don't know from vows. That's Mother Nature's little way of causing trouble. We're animals. Plain and simple animals, no more sophisticated than dogs or cows or pigs. He took one whiff of you, and he's hooked."

"I don't think so." I can't help but laugh.

"Jack Mac is an idiot. Letting you loose in Italy. Alone! You'd have to be dead here not to be thinking about sex twenty-four–seven. Is your husband insane? Leaving you alone in a pastoral friggin' setting with lighting so flattering we all look sixteen? A woman alone in Florence? It's like throwing raw hamburger to a starving rottweiler." Gala winks at a man as he passes. He stops, smiles, and continues on. "How I love my mother country!"

As Pete promised, the churches in Florence are filled with art so astonishing that I almost cannot take it in. In the Cathedral of Saint Monica, there is a mural of the saint with her son, Saint Augustine. It's the moment when he becomes a priest, a dream she held for her rogue son all of his life. The look in her eye, of complete joy at giving her only son to God and yet deep grief at losing him, makes me cry. I look at the corals and pinks in the painting and think of my own son's skin, how it changed from pink to pale yellow bruises when the fever came just before he died.

"Are you okay?" Pete whispers.

"How do they know?"

"Who?"

"Artists. How do they know how I feel?"

"That's their job," Pete tells me. Then, as quickly as I can, I find a door and go outside. Pete follows me.

The girls ask to go for gelato around the corner. Pete and I sit on a bench.

"What happened in there?"

"I don't know." I feel the tears come to my eyes again. He puts his arm around me. "Don't," I tell him. Quickly, he pulls it away.

"I'm sorry."

"Etta's here."

Why did I say that? So he'll think that it's okay to put his arm around me when Etta isn't around? I don't want that. Or do I?

"Why did that painting make you cry?"

"I don't want to talk about it."

"Okay," he says gently.

But as soon as he backs off, I realize I *do* want to talk about it. This is precisely what I have shut down and shut off for four years. Isn't this why I came here? Didn't I come home to Italy to learn how to feel again? I look at Pete's face, full of concern. "I . . . we had a son. After Etta. His name was Joe. He died three years ago."

"How?"

"Leukemia."

"I'm sorry."

"It was the colors of the paint and the brush strokes. They looked like Joe's bruises." I look up at Pete, and I swear he understands what I saw. I don't know how or why, but he does. Married or not, it doesn't matter to me: I need the comfort of another human being, so I let Pete hold me; but I'm not in his arms, I'm somewhere else, with my son.

Etta and Chiara have not returned. I look for them in the crowd. Pete says, "The line was long at the café, the girls won't be back for a while." I sit back. Then, Pete catches my eye in a way that tells me that he's going to kiss me. I shoot up off the bench and call for Etta. Chiara comes around the corner, followed by Etta. They're laughing. I motion for them to join us.

"Mama, are you okay?" Etta looks at me, then at Pete.

"I'm okay. I was thinking about Joe."

"Oh," she says.

"Who is Joe?" Chiara wants to know.

"I'll tell you all about him," Etta tells her.

"Who needs siesta?" Pete asks and picks up my book and bag. The girls and I take our room at the hotel. Pete goes to his room and tells us he has big plans for our dinner.

Pete takes us to Cielo, a little restaurant on a side street. It is quaint—the walls filled with old pottery and the ceiling covered with tiny white lights on wires. After the most delicious dinner of my life, gnocci (tiny, light pasta ovals made of potato—"gnocci" means knees) in delicate white cream, baby lamb chops grilled with fresh sage, a glass of hearty Chianti, hot espresso, and a bite of Etta's cream puff, I feel better.

After supper, on our way to the Ponte Vecchio, Pete surprises me and takes us by Elizabeth Barrett and Robert Browning's apartment on the corner of the Piazza San Felice. He points up to the windows and I imagine Elizabeth there, recording the parade on the street below in vivid detail. "You think of everything," I tell Pete. He just smiles.

Gala is off to Venice with her busload of Americans. (She had to skip dinner with us to take her tourists to the Opera.) We're leaving in the morning, back to Schilpario. As the girls run ahead, I can hear their laughter as it echoes off the stone walls of the narrow side streets.

"When I get you home to Schilpario, I have to go down to Rome."

I feel a pang of disappointment. What did I think, that Pete was here to entertain me ad infinitum? Or at least until my vacation ended and I was ready to pack up and go home. "Business?" I ask as nonchalantly as I can manage.

"Yeah." He pauses. "I probably won't see you again."

"I understand." Of course I do. Pete saw me fall apart about my son and realized that there is more to this picture than he realized. Fine. It's best if he goes now. I shouldn't look forward to seeing him, and I don't like counting on him to take us places and show us around and make us laugh.

"I'm getting too wrapped up here," Pete tells me as we walk.

"I know," I tell him. Boy, do I know.

CHAPTER NINE

There's a puppet show in Bergamo that Giacomina wants to take the girls to, so Papa plans a day down in the city with them. Zia Meoli will have us all over for dinner. I decide to go along at the last minute. I want to shop while the girls are at the show. I haven't heard from Pete since he dropped us off after the trip to Florence. It's been about a week, and the longer he's gone, the clearer I become. It's amazing how everyday feelings can get out of control in Italy. As the date of our departure draws closer, I turn to practical matters. I really need to shop. The dollar is pretty strong, and I haven't bought gifts for Iva Lou and Fleeta. They want leather purses, and I am going to deliver northern Italy's finest to them.

The shops in Bergamo are small and exclusive, but the prices are good. I am supposed to haggle with the shopkeepers; I even practiced the technique with Papa. He tried to drill it into my brain that the shopkeepers never expect the customer to pay the price on the tag, they want you to negotiate. But I am just too much of a people pleaser, and too chicken to haggle. I just want to pick and pay. So the shopping excursion turns into a chore almost immediately. I give up and go for an espresso. There are cafés tucked in between shops and on every corner. I choose the largest one, with friendly red-and-green-striped umbrellas and small tables with curvy little chairs that face the Fountain of the Angels. The umbrellas look like a sea of wide-brimmed hats. I settle into my chair, propping my feet on the portable fence that protects the café from the street. I close my eyes and breathe.

"Hey, look who's here."

I open my eyes and look up at Pete Rutledge. My heart skips a beat, but I cover it nicely by swinging my legs off of the fence.

"How was Rome?" I ask, too abruptly.

"I bought some terrific marble from a middleman."

"Good for you."

"I have to get home and install it. We have a customer in Basking Ridge whose middle name is Rococo." I laugh. Pete sits down. "When do you leave?"

I don't answer him at first. I want to watch the white angels pour water from their pitchers into the seashells in the fountain. "The end of next week."

"Me too."

The waiter approaches. Pete orders for the two of us. We sit in silence; what is there to say? The waiter brings the espresso.

"I need your help, Pete. I have to buy a purse for Iva Lou and one for Fleeta. And I can't haggle. Will you come with me and haggle?"

"Geez," Pete says under his breath, and then he laughs. He pays for the espresso and leads me by the elbow through the umbrellas to the sidewalk. As we start down the street, I pat his back like an old dog, hoping that my platonic warmth will soothe him. "There's a good leather place down this street. Papa told me about it." Pete grabs my hand and stops me.

"This is my hotel," he says, pointing to a simple white-brick building with a black-and-white-striped awning. HOTEL D'ORSO, it says on the brass plaque in black cursive letters.

"It looks nice."

"It was."

"It's good to know: You know. Good hotels."

I continue walking down the street. Pete stops me again. "Let's go in," he says.

I look up into his eyes. The blue of them is so clear, even though he squints. He leans down. His lips are so close to mine, I can practically taste them. If I kiss him, I know we will go to his room. I know it. My hands are deep in my pockets. I try to make the left hand into a fist. Did I remember to wear my rings today? I feel the cool gold metal against the fabric. I did remember!

"I can't." I step back.

"Why?"

"Because I'm married." Now I know why there's an ancient custom of wearing wedding rings. They're there to remind you that you're married and keep you out of trouble.

"Ave Maria! Ave Maria!" I turn to see Stefano, Etta's future husband, on a bicycle. Great. Caught in the act. Perfect.

"Ciao, Stefano."

Stefano looks up at Pete.

"This is Pete."

They exchange pleasantries and I step back, relieved. Stefano's interruption has given me a few seconds to regain my composure. I realize that Stefano could have easily been Etta; I have to stop this. This is wrong, and I don't want any part of it. I almost went into that hotel, and I hate myself for it. Stefano pedals off.

"Come to my room."

"No."

"All right. Fine. But I want to know just one thing."

I dread the next question, so much so that I close my eyes.

"Do you want to?" he asks me.

"Of course I want to. And I hate myself for it. I don't even like saying it!"

"Stay with me."

"I told you, I'm not going into that hotel with you."

"No, I mean Italy. Let's not go back. Ever. Let's just stay here. Look at this."

I look down at the cobblestones, and around at the buildings with their summer awnings, and at the people, who never rush, who always seem to savor the beautiful weather and the good food. The people move through the streets in this small town just as they do in Big Stone Gap. They look at us as they pass. And I shouldn't kid myself; they know me. They may not know my name, but they see me, a married woman on the sidewalk outside a hotel, full of guilt, trying to resist the charms of a man who is not her husband.

"Pete?"

"Yeah?"

"You're crazy." I tell him this, but I know it's really me. I'm the one who's crazy; I think I have this under control, and deep within me, I don't.

I found a gorgeous burgundy crocodile shoulder bag for Iva Lou and a buttery beige leather tote for Fleeta (perfect for candy deliveries). I look at all of my Italian vacation booty on the bed and am very proud of myself. I came, I saw, I haggled. Well, not exactly. I let the purse-shop lady haggle for me. I'd ask how much something was, then, instead of haggling, I'd shrug and she'd start driving the price down.

I bought a puffy black ski jacket for Jack Mac. And a pair of boots for me. Pearl will have a handmade white lace shawl to wear on her wedding day. We won't have to do any back-to-school shopping for Etta; her grandfather has spoiled her with clothes, clogs, and even a gold chain with a dangling angel.

We haven't seen Pete Rutledge since the day he almost kissed me. He begged out of dinner at Zia Meoli's. He called once during the week to say he was checking out some marble farther into the Dolomites before he flew back to New Jersey. I don't think about him.

That's a lie. I do think about him, and to be perfectly honest, I imagine what would have happened had I decided to kiss him on the sidewalk in front of the Hotel d'Orso.

"Ave Maria! *Teléfono!*" Mafalda calls to me from the base of the stairs.

"Ciao?"

"Girl, it's me, Iva Lou."

"Hi, honey. How are you? Wait till you see the purse—"

"I don't have a lot of time. James Varner has a summer cold he can't shake, so I took over the Bookmobile run."

"Okay. What's up?"

"When are you gittin' home?"

"Next week."

"Damn. You'll be too late. Honey, this is an emergency situation."

"Is Jack all right?"

"He's fine." Iva Lou stretches out the word "fine" until it goes from a hum to a hiss.

"Are you all right?"

"Oh God, girl, everybody is fine. But you need to git home. You got to hurry."

"Why?"

"The word up in Coeburn is not good."

"What?" My legs give out on me. I sit down on the steps.

"Yes. I don't want to hurt you, but honey, the word is that Jack Mac wants to divorce you and murry that low-to-the-ground little witch Karen Bell. We all think that he's just goin' through some silly midlife crisis or somethin', and we don't think it's anything but loneliness. I think the man misses you somethin' turr-ible. You need to git home and tend to yer business, honey. The barn is burning. Understand?" I hear Iva Lou taking a drag off a cigarette; she smokes only in times of complete duress.

"How could he do this? He said he'd wait." This is all my fault. I've been spending the summer with Pete while, thousands of miles away, Jack Mac sensed that I left him emotionally, so he has left me.

"I have got to figure out a way to get that sow out of the picture."

"Iva Lou, don't do anything."

"A man never leaves a woman unless he's got someone to go to. If she wasn't around, you wouldn't have a problem."

I must have said good-bye to Iva Lou, but I don't remember it. I hold the receiver like a tasting spoon. The buzz of the telephone line must have gotten Mafalda's attention; she takes the receiver out of my hand and hangs up the phone.

"Where are the girls?"

"They went to the waterwheel."

I go up to my room and sit on the bed. I have an amazing sense of calm all of a sudden. I believe in long leashes for men; if you give them space, they'll find their way back to you. Maybe Jack Mac is testing the length of the leash, and if he is, that's his journey. It was, after all, the point of our spending the summer apart. So we could make the journeys. Decide what we want. And there is nothing I can do about it until I get home. I am not going to poison my glorious Schilpario with schemes involving Karen Bell. I am not going to call Jack, either. I am going to remain calm. For the first time in my life, I am not going to panic and I am not going to worry about what I cannot control.

I slip out of my new pale blue suede loafers (how I love Italian shoes) and into my hiking boots. I'm going to climb the mountain. That will take the edge off any anxiety that might creep in. I tell Mafalda where I'm going, and she promises to watch the girls. I walk up the street, past the houses, and through the town square. The benches are empty, and the chess tables are plain checkerboards until *la passeggiata*, when they will be filled to capacity.

As I reach the path that will lead me up to the pastures above town, I see the door to the chapel La Capella di Santa Chiara propped open with a can of paint. This is the very place where I married Jack Mac-Chesney so many years ago (we had a second ceremony here in Italy so that my father could officially give me away). Something tells me to go inside.

The smell of paint sails over musky notes of church incense. I climb up to the choir loft, and it's as though I lost something and all of a sudden remembered where to find it. I look up and around, hoping my memory serves me well. And it does. There she is, the Blessed Lady in her turn-of-the-century ankle-length coat and a hat with stars pinned to it. This is the stained-glass window my great-grandfather made—I climb up and touch the grooves of each pane of stained glass, murky blues and brilliant burgundies; the pieces fit together perfectly. But it is only when you stand back that you can see what the picture means. I remember my namesake, Ave Maria Albricci, who took care of my mother when she was pregnant with me and on her way to America. I must never forget what I was before I married Jack MacChesney. I was a work of art. My mother's work of art. All the things I thought I was—simple and plain and sometimes funny—are very small words. They do not begin to describe me. They do not begin to express what is inside of me. I have value, and I have worth. I cannot be replaced like old shoes or taken for granted like tap water. I am more than Jack MacChesney's wife, the woman he tired of and traded in for a smart and sexy lumber supplier. Come on, Jack, you can do better than that. You married *me*, remember! So you think I'm a terrible wife. Well, maybe I am. Maybe I stopped making love to my husband, but give me a break, it slipped away from me after Joe died, I was mourning. I couldn't tend to Jack's needs when I was suffering. I couldn't even take care of myself. And then it became a habit; I started to avoid intimacy. I was hurting too much. I wanted to retreat and be alone. I couldn't share myself. If I made love to Jack, it would have been like I was cheating on myself. I wanted to control the only thing I could when Joe was taken from me. And the only thing I could control was who I let in. If Jack MacChesney doesn't understand that, if he is so shallow and so selfish, then he is not the man I thought he was. Karen Bell. Honestly.

I kiss the window of the Blessed Lady. I am not thinking of sacred relics but of my mother. She would know what to do at a time like this; she could talk some sense into me. In a way, I hope that wherever she is, she doesn't know about how I've been spending my summer. (How appropriate that I should have a little dose of Catholic shame in this perfect chapel.)

As I leave the vestibule, the midafternoon sun hits my eyes, so I close them. When I open them, Pete Rutledge is at the bottom of the path, leaning against his rental truck from the quarry. At first I don't think he's real. Why am I running down the path to him and throwing myself into his arms? And why am I crying?

"What happened to you?" he says, holding me away from his body and looking me over from head to toe.

"I haggled and got a good deal on a purse for Iva Lou," I say as I quickly wipe the tears from my eyes.

"Good girl. Sorry I couldn't come and help you drive down the prices."

"You came back."

"I had to see you again."

"Why?"

"You owe me money," he says with a straight face. "Forty-seven bucks. The train tickets to Florence."

"I'm sorry. I have the money at the house."

"I don't want the money," he says with a slight smile, pulling me close and burying his hands in the back pockets of my jeans. The timing of this is too perfect. I could have him and it would be only fair. My husband is carrying on with a woman thousands of miles away. Who would ever know?

"Do you want to see the field of bluebells?" I ask him.

"Okay."

So, surefooted and strong, my legs like sculpted stone from a month of climbing around these Alps, I lead Pete Rutledge up the path to the ridge above Schilpario. I kneel and watch him as he looks at the field of bluebells for the first time. The hum of the bees drowns out the way my heart is thumping from the climbing (or, more likely, from my nerves). I catch my breath.

"God. I've never seen anything like this."

"And look. Look. Goats." I point to a far ridge, where goats mill around a pasture and a boy herds them from the edge. "Doesn't that look like something out of the Bible?"

"It does," Pete says, squinting.

I want to tell Pete about Karen Bell, but I can't. If I tell him that, he'll think Jack is terrible, and I don't want him to think that. I want him to think that I am going home to a husband who cherishes me. A husband who worked hard all summer and missed me every night and dreamed of the sex we would have upon my long-awaited return. A husband who can't look at other women because none of them measure up, not even the young ones or the beautiful ones or the ones who flirt madly. A husband who wants sex only with me, even in his fantasies. A husband who pictures my face when he's putting up a Sheetrock wall and finishes the job perfectly in my honor. A husband who, when I have fantasies about another man, dismisses it as healthy, normal, and good for our relationship. A husband so dutiful that I could treat him badly and he'd love me anyway. A husband who doesn't expect me to put up a fight when I go ahead on vacation without him, as though he's a blow dryer I accidentally forgot to pack.

A clean, cool breeze ripples through the bluebells as one perfect white cloud hangs overhead.

"I want you, Ave Maria." Pete doesn't look at me when he says this. Instead, I study him. The breeze musses his hair, and his eyes, as they narrow in the sun, are the very color of the bluebells.

"You have a way of saying things that . . ."

"That what?"

"Unglue me." I roll over and start rolling down the hill like a child. Pete tucks and rolls beside me. Finally, we stop and I crawl back toward him. We're laughing so hard, I swear the goatherd, who must be ten miles away, looks in our direction with disgust for disturbing this perfect pastoral setting.

"Pete. You don't want me."

"Why shouldn't I want you?"

"Because I can't handle anything."

"What can't you handle?"

"Haggling. Grief. Lust. My husband's midlife crisis. You name it. I can't handle anything. I just run. Find a brave girl to love. That's what you need."

"I don't think you're the best judge of what I need."

No one has pursued me or wanted or needed me in this way in ten years. How new it all sounds. When I first heard words like these from Jack, I couldn't believe it. I love the first moments of discovery with a man. When he tells you that you're beautiful, and that there is no one like you, and that you're the only person in the world he can really talk to. What a feeling of connection and purpose!

"Why did you bring me up here?" Pete wants to know.

"I wanted you to see the bluebells."

"I've seen bluebells before," Pete says in a way that makes me laugh.

"Not like these."

"No. Not like these." He looks at me. "You asked me why I came back. Now can I tell you?"

"I owe you forty-seven dollars."

"No jokes."

"Okay. No jokes."

"When you left me at the hotel in Bergamo, I had a rough night.

That's why I didn't come up to Schilpario again. I wanted to shake the idea of you and me. And I couldn't. I had to see you one more time."

"Why?"

"For the same reason you had me climb this mountain. You want this too."

I don't answer him. We lie on our backs, talking up into the sky just like the flowers. Pete rolls over onto me. I move my leg so I can grip my boot into the earth to slide out from under him, but he hooks his leg around mine and I can't move. I could say something like "get off of me," but I love the way he smells and the feeling of his breath on me and the way his leg hooks around mine. He slides his hands under my back and lifts me off the ground a little. He kisses my neck. Now there is no place for me to put my hands, so I give up. I wrap my arms around him, and I feel his back and his shoulders, and then I take his face in my hands. I know for sure that I am in Big, Big Trouble.

His lips find mine, so tenderly that I am compelled to say something. But I don't want to talk. I want to kiss this man right off this mountain. For the first time in years, I am in my body. I feel my bones, my heartbeat, and my breath. My lips burn into his mouth like hot honey. I am beyond what I am. I am so far from what I know, I don't even have a name. The air cuts through me as though I'm a vapor. I feel his body begin to move against mine. We roll into the bluebells. I want to let him in. The sun blinds me. Pete covers my eyes and kisses me again. He unbuttons my jacket and slides his arms around my waist. I must have a temperature of two hundred degrees—I am throwing heat like a furnace. I pull away from him to breathe and look up over the ridge. The goats and their herder are gone. There are no witnesses! We are alone. I can do what I feel, be what I am, have something just for me! Haven't I earned this? Isn't life supposed to be about pleasure and connection and wild kisses? What else is there? To be alive—but how? Isn't my husband, right this second, probably having sex with a woman who carries a clipboard and wears too much Charlie cologne? Kiss this man, I cheer myself on. This man understands you.

"Pete. Stop." I say it so quietly he stops.

"Why?"

"I can't. That's the wrong word. I can do this. But I won't do this."

"Ave."

"No. I won't. I want to. But I won't. People can't just do things for selfish reasons. It has to matter."

"Who are you talking about? People? Do you mean you?"

I shake my head. Somewhere I've heard this tone and these words before. Jack MacChesney made the same observation. When someone gets too close, I always talk in generalities and speak on behalf of a large group, in this instance a worldwide community of women who are tempted to have sex with men outside of their marriages. I'm talking about Those Women—I do not say "I."

"Yes, I mean me. You make me feel good. But this is wrong."

I button my jacket and tighten the laces on my boots, which loosened when I was rolling around.

"It isn't wrong. We're not wrong," he says quietly.

"No, we're not. We could be absolutely right for each other. But I have a husband."

He stands and brushes his hair back with his fingers, as he always does. He walks several steps down the path toward the ridge. I look at him, tall, gleaming in the sun, backlit like an MGM-musical moment—silent, looking at me, waiting for the music to begin.

"Pete?" I kick the bluebells squashed by our kiss-tuck-and-roll back into their standing position with the toe of my boot. "I want to, but I'm not in love with you. I'm sorry. Once there was a man who had one rule. He'd make love only when he was *in* love."

"That guy was a saint."

"No, he's no saint. He's my husband." If only I could tell Pete the truth: Jack Mac has not been acting like my husband, and he's probably been breaking his own rule all summer.

I want to savor my last night in Schilpario, so I go to bed early. After rolling around Heidi's pasture above Schilpario with the Marble Man from New Jersey, I think it's best if I take some time to be alone. When I told Pete good-bye last night, Etta and Chiara were with me. They seemed more upset than I did. Pete just seemed resigned to the whole thing. I need my solitude and my rest. I am going home to battle. And I have a hunch that I am going to lose.

I turn over onto my side and try not to remember Pete's kisses. When I lie on my back, I can feel him on top of me. It's as though he is right here in this bed. Yes, his kisses were real. And real kisses are dangerous. I could go find him and ask for more. Thank God he lives far away!

Maybe I like the idea of that; maybe I like the idea that Pete will be in New Jersey pining for me. I could have made love to him and evened the score with Jack MacChesney. But my conscience is mine. I can't control what anyone else does, including my husband. I know only my own heart. I couldn't live with myself if I made love to another man outside my marriage. I'm going to glue this wedding band on my finger from now on. I'm sure there will be days when the idea of Pete and marble fireplaces and the woods of southern New Jersey will call to me like a corner of heaven right here on earth. I just won't choose that little piece of heaven. I have my safe place, my home in Cracker's Neck Holler. But it may not be mine anymore. Karen Bell might have taken it from me. I know one thing for sure: I have never been this confused in my life. This mess I am in has made me yearn for my days as an old maid; how simple it all was. This femme-fatale business is a lot of work.

Etta is exhausted on the flight home. She sleeps so peacefully; while she didn't sleep a wink on the way over, now she's just another blasé American who uses time on airplanes to catch up on sleep. My daughter became more beautiful this summer. More self-assured.

And her personality and humor came through. How lucky I am to have this great kid. She has written "Stefano" seventy-two times on the back of her notebook. Even Etta developed new romantic muscles in Italy.

I don't think she senses how much I dread going home. Most of the time I think I'm doing a good job of shielding her from my angst. Maybe I'm fooling myself; maybe she's like the coral sponge she brought from the beach of Sestri Levante. Maybe she soaks up everything and it becomes a part of her eternal self. Maybe she'll realize this later and resent me for it. I hope not.

The airport at Tri-Cities is empty. Etta and I deboard the little prop plane and go inside for our bags. I look up to the viewing window on the second floor of the airport and expect to see Jack there, behind the glass like a mannequin in the Big & Tall Men's Shop. But there is no one there. Etta and I walk into the luggage area.

"Daddy!" Etta screams and rushes toward her father.

He scoops her up in his arms and kisses her. She hugs him and kisses him. Jack looks good; too good, with a tan and a perfect patch of pink sunburn on the bridge of his nose. He looks slim too. His jeans hug his thighs. Must be from the construction work. I don't want to think about what else he might have been doing, or with whom. I'm all Mommy right now, watching the two of them fussing over each other. I will forever be a sucker for fathers and daughters. Jack looks up at me and grins.

"Isn't Mama pretty?" Etta says loudly.

"Yes, she is," Jack says, and kisses me on the lips lightly.

I want to say, "Pretty enough to keep you faithful?" but instead I say, "Thank you."

"Etta, honey, guess who's in the truck?"

"Who, Daddy?"

"Why don't you take a look?"

Etta opens the door of the cab, and Shoo the Cat tiptoes across the front seat with his tail in a stiff loop like a Christmas ornament hanger. He jumps into her arms.

"God a-mighty, did your luggage give birth over there?" Jack laughs as he hoists our bags into the back.

"What can I tell you, I learned how to haggle," I tell him, doing my best impression of Gala Nuccio.

Etta talks nonstop on the trip home to Big Stone Gap, and I'm glad. I don't want to start a conversation with my husband, because I know it will get serious fast. It's best for all of us if I keep it light. As we roll into the Gap, from the top of the hill on the descent into town, I see the stage lights from the Outdoor Drama. Rose and white beams shoot out into the blue twilight. I have always loved this time of day best. It wasn't so many years ago that I spent every night at the theater. We drive past, and I don't mention it. As we make the curve off of Shawnee Avenue, on our way out of town through the southern section and then on to Cracker's Neck, Etta looks up at her father.

"Daddy, can we stop in Glencoe? I brought Joe something."

Jack makes the right onto Beamontown Road. When we get to the entry arch, the curlicue gates are locked with a chain. Jack starts to turn around and head for home.

"Park. We'll jump the fence," I say. Jack gives me a look. "We do it all the time." I get out of the truck and go around the arch and over the low fence into the cemetery. Etta hands Shoo to me, then I help Etta scale the fence. Jack follows her. Night is falling and settling on the stones in a haze. I climb the hill to the Mulligan plot. I don't even feel it in my legs; all those Alpine hikes made me strong. When I climb the last little bit to the plot, I am glad that there is still enough light to see Joe's headstone. I run my fingers in the gold grooves of his name and through the words "Beloved son and brother." Black marble. White streaks.

"How do you like the impatiens?" Jack says from behind me. Etta puts Shoo down on the ground, and he trots right over to the head-stone and sniffs around it. The red and white impatiens form a beautiful bright border.

"It's lovely."

"Mommy, it's like the marble on Assunta Mountain."

"You know what I wish?" I tell Etta. "I wish it was the blue kind with the black glitter in it."

"What are you talking about?" Jack says gently.

"We visited a marble quarry in Italy."

"Mama, take that rock off the stone," Etta says.

"No, leave it," Jack says.

"Why?"

"Lew Eisenberg left it there. Says it's something they do in the Jewish faith."

So we leave the rock. I dig deep into my pocket and place the lapis marble square Pete gave me next to Lew's rock. "Honey, get Shoo," I tell Etta. She picks him up. It's too dark in the cemetery to read the stones. It's time to go home.

I take a long bath and realize how much I missed my big four-legged white enamel tub and the way our water gushes out of the pipes. In Italy, you always feel like you're trying to save water. Water barely streams out of their faucets. It's the only negative thing I can say about the entire country. In fact, if they had better plumbing, it would be a perfect place.

I climb out of the tub without even holding on to the sides. I'm in such good shape, I just lift myself out of the water like Venus. I grip the stopper with my toe and yank it out. I guess my feet got stronger too. I dry off and slip into a new nightgown, white cotton with spaghetti straps and small red-ribbon rosettes on the neckline, a good-bye gift from Giacomina. She's more a sister to me than a future step-mother.

Jack is in bed when I get there. He's awake. I slide into my side of the bed and under the covers.

"You look good," Jack says to me. But it isn't a come-on. It sounds like a compliment you pay to a really nice dish of chipped beef.

"Thanks. I hiked a lot. I think I'm going to start running. It's nice to be in shape."

"Great."

"Jack?"

"Yeah?" He answered me really fast, so maybe that means he has something to tell me.

"How was your summer?"

"It was pretty good."

"Did you miss me?"

"It ain't the same around here without you and Etta."

"No, I know you missed Etta. But me. Did you miss me?"

Jack looks up at the ceiling. His hands are clasped behind his head. " 'Course I missed you," he says to the ceiling.

"Just checking," I tell him as I turn over. He turns over to spoon against me, but he doesn't reach around and pull me close. He puts his hand on the side of my thigh instead.

"You really did build some muscles in the Alps," he says.

And that's the last thing I remember before I wake the next morning.

Iva Lou meets me at the Mutual's for breakfast. I have her new purse, and she has a boatload of gossip. The Tayloe Lassiter story is true; she's been sporting one-carat diamond studs in her ears. Doc Daugherty has put Zackie on antianxiety pills to help him cope with his burglar paranoia. Pearl and Dr. Taye Bakagese are getting very serious.

"Now. Let's get down to It," Iva Lou says, buttering her toast.

"Are you sure about Jack Mac and Karen Bell?"

"Well, I haven't caught him in the act. But I'm pretty certain. Let me tell you what I know. And don't think it hasn't been an effort for me. James Varner got over his cold and is itching to get back on the Bookmobile, but I won't let him, 'cause if I let him, I lose that run up to Coeburn, and then my source dries up on me."

"Who's the source?"

"Karen Bell's best friend. Benita Hensley. The librarian up in Wise."

"Great."

"How's Jack Mac treatin' you?"

"Like a sister."

"Not good."

"Maybe it's over, Iva Lou."

"Don't say that! Don't ever say that! Y'all are true lovers! Look how long you waited to get together. Come on."

"That doesn't mean anything."

"You waited so long, to lose it all like this? Over what? Sex? What's the matter with you? Don't you care?"

"Iva Lou. Something happened to me."

"A horrible thing. I know, honey. You've been betrayed. I feel turrible about it." Iva Lou glops orange marmalade onto her toast.

"I mean something else."

"What?" Iva Lou looks up. From my tone, she guesses it must be a man. "Have you fallen in love with someone new, is that what you're sayin'?"

"No. I'm not in love. But he might be in love with me."

"Who is he?"

I tell Iva Lou all about Pete Rutledge, all the stories, all the way through the kisses in the field of bluebells.

"Well, look. On one level it's so goddamn romantic I can hardly take any more details. But you say you're not in love with him. So why would you leave what you got?"

"I wouldn't. I don't know how to explain this, Iva Lou. I really don't. But the love I have for Etta and for Joe sort of replaced the romantic love I had with Jack. And the love I have for my kids is more important to me than the love I have for Jack or the lust I had for Pete. Or any man who might come along. I'm not proud to admit it. I know I'm supposed to put my husband first, and then from there, from what's supposedly the center of everything, comes your love for the kids. But I realized when Joe got sick that things had changed between Jack and me as soon as Etta was born. She replaced him as the love of my life. And then when Joe came, I was thrilled that I could give Etta a brother and Jack a son, but I also knew that there was no question: Jack was number three. For sure. Behind Etta and Joe, my new true loves."

"Oh, you're all confused." Iva Lou rifles through her purse and finds her cigarettes. "You know, I quit." She grips a cigarette between her lips and urges me to continue as she flicks the lighter.

"I don't mean to make this sound complicated."

"Honey-o, that ain't right. It's two different kinds of love. One is not more important than the other. They're different. Love for your husband is about you. Love for your kids is about them."

"I know. It goes against everything I believe. But don't you think Jack knows that he's number three? He's not stupid."

"No, he's not. That's the first true thing you've said all the mornin'."

"I'm not even mad at him. What's the matter with me?"

"That's just a defense. You're giving up because you're afraid you'll lose him altogether."

"We don't have anything to talk about anymore."

"Do you talk about Joe?"

"No."

"There's your problem. It's all you two are thinking about, and no one's saying anything about it. You're blaming him. He didn't give Joe the cancer."

"No, but he didn't save him either, did he?" I can't believe I said it. I've only ever thought it, I've never admitted it out loud.

"Ave, you listen to me. Jack couldn't save Joe. No one could."

"But—"

"But nothin'. You stop this. You're killin' your marriage with blame. And you're holding on to bad feelings that have no place in the present."

"I know." Iva Lou is right.

"What's your plan?" She looks at me. " 'Cause, honey, I guaran-damn-tee you that Karen Bell has got a plan. What's *your* plan?"

# CHAPTER TEN

Fleeta, who swore she'd have nothing to do with the Soda Fountain, now stays late and bakes the desserts. And they're not simple ones, either. Pearl bought those aluminum cake stands with the glass domes to show off Fleeta's red velvet cake, her pecan and cinnamon pound cake drizzled with glaze and topped with crunchy sugar-dipped walnuts, and her mile-high chocolate cake with white butter-cream frosting. ("The secret to that one is the cup of strong coffee instead of cold water in the batter," Fleeta told me.) There is a SPECIALS! sign behind the counter and a chalkboard with folks' birthdays listed (you're entitled to a free sundae on your big day). This is unbelievable. In a few months, Pearl has hit a home run. Look out, Norton.

"I'm tellin' ye. It's a lot of work, but I love it," Fleeta says as she goes behind the counter.

"I thought you didn't want a soda fountain in the Pharmacy."

"I didn't. Till it was here. Then once it was here, I got to like doin' the bakin'. And makin' the lunches. I just added soup beans and cornbread to the menu. See?"

"Fleets, you have found your passion."

"Maybe." Fleeta blushes; she doesn't think of herself as passionate.

Ed Carleton has done a good job subbing for me in the pill department. He's caught up; the new orders are only as of this morning. I feel good as I slip into my smock and take my place on my bar stool behind my counter. I missed my job. I sort through the new orders. There is one for Alice Lambert for a very potent drug usually prescribed for cancer patients to counter the nausea that comes from chemo and radiation.

"Fleets? What's happening with Alice Lambert?"

"I told Eddie to refer her orders over to the Rite Aid in Appalachia."

"No, it's okay."

"She has cancer. I guess her meanness done turned on her."

Fleeta walks away. Now, there's loyalty for you. Fleeta cannot forgive Alice for the way she behaved after my mother died. As I count out twenty-four tiny pink pills and load them onto the knife to place them in the bottle, I wonder why I feel sad. Is it because Alice Lambert is the last person left from my old life? When she's gone, will it all be ancient history?

Etta is in town, spending the night with her girlfriends. I'm sure she will tell them all about her crush on Stefano and about Pete Rutledge and peach lip gloss. She hung a picture of Tom Cruise over her bed; Pete must have triggered her new taste for brunette men with flashy smiles.

Jack is working late. Or so he says. I go to bed at my usual time; often, when I wake up, he's already up and dressed and making coffee. I try to stay awake to see if he even comes to bed at all; I know at least one night he fell asleep in the living room in the easy chair with the television on. I keep waiting for the right time to have our talk, but there doesn't seem to be a right time. Maybe he is avoiding me. I'm not sure.

I have a chance to go through the house for the first time since our return last week. I have a stack of pictures from vacation to put away. I've bored everyone I know from St. Paul to Pennington Gap with the pictures of the summer snowcaps in the Alps—enough is enough. I sent some off to Papa, and I'll put the rest in the box where they stay until I fill albums with them. I pull the box out of the hall closet. I hear a mew. Shoo the Cat peers out at me, annoyed that I've found his hiding place. I give him a quick kiss on the head.

I sort through the box. I really need to get some photo albums. The box is practically full. I study the faces in the pictures. We look so happy; we are a family. The pictures from last Christmas are as clear and bright as the ones from years before. We were back on track. Ready to celebrate again. Weren't we happy last Christmas? And yet I sensed something. I was scared, even then, that Jack Mac was slipping away from me. I wasn't just being paranoid. I know that all men look at women. But I couldn't get that stupid Halloween Carnival out of my head. I remember it in such vivid detail, right down to the way the popcorn balls smelled so sickeningly sweet as I watched my husband chitchat with Karen Bell. What is that little voice in our head that tells us to Watch Out? How do we know when to heed the warning signs instead of chalking them up to PMS, or getting older, or just having a bad day?

I put the pictures in the box. Jack's canvas work vests are hanging in the closet. He didn't wash them while I was gone (obviously); he just wore them and hung them up again. I pull them off the hangers and head for the sun porch to wash them.

I pull keys and nails and bolts and scraps of paper out of the pockets. I make a neat stack of all the junk on the dryer. As I toss the vests into the machine, I hear something crackle. So I pull the vest out of the machine and go through the pockets one more time.

There's a square of loose-leaf paper folded many times. It reminds me of a note passed in high school study hall. The edges of the paper are ripped fringe. I unfold the paper and read:

My dear Jack: This has been the best summer of my life. Remember that I ♥ you. I'll wait. Karen.


I fold the note carefully back into a small square, just as I found it. (Why am I doing this?) I'm numb. This note makes it real, right down to the heart she put in the word "love" where the "o" goes. I met Karen Bell. She was no rival! What would my husband see in her when he had me? My ego makes a valiant effort, but it's not long before it gives way to despair and self-loathing. I feel the numbness leave me and the anger set in. I am so furious I could destroy this house, burn it to the ground and not look back. It's dangerous for me to be inside. I have to get out of here.

I look around for my keys to the Jeep. I usually leave them on the front table. When I can't find them, I begin to tear the house apart. I find myself ripping the cushions off of the sofa, then turning over the straight-backed chairs, then opening the cabinets in the kitchen, shoving out their contents—glass smashes, jars of jelly and cans of spices and boxes of rice shower the floor like rain. I go into my bedroom and rip off the coverlet, the sheets, and I tear the feather pillows apart; I'm sweating, soaked to the skin, and so angry that I cry out. I lift the mattress off the bed and shove it to the floor. What am I looking for? I am losing my mind. *Where are those keys?* I hear a deafening screech inside my ears, one so loud, I would stab myself to stop the noise.

"What are you doing?" A voice cuts through the pounding in my head. Jack stands in the doorway of our bedroom.

"You, you . . . I hate you!"

"What's going on?" he says, his voice breaking. I've caught him, and he knows it.

"Why don't you tell me the truth!"

"What are you talking about?" Now he has the look of a gentle person, a look that tells me he doesn't want to hurt me with the truth or anything else.

"You . . . you." I fish around my pockets—where did I put that letter? I find it and take it out and carefully, like a judge, unfold the clue. "Look. Look right here. You love this woman!"

"Ave. Listen to me."

"Why? You're a liar. You're just going to lie to me. I want these mattresses out of here. You fucked her all summer right here in this room. In our bed. Where my children were. How could you do that? I will hate you until the day I die."

I shove past him, out of the bedroom and to the front door. Suddenly, in the first moment of clarity I've had since I found that note, I remember where my keys are. I left them in the Jeep.

"Where are you going?"

"Don't talk to me," I tell him. I run to the Jeep. I feel him behind me. I get into the driver's seat. He reaches in and tries to pull me out of the Jeep. He has me by the waist. I swing my legs out and begin kicking him, and I'm grateful for my strong legs as I fend him off. He tries to control my kicks, but he cannot.

"You made your choice. Now go to her. Go on. Go!" He steps back. I turn the key and throw the Jeep in reverse. Before he can make another move, I am down the mountain. I don't look back.

It's a long drive to Knoxville, Tennessee. Even longer when you don't have any money. I left my purse in Cracker's Neck Holler. Thank God I have an emergency gas card taped to the bottom of the driver's seat. As I pay the man for the gas, I ask him if I can charge some food on the card. He shrugs. So I go through the Quik Mart and buy pretzels and Diet Coke, two apples, a cup of coffee, and a bottle of Tylenol for my throbbing head.

The road to Knoxville is a straightaway into the hills of Tennessee. I am glad I don't have to think too much as I drive. I go about eighty miles an hour. I hope a cop stops me. Have I got a story for him.

I feel oddly relieved after my tantrum, almost exhilarated. The pain and rage gave way to endorphins that pulse through my system, soothing me. Iva Lou was right. I had my defenses up; my lack of feeling about my husband's affair was just a facade. There's a lot inside me that I haven't addressed. The worst part is the realization that my husband is not the man I thought he was. I thought he loved me so much that there wasn't room for Karen Bell or any other woman to wheedle in and take him. How pathetic he looked when I told him I knew. There is no worse face in the world, the face of a man who gave it all away. I'll never forget it.

My marriage is over. It's sad, but it isn't nearly as sad as losing Joe. I instantly compare the two, because now, and for the last three years, everything is measured against that loss. I can't help it. And I realize that everything I've done since Joe's death has been busywork. My strategy has been to keep myself occupied until I can be with my son again. I can fill up my life with work and games and trips and even have moments when seeing Joe again isn't the only thing I think about; but as surely as I am diverted, the thought comes back. The ache of my loss never stops. It is as real to me as my breathing.

I find Theodore's house quickly (I'm surprised; my sense of direction is usually terrible). It's late. Thank God there's a light on. I knock on the door. Theodore looks out the window; when he sees it's me, he comes to the door and flings it open.

"What's wrong?"

"Jack has another woman. That woman I told you about. From the Halloween Carnival. It's all true."

"Come in."

The second I enter Theodore's living room, I am better. I need to be around things that are familiar and someone I can count on. I love his home. It smells like him. The same albums that he had in his log cabin in Big Stone Gap line the bookshelves. The same couch. The same coffee table. The same easy chair. Nothing has changed. I enter a safe realm when I'm with Theodore, the one constant in my life.

"You look like a banshee."

"I don't have any money."

"What?"

"I don't have my purse."

"You just left?"

I nod.

"Does Jack Mac know where you are?"

"No."

"We should call him and tell him you're safe."

"I don't know Karen Bell's phone number." I burst into tears and throw myself on the futon.

"That's her name?" Theodore hands me the box of Kleenex. "That's a crappy name."

The way Theodore says "crappy" makes me laugh. Great. I'm laughing and crying, just like the head case this whole ordeal has turned me into. "I'm not calling him."

"But what about Etta?"

"She's spending the night with her friend Tara. It's Tara's birthday."

Theodore picks up the phone.

"What are you doing?"

"I'm calling your house. Okay? Just let me call your house."

I'm too tired to put up a fight. I hear Theodore tell Jack that I am here, and then there's a long time when Theodore listens and doesn't talk. Great. Jack is telling him the whole sordid tale. Is my husband including the fact that his girlfriend coats herself in Man Tan? She is inappropriately *bronzata* in seasons that she should not be. Theodore hangs up the phone.

"Well, now I know his side."

"I left the clue in the house!" I tell him, sitting up.

"What clue?"

"The letter. She wrote him a letter, told him she loved him and was waiting for him."

"Honey, you found a letter she wrote—not one he wrote. That's her side of things. She may be in love with him, but he's not in love with her."

"How do you know?"

"He told me."

"And you believe him? Wake up. He has a girlfriend. He's had her a long time—and he spent the summer with her. How much proof do you need?"

"I know. I get it. It sounds like the plot of a bad Connie Francis movie, not that there ever was a bad one. Let's say your husband had an affair this summer, and now it's over. Now, I don't know what 'affair' means to him—maybe they just talked about it, or fooled around a little, or maybe even a lot. But that doesn't matter now. It's over. He wants you to come home."

"Just like that."

"Well, not 'just like that,' but yeah, he wants you to come home and work through this with him."

"Theodore, why are you so calm?"

"Because you're a lunatic."

"What? Excuse me, please! Could somebody be on my side? I'm the one who's been cheated on!"

"Yeah, yeah, yeah. Poor you."

"Theodore!"

"You tore up pillows—he's spent the past four hours trying to gather up goose feathers."

"Too bad."

"You love him. Why put yourselves through this?"

"Because I'm *right*. I've been true."

"Let me tell you about men." Theodore sits down next to me.

"I don't want to talk about men."

"All right, then, let's talk about the Man. The American guy over in Italy that you were dancing with. And then you spent how many day trips with him. And meals and so on. What about him?"

"That was different."

"How so?"

"I resisted!"

"Really?"

"Yes. I have morals. Principles. I could've done whatever I wanted, but I didn't—out of respect for my marriage!"

"I'm so impressed. So you're rolling around the Alps with a guy from New Jersey. And your husband is home because he disinvited himself and you didn't beg him to reconsider; and he reaches out to someone while you're gone—and you're mad at *him*?"

"How many times do I have to tell you: I didn't have sex with Pete!"

"But you wanted to."

"That's not the same as doing it!"

"Thank you for that clarification." Theodore gets up and goes to the kitchen. I follow him. "Now, we don't know if Jack had sex with Sharon. Karen Bell."

"My husband likes a lot of sex. Okay?"

"I didn't need to know that."

"And we haven't been having any. I got back from Italy and nothing. Nothing. I mean nothing."

"Let's put this in perspective, shall we?" Theodore sounds like the professor that he is. "You're tired. And you're hurt. And you're angry. And you're—"

"Betrayed."

"Betrayed. But what you aren't is honest."

"What? I am so honest!"

"You're not. You think that you're allowed to go off and have a summer romance, consummated or not, and that's your own private domain. But you expect Jack to stay home and do the chores and be loyal and wait for you to go through whatever it is you're going through, and then you come home and he gets the great privilege of being your husband again. If he didn't have a Karen Bell, you would have to leave him."

"Why?"

"You wouldn't have a man at home. You'd have a doormat. You

want to cut off his balls, and then when you do, you're mad at him because he's not man enough."

"I don't understand."

"How dare you treat him poorly for years and expect him to take it? I'm surprised he hasn't slept with half of Big Stone Gap. At least he chose a woman in Coeburn—it's hard for gossip to travel uphill. He tried not to embarrass you, and whatever he did, he ended it when you came home. So what do you want?"

"I want . . ."

"You don't know, do you?"

I don't. (But I damn sure know that if I ever rip up the house in Cracker's Neck Holler again, the last place I'm coming for comfort is here.)

"You know, that wedding ring doesn't have magical powers. It doesn't give you license to be cruel, and it can't keep you faithful. You believe you're allowed to act in whatever ugly way you choose because you have a lifetime guarantee that he's not going anywhere. You can abuse Jack, but by God, you're married for keeps. You think you're a woman of substance and commitment and high morals, but you're the worst kind of phony."

"How can you say something like that to me? You know me."

"Right. I know you, and you didn't have sex with that Pete character because you were afraid you weren't good enough. You knew he'd have sex with you and figure out that you're just like every other lay with a smart, good-looking woman—it's lots of fun in the moment but no staying power beyond the thrill. You wanted him to want you, and you led him on, with no intention of delivering the goods. You owe that guy an apology too."

I curl up into a ball of shame on the futon. Theodore is right.

"Now I'm tired. There's a nightgown in the top drawer of the bureau in your room. You left it here last time you visited. Go to bed."

Theodore goes off to his bedroom and closes the door. I hear him turn on the television. A panel of light under the door flashes and changes as the muffled voices and canned laugh track play through. I stretch out on the futon on the floor and cry. I won't sleep tonight. I don't want to.

The ride back from Knoxville goes way too fast. I stay within the speed limit. I guess I'm trying to drag out the trip. I wish it would take a week to get home. But it doesn't. It takes me exactly three hours. Since I left at dawn, I will be home long before Etta returns from her sleepover this afternoon.

Jack's truck is parked in its usual spot next to the house. I park the Jeep and sit in it for a while. I hear the creak of the screen door. Shoo the Cat has pushed the door open and comes running out onto the porch. He lifts his head and sniffs the breeze. Then he looks over at me like I'm crazy for sitting in the Jeep. He's never seen me do this. You park and get out. But he's never seen Ave Maria the Coward before. I'm not mad at Theodore for being honest with me, but maybe I didn't want to own up to what a terrible person I've been. Shame is keeping me in this Jeep.

Maybe I thought my life would settle down and take care of itself naturally. Iva Lou's words ring in my head: "What's your plan, what's your plan?" I should have known I needed a plan. I have to work for everything I get, normalcy and routine included. So I throw my legs of lead out of the Jeep and climb the stairs and go in.

The house is orderly. I can still smell the spices I spilled all over the kitchen floor; the scent of cumin and cinnamon lingers in the deep cracks of the old wood. I walk into the kitchen, which has been put back together in perfect order. I turn and look into our bedroom, which is neat. The bed is made, with the exception of pillows. There are no pillows. I'll have to buy new ones. No way to put the old ones back together again.

I go through the kitchen and out the sun porch and into the field behind our house. Jack is there in the yard, stacking firewood in that way he does, where it looks artistic, like a latticework fence. He looks up at me. He stops his work. I know I have to make a decision, and whatever I do in this moment will determine the fate of our marriage. Now that I have been honest with myself (thank you, Theodore), there is no turning back. I have to be clear. Other lives are involved here. My daughter's. My husband's. Our extended family.

I wish I had a picture in my mind of what I think marriage ought to be. The old movies never helped; those people were always happy. And my mother and Fred Mulligan's marriage was so cold, I knew long before he wasn't my real father that mine should not be like theirs. And for a girl, now a woman, who never thought she'd marry, to be in the thick of one is surreal.

I realize now that I have not chosen this. Jack MacChesney chose me; and never once, in all these years, have I chosen him. Of course, I said yes when he wanted to marry me. But I said yes because he asked, not because I really chose. How must it have been for him, all these years of trying to please me? Of hoping every day that this would be the one that Ave Maria would choose him? But I never did. I loved him, no question. And his babies came through me and into the world. But never once did I choose him. Not really.

This field that used to overwhelm me looks like a small patch of grass. The mountains shrink back into small mounds of dirt that disappear into the wet earth. And the sky, tacked up like a pale blue sheet, looks temporary. The only eternal things are what we choose. The things we would die for. What would I die for? My children, yes. But would I die for Jack MacChesney? I walk across the field to him. He looks at me. I sit on his pretty fence of firewood. I rehearsed so many ways to tell him what he means to me on the ride back from Knoxville, but now that I'm here, I don't know where to start.

"I'm sorry I trashed the house." This is my opener?

"I had a hard time getting up the rice. It took me the better part of the day to sweep it up. How was your trip?"

"Weird."

"Ave, do you want to know what happened?" Jack is speaking of Karen Bell, I assume.

"No," I tell him.

"I can tell you," he offers.

"No, honey. That's yours. That's not mine." The only strategy I have, the only one I know for sure I must stick to, is that I mustn't have real pictures of the two of them together in my mind. Those pictures would make it impossible for me to go forward. This much I know about myself.

My husband sits down next to me. We sit there a very long time.

"Jack. What should we do?"

"What do you want to do?"

"Well, I guess most of the time, I wish you could take my pain away," I tell him.

"I can't do that."

"I know."

"If you want me to go, I will. You can have everything. This house. But I want Etta half of the year. That would be the only thing I would want," he says quietly.

"You've given this some thought."

"Because I can't bear to see you like this."

"You really love me, don't you?" I take his hand.

"Yes, I do."

"That's always been amazing to me, you know."

"What do you mean?"

"That love you've always had for me. I never could quite believe it."

"Why?"

"Maybe because I never thought I deserved it. And maybe because it's easy for me not to feel. It worked so well for me all of my life. You married a real cold cookie."

"You're not cold. You've just been hurt." Jack gets up. And then he does the strangest thing. He kneels in front of me. "And I can't believe I hurt you more."

My husband puts his head in my lap and cries. And I realize a very important thing about him, and maybe it's the thing that will help us go forward: he never blames me for what I am; and he doesn't judge me. He accepts me. And that's the one thing I never gave him in return. This guy never had a chance with me; not really. He was never enough. But who could be? No man could measure up to my standards.

"Jack, look at me." He does. "I thought I had changed. I thought you changed me with your love, by giving me the kids, by sharing this life with me. I thought I let you in, but I never really did."

"I knew what you were when I fell in love with you. I knew it was going to be hard. I knew that when I signed on. Remember when you went into that Deep Sleep?"

Of course I remember. Years ago, I collapsed and slept for one week straight. At the time, Doc Daugherty called it a nervous breakdown.

"I almost decided not to go after you anymore. I thought, there's something going on inside this woman that no one will ever know or understand. But I couldn't give up. I couldn't give you up. I had the out, I had the chance, but something made me stay. I think about that a lot. Why did I stay? Is it because I love you? Or is it more than that? I know you need me, and maybe that's my purpose, to be needed. I don't know."

"That's not your purpose."

"What is, then?"

"To be chosen." Now it's my turn to cry. "And I never chose you. But I do now. Today. If you'll still have me."

My heart is breaking. This good and decent man has been dragged through my crazy life like a wagon. It wasn't all terrible, and maybe there were times when he wasn't dragged. We've had great times together. And tragedy. And routine. Great sex. No sex. But it has all been built upon sand. There is no foundation here because I never truly committed to this. I was thirty-six years old, and I thought it was time. That's why I got married. Yes, I loved him, but I also knew that this was an opportunity that would not come again. I made myself walk into my fear and seize control. I wasn't going to let anything hold me back anymore. I was going to live. I didn't think about how I was going to live, only that I had a right to live. A right to a life with a good man who loved me.

I thought I knew my issues. I thought it was my childhood, with the strange secrets hidden under the surface. I believed that once I found my real father, everything would fall into place. Mario da Schilpario would have all the answers. I was sure of it! But he was only part of the answer. When I made peace with Fred Mulligan, I felt release. When I accepted the lie my mother told to protect me, I felt galvanized. I knew all of these things, and I thought the knowledge of them, the recognition of them, had changed me. But just because I figured it out did not mean that I had fixed it. I am shocked that I know better and yet routinely fall back into my old patterns. I shut off. I shut down. I don't feel. And I hold myself above everyone else as though I am better. I think my pain elevates me above everybody else. That weak people are destroyed by the bad things that happen to them. That weak people need sex to validate their egos. That weak people can't follow the rules. I wasn't weak! I was strong, so strong nothing could penetrate me. What a glorious prize you get for not needing people. You get to be safe and alone, even in your marriage! But all those people who live and let go and let life happen to them, good or bad, wild or serene, they aren't weak—they're human. Somewhere in my past, I learned that if you separate yourself, you don't get hurt. Pain can be avoided. And if you stuff it down deep enough, you will forget it's there. Do not acknowledge it, and it will not hurt you. Theodore is right. I do owe this man an apology. But what else do I owe him?

"When will Etta be home?"

"Iva Lou is picking her up and taking her over to her house after the slumber party. She said she'd keep her overnight."

"Good." I stand up. "I don't want to go back to what we were."

"We can't."

"I want to begin again. With what I know now."

"I don't know if you can change. Or if I can."

"It's bigger than change, Jack. It's reinventing the whole thing."

"Do you know how to do that?"

"We'll figure it out."

I lead my husband into the house. We go through the sun porch and the kitchen to our bedroom and the bed with no pillows. I will begin with how I make love to my husband. I will be present in his arms, every cell of my body in tune with his, I will listen and I will pay attention and I will treat him like the rare and precious treasure that he is. For this time and every time that will come hereafter, I choose him. My beautiful husband with the big shoulders (good thing, they carried two of us all this time) and the sweet hazel eyes. I won't wait for him to kiss me; I kiss him.

"This is new," he says, and smiles.

"Work with me," I tell him, and he laughs.

I take off his clothes slowly. First his work boots. Then his socks. I take his bare feet and rub each one tenderly. He begins to pull his shirt off over his head; I won't let him. I work the shirt off of him and, for the first time, look at his neck and the way his shoulders connect to his upper arms, and the way the muscle twists from the top of his arm around the back and down the elbow. Would I know my husband's body from any other man's in the world? I will now, as I kiss each freckle on his strong brown arm, down to his wrist. His hand, the long fingers, the tiny cuts on his thumb from stacking the wood, his square pink fingernails. How strong his chest is; as I lie on top of him, I feel his breath rise and fall underneath me, as our skin touches and then fits together in the way only longtime couples know. All of this I took for granted. How did I let so much time pass? Why did I ever think that this was expendable, that I could cut this man out of my life? What was I thinking? That I could walk out of here and find someone else? Someone better? As I run my hands down his back, I know there is no one better. In the very moment that love is mundane, it can become new. Why didn't my mother tell me that? I am able to see new things simply because I'm looking for them. How sad I am that they were here all along and I gave them away as though they had no value. Simple things: my husband's love, his faith in me, and his steadfastness. All of those things I pretended did not matter. Love is so fragile. I kiss his eyes. I really want him to see me now.

Monday brings a perfectly sunny, yet cool, first day of school. I am happy for Etta, who didn't want to wear a rain slicker to her first day of fourth grade. She wanted to show off her striped Alpine sweater from her grandfather, and happily, the weather agreed. She kisses me and jumps out of the Jeep. I feel something gooey on my cheek. It's Chiara's peach lip gloss.

I'm about to turn to drive back home (I thought I'd clean out a closet), but instead I head for the Cadet section of Big Stone Gap, in the western part of town, over the bridge and down by the Powell River. It's changed a lot; I try to remember the last time I was here. Had to be over a year ago; I delivered some pills to Oneida Mitchell. As I follow the river road, I see that they've added a trailer park and a convenience market.

There's a pink house on the dead end of Morrissey Street. It's been over thirty years since I've been here. Alice Lambert lives at Number 11. The simple ranch house has a deck on the front. The yard is overgrown; nestled in the brush are white concrete statuettes of a boy and girl who appear to be Dutch.

You can hear the river rushing by; the brown water is visible through the mud trees that line the river side of the road. The mailbox is slung open and full of flyers and junk mail. I clean it out on my way to the front door.

The old silver screen door has WELCOME written in cursive in the center panel, flanked by two rusted daisies. The plastic Greek urns that anchor either side of the door are full of weeds. A couple of wild yellow blooms choke through. I knock on the door. I see the Lamberts' old Cadillac in the carport, so I assume she's home. I hear a shuffling from the back of the house. Finally, the door opens. I am shocked when I see Aunt Alice. I hardly recognize her. She might weigh one hundred pounds.

"Aunt Alice?"

"Hello," she says through the screen door.

"I wanted to stop by and say hello. I was thinking about you."

"You was?"

"Yes ma'am."

"Why is 'at?"

"I was thinking about how you came to my son's funeral so many years ago and how I never thanked you."

"It weren't nothin'," she says, looking away.

"No, no, it was very kind of you. Thank you." After I filled Alice's prescription at the Pharmacy, I felt bad every day for not calling or stopping by.

Aunt Alice stands there. She doesn't move to close the door, but she doesn't invite me in, either. This was always the way it was with my father's side of the family. They never knew what to do to make people feel at home. Or at ease. Maybe they had good intentions underneath it all, but basically, they had no manners. My mother used to say that they didn't have *creanza,* proper upbringing.

"May I come in?" I ask her.

"Sure," she says, and shrugs.

I push the door open. Her little house is neat as a pin, but it's dirty. There is a layer of dust on everything, the windows are cloudy, and the rug needs sweeping. Poor thing. She is too weak to do the chores.

"Would you like a cup of tea?"

"No, thank you."

"I ain't got much in the house."

"I don't need a thing."

We sit quietly until Alice blurts, "I got the cancer."

"I'm sorry."

"You know'd I lost Wayne."

"Yes ma'am."

"He had him the black lung. That's worse than what I git. He couldn't hardly breathe at the end; they put him on a tank. He done filled up with water and choked to death."

"I'm sorry."

"It were turr-ible. And Bobby ne'er did come home to see 'im. That were the greatest tragedy of all. I don't got a son no more."

Wayne and Alice's son, Bobby, was the light of their lives. I never liked him at all. He was several years older and a tease. I heard that he moved to Kingsport and took to drinking. He was on his fourth wife at last count.

"Sure you still have a son. Bobby just gets sidetracked, that's all."

Alice chuckles. "That there's a good word fer it: sidetracked."

"So what does Doc Daugherty say?"

" 'Bout me? Not much."

"What kind of cancer do you have?"

"It was breast. Then it done went to the bone. On account of I wouldn't let 'em take my breast. No. I come in with 'em, and I'm a-gonna go out with 'em too."

"Do you have a lot of pain?"

"I can't hardly sleep a'tall it gits so bad of the night. I can't find a good spot, you know."

"What do you eat?"

"I ain't hungry much. Once in a while I have me some Nabs. Coca-Cola."

"Aunt Alice?" My tone of voice causes Alice's spine to stiffen.

"Yes?"

"I know we've had our problems—"

"Nah, don't dredge all that there up. It's not nothin' no more."

"I wasn't very nice."

"You got a temper on ye, that's all. You're Eye-talian. They's like 'at." Her slur, instead of upsetting me, makes me smile. She's right. Italians *are* like that.

"I'd like to help you out. Can I come over once in a while?"

I go to Buckles Supermarket and shop for Aunt Alice. I pick up easy things, like eggs and bread and cheese and cold cuts. Soup. Pasta. Pancakes. I pick up magazines and puzzle books. Nellie Goodloe is at the next register checking out.

"Hello, Ave Maria. How was your summer?"

"It was good."

"I see Jack Mac's mighty busy."

"That's for sure," I say. "They have lots of work."

"Did they finish that rec center up in Coeburn, by the by?"

Then the strangest thing happens. I feel surrounded. Maybe it's because it's Monday and folks go trading, but it's also something else. I can't put my finger on it. The Methodist Sewing Circle is ready to check out: Mrs. Shoop, Mrs. Quillen, Mrs. Grubb, Mrs. Zander, and Mrs. Messer, each has a shiny cart, and they're lined up like train cars on a track. The smiles on their faces are so sweet, like they're glad to see me. But why are they all listening?

"It was a right long month with you gone. It was about a month, wasn't it?" Mrs Quillen asks.

"Yes ma'am."

"That's a long time to be gone from your husband," Mrs. Shoop chimes in.

"He thought so," I say with a smile.

"It-lee is mighty far. You know, if there was an emergency or something," Mrs. Messer says in a sweet singsong voice, half chiding me.

"I think my husband can handle anything."

"I'm sure he can," Nellie chimes in. "And I'm sure he did." She looks over her bifocals at the ladies.

"Well, it's sure good to see y'all again." I grab my groceries and get the hell out of there. As I drive back to the Cadet section, I realize why: the ladies wanted to see how A-vuh Marie survived her husband's affair. They smelled blood and they came to check out the casualty. I expect they thought I might just throw myself on the checkout and stab myself repeatedly with the outdoor barbecue tongs they had on sale.

Alice is napping when I get there. I make up a tray of macaroni and cheese and boil up some broccoli. Before long, she joins me in the kitchen.

"Smells good."

"You sit." I help her to the table. She is so tiny, I can feel her ribs as I guide her to a chair. As soon as I put the plate of food in front of her, she eats. She gulps down the macaroni and cheese and mashes up the broccoli with her fork before eating it.

"Thank ye for all this." Alice pats my hand.

"It's my pleasure." I give Alice a hug, something that I have never done. And I hold her for a good long time.

Fleeta has a lot on her plate. She won't give up cashiering, but she won't take the Soda Fountain over, either. So she's doing both, and she's worn out. She insists upon fixing Iva Lou, Pearl, and me grilled-cheese sandwiches. It's closing time, so we let her.

"Guess who I went to visit?" I say.

"Law me. You weren't up in Coeburn, were ye?"

"Fleeta. That is not nice!" Iva Lou admonishes her.

"I ain't nice."

"I think we should have a rule," Pearl says. "No mention of Coeburn ever again."

"How'd you hear about Karen Bell?" I ask Pearl.

"In Norton."

"Who cares in Norton?"

"Whoever's up there shopping from Big Stone Gap."

"Lord a-mighty." I sit back on the bar stool.

"I told you that this entire county is filled with vipers. And they's got feet. 'Cause everything that happens 'round here travels. So if you want to keep your husband's cheatin' under wraps, you got to kill him, kill her, then send them bodies north and let them Eye-talians take care of 'em." Fleeta slides the golden-brown grilled-cheese sandwiches from her double-wide spatula onto our plates on the counter.

"What? No garnish?" Pearl teases.

"I went to see Alice Lambert."

"Why would you bother with her?" Iva Lou asks.

"She's dying."

Fleeta, Iva Lou, and Pearl sit with this new information for a moment.

"Better send Reverend Bowers over there so she can repent, or she'll be frying like hot lard in the outskirts of hell," Fleeta says as she brushes potato-chip crumbs off of her smock. "I only say send him 'cause he's known to make house calls."

"Fleeta, make her some fudge. And Iva Lou, she needs some books to read."

"I don't believe my ears," Iva Lou exclaims.

"Me neither." Fleeta shakes her head.

"Find out what medicine she needs and give it to her for free," Pearl says quietly.

"I hope that when I'm sick and distended and bloated and full of the cancer, you send me some medicine for free. I work in this joint, and all I ever git is a ten percent discount." Fleeta ashes her cigarette into the sink.

"And all the Estée Lauder you can poach." Pearl winks at her.

Etta is in full swing with her schoolwork and her new social life, which includes gathering her girlfriends together to paint their nails and make crank calls to boys. It's very annoying, but I try to be patient.

I remind myself that this is just another phase of child rearing, no different from dealing with teething or mouth breathing. The entry into the Boy Years sure can get loud.

Jack comes home from work in a great mood.

"Let's go to the Fold tonight," he suggests.

"I can't. I have the Lip Gloss Girls in there for a slumber party."

"Is Fleeta around?" Jack asks.

"I hate to ask her again."

"She loves Etta." Jack picks me up and spins me around.

"Is that your hand on my ass?" I ask my husband.

"I think so. And I hate to tell you, but that situation is only gonna get worse." He kisses me.

"Okay, okay. I'll call Fleeta."

I call Fleeta. Of course, she complains a little, she wants to see a story on *20/20* about granny dumping, but I promise her we get better cable reception up here in the holler.

So she comes.

The Carter Family Fold is overflowing with folks. It's just the right time of year to gather up in the Carter family's barn and listen to music and dance. Jack wanted to come because he heard on the job that one of the Stanley Brothers was showing up. And indeed he did, so the music is glorious. I never heard such fine fiddling. We dance so much and so hard, my denim shirt is soaked.

Lew Eisenberg has turned out to be the best clogger in Southwest Virginia. He shows me a two-step that reminds him of the hora he did at his bar mitzvah many years ago. We have a good laugh over that one.

"Honey, you need to towel off," Iva Lou says to me as I collapse on the bleachers.

"I'm having a ball," I tell her.

"How's it going with your husband?"

"Very well, thank you. It's good to have him back."

"Are you kidding? It's great. It's the best of all things. It's the triumph of true love over base lust. It's a story of forgiveness and redemption, honey. You want me to go on?"

"No."

"Then I won't. I'm doin' my own brand of celebratin' tonight. Lyle stopped drinkin' again and we are flush solid, honey."

"Good for him and good for you."

"Maybe there is something to astrology. You know, maybe the planets do line up and everybody has good vibes at the same time."

"That's totally possible."

The Methodist Sewing Circle is gathered by the door, chatting furiously.

"Jesus Christmas, what has got them so agitated?" Iva Lou wonders.

"Somebody probably came up with a better apple-butter recipe."

The Sewing Circle stops chattering. Their little circle widens and fans out.

"Or not," Iva Lou says in a tone that forces me to look up. "Oh my," she says quietly.

Karen Bell stands in the doorway wearing black leather pants, a white blouse, a chain belt, and a white cowboy hat cocked on the back of her head. She rolls her pink lips together as though she's trying to bite off a bit of chapped lip. She looks worried, and the groove between her eyes is deep. Of course she's worried. I'm here, aren't I? I look around the room for my husband; he's not here, but he said he was going for a chili dog. I wonder if she's looking for him. I can see from one look at the Methodist Sewing Circle that they have the same idea. Their heads are swiveling around on their necks like geese looking to land.

"I'll be right back," I tell Iva Lou.

I ignore her call of "Where are you going?" as I walk away. The Other Woman, the Girl on the Side, the Strumpet from Coeburn, is unaware that I am walking toward her, but she is the only woman in the room unaware of me. All eyes are on the battle-ax, the wife who hung in there till her dang knuckles bled; the poor little ole thing, me. Joe Smiddy's Reedy Creek Band plays an old ballad that underscores my steps; I feel the layers of onlookers fall away as I pass. The Sewing Circle turns into a nervous Greek Chorus as they whisper what gore may ensue if Ave Maria gets mad enough. I can feel the nervous tension as it flows through the crowd and makes a path to the Other Woman. I follow that path to its bitter end.

"Karen?"

She turns to me. When she connects me, the real person, to her life, she has a moment of surreal disbelief. I am someone whose face she tried hard to remember, having met me only once. Maybe if she could find some flaw in me, it would make her plan to steal my husband all right. But all that stands before her is a sweaty Eye-talian wearing good lipstick. She can't quite make the connection, so I will do it for her.

"I'm Ave Maria. I don't know if you remember me."

She looks at me oddly, and at first her little chin juts out as though she's looking to fight. I've confused her, so the thought crease between her eyes deepens even more.

"We met at the Methodist Church," I remind her.

"Yeah. A while back." She looks away. I guess she's had enough eye contact.

"I'd like to thank you for being such a good friend to my husband this summer."

She doesn't know what to say. She's so nervous, the cowboy hat slides off the back of her head and down her back. The chin string catches on her throat. "You're welcome," she stammers.

I turn and walk back to the bleachers, past the whispers of the well-meaning Christian ladies and to my spot next to Iva Lou.

"Girl, where on God's green did you get the courage?"

"Bette Davis. There's that scene in *Jezebel* where she wears the red dress to the ball where all the nice girls are supposed to wear white. I imagined myself in the red dress, walking across that dance floor, defying all of society. Nobody ever messed with Bette Davis, and by God, nobody is ever gonna mess with me."

"Did you tell her you'd whoop her ass if she took off after your husband agin?"

"Oh yeah."

"That's my girl," Iva Lou says as she cocks her head back and takes a gulp from her beer. "In all my years and all my married men, I only had one confrontation."

"Only one?"

"Yeah. Billie Jean Scott met me up at Skeen's Ridge one night, right after I'd been with her husband. And she looked me in the eye, after she'd blocked the road and stopped my car, of course, and said, 'Iva Lou Wade, were you with my Hank?' I was caught and I knew it, so I 'fessed up. I told her, 'Yes ma'am.' And she said, 'Thank you, kindly. I've been trying to get rid of that son of a bitch for forty-one years. And you just give me the perfect excuse to give him the old heave-ho.' "

Iva Lou and I laugh so hard, the Methodist Sewing Circle looks at us as though we're crazy. And I think we just might be.

# CHAPTER ELEVEN

*W*hen folks say that Big Stone Gap is for the newlywed and the nearly dead, they ain't kidding. Alice Lambert is getting a send-off worthy of a statesman. The women in town have come down and taken over her little pink house by the brown river. They've scrubbed the windows, vacuumed, and waxed the kitchen floor; they wash her clothes, they bathe her; and the delectable food dropped off in shifts is not to be believed. Ethel Bartee even came over and did Alice's hair. And folks can't help but comment that "Alice Lambert is as sweet as pie." And she is.

Doc Daugherty told me that it's a matter of days for Alice. He can't say how many, and in a way, I don't want to know. I go and see her every day (as do the other ladies), and it's strange to say this, but I think these are the happiest days of her life.

I am sitting in the living room with Aunt Alice. Ethel gave her an upsweep with tendrils worthy of the great Loretta Lynn at the Grand Old Opry. She even wears a little lipstick. There's a rap on the door; it's Spec.

"My wife done made you a cobbler, Alice. How do you like rhubarb?" he asks.

"Thank 'er for me. I love it," Alice says.

"So how are we doin', girls?" Spec says as he sits down.

"Fine," I tell him.

"Alice, I done want to run somethin' by ye."

"Yeah?"

"Bobby's outside."

"My Bobby?"

"Yes ma'am. Yer son. I went over to Kingsport and fetched him. Now, number one: he's sober. Number two: he feels like a shit-heel for not gittin' over here sooner. Number three: I don't have a number three. He just wants to talk to ye. Are ye up fer it?"

Alice nods that she is.

Spec doesn't move from his seat, he simply shouts. "Bobby, git in here."

Bobby Lambert, forty-six years old, comes in the door. He is short like Alice but has his father's face, long and hangdog, with eyes that droop in the corners, a wide mouth, low ears, and a shock of thick hair that hangs down the center of his forehead in one curl. He is thin and has the purple-veined nose of a drinker. He's very nervous and shifts from one foot to the other. He is wearing his best clothes, but the cotton button-down shirt is yellowed, and the hems of his pants are frayed where they rest against the top of his shoes. His fourth wife must have left him.

"Hey, Mama," he says, holding on to either side of the doorframe.

"Git over here and hug yer mama's neck!" she says with a bass tone to her voice I've never heard before.

Then Bobby starts talking so fast it's as though he's conducting an auction. He's dazzling his mother with information, about this deal and that deal and this new car he got and how the transmission's the best and what kind of leather seats take the heat and which ones don't, and I look at Spec and he looks at me and we're thinking the same thing: this guy is a first-class huckster.

But Aunt Alice loves it. And him. This is her only son, and she loves everything about him. Her eyes travel over his face as though she has found a precious jewel that throws back her own reflection. She doesn't let go of his face, she is so madly in love with it. And she just nods as he drones on. Soon he's kneeling, and the picture of that, of a son at the feet of his mother, begging for her forgiveness without asking for it, is one of the most beautiful things I have ever seen. No matter what Bobby would ever do, she would forgive him. No matter what, he would always have a place here, and the only reason he didn't was his own shame. Now that he sees that his mother still loves him and always will, he can stay. And he will, until the very end.

In just three days, Alice Lambert goes to bed for good. Fleeta helps me get her to the bed. She thinks Alice didn't digest Annie Hunter's apple dumplings too well and that's why she's taken the turn. I tell Fleeta that it isn't anything that Alice has eaten, it's the cancer. Cancer is very strange; it grips a patient, and then it seems to go, then it can rage back like a fever and take you. This is what has happened to Alice. Bobby helps with the sheets, smoothing them under Alice as we turn her. I tell Fleeta to run and call Doc Daugherty.

Bobby sits on the corner of the bed and holds his mother's hand. I see in his face all the things I went through when my mother passed. The great sorrow of being separated from the one who brought you, the guilt at not doing enough for her (there is never enough we can do for our mothers), and the desperate hope that the pain will be minimal. He is trying not to cry, for her sake.

"Bobby, hon, I need me a minute with Ava." I decide to let it go. She has always mispronounced my name and that's that. Bobby looks at me kindly and leaves the room.

"Yes, Aunt Alice?"

"Do you know why I came to your boy's funeral?"

"No ma'am."

" 'Cause I lost a son too."

I'm confused, and I look at Alice quizzically.

"Not Bobby. Calvin. Calvin died at four months."

"I didn't know that."

"You wouldn't. He was born right around the time you was. I never got over it. Some folks think it turned me bitter. I don't know about that."

"Aunt Alice, will you do me a favor?"

She nods.

"When you get there, will you — could you — look out for my Joe?"

"Yes ma'am, I will."

I hear the screen door slam. Doc Daugherty must be here. I kiss Alice on the forehead. What happens next is all a haze; Doc comes in with Bobby; and Spec takes his place by the door. I feel myself leave my body as I watch this scene with me in it. And I see something that I could not have known before this moment; I watch Alice let go. She lets go of her life, of her problems, her pain, and her secrets. A burden lifts off of her as she lays dying. A smile crosses her face, one of peace and duly earned solitude.

In her final moments, her thoughts were of her sons, Bobby and Calvin. Isn't this the truth of any good mother? That in all of our lives, we worry only about those we brought into this world, regardless of whether they loved us back or treated us fairly or understood our shortcomings. As Alice lets go, so do I. I let go of my mistakes, the un-attainable standards I have for my husband, my daughter, and my-self, and my bitterness toward those who hurt me; mostly, I let go of my pride, which I thought had kept me whole but in reality almost ruined me. I was holding on so tightly to being right, to being perfect. There is only one lesson in all of this: let go. And when you think you've let go completely, let go again. Aunt Alice sailed out of here with such grace. She really did it right.

"She's gone." Bobby weeps and holds his mother. Doc Daugherty turns to me. But I already knew. I close my eyes and smile; Aunt Alice will find my son. She will make sure he's all right.

Johnny Teglas over at *The Post* asked me to write Alice Mulligan Lambert's obituary. And in so doing, I learned many things about her. She was a WAC in World War II; she took enough courses at Mountain Empire Community College to earn an associate's degree in business (who knew?); and those weren't her real teeth (I won't put that part in the paper). But I do mention baby Calvin, and Bobby, of course. I type up the story of her life and seal it in an envelope. I holler to Fleeta back in the Soda Fountain that I'm leaving and will see her tomorrow. When I get outside, I feel the first cool breeze of autumn as it blows through. Monday is Labor Day.

I put the obit in the slot of the newspaper office. I think old Johnny's in for a surprise when he reads about Alice Lambert.

When I get home, I smell fresh butter and garlic simmering; I follow the delicious aroma into the kitchen. Jack is barefoot, in his jeans and an old sweatshirt, making us dinner.

"Hi." He looks up and smiles at me.

"What are you cooking? It smells divine!"

One of the bonuses of marrying Jack is that he is attentive in the kitchen. He's a better Italian cook than I am now. I give him a big kiss.

"Linguini carbonara, with Virginia ham. Who's Pete?" he asks casually.

"Pete who?" I try not to choke on the name.

"Pete Rutledge."

"Oh, him. We met him in Italy."

"Oh, the guy Etta talks about. The marble guy."

"Really. She told you about him?" I say casually but my vocal tone gives me away: I squeak. That kid. Does she have to tell her father everything?

"Yeah."

"Why do you ask?"

"He called."

"That's nice."

"He's in town."

"What?"

"He's here."

I don't know what to say. I figured the guy had a crush, we kissed, and that was it. What is he doing here?

"Ave, honey, tell me what's going on."

"Nothing's going on. I love you." Man, if blurting "I love you" isn't a dead giveaway for guilt developed after an Alpine make-out session, I don't know what is.

"Here's his number. He's at the Trail."

Jack puts the number on the table, as though I should call Pete Rutledge right here on our phone in this house, this house where we, a newly devoted married couple, live. I do not want to make this call.

"I'll call tomorrow."

"Call him now. Invite him to dinner. I'm making plenty."

Jack stirs the garlic in the pan. My eyes bulge out of my head like rockets. Is he serious? Have him to dinner? He's the enemy, you idiot. He wanted me to stay in Italy with him for all eternity. Tear up that number if you know what's good for you.

"Go on. Call him."

I drag myself to the phone and dial. It rings a billion times. Conley Barker, the night receptionist (as well as the airport cab driver), finally answers the phone and puts me through.

"Hello?" The sound of Pete's voice makes me happy, but just for a second.

"Hi. This is Ave Maria."

"Oh, hey, thanks for calling me back."

"What are you doing here?" I say gaily.

"Hiking the Appalachian Trail. Remember? I told you I was coming through in the fall. Well, guess what? It's fall."

"Isn't that great?"

"Yeah. I'd like to see you."

"Sure. Why not?"

"Great. Where do you live?"

I decide that it's easier for me to ride down into town and pick him up rather than give him the complicated directions to get here. When I get to the Trail, Pete is waiting for me out front. He leans up against one of the entry columns, reading the town paper. He looks like he belongs here. And he looks every bit as good in southwestern Virginia twilight as he did in the dusk of northern Italy.

"Hi!" I say too loudly and too long, with about eighteen overenthusiastic syllables.

"How are you, babe?" Pete gives me a big kiss on the cheek. "What a place you live in. It's amazing. So beautiful."

"Thank you. Can't take any credit for it. These mountains were here long before I was."

I point out a few sights on the way back to Cracker's Neck. I am determined to be a tour guide, and determined that there will be no talk of Alpine kissing or dancing. Pete seems respectful, and I'm relieved. When we climb out of the Jeep, Etta is waiting for us on the porch.

"Pete!" she squeals, and runs down the field to meet us. She throws herself into his arms.

"Chiara's not here. She's in Italy. It's only me here."

And what is that on Etta's mouth? Oh dear God, it's my Gina Lollobrigida magenta lipstick from the Moderna beauty shop in Piccolo Lago. My daughter looks like a hooker.

Jack greets us at the door. I love how warm and gracious he is to Pete. Shoo the Cat runs out from under a chair, sinks his teeth into Pete's ankle, and sprints off. We check Pete's ankle, but there's barely any blood. Between the attack cat and my trampy daughter, this is going to be a long night.

Jack takes Pete (and Etta, of course, who follows) into the kitchen.

Pete and Jack will have a beer, and the way this night is going, Etta may have her first Jack Daniel's on the rocks. The phone rings; Etta rushes to answer it.

"She never used to run for the phone." Jack Mac shrugs. "Now she's either running to it or she's on it."

"It's called being a girl, honey."

"Ma, it's Uncle Theodore."

I excuse myself. I am relieved to be out of the hot kitchen. I close the bedroom door, pull the phone off the nightstand, and sit on the floor, so no one can hear me.

"Thank God it's you."

"What's wrong?"

"He's here."

"Who?"

"Pete."

Theodore laughs. "The inamorata? No way."

"It's not funny! He's hiking around here and he stopped and called and Jack invited him to dinner. I'd like to die."

"What are you going to do?"

"It's awful. I'm so embarrassed."

"Imagine how Jack Mac feels."

"He doesn't know anything."

"Right, you're hiding under the bed whispering on the phone, and he doesn't suspect a thing."

"No, he doesn't. It would be nice if you could make me feel better in this situation."

"How does he look?"

"Oh God. Even better than he looked in Italy."

"You're in trouble."

"It's like tenth grade. Why couldn't I go through this nonsense at an age-appropriate level? No, here I am now, in middle age, dealing with this stupidity."

"It wasn't that stupid up in the cockerbells."

"Bluebells."

"You'll have to tell Jack."

"I will never tell him! Never."

"Don't you think he's going to wonder why you're acting like a fool?"

"I'll tell him I'm sick or something."

"Sexual tension isn't a disease."

"You're not helping."

"Call me later." He laughs. "Good luck."

I cannot believe how weird it is to eat dinner with my husband and my summer almost-boyfriend, who with some amazing kisses could have brought down the House of MacChesney entirely. I look across the table at the two of them, doing a compare-and-contrast. They are different, and yet there is an all-boy quality to both of them. They instantly like each other (how bizarre is that!), and they seem to have lots to talk about. Etta interrupts whenever she can think of ways to get Pete's attention. My daughter is never going to be the town spinster, that's for sure. She can't wait to be a grown-up woman. She awaits her first period like it's the Preakness of Womanhood.

Headlights flash across the living room; we see the end of the beams against the wall outside the kitchen. Jack looks at me.

"Expecting anybody?"

I shake my head and take a look out the window. It's Iva Lou.

"Sorry to barge in," Iva Lou says as she throws open the door without knocking.

"Hi, honey. We have company. Pete Rutledge."

Iva Lou's eyes roll around as she tries to place the name, and when she does, it's her turn to have her eyeballs bulge out of her head like rockets. I quickly motion for her to act casual (my first mistake) as she puts a frozen smile on her face that borders on ghoulish.

"Hi-dee. Pleased to meet you, Pete."

"I spent a lot of time with Peter in Italy this summer, Iva Lou," Etta says in an accent no one has heard since Grace Kelly used it in *High Society*.

"Yeah, well, I would've too." Iva Lou winks at Pete.

"Iva, can we get you something to eat?"

"No, no. I just had a chili dog at the Mutual's. I just stopped by on my way home to tell y'all about Spec."

"Something wrong?"

"He's having an emergency triple bypass tomorrow at Holston Valley Heart Center."

"Oh my God."

"Don't worry. He's okay for now. In fact, he drove himself over there in the Rescue Squad. He said if it got rough, he could give himself his own oxygen. Well, I've got to go."

"I'll walk you out."

Iva Lou says her good nights and meets me in the hallway.

"Man alive, and I mean man alive!" she whispers. I motion for her to hush until we get outside.

"What is he *doing* here?"

"He's hiking the Appalachian Trail."

"Well, you tell him to get himself down to the trailer park and practice on Mount Iva Lou."

I push Iva Lou out the door; when she's worked up like this, there is no telling what she'll say or do.

I drive Pete back to the motel; I wanted Etta to come along, but Jack made her stay behind to do her homework. I didn't want to look suspicious, so I didn't press it. I cannot explain how strange it feels to be in my Jeep with Pete Rutledge. I am not comfortable entertaining him here at home; he is strictly a European vacation fantasy.

I pull up in front of the hotel. I can see the top of Conley Barker's crew cut behind the desk.

"Well, have a great hike."

"Thanks."

"You want to come in?" Pete asks.

"No," I tell him so loudly it's a shout.

"You don't have to."

"I can't. But thank you." I say this with a cool I didn't think I had.

"Have you thought about me at all?"

"Pete."

"Just a little?"

"Here's the only way I can explain it. I live in a holler here in these mountains, where the weather is pretty good most of the time. And once in a while, a hell of a storm comes through, and it stirs everything up. When it's over, this amazing blue sky appears, and things become so clear and clean that I actually see better; and from my field in Cracker's Neck Holler, I can see as far as Tennessee, in such detail that I can make out the veins on the leaves. Without that storm passing through, you'd never get that crystal-clear vision that follows. You came through my life like a hurricane. You stirred me up and made me look at myself. You made me look at what I wanted and what I needed to choose. And there is a part of me that wishes I had thrown you down in that field of bluebells and had the wildest sex I could imagine, just for the thrill of it. But a thrill comes and goes, and we both know that. We did the right thing. I'm happy with Jack Mac-Chesney. I really love the man. And I'm really happy that you're my friend."

"Okay, babe. I know when I'm licked." Pete opens the door of the Jeep and swings his long legs out to the ground. He swivels and looks at me. "Thanks for dinner. And Etta. And Jack. I really like Jack." Pete leans over and kisses me on the cheek. Then he gets out of the Jeep.

"Pete?" I call after him. "Good luck."

"Thanks." He smiles and waves.

I watch him walk into the lobby of the Trail Motel. He has to drop his head under the walkway awning. And he looks to me a little like the great Gary Cooper—Pete sort of rode into town, set things straight, and is gone.

When I get home, the kitchen is clean, Etta is in bed, and Jack is in our bedroom, in the overstuffed old club chair, reading *The Post*.

"He's taking off tomorrow morning. He's meeting the hikers in Asheville."

"Great." Jack puts his newspaper down. "How come you were so nervous?"

"Oh, the news about Spec really threw me."

"No, it was before that. You didn't want to call Pete at the hotel. How come?" Jack looks at me, and I'm thinking, this is what marriage is. It's like a giant washing machine. You throw everything in there, and you pour on the soap, and the water gushes in, and you think you're gonna wash it all away. But no matter what, even after it's spun around, you open that tub and right there at the top is the thing you tried to bury at the bottom. The thing you tried to deny and walk away from. The truth about Pete Rutledge was bound to come out, because I am not a good liar. And more importantly, I don't want to keep anything from my husband anymore. The truth is so much easier. (Another thing Mama taught me that has turned out to be true.)

"Honey, when I was over in Italy with Etta, I was trying to forget about you. It was just too painful. I'm not proud of that. I got so tired of the knife in my gut that I just wanted it out. And so I got a haircut."

Jack laughs. "Okay."

"It's insane, I know, but it transformed me. I heard the scissors and I saw the clumps of my hair on the floor and it changed me."

"How?" Jack leans in and listens.

"I went out that night, and that's when I met Pete. I felt so good, I forgot about our troubles and danced. Pete saw me in that moment. And he sort of fell for me. But I wouldn't get involved with him."

"Why?" Jack asks me this with a catch in his voice.

"The truth?"

"The truth."

"I'd like to say that it was something noble, like our marriage vows. But the truth is, I didn't go to bed with him because he thought I was perfect. And as someone who worked her whole life to be perfect, I didn't want to shatter the illusion. If I had the affair it would have made me a cheater. And I wanted to stay on that pedestal; otherwise I'd just be another summer lay for an American in Italy."

"Honey?" Jack gets up and sits with me on the bed.

"What?"

"I'm glad you didn't."

"Me too." I put my arms around my husband. "Do you want to know why you . . . went with Karen? Because I made you feel bad about yourself. I wasn't there for you when the mines closed, I didn't get behind your business; I didn't think that what was happening to you was serious. I treated your crisis like a glitch. And I was holding on to stuff, holding you accountable for things that you had no control over, because I had to blame somebody. Like when Joe got sick, I blamed you, because I wanted you to be the hero who comes in and fixes everything so I didn't have to worry about it. I was horrible to you. But now I understand what I did. And it won't happen again."

"If it did happen again, we'd be able to name it. For the longest time, we just couldn't name it." Jack kisses me tenderly. "So that's the story of Pete, huh? How about a cup of tea?"

"How about Jack Daniel's? Or did Etta finish the bottle?"

"I meant to ask you, what was with the lipstick?"

"Welcome to womanhood."

"Great." Jack groans. He puts his arm around me as we go into the kitchen.

Spec's triple bypass became a quintuple. When Doc Turner got inside, he "found enough goo to fill a shoe box." (That's Spec's description, not mine.) So as I tiptoe through the halls of the Holston Valley Heart Center, I am expecting the worst. The get-well balloons I bought at L. J. Horton Florists keep getting caught on the pressboard ceiling ducts overhead. I hold them down by my waist. Finally, Room 456.

"Spec, now you listen here. I ain't sharin' you with no goddamn whore. You got to choose. You choose me or her. Now that's that. I didn't give up my goddamn life since the age of goddamn fifteen to get to this point and be by my goddamn self. If you wanted out, you should've gotten out when I could still get me out there and find me another man. Who is gonna want me at sixty-four? You might as well set me on fan right here, right now in this room, and watch me burn. Now that's the goddamn truth."

The barrage keeps me in the hallway. Soon I hear the sound of soft sneakers on linoleum.

"Hi, Leola."

"Hey, A-vuh."

Leola has a yellow bouffant hairdo and big Oscar de la Renta glasses. Her face is small, so the glasses cover most of it. She has an unlit cigarette dangling from her mouth. She is tiny, and you can see the remnants of a great figure from her youth. She was always busty, but now she's low-busty. She wears tight pink stirrup pants that pick up the pink letters on her oversize sweatshirt, which reads MYRTLE BEACH MAMA.

"Are you okay?"

"I need a smoke. Nice balloons." Leola walks up the hallway.

Spec is lying in the bed attached to tubes of all kinds. He's wearing his sunglasses, which I think is weird.

"Hey, Spec. I heard it went great."

Spec holds up five fingers.

"I heard. Quintuple. Well, might as well unclog all the pipes while the doctor's in there."

Spec nods. "Doc Turner split my breastbone in two with an ax. He's a fine surgeon. The scar is vurry thin, but it's right long." Then he whispers, "Is she gone?"

"Leola?"

He nods.

"She went for a smoke."

"I got caught," he says quietly, rolling his head back into the groove of the pillow.

"What do you mean?"

"Just what I said. Twyla was over here last night. She come to see me."

"Oh no."

"And I got caught."

For years, Spec has led a double life, seeing Twyla Johnson, his off-and-on girlfriend, while married to Leola, the mother of his five children. Twyla works at the Farmers and Miners Bank down in Pennington. She's a petite brunette with a gorgeous smile and lots of time on her hands (bank hours are ten to three). She's probably sixty now, still a young thing to old Spec.

"I'm sure Leola thinks she saw more than she saw. Didn't she?"

"No, she pert near saw it all."

"Well, what did she see?"

Spec won't say.

I press him. "Did Twyla kiss you or something?"

"No."

"Was she holding your hand?"

"Not my hand."

"Oh no."

"Yeah, she was, well, you know what she was doing. It's been a vurry vurry stressful time for me. Vurry much so. And Twyla come all this way, and frankly, she wanted to make me feel good."

"Oh, Spec."

"I know. It's like your worst nightmare. It's like your mother catchin' ye, for Godsakes. It could turn you off entirely. You know what I'm sayin'."

"Yes, I do."

"I mean. Is it so wrong? Is comfort so wrong? I mean, let's say I was about to die in here, which I was, they practically spelled it out, I mean, I was a goner. Every damn avenue to my heart was clogged,

Ave. It was dirt nap, *Good Night, Irene,* and kiss-your-ass-good-bye time. And if I had my pick of ways to spend my last moments, it sure weren't gonna be with my sorry kids and my hateful wife gaping at me like a carp in a fish tank. I wanted my Twyla." Spec sounds pitiful.

"Well, what's gonna happen now?" I sit down on the bed. The movement jostles the cloudy tubes connecting in and out of him like overpasses on Appalachia Strait.

"That remains to be seen. Leola's not left the room since. Poor Twyla burst into tears and run out of here. I ain't seen her since. She ain't called, neither."

"She's probably afraid."

"It's just a mess."

"Yes, it is."

"What ought I do?"

"What do you want to do?"

"I want out of this hospital. And then I want to be happy."

"Who makes you happy?"

"The truth?"

"Yes. The truth."

"Twyla."

"Well, then you have to choose Twyla."

"But what about Leola?"

"Leola can get another man."

"You think?"

"Yes."

"But she done took care of me when I was sick."

"Give her combat pay."

"That's true. I can't believe you're sayin' this. You bein' a Cathlick and all. Y'all ain't never supposed to go for divorce."

"Well, Spec, we've known each other a long long time. And I think I know you pretty good." I don't want to say what I'm thinking, but something tells me I should. "Spec, I think you deserve more than a hand job on a gurney. I think you should be happy all the time."

Spec is a little stunned at my blunt assessment. He appreciates it, though, and twists the food IV needle stuck in his hand like a sewing needle in a pin cushion. "Well put. Well put." Spec looks away, but I can't tell what he's looking at through the sunglasses. "Thank you for that," he says, and looks toward the window.

"Spec, I read something once that helped me a lot."

"What was that?"

"Sometimes it's hard to tell the difference between true love and lust."

"Yes ma'am, it surely is."

"Do you want to know how you tell the difference?"

"I think it would shed some light," Spec says from behind his sunglasses.

"True love energizes you; lust exhausts you."

"And women will ruin you."

"That wasn't in the book, Spec."

"It ought to be."

# CHAPTER TWELVE

Pearl Grimes and Dr. Taye Bakagese are to be married tonight on the stage of the Trail of the Lonesome Pine Outdoor Drama Theatre. Pearl chose the Friday night after Thanksgiving because she knew most folks had the day off and could party into the wee hours. I am rushing around, ironing Jack's shirt, hunting for Etta's tights, and trying not to nick my freshly painted toenails on anything.

"Theodore?"

"What?" he says from inside the bathroom.

"Do you see Etta's tights in there?"

Theodore hands me Etta's tights through a crack in the door. He drove up to spend Thanksgiving with us. I convinced him that he shouldn't miss Pearl's wedding. The entire cast of the outdoor drama is invited, and they all wanted to see him.

Etta grabs her tights. I finish Jack's shirt and pull the curlers out of my hair. Jack comes in from the kitchen.

"Your hair looks nice."

"Thank you."

We decide to go in Theodore's car, since it's a four-door. When we get to the theater, it looks like a sold-out show. Pearl Grimes has cast a wide net in her life already: she went to college, then she opened a second pharmacy in Norton, with a third scheduled to open in Pound. She's amazing. As we join the folks filtering in, Otto sits by the door asking each person for tickets. Of course, everyone laughs at his joke.

"Can you believe my little grandbaby is gettin' murried?"

"Isn't life something?" I give him a hug.

"I mean, she's my new grandbaby, little Pearl, since my son murried her mother. But I can claim her, can't I?"

"Of course you can."

As we gather onstage, the ceremony is simple and elegant. It's a mix of Indian and Bluegrass, two cultures that have some things in common, like love of nature and family. Leah, radiant in a long red velvet dress, takes her place with Worley, who is wearing a new suit. Albert Grimes, hair slicked down, wearing gray slacks, a navy blazer, and a tie, fidgets nervously in the row behind Leah. (I think the insurance claim that the fire at the theater was caused by faulty wiring has taken the heat off of Albert.)

Taye looks at Pearl with so much love, it makes the hardest among us tear up. Nellie Goodloe runs out for more tissue (or maybe she's jittery because the crowd is too big and she didn't order enough mints).

Pearl's simple white gown is exquisite. It has a scoop neck and long sleeves, the kind that trumpet out. The tiny seed pearls on the bodice catch the light. She wears the shawl I brought her from Italy over her shoulders. Her hair, soft in the cool air, curls down to her shoulders like a loose ribbon. She has placed tiny sprigs of baby's breath throughout. As Taye puts the ring on Pearl's hand, Otto nudges me.

"That there is my Destry's ring."

I put my arm around Otto. He has tears in his eyes as he thinks of the love of his life, the beautiful Melungeon girl who died in child-birth bringing Worley into the world. Pearl holds her hand and looks down at the ring and adjusts it with her other hand. The judge pronounces Taye Bakagese and Pearl Grimes man and wife, and the applause echoes up and into the mountains behind us.

I feel Fleeta's breath on the back of my neck. "Them babies of theirs is gonna be real brown," she whispers.

"And beautiful," I whisper back.

"Yup," she says. I turn and look at Fleeta. Could she be softening up after all these years?

The tent, lit by tiny blue lights, showcases a feast of Southwest Virginia and Indian cuisine. Who knew that buttery sautéed kale tasted so good with grilled lamb kabobs?

"Hey, Ava!" Sweet Sue Tinsley says as she pats me on the back. In Big Stone Gap, we have open-church weddings (in this case, open-theater); they are announced in the paper and everyone is welcome. Sweet Sue Tinsley evidently kept her subscription to *The Post*, so she stays in the loop and on our party circuit. I take a good look at Jack Mac's old girlfriend. She is aging just as I thought she would: very well. She's cut her hair very short. Little spikes of white-yellow hair stick out all over her head. She wears a strapless white dress with a red patent-leather belt.

"How's Kingsport?"

"The boys love it. Mike is working at the paper plant."

"Great."

"How are you?"

"Busy. But fine."

"I'm a grandmother, you know."

"I didn't know!" I look at Sweet Sue. It seems impossible that she could be a grandmother.

"Yeah, my oldest, Chris, fell in love with his high school sweet-heart. And she got pregnant. Little Michael is three months old."

"Congratulations. You're the foxiest grandma I've ever seen," I tell her, and I mean it.

"Thank you, honey. I appreciate that. I do. You're lookin' good yourself!"

Sweet Sue excuses herself and runs off to say hello to lots of folks she hasn't seen in a long while. I knock back an egg roll. I may look all right, but it's depressing to think that I am actually old enough to be a grandmother.

"I'll give you a hundred bucks if you dance with me right now," Theodore says in my ear.

"I'm eating."

"Starve." He grabs me for a slow dance by the Jerome Street Ramblers.

"What is your problem?"

"Sarah Dunleavy has a jones for me like you wouldn't believe."

"She's harmless."

"She's forty."

"You're forty-four."

"Yeah, but I'm not trying to score a husband and a baby in the next six months. She's on a mission."

Then, as though we have glided into an old memory, Jack cuts in.

"I'd like to dance with my wife," Jack says, and smiles.

"I'd like you to dance with Sarah Dunleavy," Theodore tells him.

"No way!" I step into my husband's arms and out of Theodore's. Theodore heads for the dessert table as Jack sways with me under the glittery canopy (the same one used every year at the Powell Valley High School prom).

"What was that all about?"

"Nothing."

"Why'd you cut in?"

"I don't know. Sometimes you've got to dance with your wife."

"Don't you want to dance with Sarah Dunleavy?"

"She's too skinny."

"But she's quiet, and she choral-reads Shakespeare."

"I like noise, and I hate Shakespeare."

"Uh, Jack?"

"Yes, darlin'?"

"Honey, is that your—" As we sway on the dance floor, I carefully move Jack's hand from my butt to my waist.

"It better be my hand," he says.

Pearl and Taye kiss by the band; Spec presses his fork into Nellie Goodloe's cherry jubilee; Leola has a smoke with Fleeta (I'm sure Leola is catching her up on all the News); Iva Lou and Lyle stand over the steam tables surveying the choices; and Theodore takes the last seat at the table with Rick and Rita Harmon and their kids, so he doesn't have to sit at Sarah Dunleavy's, where there are two open seats on purpose. Etta waves to me from the corner of the tent, where the kids eat sugared mints and tell silly jokes. I wave to her; she smiles.

As the clock hits midnight, Pearl and her new husband take to the dance floor for one final go-round. The remaining guests, and there's just a few of us, leave the floor to the bride and groom. Otto rigged up a couple of portable heaters under the tent, so it's warm inside. The stage of the Outdoor Drama, fully lit and bathed in pink light, is empty now.

"Your shoes," my husband says to me as he hands me the strappy sandals that stayed on my feet for about ten minutes into the reception. "Why do you wear shoes that hurt?"

"Because they're pretty."

Jack shakes his head and motions for Etta to join us. Theodore waits by the flap of the tent.

"Wasn't it beautiful?" I ask Theodore as I look back at Pearl and Taye on the dance floor, shimmering beneath the canopy.

"It was fine. It would have been better if I didn't have to play Hide the Band Director with Sarah Dunleavy."

Etta climbs into the front seat with Theodore; Jack and I settle into the backseat.

"Mama, is Daddy drunk?"

"No honey, he's just very very happy for Pearl and Dr. B."

Theodore looks at me in the rearview mirror and smiles.

As we circle around the cul-de-sac and back onto Shawnee Avenue, we stop at the turnoff to Beamontown Road at the light. The black gates of Glencoe Cemetery glisten in the middle distance where the road meets the river. For a moment, I think to ask Theodore to make the turn. But I think better of it and let it go.

"Cracker's Neck?" Theodore asks.

"Yeah."

Jack puts his head on my lap as Etta tells Theodore about a small drama at the wedding between her friend Tara and some cute older boy named Chad. Soon the lights of Big Stone Gap blur behind us, and we're speeding in the dark toward home.

## ACKNOWLEDGMENTS

The first and best thing that ever happened to me was to have Ida Boni-celli Trigiani for my mother. What a beauty! What smarts! She gave up her career as an architectural librarian to raise our family, but she never gave up her love of books, which she passed along to me. Mom's twin sister, Irma B. Godfrey, another fabulous librarian, is an inspiration to me, too.

Because my mother was a librarian, I always took to them: so to Bil-lie Jean Scott, Ernestine Roller, and James "Wheels" Varner of the Wise County Bookmobile, thank you. You introduced me to some great ladies of literature: Beverly Cleary, Astrid Ericsson Lindgren, Kay Thompson, Betty MacDonald, Madeleine L'Engle, Margery Williams, Carolyn Keene, Laura Ingalls Wilder, Johanna Spyri, and Louise Fitzhugh. And when it was time, you gave me Charlotte Brontë, Jane Austen, Margaret Mitchell, and Gwendolyn Brooks (thank you, Frances Lewis). Miss Scott always made sure I read the periodicals in high school, so from there, I read the great Erma Bombeck, Judith Viorst, and Meg Green-field. Thanks to my dad's subscription to Esquire magazine (it was stamped "For men only"), I read the wonderful essays of Nora Ephron.

At mighty Random House, I thank my brilliant, tireless editor, Lee Boudreaux, and Ann Godoff, Andy Carpenter, Todd Doughty, Beth Pearson, and Pamela Cannon; and at Random House AudioBooks, Sherry Huber. And at Ballantine: the Italian force of nature, Gina Centrello, and the Irish typhoon, Maureen O'Neal. To Suzanne Gluck, the best agent on earth and an even better friend, my thanks and a new purse. New purses also to ICM's Caroline Sparrow, Karen Gerwin, and Margaret Halton. Lorie Stoopack, you're amazing. In Movieland, thank you to Lou Pitt, John Farrell, Michael Pitt, Jim Powers, and Todd Steiner.

Michael Patrick King, this would be a weary, impossible road without you; Elena Nachmanoff and Dianne Festa, you rule; Caroline Rhea, I adore you. My endless love and thanks to: Rosanne Cash, Ruth Pomerance, Tom Dyja, Mary Testa, Jennifer Rudolph Walsh, June Lawton, Nancy Josephson and Larry Sanitsky, Jill Holwager, Jeanne Newman, Debra McGuire, John Melfi, Dee Emmerson, Gina Casella, Cara Stein, Sharon Hall, Wendy Luck, Faith Cox, Sarah Jessica Parker, Sharon Watroba Burns, Nancy Ringham, Mike Allen, Constance Marks, Cynthia Rutledge Olson, Jasmine Guy, Susan Toepfer, Joanne Curley Kerner, Doris Shaw Gluck, Whoopi Goldberg, Max Westler, Susan and Sam Franzeskos, Jake and Jean Morrissey, Beata and Steven Baker, Brownie Polly, Aaron and Susan Fales-Hill, Kare Jackowski, Bob Kelty, Carol Ann Story, Christina Avis Krauss, Rachel DeSario, and Beth Thomas.

My thanks and eternal love to my dad, for the title; also to my brothers and sisters, our family in Italy, the Spada, Mai, Bonicelli, and Trigiani families. To my girls back in the Gap—Iva Lou, Kaye, Debbie, Beth, Tammy, Janet, Teresa, Mary Ann, Joyce, Cindy, and Jean—thank you for your friendship and memories; to the folks of Big Stone Gap, thanks for your support and encouragement; and to my husband, Tim, for everything.

# Big Cherry Holler

ADRIANA TRIGIANI

*A Reader's Guide*

# A Conversation with Adriana Trigiani

*Fleeta Mullins, the cashier and cook at the Mutual, sits down with Adriana Trigiani to discuss the finer points of* Big Cherry Holler, *Trigiani's sequel to* Big Stone Gap *set in, where else?* Big Stone Gap.

**Fleeta Mullins: Okay, now just let me turn this thing on.**

Adriana Trigiani: Fleeta?

**FM: What?**

AT: Is there a reason we're doing this interview in your car?

**FM: Yes ma'am. I didn't want a bunch of input from those layabouts at the Mutual Soda Fountain. I don't need me Spec Broadwater tellin' me what to ask and how to ask it.**

AT: No problem.

**FM: Now, my first question is: did Jack Mac cheat on Ave Maria—some of us think he did and some of us think maybe not.**

AT: What do you think?

**FM: I think men are men and he definitely had himself a fine time whilst Ave Maria was runnin' around It-lee.**

AT: Okay.

**FM: So he did! I knew it! I knew it!**

AT: I didn't say he did or didn't, Fleeta. That's up to you, the reader.

FM: **Well, that just stinks. You ought to tell us.**

AT: If Ave Maria wants to find out, then you'll find out. The books are written in her voice and she makes all the decisions.

FM: **But you're the one writin' the story.**

AT: I'm just passing along what she's thinking.

FM: **Well, I guess I'll have to live with not knowing.**

AT: For now.

FM: **You mean I may find out in a future book?**

AT: I think you might.

FM: **Hallelujah. 'Cause I got me a pool goin' and I wanna win. Now, I want to know about Pete Rutledge.**

AT: Fleeta, I don't mean to be a pill, but if you're going to smoke, could you crack a window?

FM: **Sorry. I liked Pete. I wanted him to be happy—but I didn't want him to be happy at the expense of our local Jack. Now, help me with this—is Pete really in love with Ave Maria, or is he just after her 'cause he can't have her?**

AT: I think he really loves her.

FM: That's bold.

AT: Don't you think you could be married and make a friend and the feelings sometimes get intense?

FM: Of course. It's happened to me.

AT: Really.

FM: There's a man that comes to the wrestling meets over in Kingsport—and we had coffee after a GLOW show.

AT: What's a GLOW show?

FM: The Glorious Ladies of Wrestling. Anyway, I had to have a talk with him, 'cause he got fresh and I told him we had a lot in common but he didn't need to be puttin' his hand on my knee to make a point, you know what I'm sayin'?

AT: I do.

FM: I think when you're murried, you're murried and there's no room for hanky-panky. 'Course I was raised Baptist and we got us some rules.

AT: Were you surprised where the story went in *Big Cherry Holler*?

FM: I think it got serious, but I didn't mind that. I think as you go on in life, you get you some problems and things have to be worked out. And I like how everybody in town got into Ave's business, 'cause you know, that's just how it is in this town.

You can't hardly floss without half the town knowin' it. Now, them ladies at Ballantine wanted me to ask you something.

AT: Sure.

FM: When you boil it all down, what is the theme of *Big Cherry Holler*?

AT: Letting go. Letting go of the past, of expectations we have about our mates, letting go of old hurts and making room for something wonderful to happen. Growth and change are good, don't you think?

FM: I guess so. If both in the marriage is growin' and changin' together—but there ain't nothing worse than bein' on different pages—when that's happens, well, it's look-out-it's-Splitsville.

AT: What did you think the theme of the book was?

FM: Keep an eagle eye on your husband. That, and don't let your wife go off to It-lee without you.

AT: Very practical advice.

FM: Well, I'm known for that.

AT: I've heard.

FM: Well, I got to get back to the Mutual. The lunch crowd's loading in and when they're hungry, I got to get them fed.

AT: What's the special today?

**FM: Soup beans, corn bread, collard greens, spiced apples, and coffee.**

**AT: Sounds good.**

**FM: I'll save ye some.**

# Reading Group Guide and Topics for Discussion

1. *Big Cherry Holler* is a sequel to the bestselling *Big Stone Gap*. Does it help to read *Big Stone Gap* before delving into *Big Cherry Holler*? How did the author structure this book as a stand-alone novel, and how does it function as a continuation of the first book?

2. What is the significance of the title *Big Cherry Holler*, both literally and figuratively?

3. When the book opens, Ave Maria and Jack Mac have been married for eight years. How have her attitudes about herself and about relationships changed during that time? How has she remained a "spinster" in spirit?

4. Early in the book, it's disclosed that Jack and Ave's son, Joe, died after a sudden illness. In what ways do Jack and Ave deal with his death, both separately and together? How does their marriage bear the scars of their son's untimely death?

5. What role does small-town life—both in Italy and in Big Stone Gap—play in Ave's life? How do the mammoth physical attributes of the outside world play against her life?

6. Ave Maria sees Jack Mac chatting with a tanned, blond woman named Karen Bell, and immediately feels anxious. What evidence of marital estrangement accumulates after that incident? What aspects of Karen's personality do you think would appeal to Jack Mac?

7. How does Ave Maria see Karen Bell as a rival, and in which ways does she feel superior to her? Which feeling ultimately proves more accurate?

8. Were you surprised by the revelation of Theodore's homosexuality? Which clues—both in this book and in *Big Stone Gap*—are provided before his confession? How do you think this will affect his relationship with Ave?

9. When Ave's protégé, Pearl, pleads with Ave to become a partner in the pharmacy, she signs on without consulting Jack Mac (much to his chagrin). What other decisions in her life does Ave keep to herself? Is Jack justified in his anger, or does he, too, keep some aspects of his life private? Which ones?

10. Ave's daughter, Etta, is a main character in the book. Ave describes her as "wide open, and yet very private." What parallels can you draw between Ave and Etta, and how are the two characters different? How is Etta a product of Jack Mac's influence? How does she cope with her brother's death?

11. How do the women of Big Stone Gap—Fleeta, Pearl, Iva Lou—function as a sort of Greek chorus for Ave? How does Ave affect each of their lives, and how do they, in turn, influence hers? How has each woman evolved throughout the two books?

12. The reader sees Ave Maria in a brand-new environment when she travels to Italy. Which facets of her personality come to the forefront? To what factors do you attribute this change in attitude and appearance?

13. While in Italy, Ave imagines what her life would have been like had her mother not married Fred Mulligan. How do you envision Ave's life if she had grown up in Italy? Would it have been more or less fulfilling?

14. Ave's haircut spurs an absolute transformation. In which other ways does her appearance play a role throughout the book? Of which other novels is this reminiscent?

15. What does Pete represent to Ave, both literally and figuratively? How does he reawaken passion in her?

16. Theodore dismisses Ave's assertion that she didn't really have an affair with Pete. How is this juxtaposition of "word vs. deed" a recurrent motif in the book? What examples can you find in the behavior of Ave, Jack Mac, and their friends?

17. When Jack Mac and Ave have their confrontation about Karen Bell, Ave admits that she wanted him to "take her pain away." Besides Joe's death, what other issues has Ave Maria grappled with throughout her life? How has she usually dealt with any pain she has suffered?

18. Do you believe that Jack Mac consummated his affair with Karen Bell? What evidence do you have for that conclusion?

19. Jack Mac tells Ave, "I truly believed in us, and you never did." What actions echo Jack Mac's assertion? How does Jack Mac demonstrate his love for Ave?

20. At the end of Aunt Alice's life, Ave makes an effort to reconcile with her. To what do you attribute this change of heart? How does Ave's relationship with Alice compare to the one she enjoys with her "Eye-talian" relatives?

21. What significance do you derive from the fact that Jack Mac and Pete get along immediately? What does Pete's appearance in Big Stone Gap, as promised, indicate about his character? How is he similar to Jack Mac, and how is he different?

22. Do you feel that this book is a lead-up to Etta's stand-alone story? How do you envision Etta's adolescence and adulthood?

23. Adriana Trigiani, the book's author, also is an accomplished playwright. How does this novel have the feel of a play—whether through Trigiani's use of dialogue, setting, conflict, or any other literary device?

© Evan Kafka

## ABOUT THE AUTHOR

ADRIANA TRIGIANI grew up in Virginia and now lives in New York City with her husband. She is an award-winning playwright, television writer, and documentary filmmaker. *Big Cherry Holler* is her second novel. She is currently at work on the film version of her first novel, *Big Stone Gap*, for which she wrote the screenplay and which she will also direct.

Don't miss the latest Big Stone Gap novel
by Adriana Trigiani

# MILK
# GLASS
# MOON

Available in bookstores everywhere.
Published by Random House, Inc.

*For an exciting preview,
please turn the page. . . .*

CHAPTER ONE

$\mathcal{T}$he Wise County Fair is my daughter's favorite event of the year, and I think it's safe to say that includes Christmas. Etta has been on her best behavior for the past two weeks, so perfect down to the smallest detail (including unassigned chores like making *my* bed and weeding *my* garden) that I'm worried. Her face, with its clean lines, small chin, and rosebud lips, is beatific as she reviews her plans for this long-awaited night. We have the window flaps of the Jeep down; the warm August air whipping through is sweet with honeysuckle, but it is no match for Iva Lou's perfume, which wafts through from the backseat whenever we peel around a curve. Etta looks out the window for road signs, looking for actual proof that we're almost there. I've taken the quicker route, the valley road out of Big Stone Gap up to Norton. As we ascend the mountains in twilight, we pass Coeburn, nestled in the valley below, where the lights pool in a clump like a fistful of emeralds. Etta smoothes her braids and settles back in her seat.

"Here's the plan. First we eat," Iva Lou announces as she unfolds the special supplement to the newspaper. "I myself am having a jumbo caramel apple with nuts, and if I have to go see Doc Guest for a bridge on Monday, then so be it. Them caramel apples are worth a molar."

"I want the blue cotton candy," Etta decides.

"I want a chili dog with onions," I reply.

"I have a lot of money," Etta says proudly as she sifts through her change purse.

"Ask Dad to spring for dinner. That will leave you more money for the games of chance," I tell her.

Etta smiles and counts her money carefully without lifting it out of the purse. I see a five-dollar bill folded neatly into a small square (some lucky clay-pigeon operator is about to earn a windfall).

"What if we can't find him?" Etta asks.

"We'll find him."

"Just go straight to the outdoor the-a-ter. He's up there with all them men checking out the rehearsal for Miss Lonesome Pine."

"He built the stage," I remind Iva Lou in a tone that says *Don't start with that again.*

"That's as good a reason as any to be hanging around up there then." Iva Lou winks at me in the rearview mirror.

We find a parking spot under a tree overlooking the fairgrounds. Iva Lou climbs out in a pair of dark blue denim pedal pushers and a red bandana print blouse tied at the waist; her Diamonelle hoop earrings peek out from under her bob like giant waterwheels. Iva Lou is ageless; you would never know she is fifty-something. Her look, however, is best viewed from a distance, like a fine painting. You don't want to get so close that you're lost in the details; it's the overall effect that works.

Etta looks at the fairgrounds with a clinical eye. She surveys the faded striped tents surrounded by torches like birthday candles. She smiles when she spots the Ferris wheel. "Ma, will you go on the rides with me?"

"Sure." I agree to go but Etta knows that at the last second, when we're standing in line ready to go up the metal plank, I'll send her father with her instead.

"Do we have to go to the beauty pageant?" she asks.

"I thought you liked it."

"I like the dresses all right. The talent's always terrible." Etta shrugs. She's right. Last year, leggy blond Ellen Tierney, representing Big Stone Gap, did a dance routine to "Happy to Keep Your Dinner Warm"; her tap shoe flew off when she did a high kick, clocked a man in the first row, and knocked him out. The victim was rushed to the hospital and eventually revived, but may have the imprint of the metal tap on his forehead for life.

"And I hate the physical fitness part when they come out and jump around in bathing suits. Anybody can do that stuff."

"Etta, hon, it don't take a lot of talent to look good in a bathing suit. *That* you're born with." Iva Lou breathes deeply and straightens her shoulders. "I ought to know."

"I'm never gonna be in a beauty pageant," Etta announces.

"Me neither." I give my daughter a quick hug.

The benches in the outdoor theater are filling up fast. The aisles are covered in AstroTurf runners; the stage is banked in garlands of red paper roses; the backdrop is a cutout of a giant pine tree with MISS LONESOME PINE 1990 written in gold leaf.

It's August, so I've had eight months to get used to it, but I still can't believe it's 1992. Etta is twelve years old. My mother would have been sixty-six this year. I feel oddly lost between them, not old yet and not young anymore. I thought motherhood was a job with security, but it's not; it's the least permanent job in the world. It's the only job in which your skills become obsolete overnight. When I finally got a handle on breast-feeding, it was time for solid food; I worried that Etta wasn't turning over in the crib on her own, but soon she was crawling and then, almost overnight, walking; and when she went to school, I thought she'd need me more, but all of a sudden she had a life apart from me and she was just fine. And now, after we have established a routine as a family, in which Etta has responsibilities, she has a newfound independence and her own opinions. This is, of course, the point of all of this—to prepare them to leave you—yet I'm so afraid to let go. I know the next six years will fly even faster than the past eleven, and that scares me. I wish my mother were here to lead me through these changes.

"Dad!" Etta waves to Jack, who waves back to her from a platform at the side of the stage. He helps the spot operator set the light levels, then climbs down the ladder to join us. My husband is still agile; his strong arms hook down the ladder rhythmically. His faded jeans are crisp in the twilight, and his white T-shirt frames his gray hair beautifully. He's damn cute, my husband. His fine nose and lips are surrounded not by wrinkles, but expression lines. I try not to hate him for aging well.

Otto, spiffed up in new overalls, wiping his face with a bandana, and Worley, his son and partner, toting the tool kit, join us from the back of the theater.

"We barely got that stage up in time," Otto tells us.

"It was rough," Worley adds.

" 'Cause you ain't got your minds on your work. Too busy ogling the girls, I bet," Iva Lou tells them.

"We did us some looking." Worley smiles.

"Can't hardly help it, they's so purty. Of course, I ain't never seen me no ugly women, just some that's purtier than others." Otto shrugs.

Jack gives me a quick kiss and takes Etta's hand. "You want to watch from up there?" he asks Etta.

"Yeah!"

"We've got a couple of seats down front for you."

I turn to Iva Lou. "Do you want to stay?"

"What do you want to do?"

"I'd rather wander around."

"Let's wander, then." Iva Lou turns to go up the ramp.

"Okay, we'll catch up with you later." Jack Mac takes Etta to the ladder and helps her to the top. She kneels down on the platform as her father explains something about the equipment. She listens carefully and nods. I can't believe she's my kid and not afraid of heights. In fact, she's fearless about everything—stray animals, speaking in public, boys. Etta cares about how things work; in that way, she is just like her father. She is all MacChesney, and that's not always easy for me to accept.

"What are we gonna do?" Iva Lou asks.

"We're going to see Sister Claire."

"Who the hell is that? A Cath-lick?"

"No. A mystic. She's a fortune-teller."

"No voodoo for me, girlfriend."

"Come on. After she makes you drink a cocktail of eye of newt and puts a spell on you, it's all downhill."

Iva looks at me, buying it for a moment, and then she laughs.

Sister Claire has a small dark-green tent by the edge of the grounds. Two folding chairs are set up outside the flap. I'm surprised there isn't a line. Sister Claire is well known in these parts; she's from the mountains of North Carolina near Greensboro. A customer who was visiting Big Stone Gap encouraged me to see Sister if she was ever in the area. A small, gentle woman of sixty, with a heart-shaped face and skin the color of strong tea, emerges from the tent and smiles.

"Are you here to see me?" she asks.

Iva Lou turns away and grabs my arm to return to the hub of the fair, back to the music, the lights, and the fun.

"Yes ma'am. We are. I am," I tell her earnestly, not knowing exactly how to address a mystic.

"I'm Sister Claire. Welcome."

"I think most of the people are at the beauty pageant," I tell Sister, absurdly apologizing for her lack of clientele.

Sister Claire turns to Iva Lou and looks her straight in the eye. "I understand if the idea of a reading makes you uncomfortable. I don't like to have my own cards read."

"Really?" Iva Lou says in a high pitch I've never heard before.

"Really. It's a commitment to believe. It takes blind faith. Sometimes I don't have that."

"Well, it's not that I'm scared, and I certainly believe in the comings and goings of the spirit world. It's just that I, well, I live my life a certain way and I don't want to know where it's all going."

"I understand."

"Wait here then. Okay?" I give Iva Lou a wink and follow Sister Claire into her tent. There are two more folding chairs and a red lacquered table. There is an electric wire attached to a small generator, from which a bulb dangles in a protective metal sleeve. Sister Claire motions for me to sit, then pours us each a glass of water from a bottle. She sits down at the table and rests one hand on a deck of large picture cards.

"Are you an Indian?"

"Cherokee. Descendent of the great Chief Doublehead. 'Course, all of us that's Cherokee claim that." She smiles.

"Mother and father both?"

"Yes. But, I did have a grandmother who was African American and a grandfather who was Irish."

"The green eyes give you away."

"Yes, they do."

"How did you discover your talent for this?"

"It's not so much a talent as a way of being. It tends to run in families. My mother read cards and had visions, and so do I." She shuffles the cards and asks me to pick one. "How can I help you?"

I was prepared with an answer, but for some reason I can't speak. "I'm sorry."

"Don't be sorry. Let's look at you." Sister Claire shuffles the deck and then places cards down on the table, creating an intricate layered pattern.

"What is your name?"

"Ave Maria."

"That's unusual."

"Especially in these parts."

"That's the name of the Blessed Mother. Some people think she's the first goddess. But it doesn't mean that you are a goddess; it tells me that you will always be surrounded by them. You're very lucky. You are loved and protected, and I see many women around you, almost making a fence. Your mother passed?"

"Yes."

"She did and she didn't. She's with you always." Sister Claire sits back in the chair and closes her eyes. "She's wearing purple."

"My mother?"

"Yes."

I buried my mother in a purple suit, her favorite suit made of silk wool. She made it herself out of fabric she bought on one of Fred Mulligan's buying trips to New York. She told me that she didn't want to make anything out of the fabric for the longest time because it was so beautiful, she couldn't bear to cut it into pieces.

Sister Claire continues, "And she is showing me a house with many rooms. She is hanging curtains in one of the rooms."

"She used to make curtains."

"There's a boy in the room. He just walked in. He has brown eyes and curly brown hair. Who is he?"

"My son."

"He passed?" she asks me quietly.

"Yes ma'am."

"Very young."

"He was four years old."

Sister Claire laughs. "He's a funny kid. He's happy with her. She is looking out for him." She opens her eyes and looks at me.

Sister Claire goes on to tell me lots of things—about work, about Jack, about Etta. She sees us traveling together, and she sees Etta taking a new path, which validates my feelings that my kid is going to go where she wants to go and do what she wants to do with or without my blessing.

"Sister, how does the afterlife work?"

"What do you mean?"

"Will my son always be four years old and my mother the age she was when she died? And when I die . . ."

"What do you think?"

"I thought that they were in a holding pattern, waiting for Judgment Day."

Sister Claire laughs, but I wasn't being funny. "That's a possibility, and it all depends. Your mother and son wanted you to know they're okay, so they came to me in a way you would recognize them. This doesn't happen every time."

"So they are . . . somewhere, right?"

"I like to think the *idea* of them is somewhere, but that their energy is eternal and that it's very possible that they return to life as a different person to learn new things."

"So they could be here?"

"Anywhere."

"Should I be looking for them?"

"You won't have to look for them; they'll find you." Sister Claire shuffles the cards, this time lining them up in a single row. She asks me to pick another from the deck. "Now for your future."

I take a deep breath. "I'm ready."

"You've set many goals for yourself in your lifetime. And you've met most of them. But what I see here is that you have to begin anew. You have to decide where your life is going; you must re-dream."

"Re-dream?"

"You have to invent your life again. You've reached many of your personal and professional goals, and now you have to think about what you want your life to mean from here on in. Do you understand?" I nod that I do, but I don't really, or maybe I just don't want to talk about the rest of my life. Maybe I'm not ready to talk about it.

I pay Sister Claire, and she helps me up out of my seat and to the doorway; I am a little stunned that my mother and son might be looking for me but I won't know them. The smell of Iva Lou's cigarette brings me back to the present. Iva Lou is sitting in one of the folding chairs, puffing away.

"I'm ready to go," I tell her.

"Well, honey-o, since we're here, maybe I'll get a reading too." Iva Lou turns to Sister Claire and points to her with her pinkie finger. "But I'm warnin' you, Sis, don't tell me when I'm gonna die, even if you know. Okay, I amend that. You can tell me when I'm gonna die if it's at a hundred-and-one with all my faculties and a young man up in the bed next to me that thinks I'm better than pepper jelly."

"You got a deal." Sister laughs.

They go inside the tent and I can hear quiet muttering. I sit down, stretching my legs and leaning back in the chair. From this angle, I can see the spotlight at the beauty contest make a tunnel of light against the black mountain. It is a smoky beam, barely visible as it competes with the Ferris wheel spinning streaks of light like pink glitter. The mountains funnel the sound of the applause, and the wolf whistles up into the night sky; the pageant could be a thousand miles from here, the way the sound carries in these hills. How easy it is to get lost in the noise of this world, to find yourself leading a life of acceptance and resignation. I wonder if I have anything new ahead of me. What does Sister Claire mean when she tells me I have to invent myself all over again? To be what? And how?

After what seems like a much longer time than my reading took, Iva Lou emerges from the tent, fishing in her purse for a cigarette.

"So?"

"Oh, honey, I've never heard such good news. Sister Claire was chock-full of all kinds of information, I just hope I can remember it all so I can write it down."

"What did she say?"

"That I'm an eagle."

"Is that a good thing?"

"Absolutely. I'm regal and self-possessed and all that. But of course, tell me something I didn't already know for fifteen bucks. How about you?"

"Mama and Joe came to me."

"What did they say?"

"They didn't say anything. But it's okay. They showed up; that's all I needed."

Iva Lou gives me a quick hug as we head back into the lights and the noise, but I don't see them or hear it. My mind is in that house with many rooms.

I tuck Etta into bed. She wants to read one more chapter of *Harriet the Spy*, but I won't let her. Etta is fascinated with the story of Harriet, an eleven-year-old girl who doesn't play with dolls, but has a notebook and goes around the elegant Upper East Side of Manhattan spying on her neighbors and recording their activities. Etta is tired, with dark circles under her eyes. I think this is her third time reading about Harriet's escapades.

"Mama, someday can we go to New York City?"

"Sure."

"I think I'd like it."

"Okay." I kiss Etta and walk to the door. I turn out the light. I'm already in the hallway when I hear her voice softly call out to me.

"Mama?"

"Yes?"

"Am I pretty?"

"Yes, you are."

"How do they decide who's pretty?"

"Who?"

"People. You know, it's like the group knows who's pretty and then they treat that person like they're the prettiest and that person always knows it."

"I don't know, Etta. I've never figured it out."

"I mean, sometimes I can see it. But sometimes I don't think the prettiest girl is the pretty one."

"You're pretty," I tell her plainly and sincerely.

"Okay." Etta says this in a tone that says *You've got to be kidding*.

I wait for Etta to say something else, but she doesn't; she rolls over to sleep.

Jack is in the kitchen making coffee to have with the cherry pie we bought at the fair.

"That was weird."

"What?"

"Etta asked me if I thought she was pretty. Doesn't she know I think she's pretty?"

"I guess not."

"Don't I tell her?"

"I don't think you do. You tell her she's smart and a good reader and capable and all that, but you don't heap a lot of compliments on her in other ways."

"God, isn't it more important to be smart?"

"Sure. But she's a girl, Ave. A girl."

"I'll tell her she's pretty more often." I hear my tone and realize I sound defensive.

"I don't think it's anything you're doing wrong. I just think Etta's entering a new phase. Misty Lassiter told her group about sex tonight."

"What?"

"Yeah. She decided to drop the bomb."

"Oh my God. Where did Misty get her information?"

"She's two years ahead of Etta in school, and you know, she's like her mother."

Misty Lassiter is the daughter of Tayloe Slagle Lassiter, Big Stone Gap's most beautiful homegrown girl. I see Misty when I pick up Etta at school. She's The Willowy One, taller than her classmates, the leader, with blond hair in perfect yellow ropes tied with ribbons that don't look cutesy, but sophisticated. Back when I directed the Outdoor Drama, I cast her mother, Tayloe, in the ingénue lead when she was just fifteen. She wasn't a great actress, but it didn't matter; you wanted to watch her, her delicate features, long limbs, and those eyes, so blue, heavy-lidded, and clear. She was so beautiful, you thought she knew the secret to something, some ancient truth born in her and obvious in her every movement. Tayloe has taught her daughter well. Misty is every bit as popular and perfect as she was. Quite a feat in a small town, and quite a feat when Bo Lassiter (of the low-forehead Lassiters of East Stone Gap) is your daddy.

"Etta's got so much more going for her than Misty. What did Misty say about sex?"

"Everything."

"Everything?"

Jack nods and pours our coffee. He sits down and slices the pie with his fork.

"Well, what exactly did she say?"

Jack does his best to do an impression of Misty giving the girls the goods. " 'Now, first, there's a man. And the man has a different part from the woman.' "

"Oh God." I don't want to hear this, but I indicate to Jack that he should continue.

" 'And the man takes his part and lets the woman know he has one. Then, she decides if she wants his part or not. Now, if she does, it's called sex. If she doesn't want no part of it, she's a virgin.' "

"This is horrible."

"I thought it was funny."

"Did Etta tell you this?"

"I overheard them when they were waiting for their cotton candy. The line was long."

Jack says this so matter-of-factly, but for me, this is a major turning point in Etta's development. Why is it that my husband was with her when she heard the facts of life the first time and I'm off in a tent getting my cards read? This is not how I planned this! "I am going to talk to Tayloe."

"What for?"

"She needs to tell her daughter not to be scaring the kids."

"Etta's not scared."

"What do you mean she's not scared? Who isn't scared of sex—" I stop myself. Jack looks at me. I open my mouth wide and yet no words come out. Jack knows all about my repression, which I thought was long-gone and buried, but thanks to Misty's sex talk, those feelings of separation and alienation just went from a trickle to a roaring river within me. Once the town spinster, always the town spinster. "No wonder." I cut another piece of pie.

"No wonder what?"

"She doesn't come to me to tell me about it. She can tell I don't want to talk about it."

"You got that right." My husband looks at me and smiles.

"That's awful."

"Well, fix it."

"What do you mean?"

"Talk to her." Jack shrugs as if it's as simple as teaching her to drive.

I take a long sip of the hot coffee (Jack always puts in just the right amount of cream). Then I slip off my loafers and put my feet in my husband's lap. How I wish Etta could stay a girl forever.

We're having a sidewalk sale at the Mutual Pharmacy. It isn't a big deal, just a couple of folding tables borrowed from the First Baptist Church and loaded with stuff that hasn't sold—pale orange lipstick, strawberry hand cream, and shoeboxes filled with greeting cards, neatly arranged by holiday. We start the sale with everything 50 percent off, but by Friday, we'll be giving the stuff away. Folks know this, so they wait a few days, linger after lunch in the soda fountain, and then hit Fleeta up for a freebie. Fleeta, in her smock and tight black leggings, leans against the building to light a cigarette. Once it's lit, she stands up straight and lightly touches her blue-black upsweep (she's tried the new Loving Care line that just came in) to make sure it's in place. I wave to her and pull into my parking spot.

"Pearl's pregnant," Fleeta barks.

Before I can ask her to repeat the news, Pearl comes out to the sidewalk.

"Fleeta!"

"I know it's supposed to be a secret, but you know I can't keep one. You shouldn't never have told me," Fleeta says to Pearl as she takes a long drag off her cigarette. "Besides, when you upchuck three times in one morning, I ain't gonna be the only one 'round here that's suspicious."

"Is it true?" I ask Pearl, whose smile tells me it is. "How's your husband?"

"Thrilled."

I give Pearl a hug. "How far along are you?"

"Sixteen weeks."

"My God."

"I know. I just didn't want to say anything until I knew for sure."

"Sixteen weeks is knowing for sure."

I watch Pearl walk back to the soda fountain, and now I can see the pregnancy. Her waist is beginning to fill out; she's walking more slowly, feeling the burden of the new weight on her knees. I remember all the stages of pregnancy, all right. It's true that all the suffering is worth it in the end, but for every moment of that nine months, I felt as though I had rented my body out to a tenant who had no respect for the property. The morning sickness, which is really all-day sea sickness, the bloated breasts, swollen ankles, and for me, painful big toes from having to walk in a whole new way—I remember every one of these details as though it were yesterday.

Pearl turns around. "I'll be counting on you for advice."

"Oh, I have plenty of it."

"What about me?" Fleeta asks. "I done blowed out three babies, and Pavis—he was a back birth—snapped my tailbone like a cracker on his way out. I got me a lot of advice to give, 'specially about the birthing itself."

"I'll need your advice too, Fleets." Pearl goes into the kitchen.

"Pavis really broke your tailbone?"

"Yeah, and that was a goddamn omen. That boy never give me nothin' but trouble and heartache and pain, both of the physical and of the mental variety. First he stepped on my tailbone, then on my feet—you know, when he was a-crawlin'—and then when he went to prison, he done stepped on my heart."

"You ever hear from him?"

"When he gets a phone day."

Fleeta pulls out another box of greeting cards from under the folding table. "This here sidewalk sale is already a bust," Fleeta tells me, sorting through the cards like they're junk.

"You have a bad attitude."

"If it was a good idea, every vendor on the street'd have one. You don't see Mike's Department Store hauling out the Agg-ner leather goods, or Zackie putting out the Wranglers. But we have to make a show peddling crap nobody bought all year."

"What is your problem?"

At first Fleeta looks as though she may bite my head off because I dared to snap back at her, but then she softens and says quietly, "Doc Daugherty told me I have to quit smoking."

"Did he find something?"

"He saw a spot on an X ray, said it weren't nothin' now, but if I didn't quit the smokes, it would turn to the emphysema. And I'm mighty pissed about it."

"God, Fleeta. It's simple. You have to stop smoking."

"I can't."

"You have to."

"Don't you understand you'd have three dead customers by break-fast if I couldn't smoke?"

"You don't know that."

"I don't? My nerves is so bad that I shake most days. I need 'em, and I told Doc that."

"What did he say?"

"He tole me he understood but he didn't want me gittin' the em-physema, neither. He tole me to quit gradual. Keep cutting back till I'm down to one a day."

"You think you can handle that?"

"I'm not gonna be easy to be around." Fleeta takes an envelope and goes inside to get change.

Spec, Otto, and Worley are sitting at the counter in the soda fountain eating the lunch special: soup beans and corn bread, with a side of fried apples. Spec has a lit cigarette resting on a saucer. I put out the cigarette on my way to the coffee pot.

"Hey, what'd you do that fer?" Spec bellows. He adjusts the cap-tain's bars on his pressed khaki shirt. His legs are too long for the stools, so he has them slung to the side like railroad ties. Spec has taken to putting gel in his thick white hair. The sides are so shiny and close to his head, he actually reminds me of the great George Jones, who is as famous for his coiffure as for his singing.

"You need to set an example for Fleeta. She needs to quit."

"Since when is Fleeta Mullins my problem?"

"Since she went to the doctor and he told her to quit."

"Jesus, Ave. I got enough on my plate. Don't make me Surgeon General of Wise County too." Spec adjusts his glasses and fishes for his pack of cigarettes. I stop him.

"You're in here every day for lunch. She needs your support. Thank you."

I pour myself a cup of coffee, and freshen Otto's while I'm at it.

"I can stand up for my own damn self," Fleeta announces from the floor. "I don't need the support of any of y'all."

"Aw, Fleeta, relax."

"Don't tell me what to do, Otto Olinger. Just 'cause you is president of the Where's My Ass Club that convenes up in here every day for lunch don't mean I got to take any bull off of ye."

"What do you mean, 'Where's My Ass'?" Otto asks.

"Look at ye, all y'all. Not a one of ye has an ass. I don't know how your pants stay up."

"It's called a belt, Fleets," Otto says with a chuckle.

"I ain't never gotten a single complaint about my hind end," Spec tells her, sounding hurt.

"Somebody down in Lee County's bein' nice. If old Twyla was honest . . ."

The mention of Spec's girlfriend sends Otto and Worley into a giggling fit. Fleeta continues, ". . . she'd tell you the truth: it's flat and square. Looks like somebody dropped a TV set down your drawers." Fleeta goes into the kitchen.

"She's on a royal tear." Worley takes a sip of coffee.

"Jesus, does she have to get personal like that?" Spec dumps cream into his coffee.

"It's only gonna get worse, boys," Fleeta bellows from the kitchen.

I made a run over to Johnson City to pick up some olive oil Jack Mac ordered; he's become quite the Italian chef. Sometimes he jokes he wants to open a restaurant, and I guess I glare at him so intently, he drops the subject. It never dawns on him that folks around here are not interested in sampling pesto made with fresh basil; they much prefer their own cuisine, biscuits and gravy and the like. The soda fountain at the Mutual is all the food service I can handle, and it's strictly lunch fare. Pearl and I were surprised when we saw the profit sheets for 1989. With our local economy shot to hell, it's a good thing Pearl is such a risk taker; the fountain did more business than the pharmacy.

As I cut through Wild Cat Holler and head back into Cracker's Neck, I practice the opening to The Talk About Sex between Etta and me. There is so much to say on the subject, I wrestle with whether I should begin with the physical and segue into the emotions, or if I should just start out asking her about her feelings and what she knows already, or if I should make it a family meeting and invite her father into the discussion (I'm chicken to go it alone). It bothers me that I want Jack there. Why is this so hard? I want the sort of closeness I had with my mother. She was my protector and I was her defender. We never talked about sex, but I surely felt I could ask her anything if I wanted to. There weren't any gaps in our relationship. I would have done anything for her. I didn't test her, though, and I'm sure I saw the world as she did, so there were never any arguments.

As I drive up to our house, negotiating all the pits where the stones have settled on the road, I see Otto and Worley on my roof. This reminds me of the days when the father-son team used to come by my house down in town and repair everything that needed fixing. As I jump out of the Jeep, I see a third figure on the roof. My daughter.

"Etta, what are you doing up there?"

"Helping Otto and Worley."

"I want you to go inside."

"Why?"

"Because it's not safe."

"It's safe," Etta says defiantly.

"I got an eye on her, Miss Ave," Worley says without looking up.

"Me too," Otto says to reassure me.

"Go inside anyway, Etta."

Etta looks so small from the ground below. As she gingerly crawls across the roof toward the window, it reminds me of when she first learned to crawl and, instead of being thrilled that my baby was learning a new skill, I was terrified that she was beginning to move in the world without me.

"Etta! Watch it!"

The toe of Etta's shoe got caught where a shingle has not been bolted. She tries to pry her shoe free, but she can't. Her other foot hits a slick spot and she begins to slide toward the gutter. I can hear the buttons on her barn jacket catch on the shingles. Otto and Worley drop their tools and crawl toward her, but Etta's weight against the slope of the roof makes her slide even faster.

"Ave, git the ladder! Git the ladder!"

The ladder is propped against the far side of the roof. For a moment, I'm frozen, thinking I can catch Etta if she falls. But I know this isn't possible. The drop is almost twenty feet, time is passing, the fabric on her jacket tears away as she slides. It brings me back to the present. I heave the ladder from the side of the house to the front gutter, where her feet are dangling dangerously over the edge. Worley has thrown his body sideways across the roof and has grabbed one of Etta's hands, which stops her from falling.

"Come up, Ave. Come up and git her." Worley pants. Otto attempts to crawl toward Etta, but he is afraid to disrupt the precarious balance of their weight on the roof, so he stops. I dig the feet of the ladder into the soft earth and climb up quickly. I feel confident when I get to Etta's feet and can get a grip on her legs. She feels so small in my arms, I remember what it was like when I could control everything to keep her safe. I carefully pull her toward me. Worley lets go when I have a good grip on her. Then, using Etta's weight, I slide her onto the first step of the ladder, shielding her with my body.

"Do you think you can climb down?" I ask her. Etta barely whispers a reply, and we descend the ladder, one step at a time. I try not to look to the ground below, it seems so far away. With each step I take, and each one Etta takes, I breathe a little easier. When we reach the ground, Otto and Worley are there to help us off the ladder.

"Sorry about that, Miss Ave. We thought she was safe up 'ere with us," Otto says quietly.

"That's okay," I tell him. Then I turn to my daughter, who examines the palms of her hands, streaked with a little blood, where the shingles burned them during her downward slide. I wince. I have never been able to stand it when she bleeds.

"Come on, let's wash up." I take Etta into the house, and hold on until we are out of Otto and Worley's earshot. I don't think I have ever been this furious at her.

"What in the hell were you thinking, Etta?" I yell so loudly, she is taken aback. "You are not allowed on the roof. You know that. I don't care who is here doing what, you know the rules. You could've fallen and broken your neck."

"But I didn't!" She turns on me.

"What?"

"I didn't!"

"Because you're lucky. Lucky I was there to catch you!"

"Yeah, I'm lucky you were there," Etta says in a tone of voice I've never heard before.

"Are you mocking me?"

"What do you care anyway?"

"What are you talking about?"

"You don't care about me."

"Where do you get that idea?"

"All the time." Etta storms off and up the stairs. I follow her.

"Stop right there!"

She turns and faces me.

"That's a very cruel thing to say to me. I care about you. Of course I care. But when you do something stupid, something you know you're not supposed to do, you can't turn around and blame me for it. You're the one who's wrong here. Not me."

"That's all you care about. Who's right and who's wrong."

"Watch your tone."

"You just don't want me to die like Joe. That's all." Etta slams her bedroom door shut. For a moment, I think of honoring her privacy, but my anger gets the best of me. I throw the door open.

"What is the matter with you?"

Etta cries on the bed. She is sobbing so hard, harder than I have ever seen her cry before. My heart breaks and I go to sit beside her. She pulls away.

"Go," she says through her tears.

"No. We need to talk about this."

"I don't want to talk to you. I want Daddy."

When I attempt to reach out to her again, she gets up off the bed and goes to the old easy chair with the broken foot and throws herself into it and away from me. I have never seen this sort of emotion from my daughter, and I am stunned. But I am also so hurt that I don't know what to say. So I rely on my rule about being consistent in my discipline. I'm not going to let her off the hook. "Dad is not going to bail you out of this one. You need to think about what you did this afternoon. And about the way you talked to me."

I leave the room and close the door quietly behind me. I walk down the front stairs and go through the screen door to the porch. I sit down on the steps as I have done so many times at twilight. Otto and Worley pack up their truck without saying a word. They take full responsibility for Etta being on the roof, and I don't want to say anything more. They get into their truck and wave solemnly as they descend the hill.

I lean back on the stairs and take a deep breath. The mountains, still green at the end of summer, seem to intersect like those in a pop-up book. This old stone house seems hidden in its folds, like an abandoned castle, with me its wizened housekeeper, taken for granted and obsolete. I feel myself hitting the wall common to all mothers: the day your daughter turns on you. And it happened on such an ordinary day in Cracker's Neck Holler. Nothing strange or different or particularly dramatic in the weather or the wind. The sky meets the top of the mountains in a ruffle of deep blue. The sun sets in streaks of golden pink as it slips behind Skeens Ridge. I get lost in the quiet, the color, and the breeze, and I'm back in simpler times, the time before we had the children, when this house was a place where we made love and ate good food and tended the garden.

The cool at twilight soothes the throbbing in my head. I am making a mess of motherhood. What do I know about children, really? I was an only child. Maybe I baby-sat here and there, but I never had a grand plan that included children. When I found out I was pregnant, I made Iva Lou order me every book on parenthood from the county library. I read each and every one, picking and choosing concepts that made sense and figuring out how to implement them. When my kids came along, I thought everything would fall into place. But my daughter is her own person, and she isn't who I thought she'd be. And I know that I have disappointed her too—she needs an outdoorsy, athletic mom, one who encourages her to take risks. My goal is to keep her safe, and she resents that. I am filled with dread at what lies ahead. How do I stop fearing the future? No book can tell me that.

The high beams on Jack's pickup truck light up the field as he takes the turn up the holler road. He slows down to check the mailbox, and I see him throw a few envelopes on the front seat. Then he guns the engine again, spitting gravel under his wheels. Soon I hear my daughter's footsteps as she skips down the stairs. The screen door flies open and she runs past me, down the steps, and over the path to meet her father as he parks. I hear the muffled start to her version of The Roof Disaster and wish for a moment that I weren't the mother, but the housekeeper, so I wouldn't have to rat her out. I have to be consistent and train her so that at some point later in her life when she must make hard decisions, she will call back to these days, find the wisdom borne of experience and make the right choice (yeah right). I have to be the bad guy. Jack puts his arm around Etta as they walk up the path. I stand up. Etta passes by in a businesslike huff without looking at me. She bangs the screen door behind her.

"Are you okay?" Jack puts his arm around me.

"I guess."

"We're going to have to come up with a doozy of a punishment."

"Great."

"It's all a part of life, Ave."

As we walk up the stairs, I want to tell my husband that I wish this wasn't my life, but I can't. I have to find a way to love my job as a mother, and I'm going to need him to help me do it.